Percy Bysshe Shelley, Harry Buxton Forman

Prose works

Edited by Harry Buxton Forman. Vol. 2

Percy Bysshe Shelley, Harry Buxton Forman

Prose works
Edited by Harry Buxton Forman. Vol. 2

ISBN/EAN: 9783337113629

Printed in Europe, USA, Canada, Australia, Japan

Cover: Foto ©Andreas Hilbeck / pixelio.de

More available books at **www.hansebooks.com**

THE PROSE WORKS

OF

PERCY BYSSHE SHELLEY

EDITED BY

HARRY BUXTON FORMAN

IN FOUR VOLUMES

VOLUME II

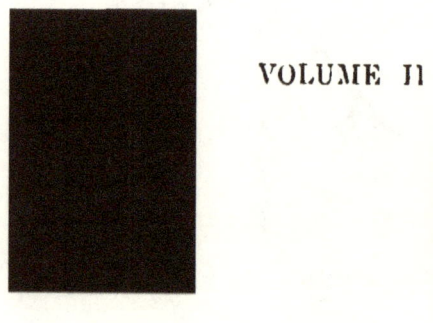

LONDON

REEVES AND TURNER 196 STRAND

1880

CONTENTS.

	PAGE
A VINDICATION OF NATURAL DIET	
EDITOR'S NOTE BEFORE THE VINDICATION	2
A VINDICATION OF NATURAL DIET	5
APPENDIX BY SHELLEY	25
A REFUTATION OF DEISM : IN A DIALOGUE	
EDITOR'S NOTE BEFORE A REFUTATION OF DEISM	30
PREFACE BY SHELLEY	33
A REFUTATION OF DEISM	35
A PROPOSAL FOR PUTTING REFORM TO THE VOTE	
EDITOR'S NOTE BEFORE THE PROPOSAL	82
A PROPOSAL &c.	85
AN ADDRESS TO THE PEOPLE ON THE DEATH OF THE PRINCESS CHARLOTTE	
EDITOR'S NOTE BEFORE THE ADDRESS	98
AN ADDRESS &c.	101

  PAGE

HISTORY OF A SIX WEEKS' TOUR THROUGH A PART OF
        FRANCE, SWITZERLAND, GERMANY, AND HOLLAND:
        WITH LETTERS DESCRIPTIVE OF A SAIL ROUND THE
        LAKE OF GENEVA, AND OF THE GLACIERS OF
        CHAMOUNI

    EDITOR'S NOTE BEFORE THE HISTORY OF A SIX WEEKS'
        TOUR   .   .   116
    PREFACE BY SHELLEY .   .   119
    JOURNAL BY MRS. SHELLEY   121
            FRANCE   123
            SWITZERLAND .   138
            GERMANY   147
            HOLLAND   154
    EDITOR'S NOTE BEFORE THE LETTERS   160
    LETTER I BY MRS. SHELLEY   161
    LETTER II BY MRS. SHELLEY   .   .   167
    LETTER III BY SHELLEY TO T. L. PEACOCK   171
    LETTER IV BY SHELLEY TO T. L. PEACOCK   185
    EDITOR'S NOTE BEFORE MONT BLANC   .   .   . 200
    MONT BLANC.   LINES WRITTEN IN THE VALE OF
        CHAMOUNI   .   201

JOURNAL AT GENEVA (INCLUDING GHOST STORIES) AND ON
        RETURN TO ENGLAND, 1816
    EDITOR'S NOTE BEFORE THE JOURNAL   206
    JOURNAL AT GENEVA .   207
    GHOST STORY No. I   .   209
    GHOST STORY No. II .   210
    GHOST STORY No. III   211
    GHOST STORY No. IV   .   212
    JOURNAL, RETURN TO ENGLAND   212

PAGE

The Assassins, a Fragment of a Romance

 Editor's Note before the Assassins . 218

 Chapter I . 219

 Chapter II . 228

 Chapter III . . 234

 Chapter IV . 239

On the Punishment of Death. A Fragment

 Editor's Note 246

 On the Punishment of Death 247

Editor's Note before Essay on Life . . 256

On Life 257

Editor's Note before Essay on Love . . 266

On Love 267

Editor's Note before Essay on a Future State . 272

On a Future State . 273

Speculations on Metaphysics

 Editor's Note before Speculations on Meta-

  physics 282

 I. The Mind 283

 II. What Metaphysics are. Errors in the Usual

  Methods of Considering Them . . 287

 III. Difficulty of Analysing the Human Mind 291

 IV. How the Analysis should be carried on . 293

 V. Catalogue of the Phenomena of Dreams, as

  Connecting Sleeping and Waking . . . 295

Speculations on Morals

 Editor's Note before Speculations on Morals 300

 I. Plan of a Treatise on Morals . 301

PAGE

SPECULATIONS ON MORALS—*continued*

    CHAPTER I

        ON THE NATURE OF VIRTUE   . 305

        BENEVOLENCE   307

        JUSTICE .   . 311

    CHAPTER II 313

    II. MORAL SCIENCE CONSISTS IN CONSIDERING THE

        DIFFERENCE, NOT THE RESEMBLANCE, OF PERSONS 316

EDITOR'S NOTE BEFORE A SYSTEM OF GOVERNMENT BY JURIES 322

A SYSTEM OF GOVERNMENT BY JURIES . 323

FRAGMENT ON REFORM 328

EDITOR'S NOTE BEFORE FRAGMENT ON THE REVIVAL OF

    LITERATURE 332

ON THE REVIVAL OF LITERATURE . . 333

ESSAY ON CHRISTIANITY

    EDITOR'S NOTE BEFORE ESSAY ON CHRISTIANITY 338

    ESSAY ON CHRISTIANITY   . 339

EDITOR'S NOTE BEFORE THE ELYSIAN FIELDS .   . 376

THE ELYSIAN FIELDS, A LUCIANIC FRAGMENT . . 377

ON THE DEVIL, AND DEVILS

    EDITOR'S NOTE BEFORE ESSAY ON THE DEVIL &c. 382

    ON THE DEVIL, AND DEVILS   . 383

FRAGMENT OF AN ESSAY ON FRIENDSHIP .   . 407

ILLUSTRATION TO VOL. II.

FAC-SIMILE OF A SKETCH MADE BY SHELLEY OUTSIDE THE

    FOLDED MS. OF "THE ELYSIAN FIELDS"   *Frontispiece*

A

VINDICATION

OF

NATURAL DIET.

[The note on vegetarianism beginning at p. 211 of Shelley's edition of *Queen Mab* was, after the issue of that poem in 1813, made the substance of a pamphlet of which the title-page is reproduced opposite. Internal evidence shews the pamphlet to have followed and not preceded *Queen Mab*. The alterations and additions are not very important; but the inclusion of this extremely rare and highly characteristic tract in the series of the Prose Works seemed more desirable than the plan of merely giving the variations with the notes to *Queen Mab*. The *Vindication* is a 12mo. pamphlet consisting of fly-title (as at back of this note), title-page as given in fac-simile opposite, pp. 1 to 39 of text, and pp. 41 to 43 of Appendix. As mentioned at p. 551 of the fourth volume of the Poetical Works (Library edition), there is a copy in the British Museum with the bottom of the title-page (including the date) torn off. The fly-title is also wanting. My own copy, from which this reprint is made, is perfect, and is the only one I ever saw or heard of beside that in the Museum. I believe this little treatise was reprinted as an Appendix to an American Medical work (Dr. Turnbull's *Manual on Health*, New York, 1835); but, not having been able to see a copy of this book, I cannot say whether the pamphlet or the *Queen Mab* note is there reprinted.—H. B. F.]

A

VINDICATION

OF

NATURAL DIET.

BEING ONE IN A SERIES OF NOTES TO QUEEN MAB
A PHILOSOPHICAL POEM.

Ιαπετιονιδη, παντων περι μηδεα ειδωσ,
Χαιρεισ μεν πυρ κλεψασ, και εμασ φρενασ ηπεροπευσασ;
Σοιτ᾽ αυτω μεγα πημα και ανδρασιν εσσομενοισι.
Τοισ δ᾽εγω αντι πυροσ δωσω κακον, ω κεν απαντεσ
Τερπωνται κατα θυμον, εον κακον αμφαγαπωντεσ.

ΗΣΙΩΔ. Op. et Dies. I. 54.

PRINTED FOR J. CALLOW, MEDICAL BOOKSELLER, CROWN
COURT, PRINCES STREET, SOHO,
By SMITH and DAVY, Queen Street, Seven Dials.
1813.

Price One Shilling and Sixpence.

B 2

A

VINDICATION

OF

NATURAL DIET.

I HOLD that the depravity of the physical and moral nature of man originated in his unnatural habits of life. The origin of man, like that of the universe of which he is a part, is enveloped in impenetrable mystery. His generations either had a beginning, or they had not. The weight of evidence in favour of each of these suppositions seems tolerably equal; and it is perfectly unimportant to the present argument which is assumed. The language spoken however by the mythology of nearly all religions seems to prove, that at some distant period man forsook the path of nature, and sacrificed the purity and happiness of his being to unnatural appetites. The date of this event, seems to have also been that of some great change in the climates of the earth, with which it has an obvious correspondence. The allegory of Adam and Eve eating of the tree of evil, and entailing upon their posterity the wrath of God, and the loss of everlasting life, admits of no other explanation, than the disease and crime that have flowed from unnatural diet. Milton was so well aware of this, that he makes Raphael thus exhibit to Adam the consequence of his disobedience.

> ————— Immediately a place,
> Before his eyes appeared: sad, noisome, dark:
> A lazar-house it seem'd; wherein were laid
> Numbers of all diseased: all maladies
> Of ghastly spasm, or racking torture, qualms
> Of heart-sick agony, all feverous kinds,
> Convulsions, epilepsies, fierce cattarrhs,
> Intestine stone and ulcer, cholic pangs,
> Dæmoniac frenzy, moping melancholy,
> And moon-struck madness, pining atrophy,
> Marasmus, and wide-wasting pestilence,
> Dropsies, and asthmas, and joint-racking rheums.

And how many thousand more might not be added to this frightful catalogue!

The story of Prometheus, is one likewise which, although universally admitted to be allegorical, has never been satisfactorily explained. Prometheus stole fire from heaven, and was chained for this crime to mount Caucasus, where a vulture continually devoured his liver, that grew to meet its hunger.—Hesiod says, that before the time of Prometheus, mankind were exempt from suffering: that they enjoyed a vigorous youth, and that death, when at length it came, approached like sleep, and gently closed their eyes.—Again, so general was this opinion, that Horace, a poet of the Augustan age, writes—

Audax omnia perpeti,
Gens humana ruit per vetetum nefas,
Audax Iapeti genus,
Ignem fraude mala gentibus intulit,
Post ignem ætheriâ domo,
Subductum, macies et nova febrium,
Terris incubuit cohors
Semotiq prius tarda necessitas,
Lethi corripuit gradum.—

How plain a language is spoken by all this.—Prometheus, (who represents the human race) effected some great change in the condition of his nature, and applied fire to culinary purposes; thus inventing an expedient for screening from his disgust the horrors of the shambles. From this moment his vitals were devoured by the vulture of disease. It consumed his being in every shape of its loathsome and infinite variety, inducing the soul-quelling sinkings of premature and violent death. All vice arose from the ruin of healthful innocence. Tyranny, superstition, commerce, and inequality, were then first known, when reason vainly attempted to guide the wanderings of exacerbated passion. I conclude this part of the subject with an extract from Mr. Newton's Defence of Vegetable Regimen, from whom I have borrowed this interpretation of the fable of Prometheus.

"Making allowance for such transposition of the events of the allegory, as time might produce after the important truths were forgotten, which this[1] portion of the antient mythology was intended to transmit, the drift of the fable seems to be this:—Man at his creation was endowed with the gift of perpetual youth; that is, he was not formed to be a sickly suffering creature as we now see

---

[1] So in Newton's book and in Queen Mab; but misprinted the in the pamphlet, as in a similar case at p. 8.

him, but to enjoy health, and to sink by slow degrees
into the bosom of his parent earth without disease or
pain. Prometheus first taught the use of animal food
(primus bovem occidit Prometheus[1]) and of fire, with
which to render it more digestible and pleasing to the
taste. Jupiter, and the rest of the gods, foreseeing the
consequences of these[2] inventions, were amused or irritated
at the short-sighted devices of the newly-formed creature,
and left him to experience the sad effects of them.
Thirst, the necessary concomitant of a flesh diet," (perhaps of all diet vitiated by culinary preparation) "ensued;
water was resorted to, and man forfeited the inestimable
gift of health which he had received from heaven : he
became diseased, the partaker of a precarious existence,
and no longer descended slowly to his grave."

> But just disease to luxury succeeds,
> And every death its own avenger breeds;
> The fury passions from that blood began,
> And turn'd on man a fiercer savage——Man.

Man, and the animals whom he has infected with his
society, or depraved by his dominion, are alone diseased.
The wild hog, the mouflon, the bison, and the wolf, are
perfectly exempt from malady, and invariably die either
from external violence, or natural old age. But the
domestic hog, the sheep, the cow, and the dog, are
subject to an incredible variety of distempers; and,
like the corrupters of their nature, have physicians
who thrive upon their miseries. The supereminence of
man is like Satan's, a supereminence of pain; and the
majority of his species, doomed to penury, disease, and

---

[1] This parenthesis is inserted by Shelley, who adds the foot-note, "Plin. Nat. Hist. lib. vii sect. 57."

[2] So in Newton's book and in *Queen Mab;* but misprinted *the* in the pamphlet.

crime, have reason to curse the untoward event, that by enabling him to communicate his sensations, raised him above the level of his fellow animals. But the steps that have been taken are irrevocable. The whole of human science is comprised in one question :—How can the advantages of intellect and civilization, be reconciled with the liberty and pure pleasures of natural life ? How can we take the benefits, and reject the evils of the system, which is now interwoven with all the fibres of our being ?—I believe that abstinence from animal food and spirituous liquors, would in a great measure capacitate us for the solution of this important question.[1]

Comparative anatomy teaches us that man resembles frugivorous animals in every thing, and carnivorous in nothing ; he has neither claws wherewith to seize his prey, nor distinct and pointed teeth to tear the living fibre. A Mandarin of the first class, with nails two inches long, would probably find them alone inefficient to hold even a hare. After every subterfuge of gluttony, the bull must be degraded into the ox, and the ram into the wether, by an unnatural and inhuman operation, that the flaccid fibre may offer a fainter resistance to rebellious nature. It is only by softening and disguising dead flesh by culinary preparation, that it is rendered susceptible of mastication or digestion ; and that the sight of its bloody juices and raw horror, does not excite intolerable loathing and disgust. Let the advocate of animal food, force himself to a decisive experiment on its fitness, and as Plutarch recommends, tear a living lamb with his teeth, and plunging his head into its vitals,

[1] Between this and the next paragraph, as printed in *Queen Mab*, there is a paragraph admitting other causes of mental and bodily derangement. See pp. 522—3, Vol. IV, *Poetical Works*.

slake his thirst with the steaming blood; when fresh from the deed of horror let him revert to the irresistible instincts of nature that would rise in judgment against it, and say, Nature formed me for such work as this. Then, and then only, would he be consistent.

Man resembles no carnivorous animal. There is no exception, except[1] man be one, to the rule of herbivorous animals having cellulated colons.

The orang-outang perfectly resembles man both in the order and number of his teeth. The orang-outang is the most anthropomorphous of the ape tribe, all of which are strictly frugivorous. There is no other species of animals[2] in which this analogy exists.* In many frugivorous animals, the canine teeth are more pointed and distinct than those of man. The resemblance also of the human stomach to that of the orang-outang, is greater than to that of any other animal.

The intestines are also identical with those of herbivorous animals, which present a larger surface for absorption, and have ample and cellulated colons. The cæcum also, though short, is larger than that of carnivorous animals; and even here the orang-outang retains its accustomed similarity. The structure of the human frame then is that of one fitted to a pure vegetable diet, in every essential particular. It is true, that the reluctance to abstain from animal food, in those who have

---

* Cuvier, Lecons d'Anat. Comp. tom. iii. p. 169. 373. 448. 465. 480. Rees's Cyclopædia, article Man. [SHELLEY'S NOTE.]

[1] In *Queen Mab*, *unless for except.* clause, *which live on different food.*
[2] In *Queen Mab*, here follows the

been long accustomed to its stimulus, is so great in some persons of weak minds, as to be scarcely overcome; but this is far from bringing any argument in its favour.—A lamb, which was fed for some time on flesh by a ship's crew, refused its natural diet at the end of the voyage. There are numerous instances of horses, sheep, oxen, and even wood-pigeons, having been taught to live upon flesh, until they have loathed their natural aliment. Young children evidently prefer pastry, oranges, apples, and other fruit, to the flesh of animals; until, by the gradual depravation of the digestive organs, the free use of vegetables has for a time produced serious inconveniences; *for a time*, I say, since there never was an instance wherein a change from spirituous liquors and animal food, to vegetables and pure water, has failed ultimately to invigorate the body, by rendering its juices bland and consentaneous, and to restore to the mind that cheerfulness and elasticity, which not one in fifty possess[1] on the present system. A love of strong liquors is also with difficulty taught to infants. Almost every one remembers the wry faces, which the first glass of port produced. Unsophisticated instinct is invariably unerring; but to decide on the fitness of animal food, from the perverted appetites which its constrained adoption produces, is to make the criminal a judge in his own cause:—it is even worse, it is appealing to the infatuated drunkard in a question of the salubrity of brandy.

What is the cause of morbid action in the animal system? Not the air we breathe, for our fellow denizens of nature, breathe the same uninjured; not the water we drink, (if remote from the pollutions of man and his in-

---

[1] In *Queen Mab, possesses.*

ventions[1]) for the animals drink it too ; not the earth we
tread upon ; not the unobscured sight of glorious nature,
in the wood, the field, or the expanse of sky and ocean ;
nothing that we are or do in common, with the un-
diseased inhabitants of the forest.   Something then
wherein we differ from them : our habit of altering
our food by fire, so that our appetite is no longer a just
criterion for the fitness of its gratification.   Except in
children there remain no traces of that instinct, which
determines in all other animals what aliment is natural
or otherwise, and so perfectly obliterated are they in the
reasoning adults of our species, that it has become necessary to urge considerations drawn from comparative
anatomy to prove that we are naturally frugivorous.

Crime is madness.   Madness is disease.   Whenever the
cause of disease shall be discovered, the root from which
all vice and misery have so long overshadowed the globe,
will lay[2] bare to the axe.   All the exertions of man, from
that moment, may be considered as tending to the clear
profit of his species.   No sane mind in a sane body re-
solves upon a real crime.   It is a man of violent passions,
blood-shot eyes, and swollen veins, that alone can grasp
the knife of murder.   The system of a simple diet promises no Utopian advantages.   It is no mere reform of
legislation, whilst the furious passions and evil propensities of the human heart, in which it had its origin,
are still unassuaged.   It strikes at the root of all evil.

[1] The necessity of resorting to some means of purifying water, and
the disease which arises from its adulteration in civilized countries, is
sufficiently apparent—See Dr. Lambe's Reports on Cancer. I do not
assert that the use of water is in itself unnatural, but that the unperverted palate would swallow no liquid capable of occasioning disease.
[SHELLEY'S NOTE.]

[2] In *Queen Mab*, *lie* instead of *lay*.

and is an experiment which may be tried with success,
not alone by nations, but by small societies, families, and
even individuals. In no cases has a return to vegetable
diet produced the slightest injury; in most it has been
attended with changes undeniably beneficial. Should ever
a physician be born with the genius of Locke, I am persuaded that he might trace all bodily and mental derange-
ments to our unnatural habits, as clearly as that philosopher has traced all knowledge to sensation. What
prolific sources of disease are not those mineral and
vegetable poisons that have been introduced for its
extirpation! How many thousands have become mur-
derers and robbers, bigots and domestic tyrants, dissolute
and abandoned adventurers, from the use of fermented
liquors; who, had they slaked their thirst only at the
mountain stream,[1] would have lived but to diffuse the
happiness of their own unperverted feelings. How many
groundless opinions and absurd institutions have not
received a general sanction, from the sottishness and intemperance of individuals! Who will assert, that had
the populace of Paris drank at the pure source of the
Seine, and[2] satisfied their hunger at the ever-furnished
table of vegetable nature, that they would have lent their
brutal suffrage to the proscription-list of Robespierre?
Could a set of men, whose passions were not perverted by
unnatural stimuli, look with coolness on an auto da fè?
Is it to be believed that a being of gentle feelings, rising
from his meal of roots, would take delight in sports of
blood? Was Nero a man of temperate life? could you
read calm health in his cheek, flushed with ungovernable

[1] In *Queen Mab* we read *with pure
water* for *at the mountain stream.*
[2] The words *drank at the pure
source of the Seine, and* do not appear in the *Queen Mab* note; nor
does the redundant *that* after *nature*
in the next line.

propensities of hatred for the human race? Did Muley
Ismael's pulse beat evenly, was his skin transparent, did
his eyes beam with healthfulness, and its invariable con-
comitants cheerfulness and benignity? Though history
has decided none of these questions, a child could not
hesitate to answer in the negative. Surely the bile-
suffused cheek of Buonaparte, his wrinkled brow, and
yellow eye, the ceaseless inquietude of his nervous system,
speak no less plainly the character of his unresting
ambition than his murders and his victories. It is
impossible that[1] had Buonaparte descended from a race of
vegetable feeders, that he could have had, either the inclination or the power to ascend the throne of the
Bourbons. The desire of tyranny could scarcely be excited in the individual, the power to tyrannize would
certainly not be delegated by a society, neither frenzied by
inebriation, nor rendered impotent and irrational by disease.
Pregnant indeed with inexhaustible calamity, is the re-
nunciation of instinct, as it concerns our physical nature;
arithmetic cannot enumerate, nor reason perhaps suspect,
the multitudinous sources of disease in civilized life.
Even common water, that apparently innoxious pabulum,
when corrupted by the filth of populous cities, is a deadly
and insidious destroyer.[2] Who can wonder that all the
inducements held out by God himself in the Bible to
virtue, should have been vainer than a nurse's tale; and
that those dogmas, apparently favourable to the intolerant
and angry passions,[3] should have alone been deemed
essential; whilst christians are in the daily practice of
all those habits, which have infected with disease and

---

[1] This first *that* does not occur
in *Queen Mab.*

[2] Shelley adds the foot-note,
" Lambe's Reports on Cancer."

[3] Instead of this clause we read
in *Queen Mab*, by which he has there
*excited and justified the most ferocious
propensities.*

crime, not only the reprobate sons, but these favoured
children of the common Father's love. Omnipotence
itself could not save them from the consequences of this
original and universal sin.

There is no disease, bodily or mental, which adoption
of vegetable diet and pure water has not infallibly miti-
gated, wherever the experiment has been fairly tried.
Debility is gradually converted into strength, disease into
healthfulness; madness in all its hideous variety, from the
ravings of the fettered maniac, to the unaccountable
irrationalities of ill temper, that make a hell of domestic
life, into a calm and considerate evenness of temper, that
alone might offer a certain pledge of the future moral
reformation of society.   On a natural system of diet, old
age would be our last and our only malady; the term of
our existence would be protracted; we should enjoy life,
and no longer preclude others from the enjoyment of it.
All sensational delights would be infinitely more exquisite
and perfect.   The very sense of being would then be a
continued pleasure, such as we now feel it in some few
and favoured moments of our youth.   By all that is
sacred in our hopes for the human race, I conjure those
who love happiness and truth, to give a fair trial to the
vegetable system.   Reasoning is surely superfluous on a
subject, whose merits an experience of six months would
set for ever at rest.   But it is only among the enlightened
and benevolent, that so great a sacrifice of appetite and
prejudice can be expected, even though its ultimate
excellence should not admit of dispute.   It is found easier,
by the short-sighted victims of disease, to palliate their
torments by medicine, than to prevent them by regimen.
The vulgar of all ranks are invariably sensual and in-

docile; yet I cannot but feel myself persuaded, that when the benefits of vegetable diet are mathematically proved; when it is as clear, that those who live naturally are exempt from premature death, as that nine is not one, the most sottish of mankind will feel a preference towards a long and tranquil, contrasted with a short and painful life. On the average, out of sixty persons, four die in three years. In[1] April 1814, a statement will be given, that sixty persons, all having lived more than three years on vegetables and pure water, are then *in perfect health*. More than two years have now elapsed; *not one of them has died;* no such example will be found in any sixty persons taken at random. Seventeen persons of all ages (the families of Dr. Lambe and Mr. Newton) have lived for seven years on this diet, without a death and almost without the slightest illness. Surely when we consider that some of these were infants, and one a martyr to asthma now nearly subdued, we may challenge any seventeen persons taken at random in this city to exhibit a parallel case. Those who may have been excited to question the rectitude of established habits of diet, by these loose remarks, should consult Mr. Newton's luminous and eloquent essay.* It[2] is from that book, and from the conversation of its excellent and enlightened author, that I have derived the materials which I here present to the public.

When these proofs come fairly before the world, and are clearly seen by all who understand arithmetic, it is

---

* Return to Nature, or Defence of Vegetable Regimen. Cadell, 1811. [SHELLEY'S NOTE.]

[1] In *Queen Mab* this promise was qualified by the prelusive words, *Hopes are entertained that.*

[2] This concluding sentence as to Newton's book does not appear in *Queen Mab.*

scarcely possible that abstinence from aliments demon-
strably pernicious should not become universal.   In proportion to the number of proselytes, so will be the weight
of evidence, and when a thousand persons can be produced living on vegetables and distilled water, who have
to dread no disease but old age, the world will be compelled to regard animal flesh and fermented liquors, as
slow, but certain poisons.   The change which would be
produced by simpler habits on political economy is
sufficiently remarkable.   The monopolizing eater of
animal flesh would no longer destroy his constitution by
devouring an acre at a meal, and many loaves of bread
would cease to contribute to gout, madness and apoplexy,
in the shape of a pint of porter, or a dram of gin, when
appeasing the long-protracted famine of the hard-working
peasant's hungry babes.   The quantity of nutritious
vegetable matter, consumed in fattening the carcase of an
ox, would afford ten times the sustenance, undepraving
indeed, and incapable of generating disease, if gathered
immediately from the bosom of the earth.   The most
fertile districts of the habitable globe are now actually
cultivated by men for animals, at a delay and waste of
aliment absolutely incapable of calculation.   It is only
the wealthy that can, to any great degree, even now,
indulge the unnatural craving for dead flesh, and they
pay for the greater licence of the privilege by subjection to
supernumerary diseases.   Again, the spirit of the nation
that should take lead in this great reform, would
insensibly become agricultural; commerce, with all its
vices, selfishness and corruption, would gradually decline;
more natural habits would produce gentler manners, and
the excessive complication of political relations would be
so far simplified, that every individual might feel and

understand why he loved his country, and took a personal
interest in its welfare. How would England, for example,
depend on the caprices of foreign rulers, if she contained
within herself all the necessaries, and despised whatever
they possessed of the luxuries of life ? How could
they starve her into compliance with their views ? Of
what consequence would it be, that they refused to take
her woollen manufactures, when large and fertile tracts
of the island ceased to be allotted to the waste of pasturage ? On a natural system of diet, we should require
no spices from India ; no wines from Portugal, Spain,
France, or Madeira ; none of those multitudinous articles
of luxury, for which every corner of the globe is rifled,
and which are the causes of so much individual rivalship,
such calamitous and sanguinary national disputes. In
the history of modern times, the avarice of commercial
monopoly, no less than the ambition of weak and wicked
chiefs, seems to have fomented the universal discord, to
have added stubbornness to the mistakes of cabinets, and
indocility to the infatuation of the people. Let it ever be
remembered, that it is the direct influence of commerce to
make the interval between the richest and the poorest
man wider and more unconquerable. Let it be remembered, that it is a foe to every thing of real worth and
excellence in the human character. The odious and disgusting aristocracy of wealth, is built upon the ruins of
all that is good in chivalry or republicanism ; and luxury
is the forerunner of a barbarism scarce capable of cure.
Is it impossible to realize a state of society, where all the
energies of man shall be directed to the production of his
solid happiness ? Certainly if this advantage (the object
of all political speculation) be in any degree attainable, it
is attainable only by a community, which holds out no

factitious incentives to the avarice and ambition of the
few, and which is internally organized for the liberty,
security and comfort of the many. None must be
entrusted with power (and money is the completest
species of power) who do not stand pledged to use it
exclusively for the general benefit. But the use of
animal flesh and fermented liquors, directly militates
with this equality of the rights of man. The peasant
cannot gratify these fashionable cravings without leaving
his family to starve. Without disease and war, those
sweeping curtailers of population, pasturage would include
a waste too great to be afforded. The labour requisite to
support a family is far lighter[1] than is usually supposed.
The peasantry work, not only for themselves, but for the
aristocracy, the army and the manufacturers.

The advantage of a reform in diet, is obviously greater
than that of any other. It strikes at the root of the
evil. To remedy the abuses of legislation, before we
annihilate the propensities by which they are produced,
is to suppose, that by taking away the effect, the cause
will cease to operate. But the efficacy of this system
depends entirely on the proselytism of individuals, and
grounds its merits as a benefit to the community, upon
the total change of the dietetic habits in its members.
It proceeds securely from a number of particular cases,
to one that is universal, and has this advantage over the

---

[1] It has come under the author's experience, that some of the workmen
on an embankment in North Wales, who, in consequence of the inability
of the proprietor to pay them, seldom received their wages, have supported large families by cultivating small spots of sterile ground by
moonlight. In the notes to Pratt's Poem, "Bread, or the Poor," is an
account of an industrious labourer, who, by working in a small garden,
before and after his day's task, attained to an enviable state of inde-
pendence. [SHELLEY'S NOTE.]

contrary mode, that one error does not invalidate all that has gone before.

Let not too much however be expected from this system. The healthiest among us is not exempt from hereditary disease. The most symmetrical, athletic, and long-lived, is a being inexpressibly inferior to what he would have been, had not the unnatural habits of his ancestors accumulated for him a certain portion of malady and deformity. In the most perfect specimen of civilized man, something is still found wanting, by the physiological critic. Can a return to nature, then, instantaneously eradicate predispositions that have been slowly taking root in the silence of innumerable ages?—Indubitably not. All that I contend for is, that from the moment of the relinquishing all unnatural habits, no new disease is generated; and that the predisposition to hereditary maladies, gradually perishes, for want of its accustomed supply. In cases of consumption, cancer, gout, asthma and scrofula, such is the invariable tendency of a diet of vegetables and pure water.

Those who may be induced by these remarks to give the vegetable system a fair trial, should, in the first place, date the commencement of their practice from the moment of their conviction. All depends upon breaking through a pernicious habit, resolutely and at once. Dr. Trotter[1] asserts, that no drunkard was ever reformed by gradually relinquishing his dram. Animal flesh in its effects on the human stomach is analogous to a dram. It is similar in the kind, though differing in the degree, of its operation. The proselyte to a pure diet, must be

[1] See Trotter on the Nervous Temperament. [SHELLEY'S NOTE.]

warned to expect a temporary diminution of muscular strength. The subtraction of a powerful stimulus will suffice to account for this event. But it is only temporary, and is succeeded by an equable capability for exertion, far surpassing his former various and fluctuating strength. Above all, he will acquire an easiness of breathing, by which the same[1] exertion is performed, with a remarkable exemption from that painful and difficult panting now felt by almost every one, after hastily climbing an ordinary mountain. He will be equally capable of bodily exertion, or mental application, after as before his simple meal. He will feel none of the narcotic effects of ordinary diet. Irritability, the direct consequence of exhausting stimuli, would yield to the power of natural and tranquil impulses. He will no longer pine under the lethargy of ennui, that unconquerable weariness of life, more dreaded[2] than death itself. He will escape the epidemic madness, that broods over its own injurious notions of the Deity, and " realizes the hell that priests and beldams feign." Every man forms as it were his god from his own character ; to the divinity of one of simple habits, no offering would be more acceptable than the happiness of his creatures. He would be incapable of hating or persecuting others for the love of God. He will find, moreover, a system of simple diet to be a system of perfect epicurism. He will no longer be incessantly occupied in blunting and destroying those organs, from which he expects his gratification. The pleasures of taste to be derived from a dinner of potatoes, beans, peas, turnips, lettice, with a dessert of

---

[1] In *Queen Mab*, *such* stands in place of *the same*.

[2] In *Queen Mab*, *more to be* *dreaded*. and *which* for *that* in the next line.

apples, gooseberries, strawberries, currants, raspberries, and in winter, oranges, apples and pears, is far greater than is supposed. Those who wait until they can eat this plain fare, with the sauce of appetite, will scarcely join with the hypocritical sensualist at a lord mayor's feast, who declaims against the pleasures of the table. Solomon kept a thousand concubines, and owned in despair that all was vanity. The man whose happiness is constituted by the society of one amiable woman, would find some difficulty in sympathizing with the disappointment of this venerable debauchee.

I address myself not only to the young enthusiast: the ardent devotee of truth and virtue; the pure and passionate moralist, yet unvitiated by the contagion of the world. He will embrace a pure system, from its abstract truth, its beauty, its simplicity, and its promise of wide-extended benefit; unless custom has turned poison into food, he will hate the brutal pleasures of the chace by instinct; it will be a contemplation full of horror and disappointment to his mind, that beings capable of the gentlest and most admirable sympathies, should take delight in the death-pangs and last convulsions of dying animals. The elderly man, whose youth has been poisoned by intemperance, or who has lived with apparent moderation, and is afflicted with a variety of painful maladies, would find his account in a beneficial change produced without the risk of poisonous medicines. The mother, to whom the perpetual restlessness of disease, and unaccountable deaths incident to her children, are the causes of incurable unhappiness, would on this diet experience the satisfaction of beholding their perpetual healths and natural

playfulness.[1] The most valuable lives are daily destroyed
by diseases, that it is dangerous to palliate and impossible to cure by medicine. How much longer will man
continue to pimp for the gluttony of death, his most
insidious, implacable, and eternal foe ?[2]

The proselyte to a simple and natural diet who desires
health, must from the moment of his conversion attend to
these rules—

NEVER TAKE ANY SUBSTANCE INTO THE STOMACH
THAT ONCE HAD LIFE.

DRINK NO LIQUID BUT WATER RESTORED TO ITS
ORIGINAL PURITY BY DISTILLATION.

---

[1] See Mr. Newton's book. His children are the most beautiful and
healthy creatures it is possible to conceive ; the girls are perfect models
for a sculptor ; their dispositions are also the most gentle and conciliating ;
the judicious treatment, which they experience in other points, may be
a correlative cause of this. In the first five years of their life, of 18000
children that are born, 7500 die of various diseases; and how many
more of those that survive are not rendered miserable by maladies not
immediately mortal ? The quality and quantity of a woman's milk,
are materially injured by the use of dead flesh. In an island near Iceland, where no vegetables are to be got, the children invariably die of
tetanus, before they are three weeks old, and the population is supplied
from the main land --Sir G. Mackenzie's Hist. of Iceland. See also
Emile, i. p. 53, 54. 56. [SHELLEY's NOTE.]

[2] The extracts from Plutarch's
treatise περὶ τῆς σαρκοφαγίας which
follow here in *Queen Mab* are not
given in the pamphlet, which ends,
instead, with the rules for " the
proselyte," and with the Appendix,
neither of which are in *Queen
Mab.*

APPENDIX.[1]

PERSONS on vegetable diet have been remarkable for longevity. The first Christians practised abstinence from animal flesh, on a principle of self-mortification.

1	Old Parr	152
2	Mary Patten	136
3	A shepherd in Hungary	126
4	Patrick O'Neale	113
5	Joseph Elkins	103
6	Elizabeth de Val	101
7	Aurungzebe	100

1 Cheyne's Essay on Health, p. 62
2 Gentleman's Magazine, vii. 449.
3 Morning Post, Jan. 28, 1800.
4 Emile, i. 44.
5 He died at Coombe in Northumberland.
6 Scot's Magazine, xxxiv. 696.
7 Aurungzebe, from the time of his Usurpation adhered strictly to the Vegetable System.   [SHELLEY'S NOTE.]

[1] In the reproduction of this Appendix the pamphlet has been followed precisely in every detail. Valuable merely as an index to the state of Shelley's mind towards the close of the year 1813, the work cannot be said to possess much intrinsic worth. As a contribution to medical science it of course has no significance, for it simply follows the leading of Newton, Lambe, and Trotter, whose books should be consulted by those who desire to ascertain how far Shelley's *Vindication of Natural Diet* is a collection of excerpts. The chief source from which the materials are drawn is "The Return to Nature, or, a Defence of the Vegetable Regimen; with some Account of an Experiment made during the last three or four years in the Author's Family. By John Frank Newton, Esq. Part the First. London Printed for J. Cadell and W. Davies, Strand, By J. M'Creery,

St. Anthony 105

James the Hermit 104

Arsenius 120

St. Epiphanius 115

Simeon 112

Rombald 120

Mr. Newton's mode of reasoning on longevity is ingenious and conclusive.

" Old Parr, healthy as the wild animals, attained to the age of 152 years.

" All men might be as healthy as the wild animals.

" Therefore all men might attain to the age of 152 years." [1]

The conclusion is sufficiently modest. Old Parr cannot be supposed to have escaped the inheritance of disease, amassed by the unnatural habits of his ancestors. The term of human life may be expected to be infinitely greater, taking into the consideration all the circumstances that must have contributed to abridge even that of Parr.

Black-Horse-Court. 1811." I am not aware of any further instalment of the Work having been published. It bears on the title-page the following motto from Spenser's *Year of Sorrow:*

Man, only man, Creation's Lord confess'd,
Amidst his happy realm remains unbless'd ;
On the bright earth, his flow'r-embroider'd throne,
Th' imperial mourner reigns and weeps alone

Newton's book is dedicated to Dr.

William Lambe, the author of the " Reports on the Effects of a peculiar Regimen in Scirrhous Tumours and Cancerous Ulcers." I have not thought it worth while to go through these medical books to ascertain whether Shelley's instances of old age are all culled from them, still less to verify the authorities cited in his note : this, however, might be an agreeable exercise for some enthusiastic vegetarian.

[1] Return to Nature. [SHELLEY'S NOTE.]

It may be here remarked, that the author and his wife have lived on vegetables for eight months. The improvements of health and temper here stated is the result of his own experience.

THE END.

[OF A VINDICATION OF NATURAL DIET.]

The imprint of *A Vindication of Natural Diet* is as follows:

SMITH AND DAVY, PRINTERS, QUEEN STREET, SEVEN DIALS.

A REFUTATION OF DEISM.

[Mr. Hogg, at pp. 484-6, Vol. II, of his Life of Shelley, gives an account of *A Refutation of Deism*, which he thinks was published at *the beginning* of the year 1814. It is another offshoot from *Queen Mab* repeating, and reconstructing in a different form, much from the Notes to that work, which notes, however, it leaves far behind in point of literary merit. In February, 1843, a small extract from this work was printed in *The Model Republic*, as from "an unpublished work" of Shelley; and in May of the same year this curious little radical monthly gave its readers a large excerpt, the passage from "Design must be proved" to "principles of reason" occupying pp. 63 to 78 of the present volume, but with the omission of the Greek note at p. 70. Thus Hogg had been forestalled in his revelation of Shelley's authorship of the book. No copy was recovered to the public till 1874: on the 19th of June in that year a copy was bought by the Trustees of the British Museum. It is a very boldly printed 8vo., consisting of title-page as reproduced opposite, pages III to V of Preface in double pica type, a leaf with list of *errata*, and 101 pages of text, with head-lines, *Eusebes and Theosophus*, throughout. Mr. Hogg describes it as " very incorrectly printed"; but beyond the seventeen verbal errors corrected in the list, and probably arising from indistinct writing, I have only found eight that are clearly printer's errors: there are of course inaccuracies of Shelley's beside these, and certain inconsistencies which may or may not be the printer's. I have made no changes without noting them, here as elsewhere. As the book is a curiosity in virtue of its scarceness, the present reproduction of it is completed by the record, in foot-notes, of the several mistakes corrected in the list of *errata*. Shelley's notes, in whatever language, are given *verbatim et literatim* from his own edition, except that he has not been followed in the accidental omission of the word *wroth* from the passage which he quotes at p. 46 from the 31st chapter of *Numbers*. — H. B. F.]

A

REFUTATION

OF

DEISM:

IN

A DIALOGUE.

ΣΥΝΕΤΟΙΣΙΝ.

London :

PRINTED BY SCHULZE AND DEAN,

13, POLAND STREET.

1814.

PREFACE.

[BY SHELLEY.]

THE object of the following Dialogue is to prove that the system of Deism is untenable. It is attempted to shew that there is no alternative between Atheism and Christianity ; that the evidences of the Being of a God are to be deduced from no other principles than those of Divine Revelation.

The Author endeavours to shew how much the cause of natural and revealed Religion has suffered from the mode of defence adopted by Theosophistical Christians. How far he will accomplish what he proposed to himself, in the composition of this Dialogue, the world will finally determine.

The mode of printing this little work may appear too expensive, either for its merits or its length. However inimical this practice confessedly is, to the general diffusion of knowledge, yet it was adopted in this instance with a view of excluding the multitude from the abuse of a mode of reasoning, liable to misconstruction on account of its novelty.[1]

[1] Hogg's account of the work (Life, Vol. II, pp. 484–5) is worth appending to this Preface: it is as follows:—

"The year 1814 had come upon us. In that year—and at the beginning of the year, I think—Shelley published a work entitled, 'A Refutation of Deism: in a Dialogue.' It is handsomely, expensively, and very incorrectly printed, in octavo. It was published in a legal sense, unquestionably; whether it was also published in a publisher's sense, and offered for sale, I know not, but I rather think, that it was: the preface informs us that it was intended it should be. I never heard that anybody bought a copy; the only copy I ever saw is that which my friend kindly sent to me: it is inscribed by his own hand on the title-page: 'To his friend, T. Jefferson Hogg, from P. B. S.' I never heard it mentioned any farther than this, that two or three of the author's friends told me, that it had been sent as a present. It is a short dialogue, comprised in 101 pages of large print. Eusebes and Theosophus discourse together, and dispute with each other, much as the author himself loved to dispute, when he could find an opponent; whenever Eusebes could find a Theosophus and get up an antagonistic dialogue. It is written in his powerful, energetic, contentious style, but it contains nothing new or important, and was composed and printed also, in a hurry. He never spoke of it to me, or in my presence. It attracted no attention; and doubtless Shelley himself soon discovered that it did not merit it. The subject of vegetable diet is brought in, dragged in, and in a crude, undigested form. The whole matter is disposed of briefly, triumphantly, and dogmatically, in a single paragraph . . ."

Hogg then quotes the paragraph, and refutes its arguments *more suo*.

EUSEBES AND THEOSOPHUS.[1]

EUSEBES.

O Theosophus, I have long regretted and observed the strange infatuation which has blinded your understanding. It is not without acute uneasiness that I have beheld the progress of your audacious scepticism trample on the most venerable institutions of our forefathers, until it has rejected the salvation which the only begotten Son of God deigned to proffer in person to a guilty and unbelieving world. To this excess then has the pride of the human understanding at length arrived? To measure itself with Omniscience! To scan the intentions of Inscrutability!

You can have reflected but superficially on this awful and important subject. The love of paradox, an affectation of singularity, or the pride of reason has seduced you to the barren and gloomy paths of infidelity. Surely you

---

[1] In place of the title, *A Refutation of Deism*, this first page bears in Shelley's edition the heading *Eusebes and Theosophus*; and, as those words are uniformly adopted for the head-lines, the other name appearing nowhere but in the title-page, it seems not unlikely either that it was originally intended to call the work *Eusebes and Theosophus*, or that Deism was to have been refuted in a Series of Dialogues, each denominated by the names of the interlocutors.

have hardened yourself against the truth with a spirit of coldness and cavil.

Have you been wholly inattentive to the accumulated evidence which the Deity has been pleased to attach to the revelation of his will? The antient books in which the advent of the Messiah was predicted, the miracles by which its truth has been so conspicuously confirmed, the martyrs who have undergone every variety of torment in attestation of its veracity? You seem to require mathematical demonstration in a case which admits of no more than strong moral probability. Surely the merit of that faith which we are required to repose in our Redeemer would be thus entirely done away. Where is the difficulty of according credit to that which is perfectly plain and evident? How is he entitled to a recompense who believes what he cannot disbelieve?

When there is satisfactory evidence that the witnesses of the Christian miracles passed their lives in labours, dangers and sufferings, and consented severally to be racked, burned and strangled, in testimony of the truth of their account, will it be asserted that they were actuated by a disinterested desire of deceiving others? That they were hypocrites for no end but to teach the purest doctrine that ever enlightened the world, and martyrs without any prospect of emolument or fame? The sophist who gravely advances an opinion thus absurd, certainly sins with gratuitous and indefensible pertinacity.

The history of Christianity is itself the most indisputable proof of those miracles by which its origin was sanctioned to the world. It is itself one great miracle.

A few humble men established it in the face of an
opposing universe. In less than fifty years an astonishing multitude was converted, as Suetonius,[1] Pliny,[2]
Tacitus[3] and Lucian attest; and shortly afterwards thousands who had boldly overturned the altars, slain the
priests and burned the temples of Paganism, were loud
in demanding the recompense of martyrdom from the
hands of the infuriated Heathens. Not until three
centuries after the coming of the Messiah did his[4] holy
religion incorporate itself with the institutions of the
Roman Empire, and derive support from the visible arm
of fleshly strength. Thus long without any assistance but
that of its Omnipotent author, Christianity prevailed in
defiance of incredible persecutions, and drew fresh vigour
from circumstances the most desperate and unpromising.

---

[1] Judæi, impulsore Chresto, turbantes, facile comprimuntur.—*Suet. in
Tib.*

Affecti suppliciis Christiani, genus hominum superstitionis novæ et
maleficæ.—*Id. in Neron.* [SHELLEY'S NOTE.]

[2] Multi omnis ætatis utriusque sexus etiam ; neque enim civitates tan-
tum, sed vicos etiam et agros superstitionis istius contagio pervagata
est. *Plin. Epist.* [SHELLEY'S NOTE.]

[3] Ergo abolendo rumori Nero subdidit reos et quæsitissimis pœnis
adfecit, quos, suo flagitio invisos, vulgus "Christianos" appellabat.
Auctor nominis ejus Christus, Tiberio imperitante, per procuratorem
Pontium Pilatum supplicio adfectus erat.   Repressaque in præsens
exitiabilis superstitio rursus erumpebat, non modo per Judæam, originem
ejus mali, sed per urbem etiam, quò cuncta, undique atrocia aut
pudenda, confluunt concelebranturque.   Igitur primo correpti, qui
fatebantur; deinde indicio eorum multitudo ingens haud perinde in
crimine incendii, quam odio humani generis convicti sunt, et pereuntibus
addita ludibria, ut, ferarum tergis contecti, laniatu canum interirent,
aut crucibus affixi, aut flammandi, atque ubi defecisset dies, in usum
nocturni luminis urerentur.   Hortos suos ei spectaculo Nero obtulerat,
et Circense ludibrium edebat, habitu aurigæ permixtus plebi, vel curri-
culo insistens.   Unde quanquam adversus sontes, et novissima exempla
meritos, miseratio oriebatur, tanquam non utilitate publicâ, sed in
sævitiam unius absumerentur.

Tacitus Annal, L. XV, Sect. XLV. [SHELLEY'S NOTE.]

[4] Omitted in the text and supplied in the *Errata.*

By what process of sophistry can a rational being persuade himself to reject a religion, the original propagation
of which is an event wholly unparalleled in the sphere of
human experience ?

The morality of the Christian religion is as original
and sublime, as its miracles and mysteries are unlike all
other portents. A patient acquiescence in injuries and
violence ; a passive submission to the will of sovereigns ;
a disregard of those ties by which the feelings of
humanity have ever been bound to this unimportant
world ; humility and faith, are doctrines neither similar
nor comparable to those of any other system.[1] Friendship, patriotism and magnanimity ; the heart that is
quick in sensibility, the hand that is inflexible in execution ;
genius, learning and courage, are qualities which have engaged the admiration of mankind, but which we are taught
by Christianity to consider as splendid and delusive vices.

I know not why a Theist should feel himself more
inclined to distrust the historians of Jesus Christ, than
those of Alexander the Great. What do the tidings of
redemption contain which render them peculiarly obnoxious to discredit ? It will not be disputed that a
revelation of the Divine will is a benefit to mankind.[2]
It will not be asserted that even under the Christian
revelation, we have too clear a solution of the vast
enigma of the Universe, too satisfactory a justification
of the attributes of God. When we call to mind the
profound ignorance in which, with the exception of the
Jews, the philosophers of antiquity were plunged ; when

---

[1] See the *Internal Evidence of Christianity* ; see also Paley's Evidences,
Vol. II, p. 27. [SHELLEY'S NOTE.]

[2] Paley's Evidences, Vol. I, p. 3. [SHELLEY'S NOTE.]

we recollect that men eminent for dazzling talents and
fallacious virtues, Epicurus, Democritus, Pliny, Lucretius,
Euripides,[1] and innumerable others, dared publicly to
avow their faith in Atheism with impunity, and that the
Theists, Anaxagoras, Pythagoras and Plato, vainly endeavoured by that human reason, which is truly incommen-
surate to so vast a purpose, to establish among philosophers
the belief in one Almighty God, the creator and preserver
of the world ; when we recollect that the multitude were
grossly and ridiculously idolatrous, and that the magistrates, if not Atheists, regarded the being of a God in the

---

[1] Imperfectæ verò in homine naturæ præcipua solatia ne Deum
quidem posse omnia. Namque nec sibi potest mortem consiscere, si
velit, quod homini dedit optimum in tantis vitæ pœnis ; nec mortales
æternitate donare, aut revocare defunctos ; nec facere ut qui vixit non
vixerit, qui honores gessit non gesserit, nullumque habere in præteritum
jus præterquam oblivionis, atque ut facetis quoque argumentis societas
hæc cum Deo copuletur ut bis dena viginti non sint, et multa similiter
ellicere non posse. Per quæ, declaratur haud dubiè, naturæ potentiam
id quoque esse, quod Deum vocamus.

Plin. Nat. His. Cap. de Deo.

Φησιν τις, ειναι δητ'εν ηρανῳ Θεὸς ;
Ουκ εισιν, ουκ εισ' .ει τις ανθρωπων λεγει,
Μη τῳ παλαιῳ μωρος ων χρησθω λογῳ.
Σκεψασθε δ'αυτα, μη'πι τοις εμοις λογοις
Γνωμην εχοντες. Φημ' εγω, τυργνιδα
Κτεινειν τε πολλὺς, κτηματων τ'αποστερειν,
Ορκηστε παραβαινοντας εκπορθειν πολεις.
Και ταυτα δρωντες μαλλον εισ' ευδαιμονες
Των ευσεβὸντων ἡσυχῃ καθ' ἡμεραν.
Πολειστε μικρας οιδα τιμὺσας Θεὸς,
Αι μειζονων κλυὸσι δυσσεβεστερων
Λογχης αριθμῳ πλειονος κρατὺμεναι.
Οιμαι δ'αν υμας, ει τις αργος ων Θεοις
Ευχοιτο, και μη χειρι συλλεγοι βιον· * * *

Euripides Belerophon. Fray. XXV.

Hunc igitur terrorem animi, tenebrasque necesse est
Non radii solis, neque lucida tela diei
Discutient, sed naturæ species ratioque :
Principium hinc cujus nobis exordia sumet,

NULLAM REM NIHILO GIGNI DIVINITUS UNQUAM.

Luc. de Rer. Nat. Lib. I. [SHELLEY'S NOTE.]

light of an abstruse and uninteresting speculation ;[1] when we add to these considerations a remembrance of the wars and the oppressions, which about the time of the advent of the Messiah, desolated the human race, is it not more credible that the Deity actually interposed to check the rapid progress of human deterioration, than that he permitted a specious and pestilent imposture to seduce mankind into the labyrinth of a deadlier superstition ? Surely the Deity has not created man immortal, and left him for ever in ignorance of his glorious destination. If the Christian Religion is false, I see not upon what foundation our belief in a moral governor of the universe, or our hopes of immortality can rest.

Thus then the plain reason of the case, and the suffrage of the civilized world conspire with the more indisputable suggestions of faith, to render impregnable that system which has been so vainly and so wantonly assailed. Suppose, however, it were admitted that the conclusions of human reason and the lessons of worldly virtue should be found, in the detail, incongruous with Divine Revelation ; by the dictates of which would it become us to abide ? Not by that which errs whenever it is employed, but by that which is incapable of error: not by the ephemeral systems of vain philosophy, but by the word of God, which shall endure for ever.

Reflect, O Theosophus, that if the religion you reject be true, you are justly excluded from the benefits which result from a belief in its efficiency to salvation. Be not regardless, therefore, I entreat you, of the curses so emphatically heaped upon infidels by the inspired organs of the will of God : the fire which is never quenched,

---

[1] See Cicero de Natura Deorum. [SHELLEY'S NOTE.]

the worm that never dies. I dare not think that the
God in whom I trust for salvation would terrify his
creatures with menaces of punishment, which he does not
intend to inflict. The ingratitude of incredulity is,
perhaps, the only sin to which the Almighty cannot
extend his mercy without compromising his justice.
How can the human heart endure, without despair,
the mere conception of so tremendous an alternative?
Return, I entreat you, to that tower of strength which
securely overlooks the chaos of the conflicting opinions
of men. Return to that God who is your creator and
preserver, by whom alone you are defended from the
ceaseless wiles of your eternal enemy. Are human institutions so faultless that the principle upon which they
are founded may strive with the voice of God? Know
that faith is superior to reason, in as much as the creature
is surpassed by the Creator; and that whensoever they
are incompatible, the suggestions of the latter, not those
of the former, are to be questioned.

Permit me to exhibit in their genuine deformity the
errors which are seducing you to destruction. State to
me, with candour the train of sophisms by which the evil
spirit has deluded your understanding. Confess the secret
motives of your disbelief; suffer me to administer a
remedy to your intellectual disease. I fear not the contagion of such revolting sentiments: I fear only lest
patience should desert me before you have finished the
detail of your presumptuous credulity.

THEOSOPHUS.

I AM not only prepared to confess, but to vindicate my
sentiments. I cannot refrain, however, from promising,

that in this controversey I labour under a disadvantage
from which you are exempt. You believe that incredulity
is immoral, and regard him as an object of suspicion and
distrust whose creed is incongruous with your own.   But
truth is the perception of the agreement or disagreement
of ideas.   I can no more conceive that a man who perceives the disagreement of any ideas, should be persuaded
of their agreement, than that he should overcome a
physical impossibility.   The reasonableness or the folly of
the articles of our creed is therefore no legitimate object
of merit or demerit ; our opinions depend not on the will,
but on the understanding.

If I am in error (and the wisest of us may not presume
to deem himself secure from all illusion) that error is the
consequence of the prejudices by which I am prevented,
of the ignorance by which I am incapacitated from forming a correct estimation of the subject.   Remove those
prejudices, dispel that ignorance, make truth apparent,
and fear not the obstacles that remain to be encountered.
But do not repeat to me those terrible and frequent curses,
by whose intolerance and cruelty I have so often been
disgusted in the perusal of your sacred books.   Do not
tell me that the All-Merciful will punish me for the conclusions of that reason by which he has thought fit to distinguish me from the beasts that perish.   Above all,
refrain from urging considerations drawn from reason, to
degrade that which you are thereby compelled to acknowledge as the ultimate arbiter of the dispute.   Answer my
objections as I engage to answer your assertions, point by
point, word by word.

You believe that the only and ever-present God begot

a Son whom he sent to reform the world, and to propitiate its sins; you believe that a book, called the Bible, contains a true account of this event, together with an infinity of miracles and prophecies which preceded it from the creation of the world. Your opinion that these circumstances really happened appears to me, from some considerations which I will proceed to state, destitute of rational foundation.

To expose all the inconsistency, immorality and false pretensions which I perceive in the Bible, demands a minuteness of criticism at least as voluminous as itself. I shall confine myself, therefore, to the confronting of your tenets with those primitive and general principles which are the basis of all moral reasoning.

In creating the Universe, God certainly proposed to himself the happiness of his creatures. It is just, therefore, to conclude that he left no means unemployed, which did not involve an impossibility to accomplish this design. In fixing a residence for this image of his own Majesty, he was doubtless careful that every occasion of detriment, every opportunity of evil should be removed. He was aware of the extent of his powers, he foresaw the consequences of his conduct, and doubtless modelled his being consentaneously with the world of which he was to be the inhabitant, and the circumstances which were destined to surround him.

The account given by the Bible has but a faint concordance with the surmises of reason concerning this event.

According to this book, God created Satan, who instigated by the impulses of his nature contended with the Omnipotent for the throne of Heaven. After a contest, for the empire, in which God was victorious, Satan was thrust into a pit of burning sulphur. On man's creation God placed within his reach a tree whose fruit he forbade him to taste, on pain of death; permitting Satan at the same time, to employ all his artifice to persuade this innocent and wondering creature to transgress the fatal prohibition.

The first man yielded to this temptation; and to satisfy Divine Justice the whole of his posterity must have been eternally burned in hell, if God had not sent his only Son on Earth, to save those few whose salvation had been foreseen and determined before the creation of the world.

God is here represented as creating man with certain passions and powers, surrounding him with certain circumstances, and then condemning him to everlasting torments because he acted as omniscience had foreseen, and was such as omnipotence had made him. For to assert that the Creator is the author of all good, and the creature the author of all evil, is to assert that one man makes a straight line and a crooked one, and that another makes the incongruity.[1]

Barbarous and uncivilized nations have uniformly adored, under various names, a God of which themselves were the model; revengeful, blood-thirsty, groveling and

---

[1] Hobbes. [SHELLEY'S NOTE.]

capricious.   The idol of a savage is a demon that delights
in carnage.   The steam of slaughter, the dissonance of
groans, the flames of a desolated land, are the offerings
which he deems acceptable, and his innumerable votaries
throughout the world have made it a point of duty to
worship him to his taste.[1]   The Phenicians, the Druids
and the Mexicans have immolated hundreds at the shrines
of their divinity, and the high and holy name of God has
been in all ages the watch word of the most unsparing
massacres, the sanction of the most atrocious perfidies.

But I appeal to your candour, O Eusebes, if there exist
a record of such groveling absurdities and enormities so
atrocious, a picture of the Deity so characteristic of a
demon as that which the sacred writings of the Jews contain.   I demand of you, whether as a conscientious
Theist you can reconcile the conduct which is attributed
to the God of the Jews with your conceptions of the
purity and benevolence of the divine nature.

The loathsome and minute obscenities to which the
inspired writers perpetually descend, the filthy observances
which God is described as personally instituting,[2] the
total disregard of truth and contempt of the first principles
of morality, manifested on the most public occasions by
the chosen favourites of Heaven, might corrupt, were they
not so flagitious as to disgust.

[1] See Preface to Le Bon Sens. [SHELLEY'S NOTE.]
[2] See Hosea, Chap. I. Chap. IX.
Ezekiel, Chap. IV. Chap. XVI. Chap. XXIII.
Heynë, speaking of the opinions entertained of the Jews by antient
poets and philosophers, says:

*Meminit quidem superstitionis Judaicæ Horatius, verum ut eam risu ex-
ploderet.*

Heyn. ad Verg. Poll. in Arg. [SHELLEY'S NOTE]

When the chief of this obscure and brutal horde of assassins asserts that the God of the Universe was enclosed in a box of shittim wood[1] "two feet long and three feet wide,"[2] and brought home in a new cart, I smile at the impertinence of so shallow an imposture. But it is blasphemy of a more hideous and unexampled nature to maintain that the Almighty God expressly commanded Moses to invade an unoffending nation, and on account of the difference of their worship utterly to destroy every human being it contained, to murder every infant and unarmed man in cold blood, to massacre the captives, to rip up the matrons, and to retain the maidens alone for concubinage and violation.[3] At the very time that philosophers of the

[1] 1 Sam. Chap. V. v. 8. [SHELLEY'S NOTE.]

[2] Wordsworth's Lyrical Ballads. [SHELLEY'S NOTE.]

[3] When Moses stood in the gate of the court and said—Who is on the Lord's side? Let him come unto me. And all the sons of Levi gathered themselves together unto him. *Thus saith the Lord God of Israel*, put every man his sword by his side, and go in and out from gate to gate throughout the camp, and *slay every man his brother, and every man his companion, and every man his neighbour.* And the children of Levi did according to the word of Moses, and there fell of the people on that day twenty three thousand men.

Exodus, Chap. XXXII, v. 26.

And they warred against the Midianites as the Lord commanded Moses, and they slew all the males; and the children of Israel took all the women of Midian captives, and their little ones, and took the spoil of all their cattle, and all their flocks, and all their goods. And they burned all their huts wherein they dwelt and all their goodly castles with fire. And Moses and Eleazer the priest, and all the princes of the congregation came forth to meet them without the camp. And Moses was wroth with the officers of the post, with the captains over hundreds and captains over thousands that came from the battle. And Moses said unto them—*Have ye saved all the women alive?*—Behold these caused the children of Israel through the counsel of Balaam to commit trespass against the Lord in the matter of Peor, and there was a plague among the congregation of the Lord. *Now therefore kill every male among the little ones, and kill every woman that hath known man by lying with him. And all the women-children that have not known a man by lying with him,* KEEP ALIVE FOR YOURSELVES.   *Numbers, Chap. XXXI.*

most enterprising benevolence were founding in Greece those institutions which have rendered it the wonder and luminary of the world, am I required to believe that the weak and wicked king of an obscure and barbarous nation, a murderer, a traitor and a tyrant was the man after God's own heart? A wretch, at the thought of whose unparalleled enormities the sternest soul must sicken in dismay! An unnatural monster who sawed his fellow beings in sunder, harrowed them to fragments under harrows of iron, chopped them to pieces with axes and burned them in brick-kilns, because they bowed before a different, and less bloody idol than his own. It is surely no perverse conclusion of an infatuated understanding that the God of the Jews is not the benevolent author of this beautiful world.

The conduct of the Deity in the promulgation of the Gospel, appears not to the eye of reason more compatible with His immutability and omnipotence than the history of his actions under the law accords with his benevolence.

You assert that the human race merited eternal reprobation because their common father had transgressed the

---

And we utterly destroyed them, as we did unto Sihon King of Heshbon utterly destroying the men, women and children of every city.
                              Deut. Chap. III, v. 6.
And they utterly destroyed all that was in the city both man and woman, young and old, and ox and sheep and ass with the edge of the sword.   *Joshua.*

So Joshua fought against Debir, and utterly destroyed all the souls that were therein, he left none remaining, but utterly destroyed all that breathed, as the *Lord God of Israel commanded.*   *Joshua, Chap. X.*

And David gathered all the people together and went to Rabbah and took it, and he brought forth the people therein, and *put them under saws and under harrows of iron, and made them pass through the brick-kiln. This did he also unto all the children of Ammon.*
          II Sam. Chap. XII, v. 29.   [SHELLEY'S NOTE.]

divine command, and that the crucifixion of the Son of
God was the only sacrifice of sufficient efficacy to satisfy
eternal justice. But it is no less inconsistent with justice
and subversive of morality that millions should be responsible for a crime which they had no share in committing; than that, if they had really committed it, the
crucifixion of an innocent being could absolve them from
moral turpitude. *Ferretne ulla civitas latorem istiusmodi
legis, ut condemnaretur filius, aut nepos, si pater aut avus
deliquisset ?* Certainly this is a mode of legislation peculiar
to a state of savageness and anarchy; this is the irrefragable logic of tyranny and imposture.

The supposition that God has ever supernaturally revealed his will to man at any other period than the
original creation of the human race, necessarily involves a
compromise of his benevolence. It assumes that he withheld from mankind a benefit which it was in his power to
confer. That he suffered his creatures to remain in
ignorance of truths essential to their happiness and salvation. That during the lapse of innumerable ages every
individual of the human race had perished without
redemption from an universal stain which the Deity at
length descended in person to erase. That the good and
wise of all ages, involved in one common fate with the
ignorant and wicked, have been tainted by involuntary
and inevitable error which torments infinite in duration
may not avail to expiate.

In vain will you assure me with amiable inconsistency
that the mercy of God will be extended to the virtuous,
and that the vicious will alone be punished. The foundation of the Christian Religion is manifestly compromised
by a concession of this nature. A subterfuge thus pal-

pable plainly annihilates the necessity of the incarnation of God for the redemption of the human race, and represents the descent of the Messiah as a gratuitous display of Deity, solely adapted to perplex, to terrify and to embroil mankind.

It is sufficiently evident that an omniscient being never conceived the design of reforming the world by Christianity. Omniscience would surely have foreseen the inefficacy of that system, which experience demonstrates not only to have been utterly impotent in restraining, but to have been most active in exhaling the malevolent propensities of men. During the period which elapsed between the removal of the seat of empire to Constantinople in 328, and its capture by the Turks in 1453, what salutary influence did Christianity exercise upon that world which it was intended to enlighten? Never before was Europe the theatre of such ceaseless and sanguinary wars; never were the people so brutalized by ignorance and debased by slavery.

I will admit that one prediction of Jesus Christ has been indisputably fulfilled. *I come not to bring peace upon earth, but a sword.* Christianity indeed has equalled Judaism in the atrocities, and exceeded it[1] in the extent of its desolation. Eleven millions of men, women and children have been killed in battle, butchered in their sleep, burned to death at public festivals of sacrifice, poisoned, tortured, assassinated and pillaged in the spirit of the Religion of Peace, and for the glory of the most merciful God.

---

[1] So in the *Errata*, but *them* in the text.

In vain will you tell me that these terrible effects flow not from Christianity, but from the abuse of it. No such excuse will avail to palliate the enormities of a religion pretended to be divine. A limited intelligence is only so far responsible for the effects of its agency as it foresaw, or might have foreseen them; but Omniscience is manifestly chargeable with all the consequences of its conduct. Christianity itself declares that the worth of the tree is to be determined by the quality of its fruit. The extermination of infidels; the mutual persecutions of hostile sects; the midnight massacres and slow burning of thousands because their creed contained either more or less than the orthodox standard, of which Christianity has been the immediate occasion; and the invariable opposition which philosophy has ever encountered from the spirit of revealed religion, plainly show that a very slight portion of sagacity was sufficient to have estimated at its true value the advantages of that belief to which some Theists are unaccountably attached.

You lay great stress upon the originality of the Christian system of morals. If this claim be just, either your religion must be false, or the Deity has willed that opposite modes of conduct should be pursued by mankind at different times, under the same circumstances; which is absurd.

The doctrine of acquiescing in the most insolent despotism; of praying for and loving[1] our enemies; of faith and humility, appears to fix the perfection of the human character in that abjectness and credulity which priests

---

[1] So in the *Errata*, but *loveing* in the text.

and tyrants of all ages have found sufficiently convenient
for their purposes.   It is evident that a whole nation of
Christians (could such an anomaly maintain itself a day)
would become, like cattle, the property of the first occu-
pier.   It is evident that ten highwaymen would suffice to
subjugate the world if it were composed of slaves who
dared not to resist oppression.

The apathy to love and friendship, recommended by
your creed, would, if attainable, not be less pernicious.
This enthusiasm of anti-social misanthropy if it were an
actual rule of conduct, and not the speculation of a few
interested persons, would speedily annihilate the human
race.   A total abstinence from sexual[1] intercourse is not
perhaps enjoined, but is strenuously recommended,[2] and
was actually practised to a frightful extent by the primitive Christians.[3]

The penalties inflicted by that monster Constantine,
the first Christian Emperor, on the pleasures of unlicenced
love, are so iniquitously severe, that no modern legislator
could have affixed them to the most atrocious crimes.[4] This
cold-blooded and hypocritical ruffian cut his son's throat,
strangled his wife, murdered his father-in-law and his
brother-in-law, and maintained at his court a set of blood-
thirsty and bigoted Christian Priests, one of whom was

---

[1] In the text, *social;* but *sexual* in the *Errata.*

[2] Now concerning the things whereof ye wrote to me. It is good
for a man not to touch a woman.

I say, therefore, to the unmarried and widows, it is good for them if
they abide even as I ; but if they cannot contain, let them marry ; it is
better to marry than burn.

                    1 *Corinthians. Chap. VII.* [SHELLEY'S NOTE.]

[3] See Gibbon's Decline and Fall, Vol. II, p. 210. [SHELLEY'S NOTE.]

[4] See Gibbon's Decline and Fall, Vol. II, p. 269. [SHELLEY'S NOTE.]

sufficient to excite the one half of the world to massacre
the other.

I am willing to admit that some few axioms of morality,
which Christianity has borrowed from the philosophers of
Greece and India, dictate, in an unconnected state, rules
of conduct worthy of regard; but the purest and most
elevated lessons of morality must remain nugatory, the
most probable inducements to virtue must fail of their
effect, so long as the slightest weight is attached to that
dogma which is the vital essence of revealed religion.

Belief is set up as the criterion of merit or demerit;
a man is to be judged not by the purity of his intentions
but by the orthodoxy of his creed; an assent to certain
propositions, is to outweigh in the balance of Christianity
the most generous and elevated virtue.

[1] But the intensity of belief, like that of every other
passion, is precisely proportionate to the degrees of excitement. A graduated scale, on which should be marked
the capabilities of propositions to approach to the test of
the senses, would be a just measure of the belief which
ought to be attached to them: and but for the influence
of prejudice or ignorance this invariably *is* the measure of
belief. That is believed which is apprehended to be true,
nor can the mind by any exertion avoid attaching credit
to an opinion attended with overwhelming evidence. Belief is not an act of volition, nor can it be regulated by
the mind: it is manifestly incapable therefore of either

[1] Shelley's recurrence to this line
of thought is very remarkable.
Compare this passage with the
Queen Mab note on the subject
(*Poetical Works*, Vol. IV, pp.
491 *et seq*), and also with the corresponding passages in *The Necessity of Atheism* and *A Letter to Lord
Ellenborough*.

merit or criminality. The system which assumes a false criterion of moral virtue, must be as pernicious as it is absurd. Above all, it cannot be divine, as it is impossible that the Creator of the human mind should be ignorant of its primary powers.

The degree of evidence afforded by miracles and prophecies in favour of the Christian Religion is lastly to be considered.

Evidence of a more imposing and irresistible nature is required in proportion to the remoteness of any event from the sphere of our experience. Every case of miracles is a contest of opposite improbabilities, whether it is more contrary to experience that a miracle should be true, or that the story on which it is supported should be false : whether the immutable[1] laws of this harmonious world should have undergone violation, or that some obscure Greeks and Jews should have conspired to fabricate a tale of wonder.

The actual appearance of a departed spirit would be a circumstance truly unusual and portentous; but the accumulated testimony of twelve old women that a spirit had appeared is neither unprecedented nor miraculous.

It seems less credible that the God whose immensity is uncircumscribed by space, should have committed adultery with a carpenter's wife, than that some bold knaves or insane dupes had deceived the credulous multitude.[2] We have perpetual and mournful experience of the latter: the former is yet under dispute. History affords us

---

[1] So in the *Errata*, but in the text *inimitable*.
[2] See Paley's Evidences, Vol. I Chap. I. [SHELLEY'S NOTE.]

innumerable examples of the possibility of the one : Philosophy has in all ages protested against the probability of the other.

Every superstition can produce its dupes, its miracles and its mysteries ; each is prepared to justify its peculiar tenets by an equal assemblage of portents, prophecies and martyrdoms.

Prophecies, however circumstantial, are liable to the same objection as direct miracles : it is more agreeable to experience that the historical evidence of the prediction really having preceded the event pretended to be foretold should be false, or that a lucky conjuncture of events should have justified the conjecture of the prophet, than that God should communicate to a man the discernment of future events.[1] I defy you to produce more than one instance of prophecy in the Bible, wherein the inspired writer speaks so as to be understood, wherein his prediction has not been so unintelligible and obscure as to have been itself the subject of controversy among Christians.

That one prediction which I except is certainly most explicit and circumstantial. It is the only one of this nature which the Bible contains. Jesus himself here predicts his own arrival in the clouds to consummate a period of supernatural desolation, before the generation which he addressed should pass away.[2] Eighteen hundred

---

[1] See the Controversy of Bishop Watson and Thomas Paine.—Paine's Criticism on the XIXth Chapter of Isaiah. [SHELLEY'S NOTE.]

[2] Immediately after the tribulation of these days, shall the sun be darkened and the moon shall not give her light, and the stars shall fall from Heaven, and the powers of the heavens shall be shaken ; and then shall appear the sign of the son of man in Heaven : and then shall all the tribes of the Earth mourn, and they shall see the son of man coming in

years have past, and no such event is pretended to have
happened. This single plain prophecy, thus conspicuously false, may serve as a criterion of those which are
more vague and indirect, and which apply in an hundred
senses to an hundred things.

Either the pretended predictions in the Bible were
meant to be understood, or they were not. If they were,
why is there any dispute concerning them : if they were
not, wherefore were they written at all ? But the God of
Christianity spoke to mankind in parables, that seeing
they might not see, and hearing they might not understand.

The Gospels contain internal evidence that they were
not written by eye-witnesses of the event which they pretend to record. The Gospel of St. Matthew was plainly
not written until some time after the taking of Jerusalem,
that is, at least forty years after the execution of Jesus
Christ: for he makes Jesus say *that upon you may come
all the righteous blood shed upon the earth, from the blood
of righteous Abel unto the blood of Zacharias son of Barachias whom ye slew between the altar and the temple.*[1] Now
Zacharias son of Barachias was assassinated between the
altar and the temple by a faction of zealots, during the
siege of Jerusalem.[2]

the clouds of Heaven with power and great Glory : and he shall send his
Angel with a great sound of a trumpet, and they shall gather together
his elect from the four winds, from one end of Heaven to the other.
*Verily I say unto you: This generation shall not pass until all these
things be fulfilled.*
Matthew, Chap. XXIV. [SHELLEY'S NOTE.]

[1] See Matthew, Chap. XXIII, v. 35. [SHELLEY'S NOTE.]

[2] Josephus. [SHELLEY'S NOTE.]

You assert that the design of the instances of super-natural interposition which the Gospel records was to convince mankind that Jesus Christ was truly the expected Redeemer. But it is as impossible that any human sophistry should frustrate the manifestation of Omnipotence, as that Omniscience should fail to select the most efficient means of accomplishing its design. Eighteen centuries have passed and the tenth part of the human race have a blind and mechanical belief in that Redeemer, without a complete reliance on the merits of whom, their lot is fixed in everlasting misery : surely if the Christian system be thus dreadfully important its Omnipotent author would have rendered it incapable of those abuses from which it has never been exempt, and to which it is subject in common with all human institutions, he would not have left it a matter of ceaseless cavil or complete indifference to the immense majority of mankind. Surely some more conspicuous evidences of its authenticity would have been afforded than driving out devils, drowning pigs, curing blind men, animating a dead body, and turning water into wine. Some theatre worthier of the transcendent event, than Judea, would have been chosen, some historians more adapted by their accomplishments and their genius to record the incarnation of the immutable God. The humane society restores drowned persons ; every empiric can cure every disease ; drowning pigs is no very difficult matter, and driving out devils was far from being either an original or an unusual occupation in Judea. Do not recite these stale absurdities as proofs of the Divine origin of Christianity.

If the Almighty has spoken, would not the Universe have been convinced? If he had judged the knowledge of his will to have been more important than any other science to mankind, would he not have rendered it more evident and more clear?

Now, O Eusebes, have I enumerated the general grounds of my disbelief of the Christian Religion.—I could have collated its Sacred Writings with the Brahminical record of the early ages of the world, and identified its institutions with the antient worship of the Sun. I might have entered into an elaborate comparison of the innumerable discordances which exist between the inspired historians of the same event. Enough however has been said to vindicate me from the charge of groundless and infatuated scepticism. I trust therefore to your candour for the consideration, and to your logic for the refutation, of my arguments.

EUSEBES.

I WILL not dissemble, O Theosophus, the difficulty of solving your general objections to Christianity, on the grounds of human reason. I did not assist at the councils of the Almighty when he determined to extend his mercy to mankind, nor can I venture to affirm that it exceeded the limits of his power to have afforded a more conspicuous or universal manifestation of his will.

But this is a difficulty which attends Christianity in common with the belief in the being and attributes of God. This whole scheme of things might have been, according to our partial conceptions, infinitely more admirable and perfect. Poisons, earthquakes, disease, war,

famine and venomous serpents; slavery and persecution
are the consequences of certain causes, which according
to human judgment might well have been dispensed with
in arranging the economy of the globe.

Is this the reasoning which the Theist will choose to
employ? Will he impose limitations on that Deity whom
he professes to regard with so profound a veneration?
Will he place his God between the horns of a logical
dilemma which shall restrict the fulness either of his
power or his bounty?

Certainly he will prefer to resign his objections to
Christianity, than pursue the reasoning upon which
they are found, to the dreadful conclusions of cold and
dreary Atheism.

I confess, that Christianity appears not unattended
with difficulty to the understanding which approaches it
with a determination to judge its mysteries by reason.
I will even[1] confess that the discourse, which you have
just delivered, ought to unsettle any candid mind engaged in a similar attempt. The children of this
world are wiser in their generation than the children
of light.

But, if I succeed in convincing you that reason conducts to conclusions destructive of morality, happiness,
and the hope of futurity,[2] and inconsistent with the

---

[1] In the original edition *ever*, an
obvious misprint, looking at the
context.

[2] In the text *fraternity;* but
futurity in the *Errata*.

very existence of human society, I trust that you
will no longer confide in a director so dangerous and
faithless.

I require you to declare, O Theosophus, whether you
would embrace Christianity or Atheism, if no other
systems of belief shall be found to stand the touch-
stone of enquiry.

THEOSOPHUS.

I DO not hesitate to prefer the Christian system, or
indeed any system of religion, however rude and gross,
to Atheism.—Here we truly sympathize[1]; nor do I
blame, however I may feel inclined to pity, the man
who in his zeal to escape this gloomy faith, should
plunge into the most abject superstition.

The Atheist is a monster among men. Inducements,
which are Omnipotent over the conduct of others, are
impotent for him. His private judgment is his criterion
of right and wrong. He dreads no judge but his own
conscience, he fears no hell but the loss of his self
esteem. He is not to be restrained by punishments, for
death is divested of its terror, and whatever enters into
his heart, to conceive, that will he not scruple to execute.
*Iste non timet omnia providentem et cogitantem, et animad-
vertentem, et omnia ad se pertinere putantem, curiosum et
plenum negotii Deum.*

This dark and terrible doctrine was surely the abortion
of some blind speculator's brain: some strange and

---

[1] In the original *sympathise*, contrary to Shelley's practice.

hideous perversion of intellect, some portentous distortion of reason.   There can surely be no metaphysician sufficiently bigotted to his own system to look upon this harmonious world, and dispute the necessity of intelligence ; to contemplate the design and deny the designer[1] ; to enjoy the spectacle of this beautiful Universe and not feel himself instinctively persuaded to gratitude and adoration.   What arguments of the slightest plausibility can be adduced to support a doctrine rejected alike by the instinct of the savage and the reason of the sage ?

I readily engage, with you, to reject reason as a faithless guide, if you can demonstrate that it conducts to Atheism.   So little however do I mistrust the dictates of reason, concerning a supreme Being, that I promise, in the event of your success, to subscribe the wildest and most monstrous creed which you can devise.   I will call credulity, faith ; reason, impiety ; the dictates of the understanding shall be the temptations of the Devil, and the wildest dreams of the imagination, the infallible inspirations of Grace.

EUSEBES.

LET me request you then to state, concisely, the grounds of your belief in the being of a God.   In my reply I shall endeavour to controvert your reasoning, and shall hold myself acquitted by my zeal for the Christian religion, of the blasphemies which I must utter in the progress of my discourse.

---

[1] In the text, *designers :* in the *Errata, designer.*

THEOSOPHUS.

I WILL readily state the grounds of my belief in the being of a God. You can only have remained ignorant of the obvious proofs of this important truth, from a superstitious reliance upon the evidence afforded by a revealed religion. The reasoning lies within an extremely narrow compass: *quicquid enim nos vel meliores vel beatiores facturum est, aut in aperto, aut in proximo posuit natura.*

From every design[1] we justly infer a designer. If we examine the structure of a watch, we shall readily confess the existence of a watch-maker. No work of man could possibly have existed from all eternity. From the contemplation of any product of human art, we conclude that there was an artificer who arranged its several parts. In like manner, from the marks of design and contrivance exhibited in the Universe, we are necessitated to infer a designer, a contriver. If the parts of the Universe have been designed, contrived and adapted, the existence of a God is manifest.

But design is sufficiently apparent. The wonderful adaptation of substances which act to those which are acted upon; of the eye to light, and of light to the eye; of the ear to sound, and of sound to the ear; of every object of sensation to the sense which it impresses prove that neither blind chance, nor undistinguishing necessity has brought them into being.

[1] There is a curious mistake in the original here: the paragraph opens thus: *Design—every design.* The correction is from the *Errata.*

The adaptation of certain animals to certain climates, the relations borne to each other by animals and vegetables, and by different tribes of animals;[1] the relation lastly, between man and the circumstances of his external situation are so many demonstrations of Deity.

All is order, design and harmony, so far as we can descry the tendency of things, and every new enlargement of our views, every new[2] display of the material world, affords a new illustration of the power, the wisdom and the benevolence of God.

The existence of God has never been the topic of popular dispute. There is a tendency to devotion, a thirst for reliance on supernatural aid inherent in the human mind. Scarcely any people, however barbarous, have been discovered, who do not acknowledge with reverence and awe the supernatural causes of the natural effects which they experience. They worship, it is true, the vilest and most inanimate substances, but they firmly confide in the holiness and power of these symbols, and thus own their connexion with what they can neither see nor perceive.

If there is motion in the Universe, there is a God.[3] The power of beginning motion is no less an attribute of mind than sensation or thought. Wherever motion exists it is evident that mind has operated. The phenomena of the Universe indicate the agency of powers which cannot belong to inert matter.

[1] In the original this semi-colon is misplaced after *relation* in the same line.

[2] In the text, *open ;* but *new* in the *Errata*.

[3] See Dugald Stewart's outlines of Moral Philosophy and Paley's Natural Theology. [SHELLEY'S NOTE.]

Every thing which begins to exist must have a cause:
every combination, conspiring to an end, implies intelligence.

DESIGN must be proved before a designer can be inferred.
The matter in controversy is the existence of design in
the Universe, and it is not permitted to assume the contested premises and thence infer the matter in dispute.
Insidiously to employ the words contrivance, design and
adaptation before these circumstances are made apparent
in the Universe, thence justly inferring[1] a contriver, is
a popular sophism against which it behoves us to be
watchful.

To assert that motion is an attribute of mind, that
matter is inert, that every combination is the result of
intelligence is also an assumption of the matter in
dispute.

Why do we admit design in any machine of human
contrivance ?   Simply, because innumerable instances of
machines having been contrived by human art are present to our mind, because we are acquainted with persons
who could construct such machines; but if, having no
previous knowledge of any artificial contrivance, we had
accidentally found a watch upon the ground, we should
have been justified in concluding that it was a thing of
Nature, that it was a combination of matter with whose
cause we were unacquainted, and that any attempt to
account for the origin of its existence would be equally
presumptuous and unsatisfactory.

[1] In the original, *infering*.

The analogy which you attempt to establish between the contrivances of human art, and the various existences of the Universe, is inadmissible. We attribute these effects to human intelligence, because we know before hand that human intelligence is capable of producing them. Take away this knowledge, and the grounds of our reasoning will be destroyed. Our entire ignorance, therefore, of the Divine Nature leaves this analogy defective in its most essential point of comparison.

What consideration remains to be urged in support of the creation of the Universe by a supreme Being? Its admirable fitness for the production of certain effects, that wonderful consent of all its parts, that universal harmony by whose changeless laws innumerable systems of worlds perform their stated revolutions, and the blood is driven through the veins of the minutest animalcule that sports in the corruption of an insect's[1] lymph: on this account did the Universe require an intelligent Creator, because it exists producing invariable effects, and inasmuch as it is admirably organized[2] for the production of these effects, so the more did it require a creative intelligence.

Thus have we arrived at the substance of your assertion. "That whatever exists, producing certain effects, stands in need of a Creator, and the more conspicuous is its fitness for the production of these effects, the more certain will be our conclusion that it would not have existed from eternity, but must have derived its origin from an intelligent creator."

---

[1] In the original *insects*, without the apostrophe,—a common lapsus of Shelley's in writing hastily.

[2] In the original *organised*.

In what respect then do these arguments apply to the Universe, and not apply to God? From the fitness of the Universe to its end you infer the necessity of an intelligent Creator. But if the fitness of the Universe, to produce certain effects, be thus conspicuous and evident, how much more exquisite fitness to his end must exist in the Author of this Universe? If we find great difficulty from its admirable arrangement, in conceiving that the Universe has existed from all eternity, and to resolve this difficulty suppose a Creator, how much more clearly must we perceive the necessity of this very Creator's creation whose perfections comprehend an arrangement far more accurate and just.

The belief of an infinity of creative and created Gods, each more eminently requiring an intelligent author of his being than the foregoing, is a direct consequence of the premises which you have stated. The assumption that the Universe is a design, leads to a conclusion that there are infinity of creative and created Gods, which is absurd. It is impossible indeed to prescribe limits to learned error, when Philosophy relinquishes experience and feeling for speculation.

Until it is clearly proved that the Universe was created, we may reasonably suppose that it has endured from all eternity. In a case where two propositions are diametrically opposite, the mind believes that which is less incomprehensible: it is easier to suppose that the Universe has existed, from all eternity, than to conceive an eternal being capable of creating it. If the mind sinks beneath the weight of one, is it an alleviation to encrease the intolerability of the burthen?

A man knows, not only that he now is, but that there was a time when he did not exist; consequently there must have been a cause. But we can only infer, from effects, causes exactly adequate to those effects. There certainly is a generative power which is effected by particular instruments; we cannot prove that it is inherent in these instruments, nor is the contrary hypothesis capable of demonstration. We admit that the generative power is incomprehensible, but to suppose that the same effects are produced by an eternal Omnipotent and Omniscient Being, leaves the cause in the same obscurity, but renders it more incomprehensible.

We can only infer from effects causes exactly adequate to those effects.—An infinite number of effects demand an infinite number of causes, nor is the philosopher justified in supposing a greater connection or unity in the latter, than is perceptible in the former. The same energy cannot be at once the cause of the serpent and the sheep; of the blight by which the harvest is destroyed, and the sunshine by which it is matured; of the ferocious propensities by which man becomes a victim to himself, and of the accurate judgment by which his institutions are improved. The spirit of our accurate and exact philosophy is outraged by conclusions which contradict each other so glaringly.

The greatest, equally with the smallest motions of the Universe, are subjected to the rigid necessity of inevitable laws. · These laws are the unknown causes of the known effects perceivable in the Universe. Their effects are the boundaries of our knowledge, their names the expressions of our ignorance. To suppose some existence beyond, or above them, is to invent a second and superfluous hypothesis to account for what has already been accounted for by the laws of motion and the properties of matter. I admit that the nature of these laws is incomprehensible, but the hypothesis of a Deity adds a gratuitous difficulty, which so far from alleviating those which it is adduced to explain, requires new hypotheses[1] for the elucidation of its own inherent contradictions.

The laws of attraction and repulsion, desire and aversion, suffice to account for every phenomenon of the moral and physical world. A precise knowledge of the properties of any object, is alone requisite to determine its manner of action. Let the mathematician be acquainted with the weight and volume of a cannon ball, together with the degree of velocity and inclination with which it is impelled, and he will accurately delineate the course it must describe, and determine the force with which it will strike an object at a given distance. Let the influencing motive, present to the mind of any person be given, and the knowledge of his consequent conduct will result. Let the bulk and velocity of a comet be discovered, and the astronomer, by the accurate estimation of the equal and contrary actions of the centripetal and centrifugal forces, will justly predict the period of its return.

The anomalous motions of the heavenly bodies, their unequal velocities and frequent aberrations, are corrected[2] by that gravitation by which they are caused. The illustrious Laplace, has shewn, that the approach of the Moon

---

[1] In the text, *hypothesis :* in the Errata, *hypotheses.*

[2] In the text, *connected* ; but *corrected* in the *Errata.*

to the Earth and the Earth to the Sun, is only a secular equation of a very long period, which has its maximum and minimum. The system of the Universe then is upheld solely by physical powers. The necessity of matter is the ruler of the world. It is vain philosophy which supposes more causes than are exactly adequate to explain the phenomena of things. *Hypotheses non fingo : quicquid enim ex phænomenis non deducitur, hypothesis vocanda est ; et hypotheses vel metaphysicæ, vel physicæ, vel qualitatum occultarum, seu mechanicæ, in philosophiâ locum non habent.*

You assert that the construction of the animal machine, the fitness of certain animals to certain situations, the connexion between the organs of perception and that which is perceived ; the relation between every thing which exists, and that which tends to preserve it in its existence, imply design. It is manifest that if the eye could not see, nor the stomach digest, the human frame could not preserve its present mode of existence. It is equally certain, however, that the elements of its composition, if they did not exist in one form, must exist in another ; and that the combinations which they would[1] form, must so long as they endured, derive support for their peculiar mode of being from their fitness to the circumstances of their situation.

It by no means follows, that because a being exists, performing certain functions, he was fitted by another being to the performance of these functions. So rash a conclusion would conduct, as I have before shewn, to an

---

[1] So in the *Errata ;* but *could* in the text.

absurdity; and it becomes infinitely more unwarrantable from the consideration that the known laws of matter and motion, suffice to unravel, even in the present imperfect state of moral and physical science, the majority of those difficulties which the hypothesis of a Deity was invented to explain.

Doubtless no disposition of inert matter, or matter deprived of qualities, could ever have composed an animal, a tree, or even a stone. But matter deprived of qualities, is an abstraction, concerning which it is impossible to form an idea. Matter, such as we behold it is not inert. It is infinitely active and subtile. Light, electricity and magnetism are fluids not surpassed by thought itself in tenuity and activity : like thought they are sometimes the cause and sometimes the effect of motion ; and, distinct as they are from every other class of substances, with which we are acquainted, seem to possess equal claims with thought to the unmeaning distinction of immateriality.

The laws of motion and the properties of matter suffice to account for every phenomenon, or combination of phenomena exhibited in the Universe. That certain animals exist in certain climates, results from the consentaneity of their frames to the circumstances of their situation : let these circumstances be altered to a sufficient degree, and the elements of their composition, must exist in some new combination no less resulting than the former from those inevitable laws by which the Universe is governed.

It is the necessary consequence of the organization of man, that his stomach should digest his food : it

inevitably results also from his gluttonous and unnatural
appetite for the flesh of animals that his frame be
diseased and his vigour impaired; but in neither of
these cases is adaptation of means to end to be perceived. Unnatural diet, and the habits consequent upon
its use are the means, and every complication of frightful
disease is the end, but to assert that these means were
adapted to this end by the Creator of the world, or that
human caprice can avail to traverse the precautions of
Omnipotence, is absurd. These are the consequences of
the properties of organized matter; and it is a strange
perversion of the understanding to argue that a certain
sheep was created to be butchered and devoured by a
certain individual of the human species, when the conformation[1] of the latter, as is manifest to the most superficial student of comparative anatomy classes him with
those animals who feed on fruits and vegetables.[2]

---

[1] In the original, *confirmation.*

[2] See Cuvier Leçons d' Anat. Comp. tom. iii. p. 169. 373. 448. 465.
480.—Rees's* Cyclopædia, Art. Man.

Ουκ αισθεσθε της ημερης καρπους αιματι και φονω μιγνυντες; αλλα
δρακοντας αγριης καλει *, και παρδαλεις και λεοντας, αυτοι δε μιαιφονειτε
εις ωμοτητα καταλιπονταις εκεινοις ηδεν. Εκεινοις μεν ο φονος τροφη, ημιν
δε οψον εστιν.

Οτι γαρ ουκ εστιν ανθρωπω κατα φυσιν το σαρκοφαγειν, πρωτον μεν απο
των σωματων δηληται της κατασκευης. Ουδενι γαρ εοικε το ανθρωπη
σωμα των απο σαρκοφαγια γεγονοτων. η γρυποτης χειλης, ουκ οξυτης
ονυχος, η τραχυτης οδοντων προσεστιν, η κοιλιας ευτονια και πνευματος
θερμοτης τρεψαι και κατεργασασθαι το βαρυ και κρεωδες. Αλλ' αυτοθεν η
φυσις τη λειοτητι των οδοντων, και τη σμικροτητι τη σωματος, και τη
μαλακοτητι της γλωσσης, και τη προς πεψιν αμβλυτητι τη πνευματος,
εξομνυται την σαρκοφαγιαν. Ει δε λεγεις πεφυκεναι σεαυτον επι τοιαυτην
εδωδην, ο βηλει φαγειν, πρωτον αυτος αποκτεινον, αλλ' αιτος δια σεαυτη,
μη χρησαμενΘ·κοπιδι. μηδε τυμπανω τινι, μηδε πελεκει· αλλα ως λυκοι και
αρκτοι και λεοντες αυτοι ως εσθιησι φονευησιν, ανελε δηγματι βην, η
σωματι συν, η αρνα η λαγωον διαρρηξον, και φαγε προσπεσων ετι ζωντος,
ως εκεινα·   Πλουτ. περι Σαρκοφαγ. Λογ. β. [SHELLEY'S NOTE.]

* In the original, *Rec's,* but *Rees's*   *Mab* and *A Vindication of Natural*
in the same note as given in *Queen*   *Diet.*

The means by which the existence of an animal is sustained, requires a designer in no greater degree than the existence itself of the animal. If it exists, there must be means to support its existence. In a world where *omne mutatur nihil interit*, no organized being can exist without a continual separation of that substance which is incessantly exhausted, nor can this separation take place otherwise, than by the invariable laws which result from the relations of matter. We are incapacitated only by our ignorance from referring every phenomenon, however unusual, minute or complex, to the laws of motion and the properties of matter; and it is an egregious offence against the first principles of reason, to suppose an immaterial creator of the world, *in quo omnia moventur sed sine mutuâ passione*; which is equally a superfluous hypothesis in the mechanical philosophy of Newton, and an useless excrescence on the inductive logic of Bacon.

What then is this harmony, this order which you maintain to have required for its establishment, what it needs not for its maintenance, the agency of a supernatural intelligence? Inasmuch as the order visible in the Universe requires one cause, so does the disorder whose operation is not less clearly apparent, demand another. Order and disorder are no more than modifications of our own perceptions of the relations which subsist between ourselves and external objects, and if we are justified in inferring the operation of a benevolent power from the advantages attendant on the former, the evils of the latter bear equal testimony to the activity of a malignant principle, no less pertinacious in inducing evil out of good, than the other is unremitting in procuring good from evil.

If we permit our imagination to traverse the obscure regions of possibility, we may doubtless imagine, according to the complexion of our minds, that disorder may have a relative tendency to unmingled good, or order be relatively replete with exquisite and subtile evil. To neither of these conclusions, which are equally presumptuous and unfounded, will it become the philosopher to assent. Order and disorder are expressions denoting our perceptions of what is injurious or beneficial to ourselves, or to the beings in whose welfare we are compelled to sympathize by the similarity of their conformation to our own.[1]

A beautiful antelope panting under the fangs of a tiger, a defenceless ox, groaning beneath the butcher's axe, is a spectacle which instantly awakens compassion in a virtuous and unvitiated breast. Many there are, however, sufficiently hardened to the rebukes of justice and the precepts of humanity, as to regard the deliberate butchery of thousands of their species, as a theme of exultation and a source of honour, and to consider any failure in these remorseless enterprises as a defect in the system of things. The criteria of order and disorder are as various as those beings from whose opinions and feelings they result.

Populous cities are destroyed by earthquakes, and desolated by pestilence. Ambition is every where devoting its millions to incalculable calamity. Superstition, in a thousand shapes, is employed in brutalizing and degrading the human species, and fitting it to endure without

---

[1] See Godwin's Political Justice, Vol. 1. p. 449. [SHELLEY'S NOTE.]

a murmur the oppression of its innumerable tyrants. All this is abstractedly neither good nor evil because good and evil are words employed to designate that peculiar state of our own perceptions, resulting from the encounter of any object calculated to produce pleasure or pain. Exclude the idea of relation, and the words good and evil are deprived of import.

Earthquakes are injurious to the cities which they destroy, beneficial to those whose commerce was injured by their prosperity, and indifferent to others which are too remote to be affected by their influence. Famine is good to the corn-merchant, evil to the poor, and indifferent to those whose fortunes can at all times command a superfluity. Ambition is evil to the restless bosom it inhabits, to the innumerable victims who are dragged by its ruthless thirst for infamy, to expire in every variety of anguish, to the inhabitants of the country it depopulates, and to the human race whose improvement it retards ; it is indifferent with regard to the system of the Universe, and is good only to the vultures and the jackalls that track the conqueror's career, and to the worms who feast in security on the desolation of his progress. It is manifest that we cannot reason with respect to the universal system from that which only exists in relation to our own perceptions.

You allege some considerations in favor of a Deity from the universality of a belief in his existence.

The superstitions of the savage, and the religion of civilized Europe appear to you to conspire to prove a

first cause. I maintain that it is from the evidence of
revelation alone that this belief derives the slightest
countenance.

That credulity should be gross in proportion to the
ignorance of the mind which it enslaves, is in strict consistency with the principles of human nature. The idiot,
the child and the savage, agree in attributing their own
passions and propensities[1] to the inanimate substances
by which they are either benefited or injured. The
former become Gods and the latter Demons ; hence
prayers and sacrifices, by the means of which the rude
Theologian imagines that he may confirm the benevolence
of the one, or mitigate the malignity of the other. He
has averted the wrath of a powerful enemy by suppli-
cations and submission ; he has secured the assistance of
his neighbour by offerings ; he has felt his own anger
subside before the entreaties of a vanquished foe, and has
cherished gratitude for the kindness of another. Therefore does he believe that the elements will listen to his
vows. He is capable of love and hatred towards his
fellow beings, and is variously impelled by those principles to benefit or injure them. The source of his error
is sufficiently obvious. When the winds, the waves and
the atmosphere, act in such a manner as to thwart or
forward his designs, he attributes to them the same propensities of whose existence within himself he is conscious when he is instigated by benefits to kindness, or
by injuries to revenge. The bigot of the woods can form
no conception of beings possessed of[2] properties differing
from his own : it requires, indeed, a mind considerably

---

[1] See Southey's History of Brazil, p. 255. [SHELLEY'S NOTE.]
[2] So in the *Errata;* but *by* in the text.

tinctured with science, and enlarged by cultivation to contemplate itself, not as the centre and model of the Universe, but as one of the infinitely various multitude of beings of which it is actually composed.

There is no attribute of God which is not either borrowed from the passions and powers of the human mind, or which is not a negation. Omniscience, Omnipotence, Omnipresence, Infinity, Immutability, Incomprehensibility, and Immateriality, are all words which designate properties and powers peculiar to organized beings, with the addition of negations, by which the idea of limitation is excluded.[1]

That the frequency of a belief in God (for it is not Universal) should be any argument in its favour, none to whom the innumerable mistakes of men are familiar, will assert. It is among men of genius and science that Atheism alone is found, but among these alone is cherished an hostility to those errors, with which the illiterate and vulgar are infected.

How small is the proportion of those who really believe in God, to the thousands who are prevented by their occupations from ever bestowing a serious thought upon the subject, and the millions who worship butterflies, bones, feathers, monkeys, calabashes and serpents. The word God, like other abstractions, signifies the agreement of certain propositions, rather than the presence of any idea. If we found our belief in the existence of God on the universal consent of mankind, we are duped by the

[1] See Le Système de la Nature : this book is one of the most eloquent vindications of Atheism. [SHELLEY'S NOTE.]

most palpable of sophisms. The word God cannot mean
at the same time an ape, a snake, a bone, a calabash, a
Trinity and a Unity : Nor can that belief be accounted
universal against which men of powerful intellect and
spotless virtue have in every age protested. *Non pudet
igitur physicum, id est speculatorem venatoremque naturæ,
ex animis consuetudine imbutis petere testimonium veri-
tatis ?*

Hume has shewn, to the satisfaction of all philosophers,
that the only idea which we can form of causation is
derivable[2] from the constant conjunction of objects, and
the consequent inference of one from the other. We
denominate that phenomenon the cause of another which
we observe with the fewest exceptions to precede its
occurrence. Hence it would be inadmissible to deduce
the being of a God from the existence of the Universe ;
even if this mode of reasoning did not conduct to the
monstrous conclusion of an infinity of creative and created
Gods, each more eminently requiring a Creator than its
predecessor.

If Power[3] be an attribute of existing substance, substance could not have derived its origin from power. One
thing cannot be at the same time the cause and the effect
of another.—The word power expresses the capability of
any thing to be or act. The human mind never hesitates
to annex the idea of power to any object of its experience.
To deny that power is the attribute of being, is to deny

---

[1] In the text, *et*; but *ex* is substituted in the *Errata.*

[2] In the original, *deniable,*—
clearly a misprint.

[3] For a very profound disquisition on this subject, see Sir William
Drummond's Academical Questions, chap. 1. p. 1. [SHELLEY'S NOTE.]

that being can be. If power be an attribute of substance, the hypothesis of a God is a superfluous and unwarrantable assumption.

Intelligence is that attribute of the Deity, which you hold to be most apparent in the Universe. Intelligence is only known to us as a mode of animal being. We cannot conceive intelligence distinct from sensation and perception, which are attributes to organized bodies. To assert that God is intelligent, is to assert that he has ideas; and Locke has proved that ideas result from sensation. Sensation can exist only in an organized body, an organized body is necessarily limited both in extent and operation. The God of the rational Theosophist is a vast and wise animal.

You have laid it down as a maxim that the power of beginning motion is an attribute of mind as much as thought and sensation.

Mind cannot create, it can only perceive. Mind is the recipient of impressions made on the organs of sense, and without the action of external objects we should not only be deprived of all knowledge of the existence of mind, but totally incapable of the knowledge of any thing. It is evident therefore that mind deserves to be considered as the effect, rather than the cause of motion. The ideas which suggest themselves too are prompted by the circumstances of our situation, these are the elements of thought, and from the various combinations of these our feelings, opinions and volitions, inevitably result.

That which is infinite necessarily includes that which

is finite.   The distinction therefore between the Universe,
and that by which the Universe is upheld, is manifestly
erroneous.   To devise the word God, that you may express
a certain portion of the universal system, can answer no
good purpose in philosophy : In the language of reason,
the words God and Universe are synonymous.[1]   *Omnia
enim per Dei potentiam facta sunt: imo, quia naturæ
potentia nulla est nisi ipsa Dei potentia, artem est nos
eatenus Dei potentiam non intelligere quatenus causas
naturales ignoramus; adeoque stultè ad eandem Dei
potentiam recurritur, quando rei alicujus, causam naturalem,
sive est, ipsam Dei potentiam ignoramus.*[2]

Thus, from the principles of that reason to which you
so rashly appealed as the ultimate arbiter of our dispute,
have I shewn that the popular arguments in favour of the
being of a God are totally destitute of colour.   I have
shewn the absurdity of attributing intelligence to the
cause of those effects which we perceive in the Universe,
and the fallacy which lurks[3] in the argument from design.
I have shewn that order is no more than a peculiar
manner of contemplating the operation of necessary
agents, that mind is the effect, not the cause of motion,
that power is the attribute, not the origin of Being.   I
have proved that we can have no evidence of the existence of a God from the principles of reason.

You will have observed, from the zeal with which I
have urged arguments so revolting to my genuine sentiments, and conducted to a conclusion in direct contradic-

[1] In the original, *synonimous.*
[2] Shelley here adds the note, "Spinosa. Tract. Theologico-Pol. chap. 1, p. 14."
[3] In the text, *works ;* but the correction is made in the *Errata.*
[4] So in the *Errata:* in the text, *used.*

tion to that faith which every good man must eternally
preserve, how little I am inclined to sympathize[1] with
those of my religion who have pretended to prove the
existence of God by the unassisted light of reason. I
confess that the necessity of a revelation has been compromised by treacherous friends to Christianity, who have
maintained that the sublime mysteries of the being of a
God and the immortality of the soul are discoverable
from other sources than itself.

I have proved, that on the principles of that philosophy to which Epicurus,[2] Lord Bacon, Newton, Locke
and Hume were addicted, the existence of God is a chimera.

The Christian Religion then, alone, affords indisputable assurance that the world was created by the power,
and is preserved by the Providence of an Almighty
God, who, in justice has appointed a future life for the
punishment of the vicious and the remuneration of the
virtuous.

Now, O Theosophus, I call upon you to decide between
Atheism and Christianity; to declare whether you will
pursue your principles to the destruction of the bonds of
civilized society, or wear the easy yoke of that Religion
which proclaims "peace upon earth, good-will to all men."

THEOSOPHUS.

I AM not prepared at present, I confess, to reply clearly
to your unexpected arguments. I assure you that no

---

[1] In the original, *sympathise*, contrary to Shelley's practice.

[2] So in the *Errata*; but *Epi-
phanes* in the text.

considerations, however specious, should seduce me to
deny the existence of my Creator.

I am willing to promise that if, after mature deliberation, the arguments which you have advanced in favour
of Atheism should appear incontrovertible, I will endeavour to adopt so much of the Christian scheme as is
consistent with my persuasion of the goodness, unity
and majesty of God.

FINIS.

The imprint of *A Refutation of Deism* is as follows :—

London : Printed by Schulze & Dean, 13, Poland Street.

A PROPOSAL FOR PUTTING REFORM TO THE VOTE.

[Of the two pamphlets issued in 1817 under the pseudonym of "The Hermit of Marlow," that whereof the title-page is reproduced opposite was clearly considerably the earlier. In an extant letter to Mr. Ollier, dated the 14th of March, Shelley asks "How does the pamphlet sell?"— a question which cannot refer to the Address on the Death of the Princess Charlotte, as that event did not occur till the 6th of November. The date given in the MS. (see p. 89) as that on which the meeting should be held at the Crown and Anchor Tavern, the 17th of March, also, of course, points to this as the pamphlet enquired after. By some good fortune the MS. used by the printer has escaped destruction and distribution, having been kept by Mr. Ollier, and sold by his family in July 1877. It is written on eighteen leaves, small 4to, on one side only, somewhat hastily, with many changes and erasures, and has the appearance of being the original draft, revised. The title-page, in Shelley's writing, with the exception of the draft imprint, originally commenced differently, *A Proposal for a National Meeting of the* . . . The MS. is now in the hands of Mr. Francis Harvey, bookseller, of 4, St. James's Street, by whose kind permission I have collated it with the printed text, and noted all variations and cancelled readings. These are not always by any means significant; but taken together they give us a glimpse of the measure of Shelley's fluency in writing such an address in the year 1817. *A Proposal for Putting Reform to the Vote* is an 8vo. pamphlet of one sheet, consisting of title-page and 13 pages of text, without head-lines and numbered centrally.—H. B. F.]

A Proposal

REFORM TO THE VOTE

THROUGHOUT THE KINGDOM.

BY THE HERMIT OF MARLOW.

LONDON:

PRINTED FOR C. AND J. OLLIER,

3, WELBECK STREET, CAVENDISH SQUARE;

By C. H. Reynell, 21, Piccadilly.

1817.

A PROPOSAL, &c.[1]

A GREAT question is now agitating in[2] this nation, which no man or party of men is competent to decide;[3] indeed there are no materials of evidence which can afford a foresight of the result. Yet on its issue depends whether we are to be slaves or freemen.

It is needless to recapitulate all that has been said about *Reform*. Every one is agreed that the House of Commons is not a representation of the people. The only theoretical question that remains is, whether the people ought to legislate for themselves,[4] or be governed by laws[5] and impoverished by taxes originating in the edicts[6] of an assembly which represents somewhat less

---

[1] The first page of the MS. is headed *An Address to the Reformers;* but the words are struck out.

[2] The word *in* is cancelled in the MS., but appears in the printed pamphlet. After *nation,* the words *which waits* are struck out.

[3] Cancelled MS. readings after *decide; or to foresce—and which—*

& the manner of the decision of which no one is able to predict. On its issue—On the issue.

[4] Cancelled MS. reading, *ought to be represented or not.*

[5] After *laws* the words *assented* and *which* are cancelled.

[6] Cancelled MS. reading *edicts of somewhat less.*

than a thousandth part of the intire community.   I
think they ought not to be so taxed and governed.   An
hospital for lunatics is the only theatre where we can
conceive so mournful a comedy to be exhibited as this
mighty nation now exhibits :[1] a single person bullying
and swindling a thousand of his comrades out of all they
possessed in the world, and then trampling and spitting[2]
upon them, though he were the most contemptible and
degraded of mankind, and they had strength in their
arms and courage in their hearts.   [3]Such a parable
realised in political society is a spectacle worthy of the
utmost indignation and abhorrence.

The prerogatives of Parliament [4]constitute a sovereignty which is[5] exercised in contempt of the People,
and it is in[6] strict consistency with the laws of human
nature that it should have been exercised for the People's
misery and ruin.   Those whom they despise, men
instinctively seek to render slavish and wretched, that
their scorn may be secure.   It is the object of the Reformers to restore the People to a sovereignty thus held in
their contempt.[7]   It is my object, or I would be silent now.

Servitude is sometimes voluntary.   Perhaps the People
choose to be enslaved; perhaps it is their will to be
degraded and ignorant and famished ;[8] perhaps custom is

---

[1] The words *as that* are struck
out before *a single*.

[2] In the MS. *trample and spit*.

[3] *To see* cancelled before *such*.

[4] Cancelled reading, *have been
exercised in contempt*.

[5] Cancelled reading, *has been for
is*.

[6] The word *obedience* is here
struck out.

[7] Cancelled MS. reading, *to restore the people to their Rights*, or

*rather to excite them to possess them-
selves of those rights ;* and again,
sovereignty which has been usurped.

[8] Cancelled passage—*perhaps the
fanaticism of custom has wooed them
to its inchantments so securely that
they would rather see their wives &
children starve by inches, rather hear
& see without indignation all the
contumelies of the proud & the
powerful, rather work sixteen hours
a day*.

their only God, and they its fanatic worshippers[1] will shiver in frost and waste[2] in famine rather than deny that idol; perhaps the majority of this nation decree[3] that they will not be represented in Parliament, that they will not[4] deprive of power[5] those who have reduced them to the miserable condition[6] in which they now exist. It is *their* will—it is their own concern. If such be their decision, the champions of the rights and the mourners over the errors and calamities of man, must retire to their homes in silence, until accumulated sufferings[7] shall have produced the effect of reason.

The question now at issue is, whether the majority of the adult individuals of the United Kingdom of Great Britain and Ireland desire or no a complete representation in the Legislative Assembly.

I[8] have no doubt that such is their will,[9] and I believe this is the opinion of most persons conversant with the state of the public feeling. But the fact[10] ought to be formally ascertained before we proceed.[11] If the majority of the adult population should[12] solemnly state their desire to be, that[13] the representatives whom they might appoint should constitute the Commons House of

---

[1] The words *& they* are here cancelled.

[2] MS. variation *pine* for *waste*.

[3] Cancelled phrase, *that they will live in squalidness & want.*

[4] The word *to* is here inserted in the MS., but does not appear in the printed text.

[5] Cancelled reading, *their power.*

[6] The words *of paying the* are struck out after *condition;* and after *exist,* Shelley has cancelled in turn *Is such* and *If such be.*

[7] MS. variation, *until suffering.*

[8] Cancelled phrase, *If that question is answered in the affirmative.*

[9] MS. variation, *desire* for *will;* and *private opinion* in the next phrase.

[10] Cancelled reading *it* for *the fact.*

[11] Cancelled line, *If the Reformers are really in the...*

[12] Cancelled reading, *shall* for *should.*

[13] Cancelled reading, *that they should be adequately represented.*

Parliament, there is an end to the dispute. Parliament would then be required, not petitioned, to prepare some effectual plan for[1] carrying the general will into effect; and if Parliament should then refuse, the consequences of the contest that might[2] ensue would rest on its presumption and temerity. Parliament would have rebelled against the People then.

If the majority of the adult population shall, when seriously called upon for their opinion, determine on grounds however erroneous, that the experiment of innovation by Reform[3] in Parliament is an evil of greater magnitude than the[4] consequences of misgovernment to[5] which Parliament has afforded a constitutional sanction, then it becomes us to be silent; and we should be guilty of the great crime which I have conditionally imputed to the House of Commons, if after unequivocal evidence that it was the national will to acquiesce[6] in the existing system we should, by partial assemblies of the multitude,[7] or by any party acts, excite the minority to disturb this decision.

The[8] first step towards Reform is to ascertain this point.

---

[1] Cancelled reading, *for the purpose*.

[2] Cancelled MS. reading, *would* for *might* and *their* for *its*. Shelley has inserted *alone* after *temerity*; but the word does not appear in the pamphlet. The next sentence was written as in the text; and *then* was afterwards transferred to a better position after *would;* but it may have been retransferred on further consideration when the proof was revised.

[3] The words *by Reform* are an afterthought.

[4] Cancelled reading, *abuse of pow[er]*.

[5] Cancelled reading, *which springs from its being made the instrument of private;* and again, *which we all...*

[6] Cancelled reading, *an unequivocal expression of the general will that they acquiesced.*

[7] MS. variation, *people* for *multitude;* and *overawe* for *disturb* in the next line.

[8] Cancelled phrases, *Let the national will be sacredly... Let the nation be free if it will to be... Let this point...*

For which[1] purpose I think the following plan would be effectual :—

That a Meeting should be appointed to be held at the *Crown and Anchor Tavern* on the[2]   of   , to take into consideration[3] the most effectual measures for ascertaining whether or no, a Reform in Parliament is[4] the will of the majority of the individuals of the British Nation.[5]

That[6] the most eloquent, and the most virtuous, and the most venerable among the Friends of Liberty,[7] should employ their authority and intellect to persuade men to lay aside all animosity and even[8] discussion respecting the topics on which they are disunited, and by the love which[9] they bear to their suffering country conjure[10] them to contribute all their energies to set this great question at rest—whether the nation desires[11] a Reform in Parliament or no ?

That the friends of Reform, residing in any part of the

---

[1] In the MS., *this*, not *which* as in the printed pamphlet. The next paragraph has two false starts, *To call a meeting*, and *That you, Sir, should call a meeting to be held*, which latter phrase seems to indicate that the work was originally intended for a Letter to some public man.

[2] In the MS. the date is given, *the seventeenth of March*.

[3] There is a cancelled passage here,—*and that all the friends of reform be invited to attend that meeting for the purpose of considering.*

[4] In the MS. *was* is cancelled in favour of *is*.

[5] The clause as to the invitation to the friends of reform is here again in the MS., and again struck out,—*That the friends of reform residing in any part of the country should be earnestly entreated to be present at this meeting.*

[6] Here again, after *That*, the words *all the friends* are struck out.

[7] The MS. reads *you* for *the Friends of Liberty*, and *all your* for *their*.

[8] The three words *animosity and even* are interpolated in the MS.

[9] Struck out in the MS., but given in the pamphlet.

[10] Cancelled MS. reading *entreat*.

[11] Cancelled reading, *Does the Nation desire*.

country, be earnestly entreated[1] to lend perhaps their last
and the decisive effort[2] to set their hopes and fears at
rest; that those who can should go[3] to London, and those
who cannot, but who yet feel that the aid of their talents
might be beneficial, should address a letter to the Chair-
man of the Meeting, explaining their sentiments: let
these letters be read aloud, let all things be transacted in
the face of day. Let Resolutions, of an import similar to
those that follow, be proposed.[4]

1.[5] That those who think that it[6] is the duty of the
People of this nation to exact such a Reform[7] in the
Commons House of Parliament, as should[8] make that
House a complete[9] representation of their will, and that
the People have a right to perform this duty, assemble
here[10] for the purpose of collecting evidence as to how far
it is the will of the majority of the People to acquit themselves of this duty, and to exercise this right.[11]

2. That the population of Great Britain and Ireland
be divided into three hundred distinct portions, each to

---

[1] Cancelled reading, *be conjured*.

[2] Cancelled reading, *the last
effort which*.

[3] The MS. shews a significant
variation here, *come* for *go*. I presume Shelley wrote the pamphlet
in London,—a supposition which
gains some support from the fact
that the last leaf is endorsed in his
writing, *Mr. Shelley, Mr. Hunt's*.

[4] Cancelled MS. reading, *Let the
following resolutions be proposed, or
something which should resemble.:.*

[5] Cancelled opening of the 1st
Resolution, — *That the Reformers
deny the imputation*.

[6] In the MS., *it* is wanting.

[7] MS. reading, *exact a full representation*.

[8] MS. reading, *shall* for *should*.

[9] Cancelled MS. reading, *full*.

[10] The variations *are now assembled* and *have assembled* are here
found in the MS.

[11] Here follow in the MS. several
cancelled passages, thus: (1) ...*for
they deny...* (2) *For that purpose they
divide the...* (3) *If the majority of the
nation determine...* (4) *If the opinion
of a majority of the nation shall be
found on examination to be determined to continue to be governed
as they are now governed, the...*
(5) *This meeting shall continue to
be held day after...* (6) *For that
purpose they divide the United Kingdom of Great Britain and Ireland
into 40 districts equal in each of
which...* (7) *For this purpose they
divide...*

contain an equal number of inhabitants,[1] and three hundred persons be commissioned, each personally to visit every individual within the district named in his commission, and to enquire whether or no that individual is willing to sign[2] the declaration contained in the third Resolution, requesting him to annex to his signature any explanation[3] or exposure of his sentiments, which he might choose to place on record. That the following Declaration be proposed for signature :—

3. That the House of Commons[4] does not represent the will of the People of the British Nation[5]; we the undersigned therefore declare, and publish, and our signatures annexed shall be evidence of our firm and solemn conviction that the liberty, the happiness, and the majesty of the great nation to which it is our boast to belong, have been brought into danger[6] and suffered to decay through the corrupt and inadequate manner in which Members are chosen to sit in the Commons House of Parliament[7]; we hereby express,[8] before God and our country,[9] a deliberate and unbiassed persuasion, that it is our duty, if we shall be found[10] in the minority in this great question, incessantly to petition; if among the

---

[1] Cancelled readings : (1) ... *number of persons, and they commission three hundred friends of reform, or persons who might be hired for the purpose, to visit...* (2)...*persons if possible disinterested, if not men ..*

[2] Cancelled readings, *to sign declaration No.* 2, and again, *the second resolution.*

[3] The words *he might think fit* are struck out of the MS. after *explanation.*

[4] The words *is not* are here struck out of the MS.

[5] Here there is the following rejected passage : *and that it is the duty of the People to require that House to originate such measures as shall remedy this enormous corruption. We therefore resolve...*

[6] Cancelled readings in the MS., *are endangered* and *are ill secured.*

[7] There are the following cancelled expressions in this sentence: (1) *The members of that assembly which falsely assumes to itself the title,*—(2) *which falsely call,*—(3) *style themselves the representatives of the nation.*

[8] The words *in the* are here struck out of the MS.

[9] After *Country,* the words *calling our* are struck out.

[10] Cancelled reading, *are found.*

majority, to require and exact that that House should
originate such measures of Reform, as would render its
Members the actual Representatives of the Nation.

4. That this Meeting shall be held day after day, until
it determines on the whole detail of the plan[1] for collecting evidence as to the will of the nation on the subject of
a Reform in Parliament.

5.[2] That this Meeting disclaims any design, however
remote, of lending their sanction to the revolutionary and
disorganizing schemes which have been most falsely imputed to the Friends of Reform, and declares that its
object is purely constitutional.

6. That a subscription be set on foot to defray the
expenses of this Plan.

In the foregoing proposal of Resolutions, to be submitted to a National Meeting of the Friends of Reform,
I have purposely avoided detail.[3]   If it shall prove that I
have in any degree[4] afforded a hint to men[5], who have
earned and established their popularity by personal sacrifices and intellectual eminence such[6] as I have not the
presumption to rival, let it belong to them[7] to pursue and
develope all suggestions[8] relating to the great cause of

---

[1] Cancelled readings, *until its
object be* and *until it shall have determined on the manner in which...*

[2] This resolution does not occur
in the MS., so that the next is there
No. 5.

[3] In the MS. there is a semicolon
here; and the sentence goes on
thus :—*it being the principal feature
in my design to excite others to a task
of which I am no less incapable
through habits of seclusion and delicacy of health, than feel...*

[4] After *degree* the words *practic-*

able and *beneficial* are struck out of
the MS.

[5] Cancelled reading,—*men of established popularity.*

[6] In the MS. *which* is here struck
out.

[7] Rejected MS. reading, *it belongs to them.*

[8] Cancelled readings : (1) *The
suggestions afforded by the...* (2)
the cause which they... (3) *suggestions which in the retirement of my
closet have involuntarily presented a
cause...*

liberty which has been nurtured (I am scarcely conscious of a metaphor) with their very sweat, and blood, and tears: some have tended[1] it in dungeons, others have cherished it in famine, all have been constant to it amidst persecution and calumny, and in the face of the sanctions of power:—so accomplish what ye have begun.

I shall mention therefore only one point[2] relating to the practical part of my Proposal. Considerable expenses[3] according to my present conception, would be necessarily incurred: funds should be created by subscription to meet these demands.[4] I have an income of a thousand a year, on[5] which I support my wife and children in decent comfort, and from which I satisfy certain large claims of general justice. Should any plan[6] resembling that which I have proposed be determined on by you, I will give £100, being a tenth part of one year's income, towards its object; and I will not deem so proudly[7] of myself, as to believe that I shall stand alone[8] in this respect, when any[9] rational and consistent scheme for the public benefit shall have received the sanction of those great and good men who have devoted themselves for its preservation.[10]

A certain degree of coalition among the sincere Friends of Reform, in whatever shape, is indispensable to the

---

[1] Cancelled MS. reading, *cherished.*
[2] The word *technical* is struck out of the MS. before *point.*
[3] Originally *expense,* and followed lower down by *This must be met by.*
[4] Cancelled reading *expense* for *demands.*
[5] In the MS. *from* is struck out in favour of *on.*
[6] Originally *Should my plan.*
[7] The words *when I confidently* are here struck out in favour of the reading of the text.
[8] The words *confident where devotion to the public good* are here cancelled.
[9] The word *temperate* is here struck out of the MS.
[10] There are three false starts for the next paragraph in the MS.:— *The leading feature in my plan is...,* *The only...,* and *An indis...*

success of this proposal.[1]   The friends of Universal or
of Limited Suffrage, of Annual or Triennial Parliaments,
ought to settle these subjects on which they disagree,
when it is known whether[2] the nation desires[3] that
measure on which they are all agreed.   It is trivial to
discuss what species of Reform shall have place, when it
yet remains a question whether there will be any Reform
or no.

Meanwhile, nothing remains for me but[4] to state explicitly my sentiments on this subject of Reform.   The
statement[5] is indeed quite foreign to the merits of the
Proposal in itself, and I should have suppressed it until
called upon to subscribe such a requisition as I have
suggested, if the question which it is natural to ask, as to
what are the sentiments of the person who originates the
scheme, could have received in any other manner a more
simple and direct reply.   It appears to me that Annual
Parliaments ought to be adopted as an immediate measure, as one which strongly tends to preserve the liberty
and happiness of the nation ; [6]it would enable men to
cultivate those energies on which the performance of the
political duties belonging to the citizen of a free state as
the rightful guardian of its prosperity, essentially de-

[1] Here follow in the MS. two
rejected beginnings, namely (1)
*The advocates of annual Parlia-
ments and Universal Suffrage...* (2)
*It requires some sacrifice of the selfish
the envious...*

[2] Cancelled MS. reading, *certain
that* for *known whether.*

[3] This was to have read *wills a'ny
Reform :* but *any Re* was cancelled
before the second word was completed ; and the MS. reads *wills
that measure,* &c.   The word *desires*
must have been substituted when

the proof was revised.

[4] Cancelled readings,—*it will be
asked w* [*hether*], and *I am bound.*

[5] This passage, from *The statement* to *direct reply,* does not occur
in the MS., where, at this point,
there are two rejected openings, *I
am* and *Annual Parliaments appear*

[6] In the MS. the original reading was, *by enabling men to cultivate
energies which have.*   This is struck
out and a new sentence begun, *It
would,* &c.

pends; it would familiarize men with liberty by dis-
ciplining them to an habitual acquaintance with its
forms. [1]Political institution is undoubtedly susceptible
of such improvements as no rational person can consider[2]
possible, so long[3] as the present degraded condition to
which the vital imperfections in the existing system of
government has reduced the vast multitude of men, shall
subsist. The securest method of arriving at such beneficial innovations, is to proceed gradually and with
caution; or in the place of that order and freedom
which the Friends of Reform assert[4] to be violated now,
anarchy and despotism will follow. Annual Parliaments
have my entire assent. I will not state those general
reasonings in their favour, which Mr. Cobbett and other
writers have already made familiar to the public mind.[5]

With respect to Universal Suffrage, I confess I[6] consider its adoption, in the present unprepared state of
public knowledge and feeling, a measure fraught with
peril. I think that none but those who register[7] their
names as paying a certain small sum in *direct taxes* ought,
at present, to send[8] Members to Parliament. The consequences of the immediate extension of the elective fran-
chise to every male adult, would be to place power[9] in
the hands of men who have been rendered brutal and
torpid and ferocious by ages of slavery. It is to suppose

---

[1] Cancelled MS. opening, *It would render innovations.*

[2] The word *as* is here cancelled in the MS.

[3] In the MS. we read here *in the present degraded condition, &c.;* and the sentence closes at *men.*

[4] Shelley began to write *complain* here but substituted *assert* before he had finished the word.

[5] Cancelled reading, *which Mr.*

Cobbett has placed already beyond the reach...

[6] The words *cannot but* are here struck out.

[7] Cancelled reading, *those who pay.*

[8] Cancelled reading in the MS., *to poss* [*ess ?*].

[9] Cancelled reading, *the happiness.*

that the qualities belonging to a demagogue are such as are sufficient to endow[1] a legislator. I allow Major Cartwright's arguments to be unanswerable ; abstractedly it is the right[2] of every human being to have a share in the government. But Mr. Paine's arguments are also unanswerable[3]; a pure republic may be shewn, by inferences the most obvious and irresistible, to be that system of social order the fittest to produce the happiness and[4] promote the genuine eminence of man. Yet, nothing can less consist with reason, or afford smaller hopes of any beneficial issue, than the plan which should abolish the regal and the aristocratical branches[5] of our constitution, before the public mind, through many gradations of improvement, shall have arrived at the maturity which can disregard these symbols of its childhood.[6]

[1] Cancelled reading, *qua [lify?]*.
[2] Cancelled reading, *it is the right abstractedly.*
[3] The following passage is here struck out of the MS. : *and who is bold enough to say that he would abolish the Lords and pull down the King, careless of all the ruin and bloodshed that must ensue. I am intimately persuaded that theoretically a pure republic is the...*
[4] Cancelled reading, *or.*
[5] Cancelled reading, *powers.*
[6] In the MS. a further paragraph is begun, thus, *Yet if the nation wills.*

FINIS.

The imprint of this pamphlet is as follows :—

C. H. Reynell, Printer,
    21, Piccadilly.

AN ADDRESS TO THE PEOPLE

ON THE

DEATH OF THE PRINCESS CHARLOTTE.

[The time at which the second Marlow pamphlet was written is ascertainable within a very few days. The Princess Charlotte died at 2.30 A.M. on the 6th of November, 1817 : on the following day the executions which so roused Shelley took place. On the 12th Shelley wrote from Mabledon Place (Hunt's residence) an unpublished letter to Mr. Ollier, enclosing what he had "written of a pamphlet on the subject of our conversation of the other evening",—to be "sent to press without an hour's delay" ; and he promised to send the rest of the MS. "before evening." He added "the subject tho' treated boldly is treated delicately." The reference is clearly to the *Address*, of which the title-page is given opposite as far as we know what it originally was. I am not aware of a copy of the original issue being extant ; but there is an early reprint bearing at the back of the title the words *Reprinted for Thomas Rodd, 2, Great Newport Street*. From this reprint the pamphlet is here given. It is an 8vo. tract of two half-sheets "stabbed" together : it consists of title-page and pages 3 to 16 of text, in eleven numbered paragraphs as here given. It is printed in large type set closely, without head-lines, and having the pages numbered centrally. It would be rash to assume the reprint to be a fac simile of the original; but it has too much character, almost, to be a bad representation of it.—H. B. F.]

"WE PITY THE PLUMAGE, BUT FORGET
THE DYING BIRD."

AN

ADDRESS TO THE PEOPLE

ON

The Death of the Princess Charlotte.

BY

The Hermit of Marlow.

AN ADDRESS, &c.[1]

———

I. THE Princess Charlotte is dead. She no longer moves, nor thinks, nor feels. She is as inanimate as the clay with which she is about to mingle. It is a dreadful thing to know that she is a putrid corpse, who but a few days since was full of life and hope; a woman young, innocent, and beautiful, snatched from the bosom of domestic peace, and leaving that single vacancy which none can die and leave not.

II. Thus much the death of the Princess Charlotte has in common with the death of thousands. How many

[1] This work is constantly spoken of as being entitled *We Pity the Plumage but Forget the Dying Bird*. That this is not the title is evident from the fact that the opening of the address is headed *An Address, &c.*; and in the setting of the title-page by which alone we know the tract, that of the reprint, there is nothing to justify the supposition that the words employed as a motto were meant for the title. Mr. MacCarthy (*Shelley's Early Life*, p. 394) points out that Shelley may probably have adopted the words from the following passage in *The Reflector* (Vol. I, p. 17): "It was pertinently said of the pathetic language which Mr. Burke, in his later writings, occasionally held on constitutional topics, that he pitied the plumage, but neglected the wounded and suffering bird."

women die in childbed and leave their families of
motherless children and their husbands to live on,
blighted by the remembrance of that heavy loss? How
many women of active and energetic virtues; mild,
affectionate, and wise, whose life is as a chain of happiness and union, which once being broken, leaves those
whom it bound to perish, have died, and have been
deplored with bitterness, which is too deep for words?
Some have perished in penury or shame, and their
orphan baby has survived, a prey to the scorn and
neglect of strangers. Men have watched by the bedside
of their expiring wives, and have gone mad when the
hideous death-rattle was heard within the throat, regardless of the rosy child sleeping in the lap of the unob-
servant nurse. The countenance of the physician had
been read by the stare of this distracted husband, till the
legible despair sunk into his heart. All this has been
and is. You walk with a merry heart through the
streets of this great city, and think not that such are the
scenes acting all around you. You do not number in
your thought the mothers who die in childbed. It is the
most horrible of ruins:—In sickness, in old age, in battle,
death comes as to his own home; but in the season of
joy and hope, when life should succeed to life, and the
assembled family expects one more, the youngest and the
best beloved, that the wife, the mother—she for whom
each member of the family was so dear to one another,
should die!—Yet thousands of the poorest poor, whose
misery is aggravated by what cannot be spoken now,
suffer this. And have they no affections? Do not their
hearts beat in their bosoms, and the tears gush from their
eyes? Are they not human flesh and blood? Yet
none weep for them—none mourn for them—none when

their coffins are carried to the grave (if indeed the parish furnishes a coffin for all) turn aside and moralize upon the sadness they have left behind.

III. The Athenians did well to celebrate, with public mourning, the death of those who had guided the republic with their valour and their understanding, or illustrated it with their genius. Men do well to mourn for the dead : it proves that we love something beside ourselves ; and he must have a hard heart who can see his friend depart to rottenness and dust, and speed him without emotion on his voyage to " that bourne whence no traveller returns." To lament for those who have benefitted the state, is a habit of piety yet more favourable to the cultivation of our best affections. When Milton died it had been well that the universal English nation had been clothed in solemn black, and that the muffled bells had tolled from town to town. The French nation should have enjoined a public mourning at the deaths of Rousseau and Voltaire. We cannot truly grieve for every one who dies beyond the circle of those especially dear to us ; yet in the extinction of the objects of public love and admiration, and gratitude, there is something, if we enjoy a liberal mind, which has departed from within that circle. It were well done also, that men should mourn for any public calamity which has befallen their country or the world, though it be not death. This helps to maintain that connexion between one man and another, and all men considered as a whole, which is the bond of social life. There should be public mourning when those events take place which make all good men mourn in their hearts,—the rule of foreign or domestic tyrants, the abuse of public faith, the wresting of old and venerable laws to the murder of the innocent, the established insecurity of all those, the flower of the nation, who cherish an unconquerable enthusiasm for public good. Thus, if Horne Tooke and Hardy had been convicted of high treason, it had been good that there had been not only the sorrow and the indignation which would have filled all hearts, but the external symbols of grief. When the French Republic was extinguished, the world ought to have mourned.

IV. But this appeal to the feelings of men should not be made lightly, or in any manner that tends to waste, on inadequate objects, those fertilizing streams of sympathy, which a public mourning should be the occasion of pouring forth. This solemnity should be used only to express a wide and intelligible calamity, and one which is felt to be such by those who feel for their country and for mankind; its character ought to be universal, not particular.

V. The news of the death of the Princess Charlotte, and of the execution of Brandreth, Ludlam, and Turner, arrived nearly at the same time. If beauty, youth, innocence, amiable manners, and the exercise of the domestic virtues could alone justify public sorrow when they are extinguished for ever, this interesting Lady would well deserve that exhibition. She was the last and the best of her race. But there were thousands of others equally distinguished as she, for private excellencies, who have been cut off in youth and hope. The accident of her birth neither made her life more virtuous nor her death more worthy of grief. For the public she had done nothing either good or evil; her education had rendered her incapable of either in a large and comprehensive sense. She was born a Princess; and those who are destined to rule mankind are dispensed with acquiring that wisdom and that experience which is necessary even to rule themselves. She was not like Lady Jane Grey, or Queen Elizabeth, a woman of profound and various learning. She had accomplished nothing, and aspired to nothing, and could understand nothing respecting those great political questions which involve the happiness of those over whom she was destined to rule. Yet this should not be said in blame, but in compassion: let us speak no evil of the dead. Such is the misery, such the impotence of royalty.—Princes are prevented from the cradle from becoming any thing which may deserve that greatest of all rewards next to a good conscience, public admiration and regret.

VI. The execution of Brandreth, Ludlam, and Turner, is an event of quite a different character from the death of the Princess Charlotte. These men were shut up in a horrible dungeon, for many months, with the fear of a hideous death and of everlasting hell thrust before their eyes; and at last were brought to the scaffold and hung. They too had domestic affections, and were remarkable for the exercise of private virtues. Perhaps their low station permitted the growth of those affections in a degree not consistent with a more exalted rank. They had sons, and brothers, and sisters, and fathers, who loved them, it should seem, more than the Princess Charlotte could be loved by those whom the regulations of her rank had held in perpetual estrangement from her. Her husband was to her as father, mother, and brethren. Ludlam and Turner were men of mature years, and the affections were ripened and strengthened within them. What these sufferers felt shall not be said. But what must have been the long and various agony of their kindred may be inferred from Edward Turner, who, when he saw his brother dragged along upon the hurdle, shrieked horribly and fell in a fit, and was carried away like a corpse by two men. How fearful must have been their agony, sitting in solitude on that day when the tempestuous voice of horror from the crowd, told them that the head so dear to them was severed from the body ! Yes—they listened to the maddening shriek which burst from the multitude : they heard the rush of ten thousand terror-stricken feet, the groans and the hootings which told them that the mangled and distorted head was then lifted into the air. The sufferers were dead. What is death ? Who dares to say that which will come after the grave ?[1] Brandreth was calm, and evidently believed that the consequences of our errors were limited by that tremendous barrier. Ludlam and Turner were full of fears, lest God should plunge them in everlasting fire. Mr. Pickering, the clergyman, was evidently anxious that Brandreth should not by a false confidence lose the single opportunity of reconciling himself with the Ruler of the future world. None knew what death was, or could know. Yet these men were presumptuously thrust into that unfathomable gulf, by other men, who knew as little and who reckoned not the present or the future sufferings of their victims. Nothing is more horrible than that man should for any cause shed the life of man. For all other calamities there is a remedy or a consolation. When that Power through which we live ceases to maintain the life which it has conferred,

---

[1] " Your death has eyes in his head—mine is not painted so."
                    CYMBELINE. [SHELLEY'S NOTE.]

then is grief and agony, and the burthen which must be borne : such sorrow improves the heart. But when man sheds the blood of man, revenge, and hatred, and a long train of executions, and assassinations, and proscriptions, is perpetuated to remotest time.

VII. Such are the particular, and some of the general considerations depending on the death of these men. But however deplorable, if it were a mere private or customary grief, the public, as the public, should not mourn. But it is more than this. The events which led to the death of those unfortunate men are a public calamity. I will not impute blame to the jury who pronounced them guilty of high treason, perhaps the law requires that such should be the denomination of their offence. Some restraint ought indeed to be imposed on those thoughtless men who imagine they can find in violence a remedy for violence, even if their oppressors had tempted them to this occasion of their ruin. They are instruments of evil, not so guilty as the hands that wielded them, but fit to inspire caution. But their death, by hanging and beheading, and the circumstances of which it is the characteristic and the consequence, constitute a calamity such as the English nation ought to mourn with an unassuageable grief.

VIII. Kings and their ministers have in every age been distinguished from other men by a thirst for expenditure and bloodshed. There existed in this country, until the American war, a check, sufficiently feeble and pliant indeed, to this desolating propensity. Until America proclaimed itself a republic, England was perhaps the freest and most glorious nation subsisting on the surface

of the earth.   It was not what is to the full desirable that
a nation should be, but all that it can be, when it does
not govern itself.   The consequences however of that
fundamental defect soon became evident.   The government which the imperfect constitution of our representative assembly threw into the hands of a few aristocrats,
improved the method of anticipating the taxes by loans,
invented by the ministers of William III, until an
enormous debt had been created.   In the war against the
republic of France, this policy was followed up, until now,
the *mere interest* of the public debt amounts to more than
twice as much as the lavish expenditure of the public
treasure, for maintaining the standing army, and the royal
family, and the pensioners, and the placemen.   The effect
of this debt is to produce such an unequal distribution of
the means of living, as saps the foundation of social union
and civilized life.   It creates a double aristocracy, instead
of one which was sufficiently burthensome before, and
gives twice as many people the liberty of living in luxury
and idleness, on the produce of the industrious and the
poor.   And it does not give them this because they are
more wise and meritorious than the rest, or because their
leisure is spent in schemes of public good, or in those
exercises of the intellect and the imagination, whose creations ennoble or adorn a country.   They are not like the
old aristocracy men of pride and honour, *sans peur et sans
tache*, but petty piddling slaves who have gained a right
to the title of public creditors, either by gambling in the
funds, or by subserviency to government, or some other
villainous trade.   They are not the " Corinthian capital
of polished society," but the petty and creeping weeds
which deface the rich tracery of its sculpture.   The effect
of this system is, that the day labourer gains no more now

by working sixteen hours a day than he gained before by
working eight.   I put the thing in its simplest and most
intelligible shape.   The labourer, he that tills the ground
and manufactures cloth, is the man who has to provide, out
of what he would bring home to his wife and children, for
the luxuries and comforts of those, whose claims are represented by an annuity of forty-four millions a year
levied upon the English nation.   Before, he supported the
army and the pensioners, and the royal family, and the
landholders; and this is a hard necessity to which it was
well that he should submit.   Many and various are the
mischiefs flowing from oppression, but this is the representative of them all; namely, that one man is forced to
labour for another in a degree not only not necessary to
the support of the subsisting distinctions among mankind,
but so as by the excess of the injustice to endanger the
very foundations of all that is valuable in social order, and
to provoke that anarchy which is at once the enemy of
freedom, and the child and the chastiser of misrule.   The
nation, tottering on the brink of two chasms, began to be
weary of a continuance of such dangers and degradations,
and the miseries which are the consequence of them; the
public voice loudly demanded a free representation of the
people.   It began to be felt that no other constituted
body of men could meet the difficulties which impend.
Nothing but the nation itself dares to touch the question
as to whether there is any remedy or no to the annual
payment of forty-four millions a year, beyond the necessary expenses of state, for ever and for ever.   A nobler
spirit also went abroad, and the love of liberty, and
patriotism, and the self-respect attendant on those glorious
emotions, revived in the bosoms of men. The government
had a desperate game to play.

IX. In the manufacturing districts of England discontent and disaffection had prevailed for many years; this was the consequence of that system of double aristocracy produced by the causes before mentioned. The manufacturers, the helots of our luxury, are left by this system famished, without affections, without health, without leisure or opportunity for such instruction as might counteract those habits of turbulence and dissipation, produced by the precariousness and insecurity of poverty. Here was a ready field for any adventurer who should wish for whatever purpose to incite a few ignorant men to acts of illegal outrage. So soon as it was plainly seen that the demands of the people for a free representation must be conceded if some intimidation and prejudice were not conjured up, a conspiracy of the most horrible atrocity was laid in train. It is impossible to know how far the higher members of the government are involved in the guilt of their infernal agents. It is impossible to know how numerous or how active they have been, or by what false hopes they are yet inflaming the untutored multitude to put their necks under the axe and into the halter. But thus much is known, that so soon as the whole nation lifted up its voice for parliamentary reform, spies were sent forth. These were selected from the most worthless and infamous of mankind, and dispersed among the multitude of famished and illiterate labourers. It was their business if they found no discontent to create it. It was their business to find victims, no matter whether right or wrong. It was their business to produce upon the public an impression, that if any attempt to attain national freedom, or to diminish the burthens of debt and taxation under which we groan, were successful, the starving multitude would rush in, and confound all orders and distinctions, and institutions and laws, in common ruin. The inference with which they were required to arm the ministers was, that despotic power ought to be eternal. To produce this salutary impression, they betrayed some innocent and unsuspecting rustics into a crime whose penalty is a hideous death. A few hungry and ignorant manufacturers seduced by the splendid promises of these remorseless blood-conspirators, collected together in what is called rebellion against the state. All was prepared, and the eighteen dragoons assembled in readiness, no doubt, conducted their astonished victims to that dungeon which they left only to be mangled by the executioner's hand. The cruel instigators of their ruin retired to enjoy the great revenues which they had earned by a life of villainy. The public voice was overpowered by the timid and the selfish, who threw the weight of fear into the scale of public opinion, and parliament confided anew to the executive government those extraordinary powers which may never be laid down, or which may be laid down in blood, or which the regularly constituted assembly of the nation must wrest out of their hands. Our alternatives are a despotism, a revolution, or reform.

X. On the 7th of November, Brandreth, Turner, and Ludlam ascended the scaffold. We feel for Brandreth the less, because it seems he killed a man. But recollect who instigated him to the proceedings which led to murder. On the word of a dying man, Brandreth tells us, that " OLIVER *brought him to this*"—that, " *but for* OLIVER, *he would not have been there.*" See, too, Ludlam and Turner, with their sons and brothers, and sisters, how they kneel together in a dreadful agony of prayer. Hell is before their eyes, and they shudder and feel sick with

fear, lest some unrepented or some wilful sin should seal
their doom in everlasting fire. With that dreadful penalty
before their eyes—with that tremendous sanction for the
truth of all he spoke, Turner exclaimed loudly and distinctly, *while the executioner was putting the rope round
his neck*, "THIS IS ALL OLIVER AND THE GOVERNMENT."[1]
What more he might have said we know not, because
the chaplain prevented any further observations.   Troops
of horse, with keen and glittering swords, hemmed in the
multitudes collected to witness this abominable exhibition.
"When the stroke of the axe was heard, there was a
burst of horror from the crowd.[2]   The instant the
head was exhibited, there was a tremendous shriek
set up, and the multitude ran violently in all
directions, as if under the impulse of sudden frenzy.
Those who resumed their stations, groaned and hooted."

---

[1] No doubt the contemporary
press if searched would yield
plenty of evidence of the hatred
and contempt with which this
government spy was regarded.
Perhaps one of the most note-
worthy utterances which he helped
to inspire was Charles Lamb's
grim poem *The Three Graves*, published in *The Poetical Recreations of
the Champion* in the year of Shelley's death, and not as well known
as it deserves to be, though given
in Mr. Charles Kent's excellent
edition of Lamb's Works (Rout-
ledge's "Popular Centenary Edition," without a date). I need not
apologize for quoting the poem
here. I give it from the *Poetical
Recreations*.

Close by the ever-burning brimstone beds,
Where Bedloe, Oates and Judas, hide their
    heads,
I saw great Satan like a Sexton stand,
With his intolerable spade in hand,

Digging three graves. Of coffin shape they
    were,
For those who, coffinless, must enter there
With unblest rites. The shrouds were of
    that cloth
Which Clotho weaveth in her blackest
    wrath :
The dismal tinct oppress'd the eye, that
    dwelt
Upon it long, like darkness to be felt.
The pillows to these baleful beds were toads,
Large, living, livid, melancholy loads,
Whose softness shock'd. Worms of all mon-
    strous size
Crawl'd round; and one upcoil'd, which
    never dies.
A doleful bell, inculcating despair,
Was always ringing in the heavy air.
And all about the detestable pit
Strange headless ghosts, and quarter'd
    forms, did flit ;
Rivers of blood, from living traitors
    spilt,
By treachery stung from poverty to guilt.
I ask'd the fiend, for whom these rites
    were meant ?
"These graves," quoth he, " when life's
    brief oil is spent,
When the dark night comes, and they're
    sinking bedwards,
—I mean for Castles, Oliver, and Edwards."

[2] These expressions are taken from the Examiner, Sunday, Nov. 9.
                          [SHELLEY'S NOTE.]

It is a national calamity, that we endure men to rule over us, who sanction for whatever ends a conspiracy which is to arrive at its purpose through such a frightful pouring forth of human blood and agony. But when that purpose is to trample upon our rights and liberties for ever, to present to us the alternatives of anarchy and oppression, and triumph when the astonished nation accepts the latter at their hands, to maintain a vast standing army, and add, year by year, to a public debt, which, already, they know, cannot be discharged; and which, when the delusion that supports it fails, will produce as much misery and confusion through all classes of society as it has continued to produce of famine and degradation to the undefended poor; to imprison and calumniate those who may offend them, at will; when this, if not the purpose, is the effect of that conspiracy, how ought we not to mourn?

XI. Mourn then People of England. Clothe yourselves in solemn black. Let the bells be tolled. Think of mortality and change. Shroud yourselves in solitude and the gloom of sacred sorrow. Spare no symbol of universal grief. Weep—mourn—lament. Fill the great City—fill the boundless fields, with lamentation and the echo of groans. A beautiful Princess is dead:—she who should have been the Queen of her beloved nation, and whose posterity should have ruled it for ever. She loved the domestic affections, and cherished arts which adorn, and valour which defends. She was amiable and would have become wise, but she was young, and in the flower of youth the despoiler came. LIBERTY is dead. Slave! I charge thee disturb not the depth and solemnity of our grief by any meaner sorrow. If One has died who was

like her that should have ruled over this land, like
Liberty, young, innocent, and lovely, know that the power
through which that one perished was God, and that it
was a private grief. But *man* has murdered Liberty, and
whilst the life was ebbing from its wound, there descended
on the heads and on the hearts of every human thing,
the sympathy of an universal blast and curse. Fetters
heavier than iron weigh upon us, because they bind our
souls. We move about in a dungeon more pestilential
than damp and narrow walls, because the earth is its
floor and the heavens are its roof. Let us follow the
corpse of British Liberty slowly and reverentially to its
tomb: and if some glorious Phantom should appear, and
make its throne of broken swords and sceptres and royal
crowns trampled in the dust, let us say that the Spirit of
Liberty has arisen from its grave and left all that was
gross and mortal there, and kneel down and worship it as
our Queen.

FINIS.

The imprint of the Address is as follows:—

Compton & Ritchie, Printers, Middle Street, Cloth Fair, London.

HISTORY

OF

A SIX WEEKS' TOUR.

[The little volume of which the original title-page is reproduced opposite has a peculiar interest, not only from its biographical value, but as
shewing what Shelley's idea of a book of travels was in 1817. Careful
readers will scarcely doubt that the journal kept by Mrs. Shelley was
revised and to some small extent interpolated by the poet; and the
responsibility of publication is expressly thrown on Shelley at p. xxi. of
Mrs. Shelley's preface to the *Essays, Letters*, &c. (2 vols. 1840), where we
read that " 'The Journal of a Six Weeks' Tour', and 'Letters from
Geneva', were published many years ago by Shelley himself. The
Journal is singular, from the circumstance that it was not written for
publication, and was deemed too trivial for such by its author. Shelley
caused it to be printed, and added to it his own letters, which contain
some of the most beautiful descriptions ever written." For some details
connected with those letters see the note at back of the fly-title *Letters*
(page 160 of this volume). I do not know positively whether this book
preceded or followed the second Marlow pamphlet in issuing from the
press; but I see no reason for doubting that the pamphlet, a single
sheet, was issued within a few days of the 12th of November, whereas
the *Six Weeks' Tour* was entered in the Stationers' Register as being
published by T. Hookham Jun. on the 10th of December, 1817. When
Mrs. Shelley says (page 121) " It is now *nearly* three years since this Journey
took place," I presume she is at the beginning of her task of transcribing
her journal : then there was all the rest of the book to get ready, print,
and bind ; and it may very well, in the busy year 1817, have been
several months before the book came out. The *History of a Six Weeks'
Tour* is a foolscap 8vo. volume, boldly printed, consisting of fly-title as
at back of this note, title-page (having at the back the imprint " Reynell,
Printer, 45, Broad-street, Golden-square"), preface pages iii to vi, text of
Journal pages 1 to 81, fly-title *Letters*, text of letters pages 85 to 172, fly-title
Lines Written in the Vale of Chamouni, and the poem of that name pages 175
to 183. The book is divided into the sections shewn in this edition ; but
there are no head-lines, the pages being numbered centrally with large
Arabic figures. This is one of the books of which Mr. Brooks seems to
have obtained a remainder ; for in 1829 an issue was made, consisting
of the 1817 sheets undisturbed in any particular except the cancelling of
the fly-title and title and the insertion of a new title only varying from
the old one after the word *Chamouni*, which is followed thus : " BY
PERCY B. SHELLEY. LONDON : PUBLISHED BY J. BROOKS,
421 OXFORD STREET 1829." Mrs. Shelley in publishing her
collection of Shelley's *Essays* &c. (referred to above), included both her
own portions of it and Shelley's,—making some revisions and additions,
which are noted in the present edition.— H. B. F.]

HISTORY

OF

A SIX WEEKS' TOUR

THROUGH

A PART OF FRANCE,
SWITZERLAND, GERMANY, AND HOLLAND:

WITH LETTERS

DESCRIPTIVE OF

A SAIL ROUND THE LAKE OF GENEVA, AND OF
THE GLACIERS OF CHAMOUNI.

LONDON:

PUBLISHED BY T. HOOKHAM, JUN.
OLD BOND STREET;

AND C. AND J. OLLIER,
WELBECK STREET.

1817.

PREFACE.

[BY SHELLEY.]

. . ... ——

Nothing can be more unpresuming than this little volume. It contains the account of some desultory visits by a party of young people to scenes which are now so familiar to our countrymen, that few facts relating to them can be expected to have escaped the many more experienced and exact observers, who have sent their journals to the press. In fact, they have done little else than arrange the few materials which an imperfect journal, and two or three letters to their friends in England afforded. They regret, since their little History is to be offered to the public, that these materials were not more copious and complete. This is a just topic of censure to those who are less inclined to be amused than to condemn. Those whose youth has been past as their's (with what success it imports not) in pursuing, like the swallow, the inconstant summer of delight and beauty which invests this visible world, will perhaps find some entertainment in following the author, with her husband and sister,[1] on foot, through part of France and Switzerland, and in sail-

[1] In the *Essays* &c. (1840) Mrs. Shelley substituted *friend* for *sister*.

ing with her down the castled Rhine, through scenes beautiful in themselves, but which, since she visited them, a great Poet has clothed with the freshness of a diviner nature. They will be interested to hear of one who has visited Meillerie,[1] and Clarens, and Chillon, and Vevai— classic ground, peopled with tender and glorious imaginations of the present and the past.

They have perhaps never talked with one who has beheld in the enthusiasm of youth the glaciers, and the lakes, and the forests, and the fountains of the mighty Alps. Such will perhaps forgive the imperfections of their narrative for the sympathy which the adventures and feelings which it recounts, and a curiosity respecting scenes already rendered interesting and illustrious, may excite.

The[2] Poem, entitled "Mont Blanc," is written by the author of the two letters from Chamouni and Vevai. It was composed under the immediate impression of the deep and powerful feelings excited by the objects which it attempts to describe; and as an undisciplined overflowing of the soul, rests its claim to approbation on an attempt to imitate the untameable wildness and inaccessible solemnity from which those feelings sprang.

---

[1] In Shelley's edition *Mellerie*, but *Meillerie* in Mrs. Shelley's.

[2] This paragraph is reprinted in the first edition of the *Essays* &c. (1840); but in later editions Mrs.

Shelley drops it, presumably because it is quoted in her note on the Poems of 1816 in her second edition of the *Poetical Works*.

It is now nearly three years since this Journey took place, and the journal I then kept was not very copious; but I have so often talked over the incidents that befel us, and attempted to describe the scenery through which we passed, that I think few occurrences of any interest will be omitted.[1]

We left London July 28th, 1814, on a hotter day than has been known in this climate for many years.
I am not a good traveller, and this heat agreed 28 July, 1814. very ill with me, till, on arriving at Dover, I was refreshed by a sea-bath. As we very much wished to cross the channel with all possible speed, we would not wait for the packet of the following day (it being then about four in the afternoon) but hiring a small boat, resolved to make the passage the same evening, the seamen promising us a voyage of two hours.

[1] It is evident from this opening paragraph that what Shelley printed was not the journal as actually kept during the tour, but an amplified version written before the end of July, 1817. As Mrs. Shelley expressly says she did not either mean it or think it worthy to be published, we must assume that she wrote it afresh either from her well-known love of writing, or from some other motive apart from publication. This section is headed with the word *Journal* in Mrs. Shelley's editions : but it has no heading in Shelley's.

The evening was most beautiful; there was but little wind, and the sails flapped in the flagging breeze: the moon rose, and night came on, and with the night a slow, heavy swell, and a fresh breeze, which soon produced a sea so violent as to toss the boat very much. I was dreadfully sea-sick, and as is usually my custom when thus affected, I slept during the greater part of the night, awaking only from time to time to ask where we were, and to receive the dismal answer each time—" Not quite half way."

The wind was violent and contrary; if we could not reach Calais, the sailors proposed making for Boulogne. They promised only two hours' sail from shore, yet hour after hour passed, and we were still far distant, when the moon sunk in the red and stormy horizon, and the fast-flashing lightning became pale in the breaking day.

We were proceeding slowly against the wind, when suddenly a thunder squall struck the sail, and the waves rushed into the boat: even the sailors acknowledged that our situation was perilous; but they succeeded in reefing the sail;—the wind was now changed, and we drove before the gale directly to Calais. As we entered the harbour I awoke from a comfortless sleep, and saw the sun rise broad, red, and cloudless over the pier.

FRANCE.

EXHAUSTED with sickness and fatigue, I walked over the sands with my companions to the hotel. I 29 July, 1814. heard for the first time the confused buzz of voices speaking a different language from that to which I had been accustomed; and saw a costume very unlike that worn on the opposite side of the channel; the women with high caps and short jackets; the men with earrings; ladies walking about with high bonnets or *coiffures* lodged on the top of the head, the hair dragged up underneath, without any stray curls to decorate the temples or cheeks. There is, however, something very pleasing in the manners and appearance of the people of Calais, that prepossesses you in their favour. A national reflection might occur, that when Edward III. took Calais, he turned out the old inhabitants, and peopled it almost entirely with our own countrymen; but unfortunately the manners are not English.

We remained during that day and the greater part of the next at Calais: we had been obliged to leave our

boxes the night before at the English custom-house, and
it was arranged that they should go by the packet of the
following day, which, detained by contrary wind, did not
arrive until night.   S*** and I walked among the fortifications on the outside of the town; they consisted of
fields where the hay was making.   The aspect of the
country was rural and pleasant.

On the 30th of July, about three in the afternoon, we
left Calais, in a cabriolet drawn by three
30 July, 1814.   horses.   To persons who had never before seen
any thing but a spruce English chaise and post-boy, there
was something irresistibly ludicrous in our equipage.   A
cabriolet is[1] shaped somewhat like a post-chaise, except
that it has only two wheels, and consequently there are
no doors at the sides; the front is let down to admit the
passengers.   The three horses were placed abreast, the
tallest in the middle, who was rendered more formidable
by the addition of an unintelligible article of harness, resembling a pair of wooden wings fastened to his shoulders;
the harnesses were[2] of rope; and the postillion, a queer,
upright little fellow with a long pig-tail, *cracked* his
whip, and clattered on, while an old forlorn shepherd with
a cocked hat gazed on us as we passed.

The roads are excellent, but the heat was intense, and
I suffered greatly from it.   We slept at Boulogne the first
night, where there was an ugly but remarkably good-
tempered femme de chambre.   This made us
30 July, 1814.   for the first time remark the difference which

---

[1] In Mrs. Shelley's editions *Our*
cabriolet was is substituted for *A*
cabriolet is; and the tense is altered
correspondingly in the subsequent

sentences.
[2] In Mrs. Shelley's editions we
read *harness was*.

exists between this class of persons in France and in England. In the latter country they are prudish, and if they become in the least degree familiar they are impudent. The lower orders in France have the easiness and politeness of the most well-bred English; they treat you unaffectedly as their equal, and consequently there is no scope for insolence.

We had ordered horses to be ready during the night, but we were too fatigued to make use of them. The man insisted on being paid for the whole post. *Ah! Madame,* said the femme-de-chambre, *pensez-y; c'est pour dedommager les pauvres chevaux d'avoir perdues leur douce sommeil.* A joke from an English chamber-maid would have been quite another thing.

The first appearance that struck our English eyes was the want of enclosures; but the fields were flourishing with a plentiful harvest. We observed no vines on this side Paris.

The weather still continued very hot, and travelling produced a very bad effect upon my health; my companions were induced by this circumstance to hasten the journey as much as possible; and accordingly we did not rest the following night, and the 31 July & 1 Aug., 1814. next day, about two, arrived in Paris.

In this city there are no hotels where you can reside as long or as short a time as you please, and we were obliged to engage apartments at an hotel for a week. They were dear, and not very pleasant. As usual in France, the principal apartment was a bedchamber; there

was another closet with a bed, and an anti-chamber,
which we used as a sitting-room.

The heat of the weather was excessive, so that we
were unable to walk except in the afternoon. On the
first evening we walked to the gardens of
the Thuilleries; they are formal,[1] in the
French fashion, the trees cut into shapes, and without
grass. I think the Boulevards infinitely more pleasant.
This street nearly surrounds Paris, and is eight miles in
extent; it is very wide, and planted on either side with
trees. At one end is a superb cascade which refreshes
the senses by its continual splashing: near this stands
the gate of St. Denis, a beautiful piece of sculpture. I
do not know how it may at present be disfigured by the
Gothic barbarism of the conquerors of France, who were
not contented with retaking the spoils of Napoleon, but
with impotent malice, destroyed the monuments of their
own defeat. When I saw this gate, it was in its splendour, and made you imagine that the days of Roman
greatness were transported to Paris.

After remaining a week in Paris, we received a small
remittance that set us free from a kind of imprisonment
there which we found very irksome. But how should we
proceed? After talking over and rejecting many plans, we
fixed on one eccentric enough, but which, from its
romance, was very pleasing to us. In England we could
not have put it in execution without sustaining continual
insult and impertinence: the French are far more tole-
rant of the vagaries of their neighbours. We resolved to

1 Aug., 1814.

---

[1] Mrs. Shelley here inserts *and
uninteresting* in the *Essays* &c.; and
in the next line inserts *any* before
grass.

walk through France; but as I was too weak for any considerable distance, and my sister[1] could not be supposed to be able to walk as far as S*** each day, we determined to purchase an ass, to carry our portmanteau and one of us by turns.

Early, therefore, on Monday, August 8th, S*** and C*** went to the ass market, and purchased an ass, and the rest of the day, until four in the afternoon, was spent in preparations for our departure; during which, Madame L'Hote[2] paid us a visit, and attempted to dissuade us from our design. She represented to us that a large army had been recently disbanded, that the soldiers and officers wandered idle about the country, and that *les Dames seroient certainement enlevées.* But we were proof against her arguments, and packing up a few necessaries, leaving the rest to go by the diligence, we departed in a fiacre from the door of the hotel, our little ass following.

8 Aug., 1814.

We dismissed the coach at the barrier. It was dusk, and the ass seemed totally unable to bear one of us, appearing to sink under the portmanteau, although it was small and light. We were, however, merry enough, and thought the leagues short. We arrived at Charenton about ten.

8 Aug., 1814.

Charenton is prettily situated in a valley, through which the Seine flows, winding among banks variegated with trees. On looking at this scene, C*** exclaimed,

---

[1] In the *Essays* &c. (1840), as C*** is substituted for *my sister*.
[2] So in Shelley's edition; but in

Mrs. Shelley's we read *Madame l'hôtesse.*

"Oh! this is beautiful enough; let us live here." This was her exclamation on every new scene, and as each surpassed the one before, she cried, "I am glad we did not stay at Charenton, but let us live here."

Finding our ass useless, we sold it before we proceeded on our journey, and bought a mule, for ten Napoleons. About nine o'clock we departed. We were clad in black silk. I rode on the mule, which carried also our portmanteau; S*** and C*** followed, bringing a small basket of provisions. At about one we arrived at Gros Bois, where, under the shade of trees, we ate our bread and fruit, and drank our wine, thinking of Don Quixote and Sancho.

9 A.M.
9 Aug., 1814.

The country through which we passed was highly cultivated, but uninteresting; the horizon scarcely ever extended beyond the circumference of a few fields, bright and waving with the golden harvest. We met several travellers; but our mode, although novel, did not appear to excite any curiosity or remark. This night we slept at Guignes, in the same room and beds in which Napoleon and some of his Generals had rested during the late war. The little old woman of the place was highly gratified in having this little story to tell, and spoke in warm praise of the Empress Josephine and Marie Louise, who had at different times passed on that road.

9 Aug., 1814.

As we continued our route, Provins was the first place that struck us with interest. It was our stage of rest for the night; we approached it at sunset. After having gained the summit of a hill, the prospect of the town opened upon us as it lay in the valley

10 Aug., 1814.

below; a rocky hill rose abruptly on one side, on the top of which stood a ruined citadel with extensive walls and towers; lower down, but beyond, was the cathedral, and the whole formed a scene for painting. After having travelled for two days through a country perfectly without interest, it was a delicious relief for the eye to dwell again on some irregularities and beauty of country. Our fare at Provins was coarse, and our beds uncomfortable, but the remembrance of this prospect made us contented and happy.

We now approached scenes that reminded us of what we had nearly forgotten, that France had lately been the country in which great and extraordinary events had taken place. Nogent, a town we entered about noon the following day, had been entirely desolated by the Cossacs. Nothing could be more entire _{11 Aug., 1814.} than the ruin which these barbarians had spread as they advanced; perhaps they remembered Moscow and the destruction of the Russian villages; but we were now in France, and the distress of the inhabitants, whose houses had been burned, their cattle killed, and all their wealth destroyed, has given a sting to my detestation of war, which none can feel who have not travelled through a country pillaged and wasted by this plague, which, in his pride, man inflicts upon his fellow.

We quitted the great route soon after we had left Nogent, to strike across the country to Troyes. About six in the evening we arrived in St. Aubin, a lovely village embosomed in trees; but on a nearer _{11 Aug., 1814.} view we found the cottages roofless, the rafters black, and the walls dilapidated;—a few inhabitants remained.

We asked for milk—they had none to give; all their cows had been taken by the Cossacs. We had still some leagues to travel that night, but we found that they were not post leagues, but the measurement of the inhabitants, and nearly double the distance. The road lay over a desart plain, and as night advanced we were often in danger of losing the track of wheels, which was our only guide. Night closed in, and we suddenly lost all trace of the road; but a few trees, indistinctly seen, seemed to indicate the position of a village. About ten we arrived at Trois Maisons, where, after a supper on milk and sour bread, we retired to rest on wretched beds: but sleep is seldom denied, except to the indolent, and after the day's fatigue, although my bed was nothing more than a sheet spread upon straw, I slept soundly until the morning was considerably advanced.

11 Aug., 1814.

S*** had hurt his ancle so considerably the preceding evening, that he was obliged, during the whole of the following day's journey, to ride on our mule. Nothing could be more barren and wretched than the track through which we now passed; the ground was chalky and uncovered even by grass, and where there had been any attempts made towards cultivation, the straggling ears of corn discovered more plainly the barren nature of the soil. Thousands of insects, which were of the same white colour as the road, infested our path; the sky was cloudless, and the sun darted its rays upon us, reflected back by the earth, until I nearly fainted under the heat. A village appeared at a distance, cheering us with a prospect of rest. It gave us new strength to proceed; but it was a wretched place, and afforded us but little relief. It had been once large and populous,

12 Aug., 1814.

but now the houses were roofless, and the ruins that lay scattered about, the gardens covered with the white dust of the torn cottages, the black burnt beams, and squalid looks of the inhabitants, presented in every direction the melancholy aspect of devastation. One house, a *cabarêt*, alone remained ; we were here offered plenty of milk, stinking bacon, sour bread, and a few vegetables, which we were to dress for ourselves.

As we prepared our dinner in a place, so filthy that the sight of it alone was sufficient to destroy our appetite, the people of the village collected around us, squalid with dirt, their countenances expressing every thing that is disgusting and brutal. They seemed indeed entirely detached from the rest of the world, and ignorant of all that was passing in it. There is much less communication between the various towns of France than in England. The use of passports may easily account for this : these people did not know that Napoleon was deposed, and when we asked why they did not rebuild their cottages, they replied, that they were afraid that the Cossacs would destroy them again upon their return. Echemine (the name of this village) is in every respect the most disgusting place I ever met with.

Two leagues beyond, on the same road, we came to the village of Pavillon, so unlike Echemine, that we might have fancied ourselves in another quarter of the globe ; here every thing denoted cleanliness and hospitality ; many of the cottages were destroyed, but the inhabitants were employed in repairing them. What could occasion so great a difference ?

Still our road lay over this track of uncultivated country, and our eyes were fatigued by observing nothing but a white expanse of ground, where no bramble or stunted shrub adorned its barrenness.   Towards evening

12 Aug., 1814.   we reached a small plantation of vines, it appeared like one of those islands of verdure that are met with in the midst of the sands of Lybia, but the grapes were not yet ripe.   S*** was totally incapable of walking, and C*** and I were very tired before we arrived at Troyes.

We rested here for the night, and devoted the follow-

12 and
13 Aug., 1814.   ing day to a consideration of the manner in which we should proceed.   S***'s sprain rendered our pedestrianism impossible.   We accordingly sold our mule, and bought an open *voiture* that went on four wheels, for five Napoleons, and hired a man with a mule for eight more, to convey us to Neufchâtel in six days.

The suburbs of Troyes were destroyed, and the town itself dirty and uninviting.   I remained at the inn writing,[1] while S*** and C*** arranged this bargain and visited the cathedral of the town; and the next morning we

14 Aug., 1814.   departed in our *voiture* for Neufchâtel.   A curious instance of French vanity occurred on leaving this town.   Our *voiturier* pointed to the plain around, and mentioned, that it had been the scene of a battle between the Russians and the French.   " In which the Russians gained the victory ?"—" Ah no, Madame," replied the man, " the French are never beaten."   " But how was it then," we asked, " that the Russians had

---

[1] In the *Essays* &c. the employment is particularized as *writing letters*.

entered Troyes soon after?"—"Oh, after having been defeated, they took a circuitous route, and thus entered the town."

Vandeuvres is a pleasant town, at which we rested during the hours of noon. We walked in the grounds of a nobleman, laid out in the English taste, and terminated in a pretty wood; it was a scene that reminded us of our native country. As we left Vandeuvres the aspect of the country suddenly changed; abrupt hills, covered with vineyards, intermixed with trees, enclosed a narrow valley, the channel of the Aube. The view was interspersed by green meadows, groves of poplar and white willow, and spires of village churches, which the Cossacs had yet spared. Many villages, ruined by the war, occupied the most romantic spots.

14 Aug., 1814.

In the evening we arrived at Bar-sur-Aube, a beautiful town, placed at the opening of the vale where the hills terminate abruptly. We climbed the highest of these, but scarce had we reached the top, when a mist descended upon every thing, and the rain began to fall: we were wet through before we could reach our inn. It was evening, and the laden clouds made the darkness almost as deep as that of midnight; but in the west an unusually brilliant and fiery redness occupied an opening in the vapours, and added to the interest of our little expedition: the cottage lights were reflected in the tranquil river, and the dark hills behind, dimly seen, resembled vast and frowning mountains.

14 Aug., 1814.

As we quitted Bar-sur-Aube, we at the same time bade a short farewel to hills. Passing through the towns of Chaumont, Langres (which was situated

15 Aug., 1814.

on a hill, and surrounded by ancient fortifications),
Champlitte, and Gray, we travelled for nearly
16 Aug., 1814.   three days through plains, where the country
gently undulated, and relieved the eye from a perpetual
flat, without exciting any peculiar interest. Gentle rivers,
their banks ornamented by a few trees, stole through these
plains, and a thousand beautiful summer insects skimmed
over the streams. The third day was a day of rain, and
the first that had taken place during our journey. We
were soon wet through, and were glad to stop at a little
inn to dry ourselves. The reception we received
17 Aug., 1814.   here was very unprepossessing, the people still
kept their seats round the fire, and seemed very unwilling
to make way for the dripping guests. In the afternoon,
however, the weather became fine, and at about six in the
evening we entered Besançon.

Hills had appeared in the distance during the whole
day, and we had advanced gradually towards them, but
were unprepared for the scene that broke upon us as we
passed the gate of this city. On quitting the walls, the
road wound underneath a high precipice; on
17 Aug., 1814.   the other side the hills rose more gradually,
and the green valley that intervened between them was
watered by a pleasant river; before us arose an amphitheatre of hills covered with vines, but irregular and
rocky. The last gate of the town was cut through the
precipitous rock that arose on one side, and in that place
jutted into the road.

This approach to mountain scenery filled us with
delight; it was otherwise with our *voiturier*: he came
from the plains of Troyes, and these hills so utterly

scared him, that he in some degree lost his reason. After winding through the valley, we began to ascend the mountains which were its boundary : we left our *voiture*, and walked on, delighted with every new view that broke upon us.

When we had ascended the hills for about a mile and a half, we found our *roiturier* at the door of a wretched inn, having taken the mule from the *roiture*, and obstinately determined to remain for the night at this miserable village of Mort. We could only submit, for he was deaf to all we could urge, and to our remonstrances only replied, *Je ne puis pas.*[1]

Our beds were too uncomfortable to allow a thought of sleeping in them : we could only procure one room, and our hostess gave us to understand   17 Aug., 1814. that our *roiturier* was to occupy the same apartment. It was of little consequence, as we had previously resolved not to enter the beds. The evening was fine, and after the rain the air was perfumed by many delicious scents. We climbed to a rocky seat on the hill that overlooked the village, where we remained until sunset. The night was passed by the kitchen fire in a wretched manner, striving to catch a few moments of sleep, which were denied to us. At three in the   18 Aug., 1814. morning we pursued our journey.

Our road led to the summit of the hills that environ Besançon. From the top of one of these we saw the whole expanse of the valley filled with a white undulating mist, which was pierced like islands by the piny mountains.

---

[1] In the *Essays* &c. *plus* is substituted for *pas*.

The sun had just risen, and a ray of red light lay upon the waves of this fluctuating vapour.   To the west, opposite the sun, it seemed driven by the light against the rocks in immense masses of foaming cloud, until it became lost in the distance, mixing its tints with the fleecy sky.

Our *voiturier* insisted on remaining two hours at the village of Noë, although we were unable to procure any dinner, and wished to go on to the next stage.   I have already said, that the hills scared his senses, and he had become disobliging, sullen, and stupid.   While he waited we walked to the neighbouring wood : it was a fine forest, carpeted beautifully with moss, and in various places overhung by rocks, in whose crevices young pines had taken root, and spread their branches for shade to those below ; the noon heat was intense, and we were glad to shelter ourselves from it in the shady retreats of this lovely forest.

On our return to the village we found, to our extreme surprise, that the *voiturier* had departed nearly an hour before, leaving word that he expected to meet us on the road.   S***'s sprain rendered him incapable of much exertion ; but there was no remedy, and we proceeded on foot to Maison Neuve, an *auberge*, four miles and a half distant.

At Maison Neuve the man had left word that he should proceed to Pontarlier,[1] the frontier town of France, six leagues distant, and that if we did not arrive that night, he should the next morning leave the *voiture* at an inn, and return with the mule to Troyes.   We were asto-

---

[1] In Shelley's edition uniformly spelt *Pontalier* ; but Mrs. Shelley corrected the name to *Pontarlier* in the *Essays* &c. in 1840.

nished at the impudence of this message, but the boy of
the inn comforted us by saying, that by going on a horse
by a cross road, where the *voiture* could not venture, he
could easily overtake and intercept the *voiturier*, and
accordingly we dispatched him, walking slowly after.
We waited at the next inn for dinner, and in about two
hours the boy returned. The man promised to wait for
us at an *auberge* two leagues further on. S***'s ancle
had become very painful, but we could procure no conveyance, and as the sun was nearly setting, we were
obliged to hasten on. The evening was most beautiful,
and the scenery lovely enough to beguile us of our
fatigue: the horned moon hung in the light of sunset,
that threw a glow of unusual depth of redness over the
piny mountains and the dark deep vallies[1] they enclosed;
at intervals in the woods were beautiful lawns interspersed
with picturesque clumps of trees, and dark pines overshadowed our road.

In about two hours we arrived at the promised termination of our journey, but the *voiturier* was not there:
after the boy had left him, he again pursued his journey
towards Pontarlier. We were enabled, however, to procure
here a rude kind of cart, and in this manner arrived late
at Pontarlier, where we found our conductor,
who blundered out many falsehoods for excuses; 18 Aug., 1814.
and thus ended the adventures of that day.[2]

---

[1] Mrs. Shelley here inserts *which* in the *Essays* &c.

[2] When Mrs. Shelley republished the journal among Shelley's *Essays* &c. in 1840, she substituted for this paragraph the following :

"In about two hours we arrived at the promised termination of our journey. We found, according to our expectation, that M. le voiturier had pursued his journey with the utmost speed. We were enabled, however, to procure here a rude kind of cart,S*** being unable to walk. The moon became yellow, and hung low close to the woody horizon. Every now and then sleep overcame me, but our vehicle was too rude and rough to permit its indulgence. I looked on the stars—and the constellations seemed to weave a wild dance, as the visions of slumber invaded the domains of reality. In this manner we arrived late at Pontarlier, where we found our conductor, who blundered out many falsehoods for excuses; and thus ended the adventures of that day."

SWITZERLAND.

On passing the French barrier, a surprising difference may be observed between the opposite nations that inhabit either side. The Swiss cottages are much cleaner and neater, and the inhabitants exhibit the same contrast. The Swiss women wear a great deal of white linen, and their whole dress is always perfectly clean. This superior cleanliness is chiefly produced by the difference of religion: travellers in Germany remark the same contrast between the protestant and catholic towns, although they be but a few leagues separate.

The scenery of this day's journey was divine, exhibiting piny mountains, barren rocks, and spots of ver-
10 Aug., 1814. dure surpassing imagination. After descending for nearly a league between lofty rocks,[1] covered with pines, and interspersed with green glades, where the grass is short, and soft, and beautifully verdant, we arrived at the village of St. Sulpice.

[1] So in Shelley's edition and the first edition of the *Essays* &c. (1840); but Mrs. Shelley reads *cliffs* in later editions.

The mule had latterly become very lame, and the man so disobliging, that we determined to engage a horse for the remainder of the way. Our *roiturier* had anticipated us, without in the least intimating his intention[1]: he had determined to leave us at this village, and taken measures to that effect. The man we now engaged was a Swiss, a cottager of the better class, who was proud of his mountains and his country. Pointing to the glades that were interspersed among the woods, he informed us that they were very beautiful, and were excellent pasture; that the cows thrived there, and consequently produced excellent milk, from which the best cheese and butter in the world were made.

The mountains after St. Sulpice became loftier and more beautiful. We passed through a narrow valley between two ranges of mountains, clothed with forests, at the bottom of which flowed a river, from whose narrow bed on either side the boundaries of the vale arose precipitously. The road lay about half way up the mountain, which formed one of the sides, and we saw the overhanging rocks above us and below, enormous pines, and the river, not to be perceived but from its reflection of the light of heaven, far beneath. The mountains of this beautiful ravine are so little asunder, that in time of war with France an iron chain is thrown across it. Two leagues from Neufchâtel we saw the Alps; range after range of black mountains are seen extending one before the other, and far behind all, towering above every feature of the scene, the snowy Alps. They were an[2] hundred miles distant, but reach so high in the heavens,

---

[1] In the *Essays* &c. (1840), we read *to us*, after *intention*, and the colon gives place to a comma.

[2] So in Shelley's edition, but *a* in the *Essays* &c.

that they look like those accumulated clouds of dazzling white that arrange themselves on the horizon during summer. Their immensity staggers the imagination, and so far surpasses all conception, that it requires an effort of the understanding to believe that they indeed form a part of the earth.

From this point we descended to Neufchâtel, which is situated in a narrow plain, between the mountains and its immense lake, and presents no additional aspect of peculiar interest.

We remained the following day at this town, occupied in a consideration of the step it would now be advisable for us to take. The money we had brought with us from Paris was nearly exhausted, but we obtained about £38 in silver upon discount from one of the bankers of the city, and with this we resolved to journey towards the lake of Uri, and seek in that romantic and interesting country some cottage where we might dwell in peace and solitude. Such were our dreams, which we should probably have realized, had it not been for the deficiency of that indispensible article money, which obliged us to return to England.

A Swiss, whom S*** met at the post-office, kindly interested himself in our affairs, and assisted us to hire a *voiture* to convey us to Lucerne, the principal town of the lake of that name, which is connected with the lake of Uri.[1] The journey to this place[2] occupied rather more

20 Aug., 1814.

---

[1] In the *Essays* &c. (1840), Mrs. Shelley here inserts the following details :—

"This man was imbued with the spirit of true politeness, and endeavoured to perform real services, and seemed to regard the mere ceremonies of the affair as things of very little value. On the 21st August, we left Neufchâtel, our Swiss friend accompanied us a little way out of the town."

[2] In the *Essays* &c., *Lucerne* for *this place.*

than two days. The country was ·flat and dull, and, excepting that we now and then caught a glimpse of the divine Alps, there was nothing in it to interest us. Lucerne promised better things, and as soon as we arrived (August 23d) we hired a boat, with which we proposed to coast the lake until we should meet with some suitable habitation, or perhaps, even going to Altorf, cross Mont St. Gothard, and seek in the warm climate of the country to the south of the Alps an air more salubrious, and a temperature better fitted for the precarious state of S***'s health, than the bleak region to the north. The lake of Lucerne is encompassed on all sides by high mountains that rise abruptly from the water;— sometimes their bare fronts descend perpendicularly and cast a black shade upon the waves;—sometimes they are covered with thick wood, whose dark foliage is interspersed by the brown bare crags on which the trees have taken root. In every part where a glade shews itself in the forest it appears cultivated, and cottages peep from among the woods. The most luxuriant islands, rocky and covered with moss, and bending trees, are sprinkled over the lake. Most of these are decorated by the figure of a saint in wretched waxwork.

The direction of this lake extends at first from east to west, then turning a right angle, it lies from north to south; this latter part is distinguished in name from the other, and is called the lake of Uri. The former part is also nearly divided midway, where the jutting land almost meets, and its craggy sides cast a deep shadow on the little strait through which you pass. The summits of several of the mountains that enclose the lake to the south are covered by eternal glaciers; of one of these,

opposite Brunen, they tell the story of a priest and his
mistress, who, flying from persecution, inhabited a cottage
at the foot of the snows. One winter night an avalanche[1]
overwhelmed them, but their plaintive voices are still
heard in stormy nights, calling for succour from the
peasants.

Brunen is situated on the northern side of the angle
which the lake makes, forming the extremity of the lake
of Lucerne. Here we rested for the night, and dismissed
our boatmen. Nothing could be more magnificent than
the view from this spot. The high mountains encompassed us, darkening the waters; at a distance on the
shores of Uri we could perceive the chapel of Tell, and
this was the village where he matured the conspiracy
which was to overthrow the tyrant of his country; and
indeed this lovely lake, these sublime mountains, and
wild forests, seemed a fit cradle for a mind aspiring to
high adventure and heroic deeds. Yet we saw no glimpse
of his spirit in his present countrymen. The Swiss appeared to us then, and experience has confirmed our
opinion, a people slow of comprehension and of action;
but habit has made them unfit for slavery, and they
would, I have little doubt, make a brave defence against
any invader of their freedom.

Such were our reflections, and we remained until late
in the evening on the shores of the lake
23 Aug., 1814. conversing, enjoying the rising breeze, and
contemplating with feelings of exquisite delight the
divine objects that surrounded us.

[1] In Shelley's edition, *avelanche.*

The following day was spent in a consideration of our circumstances, and in contemplation of the scene around us. A furious *vent d'Italie* (south wind) tore up the lake, making immense waves, and carrying the water in a whirlwind high in the air, when it fell like heavy rain into the lake. The waves broke with a tremendous noise on the rocky shores. This conflict continued during the whole day, but it became calmer towards the evening. S*** and I walked on the banks, and sitting on a rude pier, S*** read aloud the account of the Siege of Jerusalem from Tacitus.

24 Aug., 1814.

In the mean time we endeavoured to find an[1] habitation, but could only procure two unfurnished rooms in an ugly big house, called the Chateau. These we hired at a guinea a month, had beds moved into them, and the next day took possession. But it was a wretched place, with no comfort or convenience. It was with difficulty that we could get any food prepared: as it was cold and rainy, we ordered a fire—they lighted an immense stove which occupied a corner of the room; it was long before it heated, and when hot, the warmth was so unwholesome, that we were obliged to throw open our windows to prevent a kind of suffocation; added to this, there was but one person in Brunen who could speak French, a barbarous kind of German being the language of this part of Switzerland. It was with difficulty, therefore, that we could get our most ordinary wants supplied.[2]

25 Aug., 1814.

---

[1] So in Shelley's edition, but *a* in the *Essays* &c.

[2] In the *Essays* &c. (1840), Mrs. Shelley here added—"Our amusement meanwhile was writing. S*** commenced a Romance on the subject of the Assassins, and I wrote to his dictation." The next paragraph begins with *Our* instead of *These*; and after *situation* we read, in the *Essays* &c.,—"At one time we proposed crossing Mount St. Gothard into Italy; but the £28" &c.

These immediate inconveniences led us to a more serious consideration of our situation. The £28. which we possessed, was all the money that we could count upon with any certainty, until the following December. S***'s presence in London was absolutely necessary for the procuring any further supply. What were we to do? we should soon be reduced to absolute want. Thus, after balancing the various topics that offered themselves for discussion, we resolved to return to England.

26 Aug., 1814.

Having formed this resolution, we had not a moment for delay : our little store was sensibly decreasing, and £28. could hardly appear sufficient for so long a journey. It had cost us sixty to cross France from Paris to Neufchâtel ; but we now resolved on a more economical mode of travelling. Water conveyances are always the cheapest, and fortunately we were so situated, that by taking advantage of the rivers of the Reuss and Rhine, we could reach England without travelling a league on land. This was our plan ; we should travel eight hundred miles, and was this possible for[1] so small a sum? but there was no other alternative, and indeed S*** only knew how very little we had to depend upon.

We departed the next morning for the town of Lucerne. It rained violently during the first part of our voyage, but towards its conclusion the sky became clear, and the sun-beams dried and cheered us. We saw again, and for the last time, the rocky shores of this beautiful lake, its verdant isles, and snow-capt mountains.

27 Aug., 1814.

---

[1] In the *Essays* &c., *on* is substituted for *for*.

We landed at Lucerne, and remained in that town the following night, and the next morning (August 28th) departed in the *diligence par-eau* for Loffenburgh, a town on the Rhine, where the falls of that river prevented the same vessel from proceeding any further. Our companions in this voyage were of the meanest class, smoked prodigiously, and were exceedingly disgusting. After having landed for refreshment in the middle of the day, we found, on our return to the boat, that our former seats were occupied; we took others, when the original possessors angrily, and almost with violence, insisted upon our leaving them. Their brutal rudeness to us, who did not understand their language, provoked S*** to knock one of the foremost down : he did not return the blow, but continued his vociferations until the boatmen interfered, and provided us with other seats.

28 Aug., 1814.

The Reuss is exceedingly rapid, and we descended several falls, one of more than eight feet.[1] There is something very delicious in the sensation, when at one moment you are at the top of a fall of water, and before the second has expired you are at the bottom, still rushing on with the impulse which the descent has given. The waters of the Rhone are blue, those of the Reuss are of a deep green. I should think that there must be something in the beds of these rivers, and that the accidents of the banks and sky cannot alone cause this difference.

Sleeping at Dettingen, we arrived the next morning

[1] In the *Essays* &c. (1840), Mrs. Shelley here inserts the following passage :
"Most of the passengers landed at this point, to re-embark when the boat had descended into smooth water—the boatmen advised us to remain on board."

29 Aug., 1814. at Loffenburgh, where we engaged a small canoe to convey us to Mumph.   I give these boats this Indian appellation, as they were of the rudest construction—long, narrow, and flat-bottomed : they consisted merely of straight pieces of deal board, unpainted, and nailed together with so little care, that the water constantly poured in at the crevices, and the boat perpetually required emptying.   The river was rapid, and sped swiftly, breaking as it passed on innumerable rocks just covered by the water : it was a sight of some dread to see our frail boat winding among the eddies of the rocks, which it was death to touch, and when the slightest inclination on one side would instantly have overset it.

We could not procure a boat at Mumph, and we thought ourselves lucky in meeting with a return *cabriolet* to Rheinfelden ; but our good fortune was of short duration : about a league from Mumph the *cabriolet* broke down, and we were obliged to proceed on foot. Fortunately we were overtaken by some Swiss soldiers, who were discharged and returning home, who[1] carried our box for us as far as Rheinfelden, when we were directed to proceed a league farther to a village, where boats were commonly hired. Here, although not without some difficulty, we procured a boat for Basle, and proceeded down a swift river, while evening came on, and the air was bleak and comfortless.   Our voyage was, however, short, and we arrived at the place of 29 Aug., 1814. our destination by six in the evening.

[1] In the *Essays* &c., *they* is substituted for *who*.

BEFORE we slept, S*** had made a bargain for a boat to carry us to Mayence, and the next morning, bidding adieu to Switzerland, we embarked in a boat laden with merchandize, but where we had no fellow-passengers to disturb our tranquillity by their vulgarity and rudeness.   The wind was violently against us, but the stream, aided by a slight exertion from the rowers, carried us on; the sun shone pleasantly, S*** read aloud to us Mary Wollstonecraft's Letters from Norway,[1] and we passed our time delightfully.

The evening was such as to find few parallels

30 Aug., 1814.

---

[1] Presumably Mrs. Shelley had with her a copy of the little volume in which her mother had published such portions of her letters to Imlay as were not private, under the title of *Letters Written during a Short Residence in Sweden, Norway, and Denmark.*   This was published in 1796; and a second edition appeared in 1802, while, in 1798, Godwin had printed among his wife's *Posthumous Works* the private portions of the letters to Imlay.   Mr. C. Kegan Paul has recently (1879) published the personal narrative of this truly beautiful character as unfolded in her letters to Imlay; but the admirable descriptive portions published by the writer herself in 1796 are not given in Mr. Paul's book (*Mary Wollstonecraft: Letters to Imlay*).

L 2

in beauty; as it approached, the banks which had hitherto been flat and uninteresting, became exceedingly beautiful. Suddenly the river grew narrow, and the boat dashed with inconceivable rapidity round the base of a rocky hill covered with pines; a ruined tower, with its desolated windows, stood on the summit of another hill that jutted into the river; beyond, the sunset was illuminating the distant mountains and clouds, casting the reflection of its rich and purple hues on the agitated river. The brilliance and contrasts of the colours on the circling whirlpools of the stream, was an appearance entirely new and most beautiful; the shades grew darker as the sun descended below the horizon, and after we had landed, as we walked to our inn round a beautiful bay, the full moon arose with divine splendour, casting its silver light on the before-purpled waves.

The following morning we pursued our journey in a slight canoe, in which every motion was accompanied with danger: but the stream had lost much of its rapidity, and was no longer impeded by rocks, the banks were low, and covered with willows. We passed Strasburgh, and the next morning it was proposed to us that we should proceed in the *diligence par-eau*, as the navigation would become dangerous for our small boat.

31 Aug., 1814.

1 Sept., 1814.

There were only four passengers besides ourselves, three of these were students of the Strasburgh university: Schwitz, a rather handsome, good tempered young man; Hoff, a kind of shapeless animal, with a heavy, ugly, German face; and Schneider, who was nearly an ideot, and on whom his companions were always playing a thousand tricks : the remaining passengers were a woman, and an infant.

The country was uninteresting, but we enjoyed fine weather, and slept in the boat in the open air without any inconvenience. We saw on the shores few objects that called forth our attention, if I except the town of Mannheim,[1] which was strikingly neat and clean. It was situated at about a mile from the river, and the road to it was planted on each side with beautiful acacias. The last part of this voyage was performed close under land, as the wind was so violently against us, that even with all the force of a rapid current in our favour, we were hardly permitted to proceed. We were told (and not without reason) that we ought to congratulate ourselves on having exchanged our canoe for this boat, as the river was now of considerable width, and tossed by the wind into large waves. The same morning a boat, containing fifteen persons, in attempting to cross the water, had upset in the middle of the river, and every one in it perished. We saw the boat turned over, floating down the stream. This was a melancholy sight, yet ludicrously commented on by the *batelier ;*[2] almost the whole stock of whose French consisted in the word *seulement.* When we asked him what had happened, he answered, laying particular emphasis on this favourite dissyllable, *C''est seulement un*

5 A.M.,
2 Sept., 1814.

---

[1] In Shelley's edition *Manheim :* in Mrs. Shelley's, *Mannheim.* It would seem that the slowness of the *diligence par-eau* admitted of a visit to this Town, and that the voyage to Mayence from the point past Strasbourg at which the canoe was abandoned occupied the greater part of three days,—two nights (the 1st and 2nd of September) being passed in the boat, in the open air, and one (the 3rd) at Mayence.

[2] In Shelley's edition *batelier,* but *batelier* in Mrs. Shelley's.

bateau, qui étoit seulement renversée, et tous les peuples sont seulement noyés.

Mayence is one of the best fortified towns in Germany.

1 P.M.,
3 Sept., 1814. The river, which is broad and rapid, guards it to the east, and the hills for three leagues around exhibit signs of fortifications. The town itself is old, the streets narrow, and the houses high: the cathedral and towers of the town still bear marks of the bombardment which took place in the revolutionary war.

We took our place in the *diligence par-eau* for Cologne, and the next morning (September 4th) de-
4 Sept., 1814. parted. This conveyance appeared much more like a mercantile English affair than any we had before seen; it was shaped like a steam-boat, with a cabin and a high deck. Most of our companions chose to remain in the cabin; this was fortunate for us, since nothing could be more horribly disgusting than the lower order of smoking, drinking Germans who travelled with us; they swaggered and talked,[1] and what was hideous to English eyes, kissed one another: there were, however, two or three merchants of a better class, who appeared well-informed and polite.

The part of the Rhine down which we now glided, is that so beautifully described by Lord Byron in his third canto of *Childe Harold.* We read these verses with delight, as they conjured before us these lovely scenes with the truth and vividness of painting, and with the exquisite addition of glowing language and a warm

---

[1] In the *Essays* &c. (1840) Mrs. Shelley here inserts *and got tipsy.*

imagination. We were carried down by a dangerously rapid current, and saw on either side of us hills covered with vines and trees, craggy cliffs crowned by desolate towers, and wooded islands, where picturesque ruins peeped from behind the foliage, and cast the shadows of their forms on the troubled waters, which distorted without deforming them. We heard the songs of the vintagers, and if surrounded by disgusting Germans, the sight was not so replete with enjoyment as I now fancy it to have been; yet memory, taking all the dark shades from the picture, presents this part of the Rhine to my remembrance as the loveliest paradise on earth.

We had sufficient leisure for the enjoyment of these scenes, for the boatmen, neither rowing nor steering, suffered us to be carried down by the stream, and the boat turned round and round as it descended.

While I speak with disgust of the Germans who travelled with us, I should in justice to these borderers record, that at one of the inns here we saw the only pretty woman we met with in the course of our travels. She is what I should conceive to be a truly German beauty; grey eyes, slightly tinged with brown, and expressive of uncommon sweetness and frankness. She had lately recovered from a fever, and this added to the interest of her countenance, by adorning it with an appearance of extreme delicacy.

On the following day we left the hills of the Rhine, and found that, for the remainder of our journey, we should move sluggishly through 5 Sept., 1814. the flats of Holland: the river also winds extremely, so

that, after calculating our resources, we resolved to
finish our journey in a land diligence. Our water conveyance remained that night at Bonn, and that we might
lose no time, we proceeded post the same night to
Cologne, where we arrived late; for the rate of travelling
in Germany seldom exceeds a mile and a half an hour.

Cologne appeared an immense town, as we drove
through street after street to arrive at our inn.   Before
6 Sept., 1814.   we slept, we secured places in the diligence,
which was to depart next morning for Clêves.

Nothing in the world can be more wretched than
travelling in this German diligence: the coach is clumsy
and comfortless, and we proceeded so slowly, stopping so
often, that it appeared as if we should never arrive at
our journey's end. We were allowed two hours for
dinner, and two more were wasted in the evening while
the coach was being changed. We were then requested,
as the diligence had a greater demand for places than
it could supply, to proceed in a *cabriolet* which was
provided for us. We readily consented, as we hoped to
travel faster than in the heavy diligence; but this was
not permitted, and we jogged on all night behind this
cumbrous machine.   In the morning when we
7 Sept., 1814.   stopped, and[1] for a moment indulged a hope
that we had arrived at Clêves, which was at the distance
of five leagues from our last night's stage; but we had
only advanced three leagues in seven or eight hours, and
had yet eight miles to perform. However, we first
rested about three hours at this stage, where we could not

---

[1] In the *Essays* &c. (1840) Mrs.   substituting *we* for *and*.
Shelley amended this sentence by

obtain breakfast or any convenience, and at about eight o'clock we again departed, and with slow, although far from easy travelling, faint with hunger and fatigue, we arrived by noon at Clêves.

HOLLAND.

TIRED by the slow pace of the diligence, we resolved to post the remainder of the way. We had now, however, left Germany, and travelled at about the same rate as an English post-chaise. The country was entirely flat, and the roads so sandy, that the horses proceeded with difficulty. The only ornaments of this country are the turf fortifications that surround the towns. At Nimeguen we passed the flying bridge, mentioned in the letters of Lady Mary[1] Montague. We had intended to travel all night, but at Triel, where we arrived at about ten o'clock,

7 Sept., 1814.

we were assured that no post-boy was to be found who would proceed at so late an hour, on account of the robbers who infested the roads. This was an obvious imposition; but as we could procure neither horses nor driver, we were obliged to sleep here.

During the whole of the following day the road lay

---

[1] Mrs. Shelley inserts *Wortley* in the *Essays* &c.

between canals, which intersect this country in
every direction. The roads were excellent, but
the Dutch have contrived as many inconveniences as possible. In our journey of the day before, we had passed
by a windmill, which was so situated with regard to the
road, that it was only by keeping close to the opposite
side, and passing quickly, that we could avoid the sweep
of its sails.

8 Sept., 1814.

The roads between the canals were only wide enough
to admit of one carriage, so that when we encountered
another we were obliged sometimes to back for half a
mile, until we should come to one of the drawbridges
which led to the fields, on which one of the *cabriolets* was
rolled,[1] while the other passed. But they have another
practice, which is still more annoying: the flax when cut
is put to soak under the mud of the canals, and then
placed to dry against the trees which are planted on
either side of the road; the stench that it exhales, when
the beams of the sun draw out the moisture, is scarcely
endurable. We saw many enormous frogs and toads in
the canals; and the only sight which refreshed the eye
by its beauty was the delicious verdure of the fields, where
the grass was as rich and green as that of England, an
appearance not common on the continent.

Rotterdam is remarkably clean: the Dutch even wash
the outside brick-work of their houses. We remained
here one day, and met with a man in a very unfortunate
condition: he had been born in Holland, and had spent
so much of his life between England, France, and

---

[1] In the *Essays* &c., *bucked* for *rolled.*

Germany, that he had acquired a slight knowledge of the language of each country, and spoke all very imperfectly. He said that he understood English best, but he was nearly unable to express himself in that.

On the evening of the 8th of September[1] we sailed from Rotterdam, but contrary winds obliged us to remain nearly two days at Marsluys, a town about two leagues from Rotterdam. Here our last guinea was expended, and we reflected with wonder that we had travelled eight hundred miles for less than thirty pounds, passing through lovely scenes, and enjoying the beauteous Rhine, and all the brilliant shews of earth and sky, perhaps more, travelling as we did, in an open boat, than if we had been shut up in a carriage, and passed on the road under the hills.[2]

8 Sept., 1814.

The captain of our vessel was an Englishman, and had been a king's pilot. The bar of the Rhine a little below Marsluys is so dangerous, that without a very favourable breeze none of the Dutch vessels dare attempt its passage; but although the wind was a very few points in our favour, our captain resolved to sail, and although half repentant before he had accomplished his undertaking, he was glad and proud when, triumphing over the timorous Dutchmen, the bar was crossed, and the vessel safe in the open sea. It was in truth an enterprise of some peril; a heavy gale

---

[1] In Shelley's edition *August* is printed for *September*, through some oversight. Mrs. Shelley, in the *Essays* &c., 1840, corrected the error. Miss Clairmont's journal, written from day to day, makes it quite clear that the travellers slept at Rotterdam on the 8th of September, and sailed at 4 P.M. on the 9th.

[2] In the *Essays* &c., Mrs. Shelley here adds—"During our stay at Marsluys, S*** continued his Romance." The reference is presumably to *The Assassins*, begun at Brunen. (See p. 143.)

had prevailed during the night, and although it had abated since the morning, the breakers at the bar were still exceedingly high. Through some delay, which had arisen from the ship having got a-ground in the harbour, we arrived half an hour after the appointed time. 11 Sept., 1814.
The breakers were tremendous, and we were informed that there was the space of only two feet between the bottom of the vessel and the sands. The waves, which broke against the sides of the ship with a terrible shock, were quite perpendicular, and even sometimes overhanging in the abrupt smoothness of their sides. Shoals of enormous porpoises were sporting with the utmost composure amidst the troubled waters.

We safely past this danger, and after a navigation unexpectedly short, arrived at Gravesend on the morning of the 13th of September, the 13 Sept., 1814. third day after our departure from Marsluys.

M.

LETTERS.

[Letters I and II in the following series are by Mrs. Shelley, Letters III and IV by Shelley. The latter would seem to represent a considerably larger mass of Shelley's incomparable descriptive prose. In Thomas Love Peacock's important contribution to the poet's biography, viz. *Memoirs of Percy Bysshe Shelley*, Part II, published in *Fraser's Magazine* for January, 1860, we read at pages 96, 98, 99 and 100 as follows: "After leaving England, in 1814, the newly affianced lovers took a tour on the Continent. He wrote to me several letters from Switzerland, which were subsequently published, together with a *Six Weeks' Tour*, written in the form of a journal by the lady with whom his fate was thenceforward indissolubly bound.... In the early summer of 1816, the spirit of restlessness again came over him, and resulted in a second visit to the Continent.... During his absence he wrote me several letters, some of which were subsequently published by Mrs. Shelley; others are still in my possession.... During his stay in Switzerland he became acquainted with Lord Byron. They made together an excursion round the Lake of Geneva, of which he sent me the detail in a diary. This diary was published by Mrs. Shelley, but without introducing the name of Lord Byron, who is throughout called 'my companion.' The diary was first published during Lord Byron's life; but why his name was concealed I do not know. Though the changes are not many, yet the association of the two names gives it great additional interest." The concealment of Byron's name in 1817 was of course part and parcel of the anonymous scheme of the whole book; and it is scarcely remarkable that Mrs. Shelley in 1840 should have abstained from filling in the names : at all events the term *my companion* is Shelley's, not his widow's ; and for the rest, if we are to trust Peacock's memory, some of these inestimable Swiss letters are missing. The remarks from which extracts are given above are made in chronological order, and it was clearly intended to imply that Shelley wrote Peacock "several letters from Switzerland" in 1814, which were published in the volume of 1817 ; but no such letters are there ; nor are there any of the "several letters" of 1816, except the two extending from the 23rd of June to the 27th of July, which obviously constitute the "diary" referred to by Peacock. Moreover, with the exception of the two forming the diary, Mrs. Shelley did not publish any letters of Shelley's from Switzerland, nor did Peacock, when he issued Shelley's letters to him in *Fraser's Magazine*,—the earliest then printed being that of the 25th of July 1818 from the Bagni di Lucca. Furthermore, when Peacock's books and Shelley's letters to him were sold, there was but one from Switzerland beside those composing the diary ; and that one was dated "Geneva, May 15th, 1816." It is to be hoped Peacock's memory was not inaccurate in this matter, because, if it was not, there will probably be found, sooner or later, some letters of Shelley belonging to a most interesting period : if Peacock had them in 1860 several of 1814, and several of 1816—they are not likely to have perished since, one would think. Those who wish to read this series of papers concerning Shelley may perhaps refer to Vol. III of Peacock's Works (Bentley, 1875) more conveniently than to *Fraser's Magazine*.—H. B. F.]

LETTERS

WRITTEN

DURING A RESIDENCE OF THREE MONTHS IN THE ENVIRONS OF GENEVA,

In the Summer of the Year 1816.

LETTER 1.

Hôtel de Sécheron,[1] Geneva,
May 17, 1816.

WE arrived at Paris on the 8th of this month, and were detained two days for the purpose of obtaining the various signatures necessary to our pass- 8 May, 1816. ports, the French government having become much more circumspect since the escape of Lavalette. We had no letters of introduction, or any friend in that city, and were therefore confined to our hotel, where we were obliged to hire apartments for the week, although when we first arrived we expected to be detained one night only; for in Paris there are no houses where you can be accommodated with apartments by the day.

[1] *Secheron* in Shelley's edition.

The manners of the French are interesting, although less attractive, at least to Englishmen, than before the last invasion of the Allies: the discontent and sullenness of their minds perpetually betrays itself. Nor is it wonderful that they should regard the subjects of a government which fills their country with hostile garrisons, and sustains a detested dynasty on the throne, with an acrimony and indignation of which that government alone is the proper object. This feeling is honourable to the French, and encouraging to all those of every nation in Europe who have a fellow feeling with the oppressed, and who cherish an unconquerable hope that the cause of liberty must at length prevail.

Our route after Paris, as far as Troyes, lay through the same uninteresting tract of country which we had traversed on foot nearly two years before, but on quitting Troyes we left the road leading to Neufchâtel, to follow that which was to conduct us to Geneva. We entered Dijon on the third evening after our departure from Paris, and passing through Dôle, arrived at Poligny. This town is built at the foot of Jura, which rises abruptly from a plain of vast extent. The rocks of the mountain overhang the houses. Some difficulty in procuring horses detained us here until the evening closed in, when we proceeded, by the light of a stormy moon, to Champagnolles, a little village situated in the depth of the mountains. The road was serpentine and exceedingly steep, and was overhung on one side by half distinguished precipices, whilst the other was a gulph, filled by the darkness of the driving clouds. The dashing of the invisible mountain[1] streams announced to

12 or 13 May, 1816.

---

[1] Mrs. Shelley omits this word in her editions.

us that we had quitted the plains of France, as we slowly ascended, amidst a violent storm of wind and rain, to Champagnolles, where we arrived at twelve o'clock, the fourth night after our departure ^{14 or 15 May, 1816.} from Paris.

The next morning we proceeded, still ascending among the ravines and vallies of the mountain. The scenery perpetually grows more wonderful and sublime: pine forests of impenetrable thickness, and untrodden, nay, inaccessible expanse spread on every side. Sometimes the dark woods descending, follow the route into the vallies, the distorted trees struggling with knotted roots between the most barren clefts; sometimes the road winds high into the regions of frost, and then the forests become scattered, and the branches of the trees are loaded with snow, and half of the enormous pines themselves buried in the wavy drifts. The spring, as the inhabitants informed us, was unusually late, and indeed the cold was excessive; as we ascended the mountains, the same clouds which rained on us in the vallies poured forth large flakes of snow thick and fast. The sun occasionally shone through these showers, and illuminated the magnificent ravines of the mountains, whose gigantic pines were some laden with snow, some wreathed round by the lines of scattered and lingering vapour; others darting their dark[1] spires into the sunny sky, brilliantly clear and azure.

As the evening advanced, and we ascended higher, the snow, which we had beheld whitening the overhanging

---

[1] Mrs. Shelley omits the word *dark* in her editions.

rocks, now encroached upon our road, and it snowed fast as we entered the village of Les Rousses, where we were threatened by the apparent necessity of passing the night in a bad inn and dirty beds. For from that place there are two roads to Geneva; one by Nion, in the Swiss territory, where the mountain route is shorter, and comparatively easy at that time of the year, when the road is for several leagues covered with snow of an enormous depth; the other road lay through Gex, and was too circuitous and dangerous to be attempted at so late an hour in the day. Our passport, however, was for Gex, and we were told that we could not change its destination; but all these police laws, so severe in themselves, are to be softened by bribery, and this difficulty was at length overcome. We hired four horses, and ten men to support the carriage, and departed from Les Rousses at six in the evening, when the sun had already far descended, and the snow pelting against the windows of our carriage, assisted the coming darkness to deprive us of the view of the lake of Geneva and the far distant Alps.

The prospect around, however, was sufficiently sublime to command our attention—never was scene more awfully desolate. The trees in these regions are incredibly large, and stand in scattered clumps over the white wilderness; the vast expanse of snow was chequered only by these gigantic pines, and the poles that marked our road: no river or[1] rock-encircled lawn relieved the eye, by adding the picturesque to the sublime. The natural silence of that uninhabited

15 or
16 May, 1816.

---

[1] In Mrs. Shelley's editions *nor*.

desert contrasted strangely with the voices of the men who conducted us, who, with animated tones and gestures, called to one another in a *patois* composed of French and Italian, creating disturbance, where but for them, there was none.

To what a different scene are we now arrived! To the warm sunshine and to the humming of sun-loving insects. From the windows of our hotel we see the lovely lake, blue as the heavens which it reflects, and sparkling with golden beams. The opposite shore is sloping, and covered with vines, which however do not so early in the season add to the beauty of the prospect. Gentlemen's[1] seats are scattered over these banks, behind which rise the various ridges of black mountains, and towering far above, in the midst of its snowy Alps, the majestic Mont Blanc, highest and queen of all. Such is the view reflected by the lake; it is a bright summer scene without any of that sacred solitude and deep seclusion that delighted us at Lucerne.

We have not yet found out any very agreeable walks, but you know our attachment to water excursions. We have hired a boat, and every evening at about six o'clock we sail on the lake, which is delightful, whether we glide over a glassy surface or are speeded along by a strong wind. The waves of this lake never afflict me with that sickness that deprives me of all enjoyment in a sea voyage; on the contrary, the tossing of our boat raises my spirits and inspires me with unusual hilarity. Twilight here is of short duration, but we at present enjoy the benefit of an increasing moon, and seldom return until ten o'clock,

[1] In Shelley's edition, *Gentlemens'*.

when, as we approach the shore, we are saluted by the delightful scent of flowers and new mown grass, and the chirp of the grasshoppers, and the song of the evening birds.

We do not enter into society here, yet our time passes swiftly and delightfully. We read Latin and Italian during the heats of noon, and when the sun declines we walk in the garden of the hotel, looking at the rabbits, relieving fallen cockchaffers,[1] and watching the motions of a myriad of lizards, who inhabit a southern wall of the garden. You know that we have just escaped from the gloom of winter and of London; and coming to this delightful spot during this divine weather, I feel as happy as a new-fledged bird, and hardly care what twig I fly to, so that I may try my new-found wings. A more experienced bird may be more difficult in its choice of a bower; but in my present temper of mind, the budding flowers, the fresh grass of spring, and the happy creatures about me that live and enjoy these pleasures, are quite enough to afford me exquisite delight, even though clouds should shut out Mont Blanc from my sight. Adieu!

M.

---

[1] I suppose this should be *cock-chafers*; but both Shelley and Mrs. Shelley have it *cockchaffers*.

LETTER II.

Campagne C******,[1] near Coligny,
1st June.

You will perceive from my date that we have changed our residence since my last letter. We now inhabit a little cottage on the opposite shore _{1 June, 1816.} of the lake, and have exchanged the view of Mont Blanc and her snowy *aiguilles* for the dark frowning Jura, behind whose range we every evening see the sun sink, and darkness approaches our valley from behind the Alps, which are then tinged by that glowing rose-like hue which is observed in England to attend on the clouds of an autumnal sky when day-light is almost gone. The lake is at our feet, and a little harbour contains our boat, in which we still enjoy our evening excursions on the water Unfortunately we do not now enjoy those brilliant skies that hailed us on our first arrival to this country. An almost perpetual rain confines us principally to the house ; but when the sun bursts forth it is with a splendour and

[1] Mrs. Shelley supplied the name *Chapuis* in the *Essays* &c.

heat unknown in England. The thunder storms that visit
us are grander and more terrific than I have ever seen
before. We watch them as they approach from the opposite side of the lake, observing the lightning play among
the clouds in various parts of the heavens, and dart in
jagged figures upon the piny heights of Jura, dark with
the shadow of the overhanging cloud, while perhaps the
sun is shining cheerily upon us. One night we *enjoyed* a
finer storm than I had ever before beheld. The lake was
lit up—the pines on Jura made visible, and all the scene
illuminated for an instant, when a pitchy blackness succeeded, and the thunder came in frightful bursts over our
heads amid the darkness.

But while I still dwell on the country around Geneva,
you will expect me to say something of the town itself:
there is nothing, however, in it that can repay you for
the trouble of walking over its rough stones. The houses
are high, the streets narrow, many of them on the ascent,
and no public building of any beauty to attract your eye,
or any architecture to gratify your taste. The town is
surrounded by a wall, the three gates of which are shut
exactly at ten o'clock, when no bribery (as in France) can
open them. To the south of the town is the promenade
of the Genevese, a grassy plain planted with a few trees,
and called Plainpalais. Here a small obelisk is erected
to the glory of Rousseau, and here (such is the mutability
of human life) the magistrates, the successors of those
who exiled him from his native country, were shot by
the populace during that revolution, which his writings
mainly contributed to mature, and which, notwithstanding
the temporary bloodshed and injustice with which it was
polluted, has produced enduring benefits to mankind, which

all the chicanery of statesmen, nor even the great conspiracy of kings, can entirely render vain. From respect to the memory of their predecessors, none of the present magistrates ever walk in Plainpalais. Another Sunday recreation for the citizens is an excursion to the top of Mont Salève. This hill is within a league of the town, and rises perpendicularly from the cultivated plain. It is ascended on the other side, and I should judge from its situation that your toil is rewarded by a delightful view of the course of the Rhone and Arve, and of the shores of the lake. We have not yet visited it.

There is more equality of classes here than in England. This occasions a greater freedom and refinement of manners among the lower orders than we meet with in our own country. I fancy the haughty English ladies are greatly disgusted with this consequence of republican institutions, for the Genevese servants complain very much of their *scolding*, an exercise of the tongue, I believe, perfectly unknown here. The peasants of Switzerland may not however emulate the vivacity and grace of the French. They are more cleanly, but they are slow and inapt. I know a girl of twenty, who although she had lived all her life among vineyards, could not inform me during what month the vintage took place, and I discovered she was utterly ignorant of the order in which the months succeed to one another.[1] She would not have been surprised if I had talked of the burning sun and delicious fruits of December, or of the frosts of July. Yet she is by no means deficient in understanding.

[1] In the *Essays* &c. we read *one to another*.

The Genevese are also much inclined to puritanism. It is true that from habit they dance on a Sunday, but as soon as the French government was abolished in the town, the magistrates ordered the theatre to be closed, and measures were taken to pull down the building.

We have latterly enjoyed fine weather, and nothing is more pleasant than to listen to the evening song of the vine-dressers. They are all women, and most of them have harmonious although masculine voices. The theme of their ballads consists of shepherds, love, flocks, and the sons of kings who fall in love with beautiful shepherdesses. Their tunes are monotonous, but it is sweet to hear them in the stillness of evening, while we are enjoying the sight of the setting sun, either from the hill behind our house or from the lake.

Such are our pleasures here, which would be greatly increased if the season had been more favourable, for they chiefly consist in such enjoyments as sunshine and gentle breezes bestow. We have not yet made any excursion in the environs of the town, but we have planned several, when you shall again hear of us; and we will endeavour, by the magic of words, to transport the ethereal part of you to the neighbourhood of the Alps, and mountain streams, and forests, which, while they clothe the former, darken the latter with their vast shadows. Adieu!

M.

LETTER III.

To T. P. Esq.

MEILLERIE—CLARENS—CHILLON¹—VEVAI—LAUSANNE.

Montalegre, near Coligni, Geneva.
July 12th.

It is nearly a fortnight since I have returned from Vevai. This journey has been on every account delightful, but most especially, because then I first knew the divine beauty of Rousseau's imagination, as it exhibits itself in Julie. It is inconceivable what an enchantment the scene itself lends to those delineations, from which its own most touching charm arises. But I will give you an abstract of our voyage, which lasted eight days, and if you have a map of Switzerland, you can follow me.

We left Montalegre at half past two on the 23d of June. The lake was calm, and after three hours of rowing we arrived at Hermance, a

23 June, 1816.

¹ In Shelley's edition these three names appear, doubtless through a printer's error, as *MELLTERIE— CLAREN — SCHILLON.* Elsewhere in the book *Clarens* and *Chillon* are given correctly; but *Meillerie*, which Mrs. Shelley set to rights in 1840, is uniformly spelt *Mellerie* in the 1817 volume.

beautiful little village, containing a ruined tower, built, the villagers say, by Julius Cæsar. There were three other towers similar to it, which the Genevese destroyed for their own fortifications in 1560. We got into the tower by a kind of window. The walls are immensely solid, and the stone of which it is built so hard, that it yet retained the mark of chisels. The boatmen said, that this tower was once three times higher than it is now. There are two staircases in the thickness of the walls, one of which is entirely demolished, and the other half ruined, and only accessible by a ladder. The town itself, now an inconsiderable village inhabited by a few fishermen, was built by a Queen of Burgundy, and reduced to its present state by the inhabitants of Berne, who burnt and ravaged every thing they could find.

Leaving Hermance, we arrived at sunset at the village of Nerni. After looking at our lodgings, which were gloomy and dirty, we walked out by the side of the lake. It was beautiful to see the vast expanse of these purple and misty waters broken by the craggy islets near to its slant and "beached margin." There were many fish sporting in the lake, and multitudes were collected close to the rocks to catch the flies which inhabited them.

On returning to the village, we sat on a wall beside the lake, looking at some children who were playing at a game like ninepins. The children here appeared in an extraordinary way deformed and diseased. Most of them were crooked, and with enlarged throats; but one little boy had such exquisite grace in his mien and motions, as I never before saw equalled in a child. His countenance was beautiful for the expression with which it over-flowed. There was a mixture of pride and gentleness in his eyes and lips, the indications of sensibility, which his education will probably pervert to misery or seduce to crime; but there was more of gentleness than of pride, and it seemed that the pride was tamed from its original wildness by the habitual exercise of milder feelings. My companion gave him a piece of money, which he took without speaking, with a sweet smile of easy thankfulness, and then with an unembarrassed air turned to his play. All this might scarcely be; but the imagination surely could not forbear to breathe into the most inanimate forms some likeness of its own visions, on such a serene and glowing evening, in this remote and romantic village, beside the calm lake that bore us hither.

On returning to our inn, we found that the servant had arranged our rooms, and deprived them of the greater portion of their former disconsolate appearance. They reminded my companion of Greece: it was five years, he said, since he had slept in such beds. The influence of the recollections excited by this circumstance on our conversation gradually faded, and I retired to rest with no unpleasant sensations, thinking of our journey to-morrow, and of the pleasure of recounting the little adventures of it when we return.

The next morning we passed Yvoire, a scattered village with an ancient castle, whose houses are interspersed with trees, and which stands at a 24 June, 1816. little distance from Nerni, on the promontory which bounds a deep bay, some miles in extent. So soon as we arrived at this promontory, the lake began to assume an aspect of wilder magnificence. The mountains of Savoy, whose summits were bright with snow, descended in broken slopes to the lake : on high, the rocks were dark with pine forests, which become deeper and more immense, until the ice and snow mingle with the points of naked rock that pierce the blue air ; but below, groves of walnut, chesnut, and oak, with openings of lawny fields, attested the milder climate.

As soon as we had passed the opposite promontory, we saw the river Drance, which descends from between a chasm[1] in the mountains, and makes a plain near the lake, intersected by its divided streams. Thousands of *besolets*,[2] beautiful water-birds, like sea-gulls, but smaller, with purple on their backs, take their station on the shallows, where its waters mingle with the lake. As we approached Evian, the mountains descended more precipitously to the lake, and masses of intermingled wood and rock overhung its shining spire.

We arrived at this town about seven o'clock, after a day which involved more rapid changes of atmosphere than I ever recollect to have observed before. The morning was cold and wet ; then an easterly wind, and the clouds hard and high ; then thunder showers, and wind shifting to every quarter ; then a warm blast from the south, and summer clouds hanging over the peaks, with bright blue sky between. About half an hour after we had arrived at Evian, a few flashes of lightning came from a dark cloud, directly over head, and continued after the cloud had dispersed. " Diespiter, per

---

[1] The expression *between a chasm* recalls the like use of the word *between* for *through* in *Alastor*. (See Poetical Works, Vol. 1, p. 36).

[2] Terns. Littré defines *besolet* as " Hirondelle de mer dans le parler genévois."

pura tonantes egit equos:" a phenomenon which certainly had no influence on me, corresponding with that
which it produced on Horace.

The appearance of the inhabitants of Evian is more
wretched, diseased and poor, than I ever recollect to have
seen. The contrast indeed between the subjects of the
King of Sardinia and the citizens of the independent
republics of Switzerland, affords a powerful illustration of
the blighting mischiefs of despotism, within the space of
a few miles. They have mineral waters here, *eaux saron-
neuses*, they call them. In the evening we had some
difficulty about our passports, but so soon as the syndic
heard my companion's rank and name, he apologized for
the circumstance. The inn was good. During our
voyage, on the distant height of a hill, covered with pine-
forests, we saw a ruined castle, which reminded me of
those on the Rhine.

We left Evian on the following morning, with a wind
of such violence as to permit but one sail to
be carried. The waves also were exceedingly   25 June, 1816.
high, and our boat so heavily laden, that there appeared
to be some danger. We arrived however safe at
Meillerie, after passing with great speed mighty forests
which overhung the lake, and lawns of exquisite
verdure, and mountains with bare and icy points, which
rose immediately from the summit of the rocks, whose
bases were echoing to the waves.

We here heard that the Empress Maria Louisa had
slept at Meillerie, before the present inn was built,
and when the accommodations were those of the most

wretched village, in remembrance of St. Preux. How beautiful it is to find that the common sentiments of human nature can attach themselves to those who are the most removed from its duties and its enjoyments, when Genius pleads for their admission at the gate of Power. To own them was becoming in the Empress, and confirms the affectionate praise contained in the regret of a great and enlightened nation. A Bourbon dared not even to have remembered Rousseau. She owed this power to that democracy which her husband's dynasty outraged, and of which it was however in some sort the representative among the nations of the earth. This little incident shews at once how unfit and how impossible it is for the ancient system of opinions, or for any power built upon a conspiracy to revive them, permanently to subsist among mankind. We dined there, and had some honey, the best I have ever tasted, the very essence of the mountain flowers, and as fragrant. Probably the village derives its name from this production. Meillerie is the well known scene of St. Preux's visionary exile; but Meillerie is indeed inchanted ground, were Rousseau no magician. Groves of pine, chesnut, and walnut overshadow it; magnificent and unbounded forests to which England affords no parallel. In the midst of these woods are dells of lawny expanse, inconceivably verdant, adorned with a thousand of the rarest flowers and odourous with thyme.

The lake appeared somewhat calmer as we left Meillerie, sailing close to the banks, whose magnificence augmented with the turn of every promontory. But we congratulated ourselves too soon: the wind gradually increased in violence, until it blew tremendously; and as it came from the remotest extremity of the lake, produced waves of a frightful height, and covered the whole surface with a chaos of foam. One of our boatmen, who was a dreadfully stupid fellow, persisted in holding the sail at a time when the boat was on the point of being driven under water by the hurricane. On discovering his error, he let it entirely go, and the boat for a moment refused to obey the helm; in addition, the rudder was so broken as to render the management of it very difficult; one wave fell in, and then another. My companion, an excellent swimmer, took off his coat, I did the same, and we sat with our arms crossed, every instant expecting to be swamped. The sail was however again held, the boat obeyed the helm, and still in imminent peril from the immensity of the waves, we arrived in a few minutes at a sheltered port, in the village of St. Gingoux.

I felt in this near prospect of death a mixture of sensations, among which terror entered, though but subordinately. My feelings would have been less painful had I been alone; but I know[1] that my companion would have attempted to save me, and I was overcome with humiliation, when I thought that his life might have been risked to preserve mine. When we arrived at St. Gingoux, the inhabitants, who stood on the shore, unaccustomed to see a vessel as frail as our's, and fearing to venture at all on such a sea, exchanged looks of wonder and congratulation with our boatmen, who, as well as ourselves, were well pleased to set foot on shore.

---

[1] So in Shelley's edition and the first edition of the *Essays* &c.; but in later editions *knew* is substituted for *know*.

St. Gingoux is even more beautiful than Meillerie; the mountains are higher, and their loftiest points of elevation descend more abruptly to the lake. On high, the aerial summits still cherish great depths of snow in their ravines, and in the paths of their unseen torrents. One of the highest of these is called Roche de St. Julien, beneath whose pinnacles the forests become deeper and more extensive; the chesnut gives a peculiarity to the scene, which is most beautiful, and will make a picture in my memory, distinct from all other mountain scenes which I have ever before visited.

As we arrived here early, we took a *voiture* to visit the mouth of the Rhone. We went between the mountains and the lake, under groves of mighty chesnut trees, beside perpetual streams, which are nourished by the snows above, and form stalactites on the rocks, over which they fall. We saw an immense chesnut tree, which had been overthrown by the hurricane of the morning. The place where the Rhone joins the lake was marked by a line of tremendous breakers; the river is as rapid as when it leaves the lake, but is muddy and dark. We went about a league farther on the road to La Valais, and stopped at a castle called La Tour de Bouverie, which seems to be the frontier of Switzerland and Savoy, as we were asked for our passports, on the supposition of our proceeding to Italy.

On one side of the road was the immense Roche de St. Julien, which overhung it; through the gateway of the castle we saw the snowy mountains of La Valais, clothed in clouds, and on the other side was the willowy plain of the Rhone, in a character of striking contrast

with the rest of the scene, bounded by the dark mountains that overhang Clarens, Vevai, and the lake that
rolls between.   In the midst of the plain rises a little
isolated hill, on which the white spire of a church peeps
from among the tufted chesnut woods.   We
returned to St. Gingoux before sun-set, and I   25 June, 1816.
passed the evening in reading Julie.

As my companion rises late, I had time before breakfast, on the ensuing morning, to hunt the
waterfalls of the river that fall into the lake   26 June, 1816.
at St. Gingoux.   The stream is indeed, from the declivity
over which it falls, only a succession of waterfalls, which
roar over the rocks with a perpetual sound, and suspend
their unceasing spray on the leaves and flowers that overhang and adorn its savage banks. The path that conducted
along this river sometimes avoided the precipices of its
shores, by leading through meadows; sometimes threaded
the base of the perpendicular and caverned rocks.   I
gathered in these meadows a nosegay of such flowers as
I never saw in England, and which I thought more beautiful for that rarity.

On my return, after breakfast, we sailed for Clarens,
determining first to see the three mouths of the Rhone,
and then the castle of Chillon; the day was fine, and
the water calm.   We passed from the blue waters of the
lake over the stream of the Rhone, which is rapid even
at a great distance from its confluence with the lake; the
turbid waters mixed with those of the lake, but mixed
with them unwillingly. (See *Nouvelle Heloise, Lettre* 17,
Part 4.)   I read Julie all day; an overflowing, as it now
seems, surrounded by the scenes which it has so wonder-

N 2

fully peopled, of sublimest genius, and more than human
sensibility.   Meillerie, the Castle of Chillon, Clarens, the
mountains of La Valais and Savoy, present themselves to
the imagination as monuments of things that were once
familiar, and of beings that were once dear to it.   They
were created indeed by one mind, but a mind so powerfully
bright as to cast a shade of falsehood on the records that
are called reality.

We passed on to the Castle of Chillon, and visited its
dungeons and towers.   These prisons are excavated below
the lake; the principal dungeon is supported by seven
columns, whose branching capitals support the roof.   Close
to the very walls, the lake is 800 feet deep; iron rings
are fastened to these columns, and on them were engraven
a multitude of names, partly those of visitors, and partly
doubtless of the prisoners, of whom now no memory
remains, and who thus beguiled a solitude which they
have long ceased to feel.   One date was as ancient as
1670.   At the commencement of the Reformation, and
indeed long after that period, this dungeon was the receptacle of those who shook, or who denied the system of
idolatry, from the effects of which mankind is even now
slowly emerging.

Close to this long and lofty dungeon was a narrow cell,
and beyond it one larger and far more lofty and dark,
supported upon two unornamented arches.   Across one
of these arches was a beam, now black and rotten, on
which prisoners were hung in secret.   I never saw a
monument more terrible of that cold and inhuman
tyranny, which it has been the delight of man to exercise over man.   It was indeed one of those many tremendous fulfilments which render the "pernicies humani

generis" of the great Tacitus, so solemn and irrefragable
a prophecy.   The gendarme, who conducted us over this
castle, told us that there was an opening to the lake, by
means of a secret spring, connected with which the whole
dungeon might be filled with water before the prisoners
could possibly escape!

We proceeded with a contrary wind to Clarens, against
a heavy swell.   I never felt more strongly than on land-
ing at Clarens, that the spirit of old times had deserted
its once cherished habitation.   A thousand times, thought
I, have Julia and St. Preux walked on this terrassed road,
looking towards these mountains which I now behold;
nay, treading on the ground where I now tread.   From
the window of our lodging our landlady pointed out " le
bosquet de Julie."   At least the inhabitants of this village
are impressed with an idea, that the persons of that romance
had actual existence.   In the evening we walked thither.
It is indeed Julia's wood.   The hay was making under
the trees; the trees themselves were aged, but vigorous,
and interspersed with younger ones, which are destined
to be their successors, and in future years, when we are
dead, to afford a shade to future worshippers of nature,
who love the memory of that tenderness and peace of
which this was the imaginary abode.   We walked forward
among the vineyards, whose narrow terraces overlook this
affecting scene.   Why did the cold maxims of the world
compel me at this moment to repress the tears of melancholy transport which it would have been so sweet to
indulge, immeasurably, even until the darkness of night
had swallowed up the objects which excited them?

I forgot to remark, what indeed my companion remarked
to me, that our danger from the storm took place precisely

in the spot where Julie and her lover were nearly overset, and where St. Preux was tempted to plunge with her into the lake.

On the following day we went to see the castle of Clarens, a square strong house, with very few windows, surrounded by a double terrace that overlooks the valley, or rather the plain of Clarens. The road which conducted to it wound up the steep ascent through woods of walnut and chesnut. We gathered roses on the terrace, in the feeling that they might be the posterity of some planted by Julia's hand. We sent their dead and withered leaves to the absent.

27 June, 1816.

We went again to "the bosquet de Julie," and found that the precise spot was now utterly obliterated, and a heap of stones marked the place where the little chapel had once stood. Whilst we were execrating the author of this brutal folly, our guide informed us that the land belonged to the convent of St. Bernard, and that this outrage had been committed by their orders. I knew before, that if avarice could harden the hearts of men, a system of prescriptive religion has an influence far more inimical to natural sensibility. I know that an isolated man is sometimes restrained by shame from outraging the venerable feelings arising out of the memory of genius, which once made nature even lovelier than itself; but associated man holds it as the very sacrament of his union to forswear all delicacy, all benevolence, all remorse, all that is true, or tender, or sublime.

We sailed from Clarens to Vevai. Vevai is a town

more beautiful in its simplicity than any I have ever seen. Its market-place, a spacious square interspersed with trees, looks directly upon the mountains of Savoy and La Valais, the lake, and the valley of the Rhone. It was at Vevai that Rousseau conceived the design of Julie.

29 June, 1816.

From Vevai we came to Ouchy, a village near Lausanne. The coasts of the Pays de Vaud, though full of villages and vineyards, present an aspect of tranquillity and peculiar beauty which well compensates for the solitude which I am accustomed to admire. The hills are very high and rocky, crowned and interspersed with woods. Water-falls echo from the cliffs, and shine afar. In one place we saw the traces of two rocks of immense size, which had fallen from the mountain behind. One of these lodged in a room where a young woman was sleeping, without injuring her. The vineyards were utterly destroyed in its path, and the earth torn up.

The rain detained us two days at Ouchy. We however visited Lausanne, and saw Gibbon's house. We were shewn the decayed summer-house where he finished his History, and the old acacias on the terrace, from which he saw Mont Blanc, after having written the last sentence. There is something grand and even touching in the regret which he expresses at the completion of his task. It was conceived amid the ruins of the Capitol. The sudden departure of his cherished and accustomed toil must have left him, like the death of a dear friend, sad and solitary.

29 to 30 June, 1816.

My companion gathered some acacia leaves to preserve

in remembrance of him.   I refrained from doing so, fearing to outrage the greater and more sacred name of
Rousseau ; the contemplation of whose imperishable
creations had left no vacancy in my heart for mortal
things.   Gibbon had a cold and unimpassioned spirit.   I
never felt more inclination to rail at the prejudices which
cling to such a thing, than now that Julie and Clarens,
Lausanne and the Roman Empire, compelled me to a
contrast between Rousseau and Gibbon.

When we returned, in the only interval of sunshine
during the day, I walked on the pier which the lake was
lashing with its waves.   A rainbow spanned the lake, or
rather rested one extremity of its arch upon the water,
and the other at the foot of the mountains of Savoy.
Some white houses, I know not if they were those of
Meillerie, shone through the yellow fire.

On Saturday the 30th of June we quitted Ouchy, and
after two days of pleasant sailing arrived on
1 July, 1816. Sunday evening at Montalegre.

                                                        S.

LETTER IV.

To T. P. Esq.

ST. MARTIN—SERVOZ—CHAMOUNI—MONTANVERT— MONT BLANC.

Hôtel de Londres, Chamouni,
July 22d, 1816.

WHILST you, my friend, are engaged in securing a home for us,[1] we are wandering in search of recollections to embellish it. I do not err in conceiving that you are interested in details of all that is majestic or beautiful in nature ; but how shall I describe to you the scenes by which I am now surrounded ? To exhaust the epithets which express the astonishment and the admiration—the very excess of satisfied astonishment, where expectation

---

[1] The hiatus implied in this opening is filled by the long and very interesting letter of which a large portion is printed in Middleton's *Shelley and his Writings* (Vol. II, pp. 38 *et seq.*). Shelley's reason for omitting it from this book is obvious : it is not cognate to the subject, and is mainly on the choice of a house, entrusted to Peacock. What has become of the original I know not ; but it was evidently the letter, or a part of the letter, disposed of at the Dillon Sale, mentioned in Mr. Rossetti's Memoir (ed. 1878), Vol. I, p. 63. From the auctioneer's catalogue, it would seem as if Middleton's fragment and the preceding letter were originally continuous ; and the extract given by the auctioneer would rather have been in the previous letter than in the fragment. The extract is as follows :

"Lord Byron is an exceedingly interesting person ; and, as such, is it not to be regretted that he is a slave to the vilest and most vulgar prejudices, and as mad as the winds ?"

scarcely acknowledged any boundary, is this, to impress
upon your mind the images which fill mine now even till
it overflow?   I too have read the raptures of travellers;
I will be warned by their example; I will simply detail
to you all that I can relate, or all that, if related, would
enable you to conceive of[1] what we have done or seen
since the morning of the 20th, when we left Geneva.

We commenced our intended journey to Chamouni at
half-past eight in the morning.   We passed
20 July, 1816.   through the champain country, which extends
from Mont Salêve to the base of the higher Alps.   The
country is sufficiently fertile, covered with corn fields and
orchards, and intersected by sudden acclivities with flat
summits.   The day was cloudless and excessively hot,
the Alps were perpetually in sight, and as we advanced, the
mountains, which form their outskirts, closed in around
us.   We passed a bridge over a stream, which discharges
itself into the Arve.   The Arve itself, much swollen
by the rains, flows constantly to the right of the road.

As we approached Bonneville through an avenue composed of a beautiful species of drooping poplar, we
observed that the corn fields on each side were covered
with inundation.   Bonneville is a neat little town, with
no conspicuous peculiarity, except the white towers of the
prison, an extensive building overlooking the town.   At
Bonneville the Alps commence, one of which, clothed by
forests, rises almost immediately from the opposite bank
of the Arve.

[1] The word *of* occurs here in
Shelley's edition and the first edition of the *Essays* &c.; but Mrs.
Shelley drops it in her later editions.

From Bonneville to Cluses the road conducts through a spacious and fertile plain, surrounded on all sides by mountains, covered like those of Meillerie with forests of intermingled pine and chesnut. At Cluses the road turns suddenly to the right, following the Arve along the chasm, which it seems to have hollowed for itself among the perpendicular mountains. The scene assumes here a more savage and colossal character : the valley becomes narrow, affording no more space than is sufficient for the river and the road. The pines descend to the banks, imitating with their irregular spires, the pyramidal crags which lift themselves far above the regions of forest into the deep azure of the sky, and among the white dazzling clouds. The scene, at the distance of half a mile from Cluses, differs from that of Matlock in little else than in the immensity of its proportions, and in its untameable, inaccessible solitude, inhabited only by the goats which we saw browsing on the rocks.

Near Maglans, within a league of each other, we saw two waterfalls. They were no more than mountain rivulets, but the height from which they fell, at least of *twelve* hundred feet, made them assume a character inconsistent with the smallness of their stream. The first fell from the overhanging brow of a black precipice on an enormous rock, precisely resembling some colossal Egyptian statue of a female deity. It struck the head of the visionary image, and gracefully dividing there, fell from it in folds of foam more like to cloud than water, imitating a veil of the most exquisite woof. It then united, concealing the lower part of the statue, and hiding itself in a winding of its channel, burst into a deeper fall, and crossed our route in its path towards the Arve.

The other waterfall was more continuous and larger. The violence with which it fell made it look more like some shape which an exhalation had assumed, than like water, for it streamed beyond the mountain, which appeared dark behind it, as it might have appeared behind an evanescent cloud.

The character of the scenery continued the same until we arrived at St. Martin (called in the maps Sallanches) the mountains perpetually becoming more elevated, exhibiting at every turn of the road more craggy summits, loftier and wider extent of forests, darker and more deep recesses.

The following morning we proceeded from St. Martin on mules to Chamouni, accompanied by two guides. We proceeded, as we had done the preceding day, along the valley of the Arve, a valley surrounded on all sides by immense mountains, whose rugged precipices are intermixed on high with dazzling snow. Their bases were still covered with the eternal forests, which perpetually grew darker and more profound as we approached the inner regions of the mountains.

21 July, 1816.

On arriving at a small village, at the distance of a league from St. Martin, we dismounted from our mules, and were conducted by our guides to view a cascade. We beheld an immense body of water fall two hundred and fifty feet, dashing from rock to rock, and casting a spray which formed a mist around it, in the midst of which hung a multitude of sunbows, which faded or became unspeakably vivid, as the inconstant sun shone through the clouds. When we approached near to it, the rain of the spray reached us, and our clothes were wetted by the quick-falling but minute particles of water. The cataract fell from above into a deep craggy chasm at our feet, where, changing its character to that of a mountain stream, it pursued its course towards the Arve, roaring over the rocks that impeded its progress.

As we proceeded, our route still lay through the valley, or rather, as it had now become, the vast ravine, which is at once the couch and the creation of the terrible Arve. We ascended, winding between mountains whose immensity staggers the imagination. We crossed the path of a torrent, which three days since had descended from the thawing snow, and torn the road away.

We dined at Servoz, a little village, where there are lead and copper mines, and where we saw a cabinet of natural curiosities, like those of Keswick and Bethgelert. We saw in this cabinet some chamois' horns, and the horns of an exceedingly rare animal called the bouquetin, which inhabits the desarts of snow to the south of Mont Blanc : it is an animal of the stag kind ; its horns weigh at least twenty-seven English pounds. It is inconceivable how so small an animal could support so inordinate a weight. The horns are of a very peculiar conformation, being broad, massy, and pointed at the ends, and surrounded with a number of rings, which are supposed to afford an indication of its age : there were seventeen rings on the largest of these horns.

From Servoz three leagues remain to Chamouni.—Mont Blanc was before us—the Alps, with their innumerable glaciers on high all around, closing in the complicated

windings of the single vale—forests inexpressibly beautiful, but majestic in their beauty—intermingled beech and
pine, and oak, overshadowed our road, or receded, whilst
lawns of such verdure as I have never seen before occupied these openings, and gradually became darker in their
recesses. Mont Blanc was before us, but it was covered
with cloud; its base, furrowed with dreadful gaps, was
seen above. Pinnacles of snow intolerably bright, part of
the chain connected with Mont Blanc, shone through the
clouds at intervals on high. I never knew—I never
imagined what mountains were before. The immensity
of these aerial summits excited, when they suddenly burst
upon the sight, a sentiment of extatic wonder, not unallied
to madness. And remember this was all one scene, it all
pressed home to our regard and our imagination. Though
it embraced a vast extent of space, the snowy pyramids
which shot into the bright blue sky seemed to overhang
our path; the ravine, clothed with gigantic pines, and
black with its depth below, so deep that the very roaring
of the untameable Arve, which rolled through it, could
not be heard above—all was as much our own, as if we
had been the creators of such impressions in the minds of
others as now occupied our own. Nature was the poet,
whose harmony held our spirits more breathless than that
of the divinest.

As we entered the valley of Chamouni (which in fact
may be considered as a continuation of those which we
have followed from Bonneville and Cluses) clouds hung
upon the mountains at the distance perhaps of 6000 feet
from the earth, but so as effectually to conceal not only
Mont Blanc, but the other *aiguilles*, as they call them
here, attached and subordinate to it. We were travelling

along the valley, when suddenly we heard a sound as of
the burst of smothered thunder rolling above; yet there
was something earthly[1] in the sound, that told us it
could not be thunder. Our guide hastily pointed out
to us a part of the mountain opposite, from whence the
sound came. It was an avalanche. We saw the smoke
of its path among the rocks, and continued to hear at
intervals the bursting of its fall. It fell on the bed of a
torrent, which it displaced, and presently we saw its
tawny-coloured waters also spread themselves over the
ravine, which was their couch.

We did not, as we intended, visit the *Glacier de Boisson*[2]
to-day, although it descends within a few
minutes' walk of the road, wishing to 22 July, 1816.
survey it at least when unfatigued. We saw this
glacier which comes close to the fertile plain, as we
passed, its surface was broken into a thousand unaccountable figures: conical and pyramidical crystaliza-
tions, more than fifty feet in height, rise from its
surface, and precipices of ice, of dazzling splendour,
overhang the woods and meadows of the vale. This
glacier winds upwards from the valley, until it joins the
masses of frost from which it was produced above, winding through its own ravine like a bright belt flung over
the black region of pines. There is more in all these
scenes than mere magnitude of proportion: there is a
majesty of outline; there is an awful grace in the very
colours which invest these wonderful shapes—a charm

---

[1] So in Shelley's edition and the
first edition of the *Essays* &c.; but
the word *earthly* is omitted in Mrs.
Shelley's later editions.

[2] *Glacier de Boisson* in Shelley's
edition and the first edition of the
Essays &c.: in Mrs. Shelley's later
editions *Glacier des Bossons*.

which is peculiar to them, quite distinct even from the reality of their unutterable greatness.

July 24.

23 July, 1816.

Yesterday morning we went to the source of the Arveiron. It is about a league from this village; the river rolls forth impetuously from an arch of ice, and spreads itself in many streams over a vast space of the valley, ravaged and laid bare by its inundations. The glacier by which its waters are nourished, overhangs this cavern and the plain, and the forests of pine which surround it, with terrible precipices of solid ice. On the other side rises the immense glacier of Montanvert, fifty miles in extent, occupying a chasm among mountains of inconceivable height, and of forms so pointed and abrupt, that they seem to pierce the sky. From this glacier we saw as we sat on a rock, close to one of the streams of the Arveiron, masses of ice detach themselves from on high, and rush with a loud dull noise into the vale. The violence of their fall turned them into powder, which flowed over the rocks in imitation of waterfalls, whose ravines they usurped and filled.

In the evening I went with Ducrée, my guide, the only tolerable person I have seen in this country, to visit the glacier of Boisson. This glacier, like that of Montanvert, comes close to the vale, overhanging the green meadows and the dark woods with the dazzling whiteness of its precipices and pinnacles, which are like spires of radiant crystal, covered with a net-work of frosted silver. These glaciers flow perpetually into the valley, ravaging in their slow but irresistible progress the pastures and the forests which surround them, performing a work of desolation in ages, which a river of lava might accomplish in an hour, but far more irretrievably; for where the ice has once descended, the hardiest plant refuses to grow; if even, as in some extraordinary instances, it should recede after its progress has once commenced. The glaciers perpetually move onward, at the rate of a foot each day, with a motion that commences at the spot where, on the boundaries of perpetual congelation, they are produced by the freezing of the waters which arise from the partial melting of the eternal snows. They drag with them from the regions whence they derive their origin, all the ruins of the mountain, enormous rocks, and immense accumulations of sand and stones. These are driven onwards by the irresistible stream of solid ice; and when they arrive at a declivity of the mountain, sufficiently rapid, roll down, scattering ruin. I saw one of these rocks which had descended in the spring, (winter here is the season of silence and safety) which measured forty feet in every direction.

The verge of a glacier, like that of Boisson, presents the most vivid image of desolation that it is possible to conceive. No one dares to approach it; for the enormous pinnacles of ice which perpetually fall, are perpetually reproduced. The pines of the forest, which bound it at one extremity, are overthrown and shattered to a wide extent at its base. There is something inexpressibly dreadful in the aspect of the few branchless trunks, which, nearest to the ice rifts, still stand in the uprooted soil. The meadows perish, overwhelmed with sand and stones. Within this last year, these glaciers have advanced three hundred feet

into the valley. Saussure, the naturalist, says, that they
have their periods of increase and decay : the people of
the country hold an opinion entirely different ; but as I
judge, more probable. It is agreed by all, that the snow
on the summit of Mont Blanc and the neighbouring
mountains perpetually augments, and that ice, in the form
of glaciers, subsists without melting in the valley of
Chamouni during its transient and variable summer. If
the snow which produces this glacier must augment, and
the heat of the valley is no obstacle to the perpetual existence of such masses of ice as have already descended
into it, the consequence is obvious ; the glaciers must
augment and will subsist, at least until they have over-
flowed this vale.

I will not pursue Buffon's sublime but gloomy theory
—that this globe which we inhabit will at some future
period be changed into a mass of frost by the encroach-
ments of the polar ice, and of that produced on the most
elevated points of the earth. Do you, who assert the
supremacy of Ahriman, imagine him throned among these
desolating snows, among these palaces of death and frost,
so sculptured in this their terrible magnificence by the
adamantine hand of necessity, and that he casts around
him, as the first essays of his final usurpation, avalanches,
torrents, rocks, and thunders, and above all these deadly
glaciers, at once the proof and symbols of his reign ;—
add to this, the degradation of the human species—who
in these regions are half deformed or idiotic, and most of
whom are deprived of any thing that can excite interest
or admiration. This is a part of the subject more mournful and less sublime ; but such as neither the poet nor
the philosopher should disdain to regard.

This morning we departed, on the promise of a fine day, to visit the glacier of Montanvert. In that part where it fills a slanting valley, 24 July, 1816. it is called the Sea of Ice. This valley is 950 toises, or 7600 feet above the level of the sea. We had not proceeded far before the rain began to fall, but we persisted until we had accomplished more than half of our journey, when we returned, wet through.

Chamouni, July 25th.

We have returned from visiting the glacier of Montanvert, or as it is called, the Sea of Ice, a scene in truth of dizzying wonder. The path that winds to it along the side of a mountain, now clothed with pines, now intersected with snowy hollows, is wide and steep. The cabin of Montanvert is three leagues from Chamouni, half of which distance is performed on mules, not so sure footed, but that on the first day the one which I rode fell in what the guides call a *mauvais pas*, so that I narrowly escaped being precipitated down the mountain. We passed over a hollow covered with snow, down which vast stones are accustomed to roll. One had fallen the preceding day, a little time after we had returned: our guides desired us to pass quickly, for it is said that sometimes the least sound will accelerate their descent. We arrived at Montanvert, however, safe.

On all sides precipitous mountains, the abodes of unrelenting frost, surround this vale: their sides are banked up with ice and snow, broken, heaped high, and exhibiting terrific chasms. The summits are sharp and naked pinnacles, whose overhanging steepness will not even permit snow to rest upon them. Lines of dazzling ice occupy

here and there their perpendicular rifts, and shine through
the driving vapours with inexpressible brilliance : they
pierce the clouds like things not belonging to this earth.
The vale itself is filled with a mass of undulating ice, and
has an ascent sufficiently gradual even to the remotest
abysses of these horrible desarts.   It is only half a league
(about two miles) in breadth, and seems much less.   It
exhibits an appearance as if frost had suddenly bound up
the waves and whirlpools of a mighty torrent.   We walked
some distance upon its surface.   The waves are elevated
about 12 or 15 feet from the surface of the mass, which
is intersected by long gaps of unfathomable depth, the
ice of whose sides is more beautifully azure than the sky.
In these regions every thing changes, and is in motion.
This vast mass of ice has one general progress, which ceases
neither day nor night ; it breaks and bursts for ever :
some undulations sink while others rise ; it is never the
same.   The echo of rocks, or of the ice and snow which
fall from their overhanging precipices, or roll from their
aerial summits, scarcely ceases for one moment.   One
would think that Mont Blanc, like the god of the Stoics,
was a vast animal, and that the frozen blood for ever
circulated through his stony veins.

We dined (M***, C***, and I) on the grass, in the
open air, surrounded by this scene.   The air is piercing
and clear.   We returned down the mountain, sometimes
encompassed by the driving vapours, sometimes cheered
by the sunbeams, and arrived at our inn by seven
o'clock.

Montalegre, July 28th.

The next morning we returned through the rain to St.

Martin.   The scenery had lost something of its
immensity, thick clouds hanging over the highest   26 July, 1816.
mountains; but visitings of sunset intervened between the
showers, and the blue sky shone between the accumulated
clouds of snowy whiteness which brought them; the dazzling mountains sometimes glittered through a chasm of the
clouds above our heads, and all the charm of its grandeur
remained.   We repassed *Pont Pellisier*, a wooden bridge
over the Arve, and the ravine of the Arve.   We repassed
the pine forests which overhang the defile, the chateau of
St. Michel, a haunted ruin, built on the edge of a
precipice, and shadowed over by the eternal forest.   We
repassed the vale of Servoz, a vale more beautiful, because
more luxuriant, than that of Chamouni.   Mont Blanc
forms one of the sides of this vale also, and the other is
inclosed by an irregular amphitheatre of enormous mountains, one of which is in ruins, and fell fifty years ago
into the higher part of the valley: the smoke of its fall
was seen in Piedmont, and people went from Turin to
investigate whether a volcano had not burst forth among
the Alps.   It continued falling many days, spreading,
with the shock and thunder of its ruin, consternation
into the neighbouring vales.   In the evening we arrived
at St. Martin.   The next day we wound through the
valley, which I have described before, and
arrived in the evening at our home.   27 July, 1816.

We have bought some specimens of minerals and
plants, and two or three crystal seals, at Mont Blanc,
to preserve the remembrance of having approached it.
There is a cabinet of *Histoire Naturelle* at Chamouni, just
as at Keswick, Matlock, and Clifton; the proprietor of
which is the very vilest specimen of that vile species

of quack that, together with the whole army of auber-
gistes and guides, and indeed the entire mass of the
population, subsist on the weakness and credulity of
travellers as leaches subsist on the sick. The most interesting of my purchases is a large collection of all the
seeds of rare alpine plants, with their names written
upon the outside of the papers that contain them. These
I mean to colonize in my garden in England, and to
permit you to make what choice you please from them.
They are companions which the Celandine—the classic
Celandine, need not despise; they are as wild and more
daring than he, and will tell him tales of things even
as touching and sublime as the gaze of a vernal poet.

Did I tell you that there are troops of wolves among
these mountains? In the winter they descend into the
vallies, which the snow occupies six months of the year,
and devour every thing that they can find out of doors.
A wolf is more powerful than the fiercest and strongest
dog. There are no bears in these regions. We heard,
when we were at Lucerne, that they were occasionally
found in the forests which surround that lake. Adieu.

S.

LINES

WRITTEN IN THE VALE OF CHAMOUNI.

MONT BLANC.

LINES WRITTEN IN THE VALE OF CHAMOUNI.

I.

THE everlasting universe of things
Flows through the mind, and rolls its rapid waves,
Now dark—now glittering—now reflecting gloom—
Now lending splendour, where from secret springs
The source of human thought its tribute brings
Of waters,—with a sound but half its own,
Such as a feeble brook will oft assume
In the wild woods, among the mountains lone,
Where waterfalls around it leap for ever,
Where woods and winds contend, and a vast river
Over its rocks ceaselessly bursts and raves.

II.

Thus thou, Ravine of Arve—dark, deep Ravine—
Thou many-coloured, many-voiced vale,
Over whose pines, and crags, and caverns sail
Fast cloud shadows and sunbeams : awful scene,
Where Power in likeness of the Arve comes down
From the ice gulphs that gird his secret throne,
Bursting through these dark mountains like the flame
Of lightning thro' the tempest ;—thou dost lie,
Thy giant brood of pines around thee clinging,
Children of elder time, in whose devotion
The chainless winds still come and ever came
To drink their odours, and their mighty swinging
To hear—an old and solemn harmony ;

Thine earthly rainbows stretched across the sweep
Of the ethereal waterfall, whose veil
Robes some unsculptured image; the strange sleep
Which when the voices of the desart fail
Wraps all in its own deep eternity;—
Thy caverns echoing to the Arve's commotion,
A loud, lone sound no other sound can tame;
Thou art pervaded with that ceaseless motion,
Thou art the path of that unresting sound—
Dizzy Ravine! and when I gaze on thee
I seem as in a trance sublime and strange
To muse on my own separate phantasy,
My own, my human mind, which passively
Now renders and receives fast influencings,
Holding an unremitting interchange
With the clear universe of things around;
One legion of wild thoughts, whose wandering wings
Now float above thy darkness, and now rest
Where that or thou art no unbidden guest,
In the still cave of the witch Poesy,
Seeking among the shadows that pass by
Ghosts of all things that are, some shade of thee,
Some phantom, some faint image; till the breast
From which they fled recalls them, thou art there!

III.

Some say that gleams of a remoter world
Visit the soul in sleep,—that death is slumber,
And that its shapes the busy thoughts outnumber
Of those who wake and live.—I look on high;
Has some unknown omnipotence unfurled
The veil of life and death? or do I lie
In dream, and does the mightier world of sleep
Spread far around and inaccessibly
Its circles? For the very spirit fails,
Driven like a homeless cloud from steep to steep
That vanishes among the viewless gales!
Far, far above, piercing the infinite sky,
Mont Blanc appears, —still, snowy, and serene—
Its subject mountains their unearthly forms
Pile around it, ice and rock; broad vales between
Of frozen floods, unfathomable deeps,
Blue as the overhanging heaven, that spread
And wind among the accumulated steeps;
A desart peopled by the storms alone,

Save when the eagle brings some hunter's bone,
And the wolf tracks her there—how hideously
Its shapes are heaped around ! rude, bare, and high,
Ghastly, and scarred, and riven.—Is this the scene
Where the old Earthquake-dæmon taught her young
Ruin ?   Were these their toys ? or did a sea
Of fire, envelope once this silent snow ?
None can reply—all seems eternal now.
The wilderness has a mysterious tongue
Which teaches awful doubt, or faith so mild,
So solemn, so serene, that man may be
But for such faith with nature reconciled ;
Thou hast a voice, great Mountain, to repeal
Large codes of fraud and woe ; not understood
By all, but which the wise, and great, and good
Interpret. or make felt, or deeply feel.

IV.

The fields, the lakes, the forests, and the streams,
Ocean, and all the living things that dwell
Within the dædal earth ; lightning, and rain,
Earthquake, and fiery flood, and hurricane,
The torpor of the year when feeble dreams
Visit the hidden buds, or dreamless sleep
Holds every future leaf and flower ;—the bound
With which from that detested trance they leap ;
The works and ways of man, their death and birth,
And that of him and all that his may be ;
All things that move and breathe with toil and sound
Are born and die ; revolve, subside and swell.
Power dwells apart in its tranquillity
Remote, serene, and inaccessible :
And *this*, the naked countenance of earth,
On which I gaze, even these primæval mountains
Teach the adverting mind.   The glaciers creep
Like snakes that watch their prey, from their far fountains,
Slow rolling on ; there, many a precipice,
Frost and the Sun in scorn of mortal power
Have piled : dome, pyramid, and pinnacle,
A city of death, distinct with many a tower
And wall impregnable of beaming ice.
Yet not a city, but a flood of ruin
Is there, that from the boundaries of the sky
Rolls its perpetual stream ; vast pines are strewing
Its destined path, or in the mangled soil

Branchless and shattered stand; the rocks, drawn down
From yon remotest waste, have overthrown
The limits of the dead and living world,
Never to be reclaimed. The dwelling-place
Of insects, beasts, and birds, becomes its spoil;
Their food and their retreat for ever gone,
So much of life and joy is lost. The race
Of man, flies far in dread; his work and dwelling
Vanish, like smoke before the tempest's stream,
And their place is not known. Below, vast caves
Shine in the rushing torrent's restless gleam,
Which from those secret chasms in tumult welling
Meet in the vale, and one majestic River,
The breath and blood of distant lands, for ever
Rolls its loud waters to the ocean waves,
Breathes its swift vapours to the circling air.

V.

Mont Blanc yet gleams on high :—the power is there,
The still and solemn power of many sights,
And many sounds, and much of life and death.
In the calm darkness of the moonless nights,
In the lone glare of day, the snows descend
Upon that Mountain; none beholds them there,
Nor when the flakes burn in the sinking sun,
Or the star-beams dart through them :—Winds contend
Silently there, and heap the snow with breath
Rapid and strong, but silently! Its home
The voiceless lightning in these solitudes
Keeps innocently, and like vapour broods
Over the snow. The secret strength of things
Which governs thought, and to the infinite dome
Of heaven is as a law, inhabits thee !
And what were thou, and earth, and stars, and sea,
If to the human mind's imaginings
Silence and solitude were vacancy ?

July 23, 1816.

The imprint of the *History of a Six Weeks' Tour* is as follows :—

Reynell, Printer, 45, Broad-street,
Golden-square.

JOURNAL AT GENEVA

(INCLUDING GHOST STORIES)

AND ON RETURN TO ENGLAND, 1816.

[With the *History of a Six Weeks' Tour* &c. ends the series of prose volumes and pamphlets issued by Shelley during his life. The remainder is posthumous, and to a great extent fragmentary. The following Journal is taken out of its chronological position among the posthumous prose writings because it connects itself with the letters forming the latter portion of the *Six Weeks' Tour* volume, having been written by Shelley during the continental trip of 1816. Mrs. Shelley published it in the second volume of the *Essays, Letters,* &c. (1840), from which it is now simply reprinted.—H. B. F.]

JOURNAL.

Geneva, Sunday, 18th August, 1816.

SEE Apollo's Sexton,[1] who tells us many mysteries of his trade. We talk of Ghosts. Neither Lord Byron nor M. G. L. seem to believe in them; and they both agree, in the very face of reason, that none could believe in ghosts without believing in God. I do not think that all the persons who profess to discredit these visitations, really discredit them; or, if they do in the daylight, are not admonished by the approach of loneliness and midnight, to think more respectfully of the world of shadows.

Lewis recited a poem, which he had composed at the

[1] Matthew Gregory Lewis, M.P. for Hindon, author of *The Monk*, *The Castle Spectre*, *Tales of Terror*, &c., thus addressed in *English Bards and Scotch Reviewers:*—

Oh! wonder-working Lewis! monk, or bard,
Who fain wouldst make Parnassus a church-yard!
Lo! wreaths of yew, not laurel, bind thy brow,
Thy muse a sprite, Apollo's sexton thou!

Mrs. Shelley records that "when Lewis first saw Lord Byron, he asked him earnestly,—'Why did you call me Apollo's Sexton.' The noble Poet found it difficult to reply to this categorical species of reproof." Some of these stories had appeared in print when Mrs. Shelley published the Journal in 1840; but, "as a ghost story depends entirely on the mode in which it is told," these were justly thought worth preservation as having been "written by Shelley, fresh from their relation by Lewis."

request of the Princess of Wales. The Princess of Wales,
he promised, was not only a believer in ghosts, but in
magic and witchcraft, and asserted, that prophecies made
in her youth had been accomplished since. The tale was
of a lady in Germany.

This lady, Minna, had been exceedingly attached to
her husband, and they had made a vow that the one who
died first, should return after death to visit the other as
a ghost. She was sitting one day alone in her chamber,
when she heard an unusual sound of footsteps on the
stairs. The door opened, and her husband's spectre,
gashed with a deep wound across the forehead, and in
military habiliments, entered. She appeared startled at
the apparition; and the ghost told her, that when he
should visit her in future, she would hear a passing bell
toll, and these words distinctly uttered close to her ear,
" Minna, I am here." On inquiry, it was found that her
husband had fallen in battle on the very day she was
visited by the vision. The intercourse between the ghost
and the woman continued for some time, until the latter
laid aside all terror, and indulged herself in the affection
which she had felt for him while living. One evening
she went to a ball, and permitted her thoughts to be
alienated by the attentions of a Florentine gentleman,
more witty, more graceful, and more gentle, as it
appeared to her, than any person she had ever seen. As
he was conducting her through the dance, a death bell
tolled. Minna, lost in the fascination of the Florentine's
attentions, disregarded, or did not hear the sound. A
second peal, louder and more deep, startled the whole
company, when Minna heard the ghost's accustomed
whisper, and raising her eyes, saw in an opposite mirror

the reflexion of the ghost, standing over her. She is said to have died of terror.

Lewis told four other stories—all grim.

I.

A YOUNG man who had taken orders, had just been presented with a living, on the death of the incumbent. It was in the Catholic part of Germany. He arrived at the parsonage on a Saturday night; it was summer, and waking about three o'clock in the morning, and it being broad day, he saw a venerable-looking man, but with an aspect exceedingly melancholy, sitting at a desk in the window, reading, and two beautiful boys standing near him, whom he regarded with looks of the profoundest grief. Presently he rose from his seat, the boys followed him, and they were no more to be seen. The young man, much troubled, arose, hesitating whether he should regard what he had seen as a dream, or a waking phantasy. To divert his dejection, he walked towards the church, which the sexton was already employed in preparing for the morning service. The first sight that struck him was a portrait, the exact resemblance of the man whom he had seen sitting in his chamber. It was the custom in this district to place the portrait of each minister, after his death, in the church.

He made the minutest inquiries respecting his predecessor, and learned that he was universally beloved, as a man of unexampled integrity and benevolence; but that he was the prey of a secret and perpetual sorrow.

His grief was supposed to have arisen from an attachment to a young lady, with whom his situation did not permit him to unite himself. Others, however, asserted, that a connexion did subsist between them, and that even she occasionally brought to his house two beautiful boys, the offspring of their connexion.—Nothing further occurred until the cold weather came, and the new minister desired a fire to be lighted in the stove of the room where he slept. A hideous stench arose from the stove as soon as it was lighted, and, on examining it, the bones of two male children were found within.

II.

Lord Lyttleton and a number of his friends were joined during the chase by a stranger. He was excellently mounted, and displayed such courage, or, rather so much desperate rashness, that no other person in the hunt could follow him. The gentlemen, when the chase was concluded, invited the stranger to dine with them. His conversation was something of a wonderful kind. He astonished, he interested, he commanded the attention of the most inert. As night came on, the company, being weary, began to retire one by one, much later than the usual hour: the most intellectual among them were retained latest by the stranger's fascination. As he perceived that they began to depart, he redoubled his efforts to retain them. At last, when few remained, he entreated them to stay with him; but all pleaded the fatigue of a hard day's chase, and all at last retired. They had been in bed about an hour, when they were awakened by the most horrible screams, which issued from the stranger's room. Every one rushed towards it. The door was locked. After a moment's deliberation they burst it open, and found the stranger stretched on the ground, writhing with[1] agony, and weltering in blood. On their entrance he arose, and collecting himself, apparently with a strong effort, entreated them to leave him—not to disturb him, that he would give every possible explanation in the morning. They complied. In the morning, his chamber was found vacant, and he was seen no more.

III.

MILES ANDREWS, a friend of Lord Lyttleton, was sitting one night alone when Lord Lyttleton came in, and informed him that he was dead, and that this was his ghost which he saw before him. Andrews pettishly told him not to play any ridiculous tricks upon him, for he was not in a temper to bear them. The ghost then departed. In the morning Andrews asked his servant at what hour Lord Lyttleton had arrived. The servant said he did not know that he had arrived, but that he would inquire. On inquiry it was found that Lord Lyttleton had not arrived, nor had the door been opened to any one during the whole night. Andrews sent to Lord Lyttleton, and discovered, that he had died precisely at the hour of the apparition.

[1] In Mrs. Shelley's edition of 1852, *in*.

IV.

A GENTLEMAN on a visit to a friend who lived on the skirts of an extensive forest in the east of Germany lost his way. He wandered for some hours among the trees, when he saw a light at a distance. On approaching it, he was surprised to observe, that it proceeded from the interior of a ruined monastery. Before he knocked he thought it prudent to look through the window. He saw a multitude of cats assembled round a small grave, four of whom were letting down a coffin with a crown upon it. The gentleman, startled at this unusual sight, and imagining that he had arrived among the retreats of fiends or witches, mounted his horse and rode away with the utmost precipitation. He arrived at his friend's house at a late hour, who had sate up for him. On his arrival his friend questioned as to the cause of the traces of trouble visible in his face. He began to recount his adventure, after much difficulty, knowing that it was scarcely possible that his friends should give faith to his relation. No sooner had he mentioned the coffin with a crown upon it, than his friend's cat, who seemed to have been lying asleep before the fire, leaped up, saying— "Then I am the King of the Cats!" and scrambled up the chimney, and was seen no more.

Thursday, 29th August.—We depart from Geneva, at nine in the morning. The Swiss are very slow drivers; besides which we have Jura to mount; we, therefore, go a very few posts to-day. The scenery is very beautiful,

and we see many magnificent views.   We pass Les
Rousses, which, when we crossed in the spring, was deep
in snow.   We sleep at Morrez.

Friday, 30th.—We leave Morrez, and arrive in the
evening at Dole, after a various day.   30 Aug., 1816.

Saturday, 31st.—From Dole we go to Rouvray, where
we sleep.   We pass through Dijon ; and, after Dijon,
take a different route than that which we followed on the
two other occasions.   The scenery has some beauty and
singularity in the line of the mountains which surround
the Val de Suzon.   Low, yet precipitous hills, covered
with vines or woods, and with streams, meadows, and
poplars, at the bottom.

Sunday, September 1st.—Leave Rouvray, pass Auxerre,
where we dine ; a pretty town, and arrive, at two o'clock,
at Villeneuve le Guiard.

Monday 2d.—From Villeneuve le Guiard, we arrive
at Fontainebleau.   The scenery around this palace is
wild and even savage.   The soil is full of rocks, apparently granite, which on every side break through the
ground.   The hills are low, but precipitous and rough.
The valleys, equally wild, are shaded by forests.   In the
midst of this wilderness stands the palace.   Some of the
apartments equal in magnificence anything that I could
conceive.   The roofs are fretted with gold, and the
canopies of velvet.   From Fontainebleau we proceed to
Versailles, in the route towards Rouen.   We arrive at
Versailles at nine.

Tuesday 3d.—We saw the palace and gardens of Versailles and le Grand et Petit Trianon. They
3 Sept., 1816. surpass Fontainebleau. The gardens are full of
statues, vases, fountains, and colonnades. In all that essentially belongs to a garden they are extraordinarily deficient.
The orangery is a stupid piece of expense. There was one
orange-tree, not apparently so old, sown in 1442. We
saw only the gardens and the theatre at the Petit
Trianon. The gardens are in the English taste, and extremely pretty. The Grand Trianon was open. It is a
summer palace, light, yet magnificent. We were unable
to devote the time it deserved to the gallery of paintings
here. There was a portrait of Madame de la Vallière,
the repentant mistress of Louis XIV. She was melancholy, but exceedingly beautiful, and was represented as
holding a scull, and sitting before a crucifix, pale, and
with downcast eyes.

We then went to the great palace. The apartments
are unfurnished, but even with this disadvantage, are
more magnificent than those of Fontainebleau. They are
lined with marble of various colours, whose pedestals and
capitals are gilt, and the ceiling is richly gilt with com-
partments of painting. The arrangement of these materials
has in them, it is true, something effeminate and royal.
Could a Grecian architect have commanded all the labour
and money which was expended on Versailles, he would
have produced a fabric which the whole world has never
equalled. We saw the hall of Hercules, the balcony
where the King and the Queen exhibited themselves to
the Parisian mob. The people who showed us through
the palace, obstinately refused to say anything about the
Revolution. We could not even find out in which

chamber the rioters of the 10th August found the king.
We saw the Salle d'Opera, where are now preserved the
portraits of the kings. There was the race of the
house of Orleans, with the exception of Egalité, all
extremely handsome. There was Madame de Main-
tenou, and beside her a beautiful little girl, the
daughter of La Vallière. The pictures had been hidden
during the Revolution. We saw the Library of Louis
XVI. The librarian had held some place in the ancient
court near Marie Antoinette. He returned with the
Bourbons, and was waiting for some better situation. He
showed us a book which he had preserved during the
Revolution. It was a book of paintings, representing a
Tournament at the Court of Louis XIV.; and it seemed
that the present desolation of France, the fury of the
injured people, and all the horrors to which they abandoned themselves, stung by their long sufferings, flowed
naturally enough from expenditures so immense, as must
have been demanded by the magnificence of this tournament. The vacant rooms of this palace imaged well the
hollow show of monarchy. After seeing these things
we departed toward Havre, and slept at Auxerre.

Wednesday 4th.—We passed through Rouen, and saw
the cathedral, an immense specimen of the most
costly and magnificent gothic. The interior of ⁴ Sept., 1816.
the church disappoints. We saw the burial-place of Richard
Cœur de Lion and his brother. The altar of the church
is a fine piece of marble. Sleep at Yvetot.

Thursday 5th.—We arrive at Havre, and wait for the
packet—wind contrary.

THE ASSASSINS,

A FRAGMENT OF A ROMANCE.

[With *The Assassins*, apparently, begins the series of uncompleted prose works which Shelley left us. Strange, weird, and unnatural as the few incidents of the Romance, as far as it goes, may seem, the thoughtful student will not fail to discern its importance as a step in the growth of Shelley's style. There are better things in its descriptive passages than can be found in *Queen Mab;* and we even find a foretaste of the glories of style first made evident in *Alastor.* Seemingly, *The Assassins* was begun at Brunen on the 25th of August, 1814, and continued at Marsluys on the 8th and 9th of the following month. (See notes at pages 143 and 156 of this volume.) Mrs. Shelley says in her Preface to the *Essays* &c., in which collection she first gave *The Assassins*, that it "was never touched afterwards," meaning, I imagine, after September, 1814. She says, "The Assassins were known in the eleventh century as a horde of Mahometans living among the recesses of Lebanon,—ruled over by the Old Man of the Mountain; under whose direction various murders were committed on the Crusaders, which caused the name of the people who perpetrated them to be adopted in all European languages, to designate the crime which gave them notoriety." Von Hammer, whose history of this strange tribe may be consulted in English through the translation of Dr O. C. Wood (London, 1835), derives the name of the tribe (*hashishin*) from the herb *hashishe*, which they used; and this derivation appears to be accepted by the highest authorities at the present more scientific time. Richardson gives no instance of the word *assassin* earlier than the thirteenth century; and M. Littré (*Dictionnaire de la Langue Française*) gives the following account of the Etymology of the word *assassin:* "De l'arabe *haschisch*, nom de la poudre de feuilles de chanvre, avec laquelle on prépare le *haschische.* Le Prince des assassins ou Scheik ou Vieux de la montagne faisait prendre du *haschisch* à certains hommes qu'on nommait *feidawi;* ces hommes avaient des visions qui les transportaient et qu'on leur représentait comme un avant-goût du Paradis. A ce point, ils se trouvaient déterminés à tout faire, et le prince les employait à tuer des personnages ennemis. C'est ainsi qu'une plante enivrante a fini par donner son nom à l'assassinat."—H. B. F.]

THE ASSASSINS,

A FRAGMENT OF A ROMANCE.

CHAPTER I.

JERUSALEM, goaded on to resistance by the incessant usurpations and insolence of Rome, leagued together its discordant factions to rebel against the common enemy and tyrant. Inferior to their foe in all but the unconquerable hope of liberty, they surrounded their city with fortifications of uncommon strength, and placed in array before the temple a band rendered desperate by patriotism and religion. Even the women preferred to die, rather than survive the ruin of their country. When the Roman army approached the walls of the sacred city, its preparations, its discipline, and its numbers, evinced the conviction of its leader, that he had no common barbarians to subdue. At the approach of the Roman army, the strangers withdrew from the city.

Among the multitudes which from every nation of the East had assembled at Jerusalem, was a little congregation of Christians. They were remarkable neither for their

numbers nor their importance. They contained among
them neither philosophers nor poets. Acknowledging no
laws but those of God, they modelled their conduct
towards their fellow-men by the conclusions of their
individual judgment on the practical application of these
laws. And it was apparent from the simplicity and
severity of their manners, that this contempt for human
institutions had produced among them a character superior in singleness and sincere self-apprehension to the
slavery of pagan customs and the gross delusions of anti-
quated superstition. Many of their opinions considerably
resembled those of the sect afterwards known by the
name of Gnostics. They esteemed the human understanding to be the paramount rule of human conduct;
they maintained that the obscurest religious truth required
for its complete elucidation no more than the strenuous
application of the energies of mind. It appeared impossible to them that any doctrine could be subversive of
social happiness which is not capable of being confuted
by arguments derived from the nature of existing things.
With the devoutest submission to the law of Christ, they
united an intrepid spirit of inquiry as to the correctest
mode of acting in particular instances of conduct that
occur among men. Assuming the doctrines of the Messiah concerning benevolence and justice for the regulation
of their actions, they could not be persuaded to acknowledge that there was apparent in the divine code any
prescribed rule whereby, for its own sake, one action
rather than another, as fulfilling the will of their great
Master, should be preferred.

The contempt with which the magistracy and priest-
hood regarded this obscure community of speculators,

had hitherto protected them from persecution. But they had arrived at that precise degree of eminence and prosperity which is peculiarly obnoxious to the hostility of the rich and powerful. The moment of their departure from Jerusalem was the crisis of their future destiny. Had they continued to seek a precarious refuge in a city of the Roman empire, this persecution would not have delayed to impress a new character on their opinions and their conduct; narrow views, and the illiberality of sectarian patriotism, would not have failed speedily to obliterate the magnificence and beauty of their wild and wonderful condition.

Attached from principle to peace, despising and hating the pleasures and the customs of the degenerate[1] mass of mankind, this unostentatious community of good and happy men fled to the solitudes of Lebanon. To Arabians and enthusiasts the solemnity and grandeur of these desolate recesses possessed peculiar attractions. It well accorded with the justice of their conceptions on the relative duties of man towards his fellow in society, that they should labour in unconstrained equality to dispossess the wolf and the tiger of their empire, and establish on its ruins the dominion of intelligence and virtue. No longer would the worshippers of the God of Nature be indebted to a hundred hands for the accommodation of their simple wants. No longer would the poison of a diseased civilization embrue their very nutriment with pestilence. They would no longer owe their very existence to the vices, the fears, and the follies of mankind. Love, friendship, and philanthropy, would now be the characteristic disposers of their industry. It is for his mistress or his

---

[1] In the first edition, *regenerate;* but *degenerate* in later editions.

friend that the labourer consecrates his toil ; others are
mindful, but he is forgetful, of himself.   " God feeds the
hungry ravens, and clothes the lilies of the fields, and yet
Solomon in all his glory is not like to one of these."

Rome was now the shadow of her former self.   The
light of her grandeur and loveliness had passed away.
The latest and the noblest of her poets and historians had
foretold in agony her approaching slavery and degradation.   The ruins of the human mind, more awful and
portentous than the desolation of the most solemn
temples, threw a shade of gloom upon her golden palaces
which the brutal vulgar could not see, but which the
mighty felt with inward trepidation and despair.   The
ruins of Jerusalem lay defenceless and uninhabited upon
the burning sands ; none visited, but in the depth of
solemn awe, this accursed and solitary spot.   Tradition
says that there was seen to linger among the scorched
and shattered fragments of the temple, one being, whom
he that saw dared not to call man, with clasped hands,
immoveable eyes, and a visage horribly serene.   Not on
the will of the capricious multitude, nor the constant
fluctuations of the many and the weak, depends the change
of empires and religions.   These are the mere insensible
elements from which a subtler intelligence moulds its
enduring statuary.   They that direct the changes of this
mortal scene breathe the decrees of their dominion from
a throne of darkness and of tempest.   The power of man
is great.

After many days of wandering, the Assassins pitched
their tents in the valley of Bethzatanai.   For ages had
this fertile valley lain concealed from the adventurous

search of man, among mountains of everlasting snow.
The men of elder days had inhabited this spot. Piles of
monumental marble and fragments of columns that in
their integrity almost seemed the work of some intelligence more sportive and fantastic than the gross conceptions of mortality, lay in heaps beside the lake, and were
visible beneath its transparent waves. The flowering
orange-tree, the balsam, and innumerable odoriferous
shrubs, grew wild in the desolated portals. The fountain
tanks had overflowed, and amid the luxuriant vegetation
of their margin, the yellow snake held its unmolested
dwelling. Hither came the tiger and the bear to contend
for those once domestic animals who had forgotten the
secure servitude of their ancestors. No sound, when the
famished beast of prey had retreated in despair from the
awful desolation of this place, at whose completion he had
assisted, but the shrill cry of the stork, and the flapping
of his heavy wings from the capital of the solitary column,
and the scream of the hungry vulture baffled of its only
victim. The lore of ancient wisdom was sculptured in
mystic characters on the rocks. The human spirit and
the human hand had been busy here to accomplish its
profoundest miracles. It was a temple dedicated to the
god of knowledge and of truth. The palaces of the
Caliphs and the Cæsars might easily surpass these ruins
in magnitude and sumptuousness : but they were the
design of tyrants and the work of slaves. Piercing genius
and consummate prudence had planned and executed
Bethzatanai. There was deep and important meaning in
every lineament of its fantastic sculpture. The unintelligible legend, once so beautiful and perfect, so full of
poetry and history, spoke, even in destruction, volumes of
mysterious import, and obscure significance.

But in the season of its utmost prosperity and magnificence, art might not aspire to vie with nature in the valley of Bethzatanai. All that was wonderful and lovely was collected in this deep seclusion. The fluctuating elements seemed to have been rendered everlastingly permanent in forms of wonder and delight. The mountains of Lebanon had been divided to their base to form this happy valley; on every side their icy summits darted their white pinnacles into the clear blue sky, imaging, in their grotesque outline, minarets, and ruined domes, and columns worn with time. Far below, the silver clouds rolled their bright volumes in many beautiful shapes, and fed the eternal springs that, spanning the dark chasms like a thousand radiant rainbows, leaped into the quiet vale, then, lingering in many a dark glade among the groves of cypress and of palm, lost themselves in the lake. The immensity of these precipitous mountains, with their starry pyramids of snow, excluded the sun, which overtopped not, even in its meridian, their overhanging rocks. But a more heavenly and serener light was reflected from their icy mirrors, which, piercing through the many-tinted clouds, produced lights and colours of inexhaustible variety. The herbage was perpetually verdant, and clothed the darkest recesses of the caverns and the woods.

Nature, undisturbed, had become an enchantress in these solitudes : she had collected here all that was wonderful and divine from the armoury of her omnipotence. The very winds breathed health and renovation, and the joyousness of youthful courage. Fountains of crystalline water played perpetually among the aromatic flowers, and mingled a freshness with their odour. The pine boughs became instruments of exquisite contrivance, among which every varying breeze waked music of new and more delightful melody. Meteoric shapes, more effulgent than the moonlight, hung on the wandering clouds, and mixed in discordant dance around the spiral fountains. Blue vapours assumed strange lineaments under the rocks and among the ruins, lingering like ghosts with slow and solemn step. Through a dark chasm to the east, in the long perspective of a portal glittering with the unnumbered riches of the subterranean world, shone the broad moon, pouring in one yellow and unbroken stream her horizontal beams. Nearer the icy region, autumn and spring held an alternate reign. The sere leaves fell and choked the sluggish brooks; the chilling fogs hung diamonds on every spray; and in the dark cold evening the howling winds made melancholy music in the trees. Far above, shone the bright throne of winter, clear, cold, and dazzling. Sometimes there was seen the snow-flakes to fall before the sinking orb of the beamless sun, like a shower of fiery sulphur. The cataracts, arrested in their course, seemed, with their transparent columns, to support the dark-browed rocks. Sometimes the icy whirlwind scooped the powdery snow aloft, to mingle with the hissing meteors, and scatter spangles through the rare and rayless atmosphere.

Such strange scenes of chaotic confusion and harrowing sublimity, surrounding and shutting in the vale, added to the delights of its secure and voluptuous tranquillity. No spectator could have refused to believe that some spirit of great intelligence and power had hallowed these wild and beautiful solitudes to a deep and solemn mystery.

The immediate effect of such a scene, suddenly pre-

sented to the contemplation of mortal eyes, is seldom the
subject of authentic record.   The coldest slave of custom
cannot fail to recollect some few moments in which the
breath of spring or the crowding clouds of sunset, with
the pale moon shining through their fleecy skirts, or the
song of some lonely bird perched on the only tree of an
unfrequented heath, has awakened the touch of nature.
And they were Arabians who entered the valley of
Bethzatanai; men who idolized nature and the God of
nature; to whom love and lofty thoughts, and the apprehensions of an uncorrupted spirit, were sustenance and
life.   Thus securely excluded from an abhorred world, all
thought of its judgment was cancelled by the rapidity of
their fervid imaginations.   They ceased to acknowledge,
or deigned not to advert to, the distinctions with which
the majority of base and vulgar minds controul the long-
ings and struggles of the soul towards its place of rest.
A new and sacred fire was kindled in their hearts and
sparkled in their eyes.   Every gesture, every feature, the
minutest action, was modelled to benelicence and beauty
by the holy inspiration that had descended on their
searching spirits.   The epidemic transport communicated
itself through every heart with the rapidity of a blast
from heaven.   They were already disembodied spirits;
they were already the inhabitants of paradise.   To live,
to breathe, to move, was itself a sensation of immeasurable transport. Every new contemplation of the condition
of his nature brought to the happy enthusiast an added
measure of delight, and impelled to every organ, where
mind is united with external things, a keener and more
exquisite perception of all that they contain of lovely and
divine.   To love, to be beloved, suddenly became an in-
satiable famine of his nature, which the wide circle of the

universe, comprehending beings of such inexhaustible variety and stupendous magnitude of excellence, appeared too narrow and confined to satiate.

Alas, that these visitings of the spirit of life should fluctuate and pass away! That the moments when the human mind is commensurate with all that it can conceive of excellent and powerful, should not endure with its existence and survive its most momentous change! But the beauty of a vernal sunset, with its overhanging curtains of empurpled cloud, is rapidly dissolved, to return at some unexpected period, and spread an alleviating melancholy over the dark vigils of despair.

It is true the enthusiasm of overwhelming transport which had inspired every breast among the Assassins is no more. The necessity of daily occupation and the ordinariness of that human life, the burthen of which it is the destiny of every human being to bear, had smothered, not extinguished, that divine and eternal fire. Not the less indelible and permanent were the impressions communicated to all ; not the more unalterably were the features of their social character modelled and determined by its influence.

CHAPTER II.

ROME had fallen. Her senate-house had become a polluted den of thieves and liars; her solemn temples, the arena of theological disputants, who made fire and sword the missionaries of their inconceivable beliefs. The city of the monster Constantine, symbolizing, in the consequences of its foundation, the wickedness and weakness of his successors, feebly imaged with declining power the substantial eminence of the Roman name. Pilgrims of a new and mightier faith crowded to visit the lonely ruins of Jerusalem, and weep and pray before the sepulchre of the Eternal God. The earth was filled with discord, tumult, and ruin. The spirit of disinterested virtue had armed one-half of the civilized world against the other. Monstrous and detestable creeds poisoned and blighted the domestic charities. There was no appeal to natural love, or ancient faith, from pride, superstition, and revenge.

Four centuries had passed thus terribly characterized by the most calamitous revolutions. The Assassins, meanwhile, undisturbed by the surrounding tumult, pos-

sessed and cultivated their fertile valley. The gradual
operation of their peculiar condition had matured and
perfected the singularity and excellence of their character.
That cause, which had ceased to act as an immediate and
overpowering excitement, became the unperceived law of
their lives, and sustenance of their natures. Their
religious tenets had also undergone a change, corresponding with the exalted condition of their moral being. The
gratitude which they owed to the benignant Spirit by
which their limited intelligences had not only been
created but redeemed, was less frequently adverted to,
became less the topic of comment or contemplation; not,
therefore, did it cease to be their presiding guardian, the
guide of their inmost thoughts, the tribunal of appeal for
the minutest particulars of their conduct. They learned
to identify this mysterious benefactor with the delight
that is bred among the solitary rocks, and has its dwelling alike in the changing colours of the clouds and the
inmost recesses of the caverns. Their future also no
longer existed, but in the blissful tranquillity of the
present. Time was measured and created by the vices and
the miseries of men, between whom and the happy nation
of the Assassins there was no analogy nor comparison.
Already had their eternal peace commenced. The darkness had passed away from the open gates of death.

The practical results produced by their faith and condition upon their external conduct were singular and
memorable. Excluded from the great and various community of mankind, these solitudes became to them a
sacred hermitage, in which all formed, as it were, one
being, divided against itself by no contending will or
factious passions. Every impulse conspired to one end,

and tended to a single object. Each devoted his powers to the happiness of the other. Their republic was the scene of the perpetual contentions of benevolence ; not the heartless and assumed kindness of commercial man, but the genuine virtue that has a legible superscription in every feature of the countenance, and every motion of the frame. The perverseness and calamities of those who dwelt beyond the mountains that encircled their undisturbed possessions, were unknown and unimagined. Little embarrassed by the complexities of civilized society, they knew not to conceive any happiness that can be satiated without participation, or that thirsts not to reproduce and perpetually generate itself. The path of virtue and felicity was plain and unimpeded. They clearly acknowledged, in every case, that conduct to be entitled to preference which would obviously produce the greatest pleasure. They could not conceive an instance in which it would be their duty to hesitate, in causing, at whatever expense, the greatest and most unmixed delight.

Hence arose a peculiarity which only failed to germinate in uncommon and momentous consequences, because the Assassins had retired from the intercourse of mankind, over whom other motives and principles of conduct than justice and benevolence prevail. It would be a difficult matter for men of such a sincere and simple faith, to estimate the final results of their intentions, among the corrupt and slavish multitude. They would be perplexed also in their choice of the means, whereby their intentions might be fulfilled. To produce immediate pain or disorder for the sake of future benefit, is consonant, indeed with the purest religion and philosophy, but never fails to excite invincible repugnance in the feelings of the many.

Against their predilections and distastes an Assassin, accidentally the inhabitant of a civilized community, would wage unremitting hostility from principle. He would find himself compelled to adopt means which they would abhor, for the sake of an object which they could not conceive that he should propose to himself. Secure and self-enshrined in the magnificence and pre-eminence of his conceptions, spotless as the light of heaven, he would be the victim among men of calumny and persecution. Incapable of distinguishing his motives, they would rank him among the vilest and most atrocious criminals. Great, beyond all comparison with them, they would despise him in the presumption of their ignorance. Because his spirit burned with an unquenchable passion for their welfare, they would lead him, like his illustrious master, amidst scoffs, and mockery, and insult, to the remuneration of an ignominious death.

Who hesitates to destroy a venomous serpent that has crept near his sleeping friend, except the man who selfishly dreads lest the malignant reptile should turn its fury on himself? And if the poisoner has assumed a human shape, if the bane be distinguished only from the viper's venom by the excess and extent of its devastation, will the saviour and avenger here retract and pause, entrenched behind the superstition of the indefeasible divinity of man? Is the human form, then, the mere badge of a prerogative for unlicensed wickedness and mischief? Can the power derived from the weakness of the oppressed, or the ignorance of the deceived, confer the right in security to tyrannize and defraud?

The subject of regular governments, and the disciple of

established superstition, dares not to ask this question.
For the sake of the eventual benefit, he endures what he
esteems a transitory evil, and the moral degradation of
man disquiets not his patience.   But the religion of an
Assassin imposes other virtues than endurance, when his
fellow-men groan under tyranny, or have become so
bestial and abject that they cannot feel their chains.   An
Assassin believes that man is eminently man, and only
then enjoys the prerogatives of his privileged condition,
when his affections and his judgment pay tribute to the
God of Nature.   The perverse, and vile, and vicious—
what were they? Shapes of some unholy vision, moulded
by the spirit of Evil, which the sword of the merciful
destroyer should sweep from this beautiful world. Dreamy
nothings; phantasms of misery and mischief, that hold
their death-like state on glittering thrones, and in the
loathsome dens of poverty. No Assassin would sub-
missively temporize with vice, and in cold charity become
a pander to falsehood and desolation.   His path through
the wilderness of civilized society would be marked with
the blood of the oppressor and the ruiner.   The wretch,
whom nations tremblingly adore, would expiate in his
throttling grasp a thousand licensed and venerable crimes.

How many holy liars and parasites, in solemn guise,
would his saviour arm drag from their luxurious couches,
and plunge in the cold charnel, that the green and many-
legged monsters of the slimy grave might eat off at their
leisure the lineaments of rooted malignity and detested
cunning.   The respectable man—the smooth, smiling,
polished villain, whom all the city honours ; whose very
trade is lies and murder ; who buys his daily bread with
the blood and tears of men, would feed the ravens with

his limbs. The Assassin would cater nobly for the eye-
less worms of earth, and the carrion fowls of heaven.

Yet here, religion and human love had imbued the
manners of those solitary people with inexpressible gentleness and benignity. Courage and active virtue, and
the indignation against vice, which becomes a hurrying
and irresistible passion, slept like the imprisoned earthquake, or the lightning shafts that hang in the golden
clouds of evening. They were innocent, but they were
capable of more than innocence ; for the great principles
of their faith were perpetually acknowledged and adverted
to ; nor had they forgotten, in this uninterrupted quiet,
the author of their felicity.

Four centuries had thus worn away without producing
an event. Men had died, and natural tears had been
shed upon their graves, in sorrow that improves the
heart. Those who had been united by love had gone to
death together, leaving to their friends the bequest of a
most sacred grief, and of a sadness that is allied to
pleasure. Babes that hung upon their mothers' breasts
had become men ; men had died ; and many a wild
luxuriant weed that overtopped the habitations of the
vale, had twined its roots around their disregarded bones.
Their tranquil state was like a summer sea, whose gentle
undulations disturb not the reflected stars, and break not
the long still line of the rainbow hues of sunrise.

CHAPTER III.

WHERE all is thus calm, the slightest circumstance is recorded and remembered. Before the sixth century had expired one incident occurred, remarkable and strange. A young man, named Albedir, wandering in the woods, was startled by the screaming of a bird of prey, and, looking up, saw blood fall, drop by drop, from among the intertwined boughs of a cedar. Having climbed the tree, he beheld a terrible and dismaying spectacle. A naked human body was impaled on the broken branch. It was maimed and mangled horribly; every limb bent and bruised into frightful distortion, and exhibiting a breathing image of the most sickening mockery of life. A monstrous snake had scented its prey from among the mountains—and above hovered a hungry vulture. From amidst this mass of desolated humanity, two eyes, black and inexpressibly brilliant, shone with an unearthly lustre. Beneath the blood-stained eye-brows their steady rays manifested the serenity of an immortal power, the collected energy of a deathless mind, spell-secured from dissolution. A bitter smile of mingled abhorrence and scorn distorted his wounded lip—he appeared calmly to observe and measure all around—self-possession had not deserted the shattered mass of life.

The youth approached the bough on which the breathing corpse was hung. As he approached, the serpent reluctantly unwreathed his glittering coils, and crept towards his dark and loathsome cave. The vulture, impatient of his meal, fled to the mountain, that re-echoed with his hoarse screams. The cedar branches creaked with their agitating weight, faintly, as the dismal wind arose. All else was deadly silent.

At length a voice issued from the mangled man. It rattled in hoarse murmurs from his throat and lungs— his words were the conclusion of some strange mysterious soliloquy. They were broken, and without apparent connexion, completing wide intervals of inexpressible conceptions.

" The great tyrant is baffled, even in success. Joy ! joy ! to his tortured foe ! Triumph to the worm whom he tramples under his feet ! Ha ! His suicidal hand might dare as well abolish the mighty frame of things ! Delight and exultation sit before the closed gates of death !—I fear not to dwell beneath their black and ghastly shadow. Here thy power may not avail ! Thou createst—'tis mine to ruin and destroy.—I was thy slave—I am thy equal, and thy foe.—Thousands tremble before thy throne, who, at my voice, shall dare to pluck the golden crown from thine unholy head !" He ceased. The silence of noon swallowed up his words. Albedir clung tighter to the tree—he dared not for dismay remove his eyes. He remained mute in the perturbation of deep and creeping horror.

"Albedir!" said the same voice, "Albedir! in the name of God, approach. He that suffered me to fall, watches thee ;—the gentle and merciful spirits of sweet human love, delight not in agony and horror. For pity's sake approach, in the name of thy good God, approach, Albedir?" The tones were mild and clear as the responses of Æolian music. They floated to Albedir's ear like the warm breath of June that lingers in the lawny groves, subduing all to softness. Tears of tender affection started into his eyes. It was as the voice of a beloved friend. The partner of his childhood, the brother of his soul, seemed to call for aid, and pathetically to remonstrate with delay. He resisted not the magic impulse, but advanced towards the spot, and tenderly attempted to remove the wounded man. He cautiously descended the tree with his wretched burthen, and deposited it on the ground.

A period of strange silence intervened. Awe and cold horror were slowly succeeding to the softer sensations of tumultuous pity, when again he heard the silver modulations of the same enchanting voice. "Weep not for me, Albedir! What wretch so utterly lost, but might inhale peace and renovation from this paradise! I am wounded, and in pain; but having found a refuge in this seclusion, and a friend in you, I am worthier of envy than compassion. Bear me to your cottage secretly: I would not disturb your gentle partner by my appearance. She must love me more dearly than a brother. I must be the playmate of your children ; already I regard them with a father's love. My arrival must not be regarded as a thing of mystery and wonder. What, indeed, but that men are prone to error and exaggeration, is less inexplicable, than that a stranger, wandering on Lebanon, fell from the rocks into the vale? Albedir," he continued, and his deepening voice assumed awful solemnity, " in return for the affection with which I cherish thee and thine, thou owest this submission."

Albedir implicitly submitted; not even a thought had power to refuse its deference. He reassumed his burthen, and proceeded towards the cottage. He watched until Khaled should be absent, and conveyed the stranger into an apartment appropriated for the reception of those who occasionally visited their habitation. He desired that the door should be securely fastened, and that he might not be visited until the morning of the following day.

Albedir waited with impatience for the return of Khaled. The unaccustomed weight of even so transitory a secret, hung on his ingenuous and unpractised nature, like a blighting, clinging curse. The stranger's accents had lulled him to a trance of wild and delightful imagination. Hopes, so visionary and aerial, that they had assumed no denomination, had spread themselves over his intellectual frame, and, phantoms as they were, had modelled his being to their shape. Still his mind was not exempt from the visitings of disquietude and perturbation. It was a troubled stream of thought, over whose fluctuating waves unsearchable fate seemed to preside, guiding its unforeseen alternations with an inexorable hand. Albedir paced earnestly the garden of his cottage, revolving every circumstance attendant on the incident of the day. He re-imaged with intense thought the minutest recollections of the scene. In vain—he was the slave of suggestions not to be controlled. Astonishment, horror,

and awe—tumultuous sympathy, and a mysterious elevation of soul, hurried away all activity of judgment, and
overwhelmed, with stunning force, every attempt at deliberation or inquiry.

His reveries were interrupted at length by the return
of Khaled.   She entered the cottage, that scene of undisturbed repose, in the confidence that change might as soon
overwhelm the eternal world, as disturb this inviolable
sanctuary.   She started to behold Albedir.   Without
preface or remark, he recounted with eager haste the occurrences of the day.   Khaled's tranquil spirit could
hardly keep pace with the breathless rapidity of his
narration.   She was bewildered with staggering wonder
even to hear his confused tones, and behold his agitated
countenance.

CHAPTER IV

ON the following morning Albedir arose at sunrise, and visited the stranger. He found him already risen, and employed in adorning the lattice of his chamber with flowers from the garden. There was something in his attitude and occupation singularly expressive of his entire familiarity with the scene. Albedir's habitation seemed to have been his accustomed home. He addressed his host in a tone of gay and affectionate welcome, such as never fails to communicate by sympathy the feelings from which it flows.

" My friend," said he, " the balm of the dew of our vale is sweet ; or is this garden the favoured spot where the winds conspire to scatter the best odours they can find ? Come, lend me your arm awhile, I feel very weak." He motioned to walk forth, but, as if unable to proceed, rested on the seat beside the door. For a few moments they were silent, if the interchange of cheerful and happy looks is to be called silence. At last he observed a spade that rested against the wall. " You have only one spade, brother," said he ; " you have only one, I suppose, of any of the instruments of tillage. Your garden ground, too, occupies a certain space which it will be necessary to enlarge. This must be quickly remedied. I cannot earn my supper of to-night, nor of to-morrow; but thenceforward, I do not mean to eat the bread of idleness. I know that you would willingly perform the additional labour which my nourishment would require; I know, also, that you would feel a degree of pleasure in the fatigue arising from this employment, but I shall contest with you such pleasures as these, and such pleasures as these alone." His eyes were somewhat wan, and the tone of his voice languid as he spoke.

As they were thus engaged, Khaled came towards them. The stranger beckoned to her to sit beside him, and taking her hands within his own, looked attentively on her mild countenance. Khaled inquired if he had been refreshed by sleep. He replied by a laugh of careless and inoffensive glee; and placing one of her hands within Albedir's, said, " If this be sleep, here in this odorous vale, where these sweet smiles encompass us, and the voices of those who love are heard—if these be the visions of sleep, sister, those who lie down in misery shall arise lighter than the butterflies. I came from amid the tumult of a world, how different from this! I am unexpectedly among you, in the midst of a scene such as my imagination never dared to promise. I must remain here—I must not depart." Khaled, recovering from the admiration and astonishment caused by the stranger's words and manner, assured him of the happiness which she should feel in such an addition to her society.

Albedir, too, who had been more deeply impressed

than Khaled by the event of his arrival, earnestly re-assured him of the ardour of the affection with which he had inspired them. The stranger smiled gently to hear the unaccustomed fervour of sincerity which animated their address, and was rising to retire, when Khaled said. "You have not yet seen our children, Maimuna and Abdallah. They are by the water-side, playing with their favourite snake. We have only to cross yonder little wood, and wind down a path cut in the rock that overhangs the lake, and we shall find them beside a recess which the shore makes there, and which a chasm, as it were, among the rocks and woods, encloses. Do you think you could walk there?" "To see your child-ren, Khaled? I think I could, with the assistance of Albedir's arm, and yours."—So they went through the wood of ancient cypress, intermingled with the bright-ness of many-tinted blooms, which gleamed like stars through its romantic glens. They crossed the green meadow, and entered among the broken chasms, beauti-ful as they were in their investiture of odoriferous shrubs. They came at last, after pursuing a path which wound through the intricacies of a little wilderness, to the borders of the lake. They stood on the rock which overhung it, from which there was a prospect of all the miracles of nature and of art which encircled and adorned its shores. The stranger gazed upon it with a coun-tenance unchanged by any emotion, but, as it were, thoughtfully and contemplatingly. As he gazed, Khaled ardently pressed his hand, and said, in a low yet eager voice, "Look, look, lo there!" He turned towards her, but her eyes were not on him. She looked below—her lips were parted by the feelings which possessed her soul—her breath came and went regularly but inaudibly.

She leaned over the precipice, and her dark hair hanging
beside her face, gave relief to its fine lineaments, animated by such love as exceeds utterance. The stranger
followed her eyes, and saw that her children were in the
glen below; then raising his eyes, exchanged with her
affectionate looks of congratulation and delight. The boy
was apparently eight years old, the girl about two years
younger. The beauty of their form and countenance was
something so divine and strange, as overwhelmed the
senses of the beholder like a delightful dream, with in-
supportable ravishment. They were arrayed in a loose
robe of linen, through which the exquisite proportions of
their form appeared. Unconscious that they were observed, they did not relinquish the occupation in which
they were engaged. They had constructed a little boat
of the bark of trees, and had given it sails of interwoven
feathers, and launched it on the water. They sate
beside a white flat stone, on which a small snake lay
coiled, and when their work was finished, they arose and
called to the snake in melodious tones, so that it understood their language. For it unwreathed its shining
circles and crept to the boat, into which no sooner had it
entered than the girl loosened the band which held it to
the shore, and it sailed away. Then they ran round and
round the little creek, clapping their hands, and melo-
diously pouring out wild sounds, which the snake seemed
to answer by the restless glancing of his neck. At last
a breath of wind came from the shore, and the boat
changed its course, and was about to leave the creek,
which the snake perceived and leaped into the water,
and came to the little children's feet. The girl sang to
it, and it leaped into her bosom, and she crossed her fair

hands over it, as if to cherish it there.[1] Then the boy
answered with a song, and it glided from beneath her
hands and crept towards him. While they were thus
employed, Maimuna looked up, and seeing her parents on
the cliff, ran to meet them up the steep path that wound
around it ; and Abdallah, leaving his snake, followed
joyfully.

[1] Compare this passage with stanzas xvii to xx of the first Canto of *Laon and Cythna* (Poetical Works, Vol. I, pp. 115-116).

ON THE PUNISHMENT OF DEATH.

[This Fragment was first given by Mrs. Shelley in the *Essays, Letters* &c. (1840), in the Preface to which collection we read (pages xi & xii), " The fragment of his ' Essay on the Punishment of Death' bears the value which the voice of a philosopher and a poet, reasoning in favour of humanity and refinement, must possess. It alleges all the arguments that an imaginative man, who can vividly figure the feelings of his fellow-creatures, can alone conceive; and it brings them home to the calm reasoner with the logic of truth. In the milder season that since Shelley's time has dawned upon England, our legislators each day approximate nearer to his views of justice ; this piece, fragment as it is, may suggest to some among them motives for carrying his beneficent views into practice." Mr. Rossetti (Poetical Works, 1878, Vol. I, page 149) assigns this composition to the year 1815. It is here given from the edition of 1840, the word *punishment*, in line 2, page 248, omitted from that edition, being, however, supplied from Mrs. Shelley's reprints.—H. B. F.]

ON THE PUNISHMENT OF DEATH.

A FRAGMENT.

THE first law which it becomes a Reformer to propose and support, at the approach of a period of great political change, is the abolition of the punishment of death.

It is sufficiently clear that revenge, retaliation, atonement, expiation, are rules and motives, so far from deserving a place in any enlightened system of political life, that they are the chief sources of a prodigious class of miseries in the domestic circles of society. It is clear that however the spirit of legislation may appear to frame institutions upon more philosophical maxims, it has hitherto, in those cases which are termed criminal, done little more than palliate the spirit, by gratifying a portion of it; and afforded a compromise between that which is best;—the inflicting of no evil upon a sensitive being, without a decisively beneficial result in which he should at least participate;—and that which is worst; that he should be put to torture for the amusement of those whom he may have injured, or may seem to have injured.

Omitting these remoter considerations, let us inquire what *Death* is; that punishment which is applied as a measure of transgressions of indefinite shades of distinction, so soon as they shall have passed that degree and colour of enormity, with which it is supposed no inferior infliction is commensurate.

And first, whether death is good or evil, a punishment or a reward, or whether it be wholly indifferent, no man can take upon himself to assert. That that within us which thinks and feels, continues to think and feel after the dissolution of the body, has been the almost universal opinion of mankind, and the accurate philosophy of what I may be permitted to term the modern Academy, by showing the prodigious depth and extent of our ignorance respecting the causes and nature of sensation, renders probable the affirmative of a proposition, the negative of which it is so difficult to conceive, and the popular arguments against which, derived from what is called the atomic system, are proved to be applicable only to the relation which one object bears to another, as apprehended by the mind, and not to existence itself, or the nature of that essence which is the medium and receptacle of objects.

The popular system of religion suggests the idea that the mind, after death, will be painfully or pleasurably affected according to its determinations during life. However ridiculous and pernicious we must admit the vulgar accessories of this creed to be, there is a certain analogy, not wholly absurd, between the consequences resulting to an individual during life from the virtuous or vicious, prudent or imprudent, conduct of his external actions, to those consequences which are conjectured to ensue from the discipline and order of his internal thoughts, as affecting his condition in a future state. They omit, indeed, to calculate upon the accidents of disease, and temperament, and organization, and circumstance, together with the multitude of independent agencies which affect the opinions, the conduct, and the happiness of individuals, and produce determinations of the will, and modify the judgment, so as to produce effects the most opposite in natures considerably similar. These are those operations in the order of the whole of nature, tending, we are prone to believe, to some definite mighty end, to which the agencies of our peculiar nature are subordinate ; nor is there any reason to suppose, that in a future state they should become suddenly exempt from that subordination. The philosopher is unable to determine whether our existence in a previous state has affected our present condition, and abstains from deciding whether our present condition would[1] affect us in that which may be future. That, if we continue to exist, the manner of our existence will be such as no inferences nor conjectures, afforded by a consideration of our earthly experience, can elucidate, is sufficiently obvious. The opinion that the vital principle within us, in whatever mode it may continue to exist, must lose that consciousness of definite and individual being which now characterizes it, and become a unit in the vast sum of action and of thought which disposes and animates the universe, and is called God, seems to belong to that class of opinion which has been designated as indifferent.

To compel a person to know all that can be known by

[1] So in the first edition : in others, *will.*

the dead, concerning that which the living fear, hope, or
forget; to plunge him into the pleasure or pain which
there awaits him; to punish or reward him in a manner
and in a degree incalculable and incomprehensible by us;
to disrobe him at once from all that intertexture of good and
evil with which Nature seems to have clothed every form of
individual existence, is to inflict on him the doom of death.

A certain degree of pain and terror usually accompany
the infliction of death. This degree is infinitely varied by
the infinite variety in the temperament and opinions of
the sufferers. As a measure of punishment, strictly so
considered, and as an exhibition, which, by its known
effects on the sensibility of the sufferer, is intended to in-
timidate the spectators from incurring a similar liability,
it is singularly inadequate.

Firstly,——Persons of energetic character, in whom, as
in men who suffer for political crimes, there is a large
mixture of enterprise, and fortitude, and disinterestedness,
and the elements, though misguided and disarranged, by
which the strength and happiness of a nation might have
been cemented, die in such a manner, as to make death
appear not evil, but good. The death of what is called a
traitor, that is, a person who, from whatever motive,
would abolish the government of the day, is as often a
triumphant exhibition of suffering virtue, as the warning
of a culprit. The multitude, instead of departing with a
panic-stricken approbation of the laws which exhibited
such a spectacle, are inspired with pity, admiration and
sympathy; and the most generous among them feel an
emulation to be the authors of such flattering emotions,
as they experience stirring in their bosoms. Impressed

by what they see and feel, they make no distinction between the motives which incited the criminals to the actions for which they suffer, or the heroic courage with which they turned into good that which their judges awarded to them as evil, or the purpose itself of those actions, though that purpose may happen to be eminently pernicious. The laws in this case lose that sympathy, which it ought to be their chief object to secure, and in a participation of which, consists their chief strength in maintaining those sanctions by which the parts of the social union are bound together, so as to produce, as nearly as possible, the ends for which it is instituted.

Secondly—persons of energetic character, in communities not modelled with philosophical skill to turn all the energies which they contain to the purposes of common good, are prone also to fall into the temptation of undertaking, and are peculiarly fitted for despising the perils attendant upon consummating, the most enormous crimes. Murder, rapes, extensive schemes of plunder, are the actions of persons belonging to this class ; and death is the penalty of conviction. But the coarseness of organization, peculiar to men capable of committing acts wholly selfish, is usually found to be associated with a proportionate insensibility to fear or pain. Their sufferings communicate to those of the spectators, who may be liable to the commission of similar crimes, a sense of the lightness of that event, when closely examined, which, at a distance, as uneducated persons are accustomed to do, probably they regarded with horror.

But a great majority of the spectators are so bound up in the interests and the habits of social union that no

temptation would be sufficiently strong to induce them to
a commission of the enormities to which this penalty is
assigned.   The more powerful, the richer among them,—
and a numerous class of little tradesmen are richer and
more powerful than those who are employed by them,
and the employer, in general, bears this relation to the
employed,—regard their own wrongs as, in some degree,
avenged, and their own rights secured by this punishment,
inflicted as the penalty of whatever crime.   In cases of
murder or mutilation, this feeling is almost universal.
In those, therefore, whom this exhibition does not awaken
to the sympathy which extenuates crime and discredits
the law which restrains it, it produces feelings more
directly at war with the genuine purposes of political
society.   It excites those emotions which it is the chief
object of civilization to extinguish for ever, and in the
extinction of which alone there can be any hope of better
institutions than those under which men now misgovern
one another.   Men feel that their revenge is gratified, and
that their security is established by the extinction and the
sufferings of beings, in most respects resembling themselves; and their daily occupations constraining them to
a precise form in all their thoughts, they come to connect
inseparably the idea of their own advantage with that of
the death and torture of others.   It is manifest that the
object of sane polity is directly the reverse; and that
laws founded upon reason, should accustom the gross
vulgar to associate their ideas of security and of interest
with the reformation, and the strict restraint, for that
purpose alone, of those who might invade it.

The passion of revenge is originally nothing more than
an habitual perception of the ideas of the sufferings of

the person who inflicts an injury, as connected, as they
are in a savage state, or in such portions of society as are
yet undisciplined to civilization, with security that that
injury will not be repeated in future. This feeling,
engrafted upon superstition and confirmed by habit, at
last loses sight of the only object for which it may be
supposed to have been implanted, and becomes a passion
and a duty to be pursued and fulfilled, even to the
destruction of those ends to which it originally tended.
The other passions, both good and evil, Avarice, Remorse,
Love, Patriotism, present a similar appearance ; and to
this principle of the mind over-shooting the mark at which
it aims, we owe all that is eminently base or excellent in
human nature ; in providing for the nutriment or the
extinction of which consists the true art of the legislator.[1]

Nothing is more clear than that the infliction of
punishment in general, in a degree which the reformation
and the restraint of those who transgress the law does not
render indispensable, and none more than death, con-

---

[1] The savage and the illiterate are but faintly aware of the distinction between the future and the past ; they make actions belonging
to periods so distinct, the subjects of similar feelings ; they live only in
the present, or in the past as it is present. It is in this that the philosopher excels one of the many ; it is this which distinguishes the doctrine of philosophic necessity from fatalism ; and that determination of
the will, by which it is the active source of future events, from that
liberty or indifference, to which the abstract liability of irremediable
actions is attached, according to the notions of the vulgar.

This is the source of the erroneous excesses of Remorse and Revenge ;
the one extending itself over the future, and the other over the past ;
provinces in which their suggestions can only be the sources of evil.
The purpose of a resolution to act more wisely and virtuously in future,
and the sense of a necessity of caution in repressing an enemy, are the
sources from which the enormous superstitions implied in the words
cited have arisen. [SHELLEY'S NOTE.]

firms all the inhuman and unsocial impulses of men. It is almost a proverbial remark, that those nations in which the penal code has been particularly mild, have been distinguished from all others by the rarity of crime. But the example is to be admitted to be equivocal. A more decisive argument is afforded by a consideration of the universal connexion of ferocity of manners, and a contempt of social ties, with the contempt of human life. Governments which derive their institutions from the existence of circumstances of barbarism and violence, with some rare exceptions perhaps, are bloody in proportion as they are despotic, and form the manners of their subjects to a sympathy with their own spirit.

The spectators who feel no abhorrence at a public execution, but rather a self-applauding superiority, and a sense of gratified indignation, are surely excited to the most inauspicious emotions. The first reflection of such a one is the sense of his own internal and actual worth, as preferable to that of the victim, whom circumstances have led to destruction. The meanest wretch is impressed with a sense of his own comparative merit. He is one of those on whom the tower of Siloam fell not—he is such a one as Jesus Christ found not in all Samaria, who, in his own soul, throws the first stone at the woman taken in adultery. The popular religion of the country takes its designation from that illustrious person whose beautiful sentiment I have quoted. Any one who has stript from the doctrines of this person the veil of familiarity, will perceive how adverse their spirit is to feelings of this nature.

ON LIFE.

[Three fragments on Life, Death, and Love, included by Medwin under the general title of *Reflections*, appeared in *The Athenæum* for the 29th of September, 1832, and subsequently in *The Shelley Papers*. They are all included in larger fragments (that on Life in the following composition) in the *Essays Letters* &c., 1840. In the Preface Mrs. Shelley says (page xii) à propos of this Fragment, "Shelley was a disciple of the Immaterial Philosophy of Berkeley. This theory gave unity and grandeur to his ideas, while it opened a wide field for his imagination. The creation, such as it was perceived by his mind—a unit in immensity, was slight and narrow compared with the interminable forms of thought that might exist beyond, to be perceived perhaps hereafter by his own mind; or which are perceptible to other minds that fill the universe, not of space in the material sense, but of infinity in the immaterial one. Such ideas are, in some degree, developed in his poem entitled 'Heaven;' and which makes one of the interlocutors exclaim,

'Peace! the abyss is wreathed in scorn
Of thy presumption, atom-born,'

he expresses his despair of being able to conceive, far less express, all of variety, majesty, and beauty, which is veiled from our imperfect senses in the unknown realm, the mystery of which his poetic vision sought in vain to penetrate." This fragment also Mr. Rossetti assigns to the year 1815. —H. B. F.]

ON LIFE.[1]

LIFE and the world, or[2] whatever we call that which we are and feel, is an astonishing thing. The mist of familiarity obscures from us the wonder of our being. We are struck with admiration[3] at some of its transient modifications, but it is itself the great miracle. What are changes of empires, the wreck of dynasties, with the opinions which supported them; what is the birth and the extinction of religious and of political systems, to life? What are the revolutions of the globe which we inhabit, and the operations of the elements of which it is composed, compared with life? What is the universe of stars, and suns, of which this inhabited earth is one,[4]

[1] The portion referred to on the preceding page as having been given by Medwin begins with the beginning. While adopting Mrs. Shelley's text as obviously of higher authority than Medwin's, I do not think it safe to assume that every variation arises from the inaccuracy justly brought to his charge, and have therefore noted most of the variations on the chance of his having transcribed from a different MS. from that used by Mrs. Shelley.

[2] Medwin reads *and*.

[3] Medwin reads *astonishment*.

[4] In Medwin's version, "What is the universe of stars and suns, and their motions, and the destiny of those that inhabit them, compared with life?"

and their motions, and their destiny, compared with life? Life, the great miracle, we admire not, because it is so miraculous.[1] It is well that we are thus shielded by the familiarity of what is at once so certain and so unfathomable, from an astonishment which would otherwise absorb and overawe the functions of that which is its object.

If any artist, I do not say had executed, but had merely conceived in his mind the system of the sun, and the stars, and planets, they not existing, and had painted to us in words, or upon canvas, the spectacle now afforded by the nightly[2] cope of heaven, and illustrated it by the wisdom of[3] astronomy, great would be our admiration. Or had he imagined the scenery of this earth, the mountains, the seas, and the rivers; the grass, and the flowers, and the variety[4] of the forms and masses of the leaves of the woods, and the colours which attend the setting and the rising sun, and the hues of the atmosphere, turbid or serene, these things not before existing,[5] truly we should have been astonished, and it would not have been a vain boast to have said of such a man, "Non merita nome di creatore, sennon Iddio ed il Poeta." But now these things are looked on with little wonder, and to be conscious of them with intense delight is esteemed to be the distinguishing mark of a refined and extraordinary person.[6]

---

[1] The next sentence, down to *object*, is omitted by Medwin.

[2] Medwin reads *eight of the* for *nightly*.

[3] Medwin omits *the wisdom of*, and reads *what would have been our admiration!*

[4] According to Medwin, *varieties*.

[5] Medwin omits the words *these things not before existing*, and goes on, "truly we should have been wonder-struck, and should have said, what it would have been a vain boast to have said, Truly, this creator deserves the name of a God."

[6] Medwin reads "and who views them with delight, is considered an enthusiast or an extraordinary person."

The multitude of men care not for them.   It is thus with Life—that which includes all.

What is life ?   Thoughts and feelings arise, with or without our will, and we employ words to express them. We are born, and our birth is unremembered, and our infancy remembered but in fragments; we live on, and in living we lose the apprehension of life.[1]   How vain is it to think that words can penetrate the mystery of our being !   Rightly used they may make evident our ignorance to ourselves, and this is much.   For what are we ? Whence do we come ? and whither do we go ?   Is birth the commencement, is death the conclusion of our being ? What is birth and death ?

The most refined abstractions of logic conduct to a view of life, which, though startling to the apprehension, is, in fact, that which the habitual sense of its repeated combinations has extinguished in us.   It strips, as it were, the painted curtain from this scene of things.   I confess that I am one of those who am unable to refuse my assent to the conclusions of those philosophers who assert that nothing exists but as it is perceived.

It is a decision against which all our persuasions struggle, and we must be long convicted before we can be convinced that the solid universe of external things is "such stuff as dreams are made of."   The shocking absurdities of the popular philosophy of mind and matter, its fatal consequences in morals, and their violent dogmatism concerning the source of all things, had early conducted me to materialism.   This materialism is a

[1] Here the Reflection on Life, as given by Medwin, ends.

seducing system to young and superficial minds. It
allows its disciples to talk, and dispenses them from
thinking. But I was discontented with such a view of
things as it afforded; man is a being of high aspirations,
" looking both before and after," whose " thoughts wander
through eternity," disclaiming alliance with transience
and decay; incapable of imagining to himself annihilation; existing but in the future and the past; being, not
what he is, but what he has been and shall be. Whatever
may be his true and final destination, there is a spirit
within him at enmity with nothingness and dissolution.
This is the character of all life and being. Each is at
once the centre and the circumference; the point to which
all things are referred, and the line in which all things
are contained. Such contemplations as these, materialism
and the popular philosophy of mind and matter alike for-
bid; they are only consistent with the intellectual system.

It is absurd to enter into a long recapitulation of
arguments sufficiently familiar to those inquiring minds,
whom alone a writer on abstruse subjects can be conceived to address. Perhaps the most clear and vigorous
statement of the intellectual system is to be found in Sir
William Drummond's Academical Questions. After such
an exposition, it would be idle to translate into other
words what could only lose its energy and fitness by the
change. Examined point by point, and word by word,
the most discriminating intellects have been able to discern no train of thoughts in the process of reasoning,
which does not conduct inevitably to the conclusion which
has been stated.

What follows from the admission? It establishes no

new truth, it gives us no additional insight into our hidden nature, neither its action nor itself. Philosophy, impatient as it may be to build, has much work yet remaining, as pioneer for the overgrowth of ages. It makes one step towards this object; it destroys error, and the roots of error. It leaves, what it is too often the duty of the reformer in political and ethical questions to leave, a vacancy. It reduces the mind to that freedom in which it would have acted, but for the misuse of words and signs, the instruments of its own creation. By signs, I would be understood in a wide sense, including what is properly meant by that term, and what I peculiarly mean. In this latter sense, almost all familiar objects are signs, standing, not for themselves, but for others, in their capacity of suggesting one thought which shall lead to a train of thoughts. Our whole life is thus an education of error.

Let us recollect our sensations as children. What a distinct and intense apprehension had we of the world and of ourselves! Many of the circumstances of social life were then important to us which are now no longer so. But that is not the point of comparison on which I mean to insist. We less habitually distinguished all that we saw and felt, from ourselves. They seemed as it were to constitute one mass. There are some persons who, in this respect, are always children. Those who are subject to the state called reverie, feel as if their nature were dissolved into the surrounding universe, or as if the surrounding universe were absorbed into their being. They are conscious of no distinction. And these are states which precede, or accompany, or follow an unusually intense and vivid apprehension of life. As men grow up this power commonly decays, and they become mechanical and habitual agents. Thus feelings and then reasonings are the combined result of a multitude of entangled thoughts, and of a series of what are called impressions, planted by reiteration.

The view of life presented by the most refined deductions of the intellectual philosophy, is that of unity. Nothing exists but as it is perceived. The difference is merely nominal between those two classes of thought, which are vulgarly distinguished by the names of ideas and of external objects. Pursuing the same thread of reasoning, the existence of distinct individual minds, similar to that which is employed in now questioning its own nature, is likewise found to be a delusion. The words *I, you, they,* are not signs of any actual difference subsisting between the assemblage of thoughts thus indicated, but are merely marks employed to denote the different modifications of the one mind.

Let it not be supposed that this doctrine conducts to the monstrous presumption that I, the person who now write and think, am that one mind. I am but a portion of it. The words *I,* and *you,* and *they* are grammatical devices invented simply for arrangement, and totally devoid of the intense and exclusive sense usually attached to them. It is difficult to find terms adequate to express so subtle a conception as that to which the Intellectual Philosophy has conducted us. We are on that verge where words abandon us, and what wonder if we grow dizzy to look down the dark abyss of how little we know !

The relations of *things* remain unchanged, by whatever system. By the word *things* is to be understood any object of thought, that is, any thought upon which any other thought is employed, with an apprehension of distinction. The relations of these remain unchanged; and such is the material of our knowledge.

What is the cause of life? that is, how was it produced, or what agencies distinct from life have acted or act upon life? All recorded generations of mankind have wearily[1] busied themselves in inventing answers to this question; and the result has been,—Religion. Yet, that the basis of all things cannot be, as the popular philosophy alleges, mind, is sufficiently evident. Mind, as far as we have any experience of its properties, and beyond that experience how vain is argument! cannot create, it can only perceive. It is said also to be the cause. But cause is only a word expressing a certain state of the human mind with regard to the manner in which two thoughts are apprehended to be related to each other. If any one desires to know how unsatisfactorily the popular philosophy employs itself upon this great question, they need only impartially reflect upon the manner in which thoughts develope themselves in their minds. It is infinitely improbable that the cause of mind, that is, of existence, is similar to mind.

---

[1] So in the first edition and some others; but *weariedly* in that of 1832, probably through a printer's error.

ON LOVE.

[Mrs. Shelley (*Essays* &c., 1840, Vol. I, page x) seems to regard this brief effusion on Love as in a manner cognate with Shelley's Platonic labours. It seems improbable however that it belongs to so late a period of his activity. The style appears to me rather that of 1815, or even earlier, than that of 1818; and Mr. Rossetti is probably not far wrong in assigning it to 1815. Instead, therefore, of placing it after the Banquet, it appears to me better to place it after the fragment on Life. It was issued as long ago as 1829, in *The Keepsake*, edited by Frederic Mansel Reynolds, which contained three poetic fragments by Shelley (*Summer and Winter*, *The Tower of Famine*, and *The Aziola*). For these four compositions, the Editor expresses in his Preface his indebtedness " to the kindness of the author of Frankenstein" ; and Mrs. Shelley was also a contributor on her own account to this annual. Mrs. Shelley excepts from the censure of inaccuracy an " Essay on Love," published by Medwin. The following effusion, I have not found in *The Athenæum* or in *The Shelley Papers ;* and the little Reflection on Love that is to be found in both can hardly be alluded to, because Mrs. Shelley's text of it varies from Medwin's. It is possible that, in the multiplicity of details to be dealt with, the distinction between a cutting from *The Keepsake* and a series of cuttings from *The Athenæum* or *The Shelley Papers* escaped notice.—H. B. F.]

ON LOVE.

WHAT is Love? Ask him who lives, what is life; ask him who adores, what is God?

I know not the internal constitution of other men, nor even thine,[1] whom I now address. I see that in some external attributes they resemble me, but when, misled by that appearance, I have thought to appeal to something in common, and unburthen my inmost soul to them, I have found my language misunderstood, like one in a distant and savage land. The more opportunities they have afforded me for experience, the wider has appeared the interval between us, and to a greater distance have the points of sympathy been withdrawn. With a spirit ill fitted to sustain such proof, trembling and feeble through its tenderness, I have everywhere sought sympathy,[2] and have found only repulse and disappointment.

Thou demandest what is Love. It is that powerful attraction towards all we conceive, or fear, or hope beyond

[1] In *The Keepsake* we read *even of thine* for *even thine.*

[2] This word is omitted in *The Keepsake.*

ourselves, when we find within our own thoughts the
chasm of an insufficient void, and seek to awaken in all
things that are, a community with what we experience
within ourselves. If we reason, we would be understood;
if we imagine, we would that the airy children of our
brain were born anew within another's; if we feel, we
would that another's nerves should vibrate to our own,
that the beams of their eyes should kindle at once and
mix and melt into our own; that lips of motionless ice
should not reply to lips quivering and burning with the
heart's best blood. This is Love. This is the bond and
the sanction which connects not only man with man, but
with every thing which exists. We are born into the
world, and there is something within us which, from the
instant that we live, more and more thirsts after its likeness. It is probably in correspondence with this law that
the infant drains milk from the bosom of its mother; this
propensity developes itself with the developement of our
nature. We dimly see within our intellectual nature a
miniature as it were of our entire self, yet deprived of all
that we condemn or despise, the ideal prototype of every
thing excellent and[1] lovely that we are capable of conceiving as belonging to the nature of man. Not only the
portrait of our external being, but an assemblage of the
minutest particles of which our nature is composed;* a
mirror whose surface reflects only the forms of purity and
brightness; a soul within our own[2] soul that describes a

---

* These words are ineffectual and metaphorical. Most words are so—
No help! [SHELLEY'S NOTE.]

[1] So in *The Keepsake*; in the
Essays &c., *or*.
[2] In *The Keepsake* we read *our
own soul*; in the *Essays* &c., *our
soul*. As a prose expression the
earlier reading seems more probable
than the later, which, however,
corresponds more closely with the
expression in *Epipsychidion* (line
455), *a soul within the soul*.

circle around its proper Paradise, which pain and sorrow and evil dare not overleap. To this we eagerly refer all sensations, thirsting that they should resemble or[1] correspond with it. The discovery of its antitype; the meeting with an understanding capable of clearly estimating our own; an imagination which should enter into and seize upon the subtle and delicate peculiarities which we have delighted to cherish and unfold in secret; with a frame whose nerves, like the chords of two exquisite lyres, strung to the accompaniment of one delightful voice, vibrate with the vibrations of our own; and of a combination of all these in such proportion as the type within demands; this is the invisible and unattainable point to which Love tends; and to attain which, it urges forth the powers of man to arrest the faintest shadow of that, without the possession of which there is no rest nor respite to the heart over which it rules.[2] Hence in solitude, or in that deserted state when we are surrounded by human beings, and yet they sympathize not with us, we love the flowers, the grass, the waters, and the sky. In the motion of the very leaves of spring, in the blue air, there is then found a secret correspondence with our heart. There is eloquence in the tongueless wind,[3] and a melody in the flowing brooks and the rustling of the reeds beside them, which by their inconceivable relation to something within the soul, awaken the spirits to a dance of breathless rapture, and bring tears of mysterious tender-

---

[1] In *The Keepsake* we read *and* instead of *or*.

[2] The whole line of thought here and in the following sentence corresponds with the line of thought in *Alastor*, one would say, rather than with Shelley's studies and writings of 1818.

[3] Cf. *Epipsychidion*:

I questioned every tongueless wind that flew
Over my tower of mourning, if it knew
Whither 'twas fled, this soul out of my soul;

there is much in *Epipsychidion* that is reminiscent of *Alastor* and of the phase of Shelley's existence which produced that earlier poem.

ness to the eyes, like the enthusiasm of patriotic success, or the voice of one beloved singing to you alone. Sterne says that if he were in a desert he would love some cypress. So soon as this want or power is dead, man becomes the living sepulchre of himself, and what yet survives is the mere husk of what once he was.

ON A FUTURE STATE.

[The fragment on a Future State is from the *Essays* &c., but includes the Reflection on Death already mentioned (see page 256) as having been given in *The Athenæum* for the 29th of September, 1832, and in *The Shelley Papers*. Mrs. Shelley says of this Fragment (Preface, page xiii) that, "in this portion of his Essay he gives us only that view of a future state which is to be derived from reasoning and analogy"; and adds that it is "not to be supposed" Shelley's mind "should be content with a mere logical view of that which even in religion is a mystery and a wonder"; and that he "certainly regarded the country beyond the grave as one by no means foreign to our interests and hopes." Those who require this consolation in accepting Shelley may find plenty of confirmation in the series of his works; but the opposite position may be maintained with at least equal success by putting in evidence other passages from the same series of works.—H. B. F.]

ON A FUTURE STATE.

It has been the persuasion of an immense majority of human beings in all ages and nations that we continue to live after death,—that apparent termination of all the functions of sensitive and intellectual existence. Nor has mankind been contented with supposing that species of existence which some philosophers have asserted; namely, the resolution of the component parts of the mechanism of a living being into its elements, and the impossibility of the minutest particle of these sustaining the smallest diminution. They have clung to the idea that sensibility and thought, which they have distinguished from the objects of it, under the several names of spirit and matter, is, in its own nature, less susceptible of division and decay, and that, when the body is resolved into its elements, the principle which animated it will remain perpetual and unchanged. Some philosophers—and those to whom we are indebted for the most stupendous discoveries in physical science, suppose, on the other hand, that intelligence is the mere result of certain combinations among the particles of its objects; and those among them who believe that we live after death, recur to the

T

interposition of a supernatural power, which shall overcome the tendency inherent in all material combinations,
to dissipate and be absorbed into other forms.

Let us trace the reasonings which in one and the
other have conducted to these two opinions, and endeavour to discover what we ought to think on a question of
such momentous interest. Let us analyse the ideas and
feelings which constitute the contending beliefs, and
watchfully establish a discrimination between words and
thoughts. Let us bring the question to the test of experience and fact; and ask ourselves, considering our nature
in its entire extent, what light we derive from a sustained
and comprehensive view of its component parts, which
may enable us to assert with certainty, that we do or do
not live after death.

The examination of this subject requires that it should
be stript of all those accessory topics which adhere to it
in the common opinion of men. The existence of a God,
and a future state of rewards and punishments, are totally
foreign to the subject. If it be proved that the world is
ruled by a Divine Power, no inference necessarily can be
drawn from that circumstance in favour of a future state.
It has been asserted, indeed, that as goodness and justice
are to be numbered among the attributes of the Deity, he
will undoubtedly compensate the virtuous who suffer
during life, and that he will make every sensitive being,
who does not deserve punishment, happy for ever. But
this view of the subject, which it would be tedious as
well as superfluous to develope and expose, satisfies no
person, and cuts the knot which we now seek to untie.
Moreover, should it be proved, on the other hand, that

the mysterious principle which regulates the proceedings of the universe, is neither intelligent nor sensitive, yet it is not an inconsistency to suppose at the same time, that the animating power survives the body which it has animated, by laws as independent of any supernatural agent as those through which it first became united with it. Nor, if a future state be clearly proved, does it follow that it will be a state of punishment or reward.

'By the word death, we express that condition in which natures resembling ourselves apparently cease to be that which[2] they were. We no longer hear them speak, nor see them move. If they have sensations and[3] apprehensions, we no longer participate in them. We know no more than that those external[4] organs, and all that fine texture of material frame, without which we have no experience that life or thought can subsist, are dissolved and scattered abroad. The body is placed under the earth,[5] and after a certain period there remains no vestige even of its form. This is that contemplation of inexhaustible melancholy, whose shadow eclipses the brightness of the world. The common[6] observer is struck with dejection at the spectacle. He contends in vain against the persuasion of the grave, that the dead indeed cease to be. The corpse at his feet is prophetic of his own destiny. Those who have preceded him, and whose voice was delightful to his ear; whose touch met his like sweet

---

[1] The Reflection on Death given by Medwin begins here. I note the variations from Mrs. Shelley's text on the grounds already stated. See foot-note, p. 257.

[2] Medwin reads *what* for *that which*.

[3] Medwin reads *or* for *and*.

[4] In Medwin's version, *internal*.

[5] Medwin reads *ground* for *earth*.

[6] Medwin reads *commonest*, and runs this sentence and the next together by printing *and contends*.

and subtle fire[1] ; whose aspect spread a visionary light
upon his path—these he cannot meet again. The organs
of sense are destroyed, and the intellectual operations
dependent on them have perished with[2] their sources.
How can a corpse see or feel ? its eyes are eaten out, and
its heart is black and without motion. What intercourse
can two heaps of putrid clay and crumbling bones hold together ?[3] When you can discover where the fresh colours
of the faded flower abide, or the music of the broken lyre,
seek life among the dead. Such are the anxious and
fearful contemplations of the common observer, though
the popular religion often prevents him from confessing
them even to himself.

The natural philosopher, in addition to the sensations
common to all men inspired by the event of death,
believes that he sees with more certainty that it is attended
with the annihilation of sentiment and thought. He observes the mental powers increase and fade with those of
the body, and even accommodate themselves to the most
transitory changes of our physical nature. Sleep suspends
many of the faculties of the vital and intellectual
principle ; drunkenness and disease will either temporarily
or permanently derange them. Madness or idiotey may

---

[1] In Medwin's version this passage stands thus: "Those who have
perceived him, whose voice was
delightful to his ear, whose touch
met, and thrilled, and vibrated to
his like sweet and subtle fire."
The error of transcription in substituting *perceived* for *preceded* is
characteristic of Medwin ; but the
rest of the variation is characteristic of Shelley.

[2] Medwin reads *in* for *with*, and
in the next sentence *and* for *or*.

[3] In Medwin's version, " What

intercourse can there be in two
heaps of putrid clay and crumbling bones piled together ?" This
variation will not commend itself as
other than a case of making the
best of a difficult piece of copying.
The next sentence, down to *dead*,
Medwin does not give ; and he
ends the Reflection on Death with
the following paragraph :

"Such are the anxious and fearful contemplations, that, in spite of religion, we
are sometimes forced to confess to ourselves."

utterly extinguish the most excellent and delicate of those powers. In old age the mind gradually withers; and as it grew and was strengthened with the body, so does it together with the body sink into decrepitude. Assuredly these are convincing evidences that so soon as the organs of the body are subjected to the laws of inanimate matter, sensation, and perception, and apprehension, are at an end. It is probable that what we call thought is not an actual being, but no more than the relation between certain parts of that infinitely varied mass, of which the rest of the universe is composed, and which ceases to exist so soon as those parts change their position with regard to each other. Thus colour, and sound, and taste, and odour exist only relatively. But let thought be considered as some peculiar substance, which permeates, and is the cause of, the animation of living beings. Why should that substance be assumed to be something essentially distinct from all others, and exempt from subjection to those laws from which no other substance is exempt? It differs, indeed, from all other substances, as electricity, and light, and magnetism, and the constituent parts of air and earth, severally differ from all others. Each of these is subject to change and to decay, and to conversion into other forms. Yet the difference between light and earth is scarcely greater than that which exists between life, or thought, and fire. The difference between the two former was never alleged as an argument for the eternal permanence of either, in that form under which they first might offer themselves to our notice. Why should the difference between the two latter substances be an argument for the prolongation of the existence of one and not the other, when the existence of both has arrived at their apparent termination?

To say that fire exists without manifesting any of the properties of fire, such as light, heat, &c., or that the principle
of life exists without consciousness, or memory, or desire,
or motive, is to resign, by an awkward distortion of
language, the affirmative of the dispute.   To say that
the principle of life *may* exist in distribution among
various forms, is to assert what cannot be proved to be
either true or false, but which, were it true, annihilates
all hope of existence after death, in any sense in which
that event can belong to the hopes and fears of men.
Suppose, however, that the intellectual and vital principle
differs in the most marked and essential manner from
all other known substances; that they have all some
resemblance between themselves which it in no degree
participates.   In what manner can this concession be
made an argument for its imperishability?   All that we
see or know perishes and is changed.   Life and thought
differ indeed from everything else.   But that it survives
that period, beyond which we have no experience of its
existence, such distinction and dissimilarity affords no
shadow of proof, and nothing but our own desires could
have led us to conjecture or imagine.

Have we existed before birth?   It is difficult to conceive the possibility of this.   There is, in the generative
principle of each animal and plant, a power which con-
verts the substances by which it is surrounded into a
substance homogeneous with itself.   That is, the relations[1]
between certain elementary particles of matter undergo a
change, and submit to new combinations.   For when we
use the words *principle, power, cause,* &c., we mean to
express no real being, but only to class under those terms

---

[1] In the first edition, *relation.*

a certain series of co-existing phenomena ; but let it be supposed that this principle is a certain substance which escapes the observation of the chemist and anatomist. It certainly *may be ;* though it is sufficiently unphilosophical to allege the possibility of an opinion as a proof of its truth. Does it see, hear, feel, before its combination with those organs on which sensation depends ? Does it reason, imagine, apprehend, without those ideas which sensation alone can communicate ? If we have not existed before birth ; if, at the period when the parts of our nature on which thought and life depend, seem to be woven together, they are woven together; if there are no reasons to suppose that we have existed before that period at which our existence apparently commences, then there are no grounds for supposition that we shall continue to exist after our existence has apparently ceased. So far as thought and life is concerned, the same will take place with regard to us, individually considered, after death, as had place before our birth.

It is said that it is possible that we should continue to exist in some mode totally inconceivable to us at present. This is a most unreasonable presumption. It casts on the adherents of annihilation the burthen of proving the negative of a question, the affirmative of which is not supported by a single argument, and which, by its very nature, lies beyond the experience of the human understanding. It is sufficiently easy, indeed, to form any proposition, concerning which we are ignorant, just not so absurd as not to be contradictory in itself, and defy refutation. The possibility of whatever enters into the wildest imagination to conceive is thus triumphantly vindicated. But it is enough that such assertions should be either contradictory to the known laws of nature, or exceed the limits of our experience, that their fallacy or irrelevancy to our consideration should be demonstrated. They persuade, indeed, only those who desire to be persuaded.

This desire to be for ever as we are ; the reluctance to a violent and unexperienced change, which is common to all the animated and inanimate combinations of the universe, is, indeed, the secret persuasion which has given birth to the opinions of a future state.[1]

[1] An extract from a MS. Journal of Shelley's is given in the Preface to the *Essays, Letters* &c. (1840), pp. xiv and xv, and bears upon this subject :

"I had time in that moment to reflect and even to reason on death ; it was rather a thing of discomfort and disappointment than terror to me. We should never be separated; but in death we might not know and feel our union as now. I hope—but my hopes are not unmixed with fear for what will befal this inestimable spirit when we appear to die."

Unfortunately it does not appear at what date Shelley wrote this passage. A knowledge of the date would enhance the value of the passage when compared with a similar utterance at p. 177 of the present volume.

SPECULATIONS ON METAPHYSICS.

[The greater part of this fragment was published by Mrs. Shelley in the *Essays, Letters* &c., 1840; but I have been enabled to add considerably to it from a MS. placed at my disposal by Mr. Townshend Mayer, the philosophical fragment referred to in the foot-note at page 248, Vol. IV, of the Poetical Works, as being written on the same paper with the Sonnet of Guido Cavalcanti to Dante Alighieri there printed. The MS., which unfortunately begins in the middle of a sentence, is apparently continuous. It is written generally about half-way down the page to admit of annotation ; but Shelley has only inserted one note, the Latin quotation at page 290. In the paragraphs which Mrs. Shelley printed with the heading "I.—WHAT METAPHYSICS ARE. ERRORS IN THE USUAL METHODS OF CONSIDERING THEM," occurs a different version of some of the sentences in this MS. : indeed the MS. seems to me to be, mainly, a more complete version of that particular section than Mrs. Shelley printed from, though it is possible that the MS. used in 1840 consisted of fragments of a later version. I have given the whole of both versions, either as text or as notes. Mrs. Shelley assigns the fragment printed by her to the year 1815.—H. B. F.]

SPECULATIONS ON METAPHYSICS.

I.

1. It is an axiom in mental philosophy, that we can think of nothing which we have not perceived. When I say that we can think of nothing, I mean, we can imagine nothing, we can reason of nothing, we can remember nothing, we can foresee nothing. The most astonishing combinations of poetry, the subtlest deductions of logic and mathematics, are no other than combinations which the intellect makes of sensations according to its own laws. A catalogue of all the thoughts of the mind, and of all their possible modifications, is a cyclopedic history of the universe.

But, it will be objected, the inhabitants of the various planets of this and other solar systems; and the existence of a Power bearing the same relation to all that we perceive and are, as what we call a cause does to what we call effect, were never subjects of sensation, and yet the laws of mind almost universally suggest, according to the various disposition of each, a conjecture, a persuasion, or a conviction of their existence. The reply is simple; these thoughts are also to be included in the catalogue of existence; they are modes in which thoughts are combined; the objection only adds force to the conclusion, that beyond the limits of perception and thought nothing can exist.

Thoughts, or ideas, or notions, call them what you will, differ from each other, not in kind, but in force. It has commonly been supposed that those distinct thoughts which affect a number of persons, at regular intervals, during the passage of a multitude of other thoughts, which are called *real*, or *external objects*, are totally different in kind from those which affect only a few persons, and which recur at irregular intervals, and are usually more obscure and indistinct, such as hallucinations, dreams, and the ideas of madness. No essential distinction between any one of these ideas, or any class of them, is founded on a correct observation of the nature of things, but merely on a consideration of what thoughts are most invariably subservient to the security and happiness of life; and if nothing more were expressed by the distinction, the philosopher might safely accommodate his language to that of the vulgar. But they pretend to assert an essential difference, which has no foundation in truth, and which suggests a narrow and false conception of universal nature, the parent of the most fatal errors in speculation. A specific difference between every thought of the mind, is, indeed, a necessary consequence of that law by which it perceives diversity and number; but a generic and essential difference is wholly arbitrary. The principle of the agreement and similarity of all thoughts, is, that they are all thoughts; the principle of their disagreement consists in the variety and irregularity of the occasions on which they arise in the mind. That in which they agree, to that in which they differ, is as everything to nothing. Important distinctions, of various degrees of force, indeed, are to be established between them, if they were, as they may be, subjects of ethical and œconomical discussion; but that is a question altogether distinct.

By considering all knowledge as bounded by perception, whose operations may be indefinitely combined, we arrive at a conception of Nature inexpressibly more magnificent, simple and true, than accords with the ordinary systems of complicated and partial consideration. Nor does a contemplation of the universe, in this comprehensive and synthetical view, exclude the subtlest analysis of its modifications and parts.

A scale might be formed, graduated according to the degrees of a combined ratio of intensity, duration, connexion, periods of recurrence, and utility, which would be the standard, according to which all ideas might be measured, and an uninterrupted chain of nicely shadowed distinctions would be observed, from the faintest impression on the senses, to the most distinct combination of those impressions; from the simplest of those combinations, to that mass of knowledge which, including our own nature, constitutes what we call the universe.

We are intuitively conscious of our own existence, and of that connexion in the train of our successive ideas, which we term our identity. We are conscious also of the existence of other minds; but not intuitively. Our evidence, with respect to the existence of other minds, is founded upon a very complicated relation of ideas, which it is foreign to the purpose of this treatise to anatomize. The basis of this relation is, undoubtedly, a periodical recurrence of masses of ideas, which our voluntary determinations have, in one peculiar direction, no power to circumscribe or to arrest, and against the recurrence of which they can only imperfectly provide. The irresistible laws of thought constrain us to believe that the precise limits of our actual ideas are not the actual limits of possible ideas; the law, according to which these deductions are drawn, is called analogy; and this is the foundation of all our inferences, from one idea to another, inasmuch as they resemble each other.

We see trees, houses, fields, living beings in our own shape, and in shapes more or less analogous to our own. These are perpetually changing the mode of their existence relatively to us. To express the varieties of these modes, we say, *we move, they move;* and as this motion is continual, though not uniform, we express our conception of the diversities of its course by—*it has been, it is, it shall be.* These diversities are events or objects, and are essential, considered relatively to human identity, for the existence of the human mind. For if the inequalities, produced by what has been termed the operations of the external universe, were levelled by the perception of our being, uniting, and filling up their interstices, motion and mensuration, and time, and space; the elements of the human mind being thus abstracted, sensation and imagination cease. Mind cannot be considered pure.

II.

WHAT METAPHYSICS ARE. ERRORS IN THE USUAL METHODS OF CONSIDERING THEM.

WE do not attend sufficiently to what passes within ourselves. We combine words, combined a thousand times before. In our minds we assume entire opinions; and in the expression of those opinions, entire phrases, when we would philosophize. Our whole style of expression and sentiment is infected with the tritest plagiarisms. Our words are dead, our thoughts are cold and borrowed.[1]

* * * * * *

...... more than suggest an association of words, or the

---

[1] This paragraph is the opening of the section as given by Mrs. Shelley. The rest of the text of the section is here printed from the MS. referred to at p. 282. Mrs. Shelley has instead the three following paragraphs :—

" Let us contemplate facts ; let us, in the great study of ourselves, resolutely compel the mind to a rigid consideration of itself. We are not content with conjecture, and inductions, and syllogisms, in sciences regarding external objects. As in these, let us also, in considering the phenomena of mind, severely collect those facts which cannot be disputed. Metaphysics will thus possess this conspicuous advantage over every other science, that each student, by attentively referring to his own mind, may ascertain the authorities, upon which any assertions regarding it are supported. There can thus be no deception, we ourselves being the depositaries of the evidence of the subject which we consider.

" Metaphysics may be defined as an inquiry concerning those things belonging to, or connected with, the eternal nature of man.

" It is said that mind produces motion ; and it might as well have been said, that motion produces mind."

The third paragraph does not seem to have any necessary connexion with the others.

remembrance of external objects distinct from the conceptions which the mind exerts relatively to them. They
are about these conceptions. They perpetually awaken
the attention of their reader to the consideration of their
intellectual nature. They make him feel that his mind
is not merely impelled or organized by the adhibition of
events proceeding from what has been termed the
mechanism of the material universe.

That which the most consummate intelligences that
have adorned this mortal scene inherit as their birthright,
let us acquire (for it is within our grasp) by caution, by
strict scepticism concerning all assertions, all expressions; by scrupulous and strong attention to the mysteries
of our own nature.

Let us contemplate facts. Let me repeat that in the
great study of ourselves we ought resolutely to compel
the mind to a rigid examination of itself. Let us in[1] the
science which regards those laws by which the mind acts,
as well as in those which regard the laws by which it is
acted upon, severely collect those facts.

Metaphysics is a word which has been so long applied to
denote an inquiry into the phenomena of mind, that it
would justly be considered presumptuous to employ
another. But etymologically considered it is very ill
adapted to express the science of mind. It asserts a distinction between the moral and the material universe
which it is presumptuous to assume. Metaphysics may

[1] Cancelled readings, (1) *the science which regards the mind itself* (2) *in Metaphysics as in those* *sciences which regard the laws by which it is.*

be defined as the science[1] of all that we know, feel, remember and believe : inasmuch as our knowledge, sensations, memory and faith constitute the universe considered relatively to human identity. Logic, or the science of words must no longer be confounded with metaphysics or the science of facts. Words are the instruments of mind whose capacities it becomes the Metaphysician accurately to know, but they are not mind, nor are they portions of mind. The discoveries of Horne Tooke in philology do not, as he has asserted, throw light upon[2] Metaphysics, they only render the instruments requ[is]ite to its perception more exact and accurate.

Aristotle and his followers, Locke and most of the modern Philosophers[3] gave Logic the name of Metaphysics. Nor have those who are accustomed to profess the greatest veneration for the inductive system of Lord Bacon adhered with sufficient scrupulousness to its regulations. They have professed indeed (and who have not professed ?) to deduce their conclusions from indisputable facts. How came many of those[4] facts to be called indisputable ? What sanctioning correspondence[5] unites a concatenation of syllogisms ? Their promises[6] of deducing all systems from facts has too often been performed by appealing in favour of these pretended realities to the obstinate preconceptions of the multitude ; or by the most preposterous mistake of a name for a thing. They . . . .

---

[1] Cancelled reading, *The sense in which the word Metaphysics will be employed in the following pages is :* See definition given in foot-note, p. 287.

[2] The words *the science of* are here cancelled in the MS.

[3] Cancelled reading, *Locke and the disciples of his...*

[4] Cancelled reading, *What are those.*

[5] Cancelled reading, *connexion.*

[6] The word *profession* is struck out in favour of *promises.*

The science of mind possesses eminent advantages over
every other with regard to the certainty of the conclusions which it affords.   It requires indeed for its entire
developement no more than a minute and accurate attention to facts.   Every student may refer to the testi-
monials[1] which he bears within himself to ascertain the
authorities upon which any assertion rests.   It requires
no more than attention to perceive perfect sincerity in
the relation of what is perceived, and care to distinguish
the arbitrary marks by which   are designated
from the   themselves.*

*   *   *   *   *   *

We are ourselves the depositaries of the evidence of
the subject which we consider.[2]

*   *   *   *   *   *

---

* Fabulosissima quæque portenta cujusvis religionis alius crediderim
quam hæc omnia sine Numine fieri.   [SHELLEY'S NOTE.]

[1] In the MS. *authorities* was originally written here.
[2] The continuous fragment here
breaks off at the beginning of a
page. On the next page some headings of the subject are indicated
by the inscription of the words
     Infancy
     Childhood
     Youth
     Manhood
     Old Age

The first of these sections appears
to have been begun ; but all we
have of it, or all Mrs. Shelley gave
us of it, is the fragment headed
"CATALOGUE OF THE PHENOMENA
OF DREAMS," p. 295.   That, as well
as those headed "DIFFICULTY OF
ANALYSING THE HUMAN MIND" and
"HOW THE ANALYSIS SHOULD BE
CARRIED ON" are from Mrs. Shelley's edition.

III.

If it were possible that a person should give a faithful history of his being, from the earliest epochs of his recollection, a picture would be presented such as the world has never contemplated before. A mirror would be held up to all men in which they might behold their own recollections, and, in dim perspective, their shadowy hopes and fears,—all that they dare not, or that daring and desiring, they could not expose to the open eyes of day. But thought can with difficulty visit the intricate and winding chambers which it inhabits. It is like a river whose rapid and perpetual stream flows outwards;—like one in dread who speeds through the recesses of some haunted pile, and dares not look behind. The caverns of the mind are obscure, and shadowy; or pervaded with a lustre, beautifully bright indeed, but shining not beyond their portals. If it were possible to be where we have been, vitally and indeed—if, at the moment of our pre-

sence there, we could define the results of our experience,
—if the passage from sensation to reflection—from a
state of passive perception to voluntary contemplation,
were not so dizzying and so tumultuous, this attempt
would be less difficult.

IV.

HOW THE ANALYSIS SHOULD BE CARRIED ON.

Most of the errors of philosophers have arisen from considering the human being in a point of view too detailed and circumscribed. He is not a moral, and an intellectual, —but also, and pre-eminently, an imaginative being. His own mind is his law; his own mind is all things to him. If we would arrive at any knowledge which should be serviceable from the practical conclusions to which it leads, we ought to consider the mind of man and the universe as the great whole on which to exercise our speculations. Here, above all, verbal disputes ought to be laid aside, though this has long been their chosen field of battle. It imports little to inquire whether thought be distinct from the objects of thought. The use of the words *external* and *internal*, as applied to the establishment of this distinction, has been the symbol and the source of much dispute. This is merely an affair of words, and as the dispute deserves, to say, that when speaking of the objects of thought, we indeed only describe one of the forms of thought—or that, speaking of thought, we only apprehend one of the operations of the universal system of beings.[1]

[1] I give this precisely as printed by Mrs. Shelley, though some errors of transcription may be suspected. The failure to work out the sentence to any proper construction may indeed be incident to the incomplete state of the fragment; but the term *universal system of beings,* with which the fragment closes, is so unusual, so inappropriate to the context that, one can hardly doubt, a careful examination of the MS. would shew the last word to be *things,* not *beings.*

V.

I. LET us reflect on our infancy, and give as faithfully as possible a relation of the events of sleep.

And first I am bound to present a faithful picture of my own peculiar nature relatively to sleep. I do not doubt that were every individual to imitate me, it would be found that among many circumstances peculiar to their individual nature, a sufficiently general resemblance would be found to prove the connexion existing between those peculiarities and the most universal phenomena. I shall employ caution, indeed, as to the facts which I state, that they contain nothing false or exaggerated. But they contain no more than certain elucidations of my own nature; concerning the degree in which it resembles, or differs from, that of others, I am by no means accurately aware. It is sufficient, however, to caution the reader against drawing general inferences from particular instances.

I omit the general instances of delusion in fever or delirium, as well as mere dreams considered in themselves. A delineation of this subject, however inexhaustible and interesting, is to be passed over.

What is the connexion of sleeping and of waking?

———

II. I distinctly remember dreaming three several times, between intervals of two or more years, the same precise dream. It was not so much what is ordinarily called a dream; the single image, unconnected with all other images, of a youth who was educated at the same school with myself, presented itself in sleep. Even now, after the lapse of many years, I can never hear the name of this youth, without the three places where I dreamed of him presenting themselves distinctly to my mind.

———

III. In dreams, images acquire associations peculiar to dreaming; so that the idea of a particular house, when it recurs a second time in dreams, will have relation with the idea of the same house, in the first time, of a nature entirely different from that which the house excites, when seen or thought of in relation to waking ideas.

———

IV. I have beheld scenes, with the intimate and unaccountable connexion of which with the obscure parts of my own nature, I have been irresistibly impressed. I have beheld a scene which has produced no unusual effect on my thoughts. After the lapse of many years I have dreamed of this scene. It has hung on my memory, it has haunted my thoughts, at intervals, with the pertinacity of an object connected with human affections. I have visited this scene again. Neither the dream could he dissociated from the landscape, nor the landscape from the dream, nor feelings, such as neither singly could have awakened, from both. But the most remarkable event of this nature, which ever occurred to me, happened five years ago at Oxford. I was walking with a friend, in the neighbourhood of that city, engaged in earnest and interesting conversation. We suddenly turned the corner of a lane, and the view, which its high banks and hedges had concealed, presented itself. The view consisted of a windmill, standing in one among many plashy meadows, inclosed with stone walls; the irregular and broken ground, between the wall and the road on which we stood; a long low hill behind the windmill, and a grey covering of uniform cloud spread over the evening sky. It was that season when the last leaf had just fallen from the scant and stunted ash. The scene surely was a common scene; the season and the hour little calculated to kindle lawless thought; it was a tame uninteresting assemblage of objects, such as would drive the imagination for refuge in serious and sober talk, to the evening fireside, and the dessert of winter fruits and wine. The effect which it produced on me was not such as could have been expected. I suddenly remembered to have seen that exact scene in some dream of long — —

Here I was obliged to leave off, overcome by thrilling horror.[1]

---

[1] At this point the MS. from which the fragment was given in 1840 closes. Mrs. Shelley says :—

" I remember well his coming to me from writing it, pale and agitated, to seek refuge in conversation from the fearful emotions it excited. No man, as these fragments prove, had such keen sensations as Shelley. His nervous temperament was wound up by the delicacy of his health to an intense degree of sensibility, and while his active mind pondered for ever upon, and drew conclusions from his sensations, his reveries increased their vivacity, till they mingled with, and were one with thought, and both became absorbing and tumultuous, even to physical pain."

The final page of the MS. fragment referred to at pp. 282 and 290 seems to be a note for the Speculations on Morals, and is inserted at pp. 303–4.

SPECULATIONS ON MORALS.

[These fragmentary notes are from the *Essays* &c. (1840), with the exception of the list of names given at pages 303-4. Mrs. Shelley records (Preface, page xvii.) that Shelley " at one time meditated a popular essay on morals; to shew how virtue resulted from the nature of man, and that to fulfil its laws was to abide by that principle from the fulfilment of which happiness is to spring. The few pages here given are all that he left on this subject." We are not told *when* these pages were written; but it was probably about the year 1815.—H. B. F.]

SPECULATIONS ON MORALS.

I.

THAT great science which regards nature and the operations of the human mind, is popularly divided into Morals and Metaphysics. The latter relates to a just classification, and the assignment of distinct names to its ideas; the former regards simply the determination of that arrangement of them which produces the greatest and most solid happiness. It is admitted that a virtuous or moral action, is that action which, when considered in all its accessories and consequences, is fitted to produce the highest pleasure to the greatest number of sensitive beings. The laws according to which all pleasure, since it cannot be equally felt by all sensitive beings, ought to be distributed by a voluntary agent, are reserved for a separate chapter.

The design of this little treatise is restricted to the developement of the elementary principles of morals. As far as regards that purpose, metaphysical science will be treated merely so far as a source of negative truth; whilst morality will be considered as a science, respecting which we can arrive at positive conclusions.

The misguided imaginations of men have rendered the ascertaining of what *is not true*, the principal direct service which metaphysical science can bestow upon moral science. Moral science itself is the doctrine of the voluntary actions of man, as a sentient and social being. These actions depend on the thoughts in his mind. But there is a mass of popular opinion, from which the most enlightened persons are seldom wholly free, into the truth or falsehood of which it is incumbent on us to inquire, before we can arrive at any firm conclusions as to the conduct which we ought to pursue in the regulation of our own minds, or towards our fellow-beings; or before we can ascertain the elementary laws, according to which these thoughts, from which these actions flow, are originally combined.

The object of the forms according to which human society is administered, is the happiness of the individuals composing the communities which they regard, and these forms are perfect or imperfect in proportion to the degree in which they promote this end.

This object is not merely the quantity of happiness enjoyed by individuals as sensitive beings, but the mode in which it should be distributed among them as social beings. It is not enough, if such a coincidence can be conceived as possible, that one person or class of persons should enjoy the highest happiness, whilst another is suffering a disproportionate degree of misery. It is necessary that the happiness produced by the common efforts, and preserved by the common care, should be distributed according to the just claims of each individual; if not, although the quantity produced should be the same, the end of society would remain unfulfilled. The object is in a compound proportion to the quantity of happiness produced, and the correspondence of the mode in which it is distributed, to the elementary feelings of man as a social being.

The disposition in an individual to promote this object is called virtue; and the two constituent parts of virtue, benevolence and justice, are correlative with these two great portions of the only true object of all voluntary actions of a human being. Benevolence is the desire to be the author of good, and justice the apprehension of the manner in which good ought to be done.

Justice and benevolence result from the elementary laws of the human mind.

¹An essay on the progressive excellence perceptible in the expressions—of Solomon, Homer, Bion and the Seven

---

¹ In the MS. from which the additions have been made to the *Speculations on Metaphysics*, occurs this list of names &c. On the page facing the list of headings (see foot-note, p. 290) is the priceless Sonnet of Guido Cavalcanti to Dante Alighieri, published in the Library Edition of Shelley's Poetical Works (Vol. IV, p. 248); and on the next page. the final page of the MS., occurs the long list of names given in the text, apparently forming part of the plan of a "Treatise on Morals," which, if completed, would have been a very considerable and comprehensive affair.

Sages, Socrates, Plato, Theodorus, Zeno, Carneades.
Aristotle, Epicurus, Pythagoras, Cicero, Tacitus, Jesus
Christ, Virgil, Lucan, Seneca, Epictetus, Antoninus
*   *   *   *   *   *   Sulpicius, Severus.
Mahomet, Manes, The Fathers,—Ariosto, Tasso, Petrarch,
Dante, Abeillard, Thomas Aquinas—The Schoolmen.
The reformers. Spinosa, Bayle, Paschal, Locke, Berkeley,
Leibnitz, Malebranche, The French Philosophers, Voltaire.
Rousseau, the Germans—the Illuminati—Hume. Godwin
—State of General Society. Perfectibility.

CHAPTER I.

ON THE NATURE OF VIRTUE.

Sect. 1. General View of the Nature and Objects of Virtue.—2. The Origin and Basis of Virtue, as founded on the Elementary Principles of Mind.—3. The Laws which flow from the nature of Mind regulating the application of those principles to human actions.—4. Virtue, a possible attribute of man.

WE exist in the midst of a multitude of beings like ourselves, upon whose happiness most of our actions exert some obvious and decisive influence.

The regulation of this influence is the object of moral science.

We know that we are susceptible of receiving painful or pleasurable impressions of greater or less intensity and duration. That is called good which produces pleasure ; that is called evil which produces pain. These are general names, applicable to every class of causes, from which an overbalance of pain or pleasure may result. But when a human being is the active instrument of generating or

diffusing happiness, the principle through which it is most
effectually instrumental to that purpose, is called virtue.
And benevolence, or the desire to be the author of good,
united with justice, or an apprehension of the manner in
which that good is to be done, constitutes virtue.

But wherefore should a man be benevolent and just?
The immediate emotions of his nature, especially in its
most inartificial state, prompt him to inflict pain, and to
arrogate dominion. He desires to heap superfluities to
his own store, although others perish with famine. He is
propelled to guard against the smallest invasion of his
own liberty, though he reduces others to a condition of the
most pitiless servitude. He is revengeful, proud, and
selfish. Wherefore should he curb these propensities?

It is inquired for what reason a human being should
engage in procuring the happiness, or refrain from producing the pain of another? When a reason is required
to prove the necessity of adopting any system of conduct,
what is it that the objector demands? He requires proof
of that system of conduct being such as will most effectually promote the happiness of mankind. To demonstrate
this, is to render a moral reason. Such is the object of
Virtue.

A common sophism, which, like many others, depends
on the abuse of a metaphorical expression to a literal
purpose, has produced much of the confusion which has
involved the theory of morals. It is said that no person
is bound to be just or kind, if, on his neglect, he should
fail to incur some penalty. Duty is obligation. There
can be no obligation without an obliger. Virtue is a law,

to which it is the will of the lawgiver that we should conform; which will we should in no manner be bound to obey, unless some dreadful punishment were attached to disobedience. This is the philosophy of slavery and superstition.

In fact, no person can be *bound* or *obliged*, without some power preceding to bind and oblige. If I observe a man bound hand and foot, I know that some one bound him. But if I observe him returning self-satisfied from the performance of some action, by which he has been the willing author of extensive benefit, I do not infer that the anticipation of hellish agonies, or the hope of heavenly reward, has constrained him to such an act.[1]

*   *   *   *   *

It remains to be stated in what manner the sensations which constitute the basis of virtue originate in the human mind; what are the laws which it receives there; how far the principles of mind allow it to be an attribute of a human being; and, lastly, what is the probability of persuading mankind to adopt it as an universal and systematic motive of conduct.

BENEVOLENCE.

THERE is a class of emotions which we instinctively avoid. A human being, such as is man considered in his

---

[1] Mrs. Shelley says, "A leaf of manuscript is wanting here, manifestly treating of self-love and disinterestedness."

origin, a child a month old, has a very imperfect consciousness of the existence of other natures resembling
itself. All the energies of its being are directed to the
extinction of the pains with which it is perpetually
assailed. At length it discovers that it is surrounded by
natures susceptible of sensations similar to its own. It is
very late before children attain to this knowledge. If a
child observes, without emotion, its nurse or its mother
suffering acute pain, it is attributable rather to ignorance
than insensibility. So soon as the accents and gestures,
significant of pain, are referred to the feelings which they
express, they awaken in the mind of the beholder a desire
that they should cease. Pain is thus apprehended to be
evil for its own sake, without any other necessary reference
to the mind by which its existence is perceived, than such
as is indispensable to its perception. The tendencies of
our original sensations, indeed, all have for their object
the preservation of our individual being. But these are
passive and unconscious. In proportion as the mind acquires an active power, the empire of these tendencies
becomes limited. Thus an infant, a savage, and a solitary
beast, is selfish, because its mind is incapable of receiving
an accurate intimation of the nature of pain as existing
in beings resembling itself. The inhabitant of a highly
civilized community will more acutely sympathize with the
sufferings and enjoyments of others, than the inhabitant of
a society of a less degree of civilization. He who shall have
cultivated his intellectual powers by familiarity with the
highest specimens of poetry and philosophy, will usually
sympathize more than one engaged in the less refined
functions of manual labour. Every one has experience
of the fact, that to sympathize with the sufferings of
another, is to enjoy a transitory oblivion of his own.

The mind thus acquires, by exercise, a habit, as it were, of perceiving and abhorring evil, however remote from the immediate sphere of sensations with which that individual mind is conversant. Imagination or mind employed in prophetically imaging forth its objects, is that faculty of human nature on which every gradation of its progress, nay, every, the minutest, change, depends. Pain or pleasure, if subtly analysed, will be found to consist entirely in prospect. The only distinction between the selfish man and the virtuous man is, that the imagination of the former is confined within a narrow limit, whilst that of the latter embraces a comprehensive circumference. In this sense, wisdom and virtue may be said to be inseparable, and criteria of each other. Selfishness is the offspring of ignorance and mistake; it is the portion of unreflecting infancy, and savage solitude, or of those whom toil or evil occupations have blunted or rendered torpid; disinterested benevolence is the product of a cultivated imagination, and has an intimate connexion with all the arts which add ornament, or dignity, or power, or stability to the social state of man. Virtue is thus intirely a refinement of civilized life; a creation of the human mind; or, rather, a combination which it has made, according to elementary rules contained within itself, of the feelings suggested by the relations established between man and man.

All the theories which have refined and exalted humanity, or those which have been devised as alleviations of its mistakes and evils, have been based upon the elementary emotions of disinterestedness, which we feel to constitute the majesty of our nature. Patriotism, as it existed in the ancient republics, was never, as has been

supposed, a calculation of personal advantages. When
Mutius Scævola thrust his hand into the burning coals,
and Regulus returned to Carthage, and Epicharis sustained
the rack silently, in the torments of which she knew that
she would speedily perish, rather than betray the conspirators to the tyrant,[1] these illustrious persons certainly
made a small estimate of their private interest. If it be
said that they sought posthumous fame, instances are not
wanting in history which prove that men have even
defied infamy for the sake of good. But there is a great
error in the world with respect to the selfishness of fame.
It is certainly possible that a person should seek distinction as a medium of personal gratification. But the love
of fame is frequently no more than a desire that the feelings of others should confirm, illustrate, and sympathize
with, our own. In this respect it is allied with all that
draws us out of ourselves. It is the "last infirmity of
noble minds." Chivalry was likewise founded on the
theory of self-sacrifice. Love possesses so extraordinary
a power over the human heart, only because disinterestedness is united with the natural propensities. These propensities themselves are comparatively impotent in cases
where the imagination of pleasure to be given, as well as
to be received, does not enter into the account. Let it not
be objected that patriotism, and chivalry, and sentimental
love, have been the fountains of enormous mischief. They
are cited only to establish the proposition that, according
to the elementary principles of mind, man is capable of
desiring and pursuing good for its own sake.

[1] Tacitus. [SHELLEY'S NOTE.]

JUSTICE.

THE benevolent propensities are thus inherent in the human mind. We are impelled to seek the happiness of others. We experience a satisfaction in being the authors of that happiness. Everything that lives is open to impressions of pleasure and pain. We are led by our benevolent propensities to regard every human being indifferently with whom we come in contact. They have preference only with respect to those who offer themselves most obviously to our notice. Human beings are indiscriminating and blind; they will avoid inflicting pain, though that pain should be attended with eventual benefit; they will seek to confer pleasure without calculating the mischief that may result. They benefit one at the expense of many.

There is a sentiment in the human mind that regulates benevolence in its application as a principle of action. This is the sense of justice. Justice, as well as benevolence, is an elementary law of human nature. It is through this principle that men are impelled to distribute any means of pleasure which benevolence may suggest the communication of to others, in equal portions among an equal number of applicants. If ten men are shipwrecked on a desert island, they distribute whatever subsistence may remain to them, into equal portions among themselves. If six of them conspire to deprive the remaining four of their share, their conduct is termed unjust.

The existence of pain has been shown to be a circumstance which the human mind regards with dissatisfac-

tion, and of which it desires the cessation.   It is equally
according to its nature to desire that the advantages to
be enjoyed by a limited number of persons should be
enjoyed equally by all.   This proposition is supported by
the evidence of indisputable facts.   Tell some ungarbled
tale of a number of persons being made the victims of
the enjoyments of one, and he who would appeal in
favour of any system which might produce such an evil
to the primary emotions of our nature, would have
nothing to reply.   Let two persons, equally strangers,
make application for some benefit in the possession of a
third to bestow, and to which he feels that they have an
equal claim.   They are both sensitive beings ; pleasure
and pain affect them alike.

✳   ✳

CHAPTER II.

IT is foreign to the general scope of this little Treatise to encumber a simple argument by controverting any of the trite objections of habit or fanaticism. But there are two; the first, the basis of all political mistake, and the second, the prolific cause and effect of religious error, which it seems useful to refute.

First, it is inquired, " Wherefore should a man be benevolent and just ?" The answer has been given in the preceding chapter.

If a man persists to inquire why he ought to promote the happiness of mankind, he demands a mathematical or metaphysical reason for a moral action. The absurdity of this scepticism is more apparent, but not less real than the exacting a moral reason for a mathematical or metaphysical fact. If any person should refuse to admit that all the radii of a circle are of equal length, or that human actions are necessarily determined by motives, until it could be proved that these radii and these actions uni-

formly tended to the production of the greatest general
good, who would not wonder at the unreasonable and
capricious association of his ideas?

––––––––––

The writer of a philosophical treatise may, I imagine,
at this advanced era of human intellect, be held excused
from entering into a controversy with those reasoners, if
such there are, who would claim an exemption from its
decrees in favour of any one among those diversified
systems of obscure opinion respecting morals, which,
under the name of religions, have in various ages and
countries prevailed among mankind. Besides that if, as
these reasoners have pretended, eternal torture or happiness will ensue as the consequence of certain actions, we
should be no nearer the possession of a standard to determine what actions were right and wrong, even if this
pretended revelation, which is by no means the case, had
furnished us with a complete catalogue of them. The
character of actions as virtuous or vicious would by no
means be determined alone by the personal advantage or
disadvantage of each moral agent individually considered.
Indeed, an action is often virtuous in proportion to the
greatness of the personal calamity which the author
willingly draws upon himself by daring to perform it.
It is because an action produces an overbalance of
pleasure or pain to the greatest number of sentient beings,
and not merely because its consequences are beneficial or
injurious to the author of that action, that it is good or
evil. Nay, this latter consideration has a tendency to
pollute the purity of virtue, inasmuch as it consists in
the motive rather than in the consequences of an action.
A person who should labour for the happiness of mankind
lest he should be tormented eternally in Hell, would with

reference to that motive possess as little claim to the epithet of virtuous, as he who should torture, imprison, and burn them alive, a more usual and natural consequence of such principles, for the sake of the enjoyments of Heaven.

My neighbour, presuming on his strength, may direct me to perform or to refrain from a particular action ; indicating a certain arbitrary penalty in the event of disobedience within his power to inflict. My action, if modified by his menaces, can in no degree participate in virtue. He has afforded me no criterion as to what is right or wrong. A king, or an assembly of men, may publish a proclamation affixing any penalty to any particular action, but that is not immoral because such penalty is affixed. Nothing is more evident than that the epithet of virtue is inapplicable to the refraining from that action on account of the evil arbitrarily attached to it. If the action is in itself beneficial, virtue would rather consist in not refraining from it, but in firmly defying the personal consequences attached to its performance.

Some usurper of supernatural energy might subdue the whole globe to his power ; he might possess new and unheard-of resources for induing his punishments with the most terrible attributes of pain. The torments of his victims might be intense in their degree, and protracted to an infinite duration. Still the " will of the lawgiver" would afford no surer criterion as to what actions were right or wrong. It would only increase the possible virtue of those who refuse to become the instruments of his tyranny.

MORAL SCIENCE CONSISTS IN CONSIDERING THE DIFFERENCE, NOT THE RESEMBLANCE, OF PERSONS.

THE internal influence, derived from the constitution of the mind from which they flow, produces that peculiar modification of actions, which makes them intrinsically good or evil.

To attain an apprehension of the importance of this distinction, let us visit, in imagination, the proceedings of some metropolis. Consider the multitude of human beings who inhabit it, and survey, in thought, the actions of the several classes into which they are divided. Their obvious actions are apparently uniform : the stability of human society seems to be maintained sufficiently by the uniformity of the conduct of its members, both with regard to themselves, and with regard to others. The

---

[1] Mrs. Shelley says (Preface to the *Essays* &c., 1840, p. xvii.)—

"The fragment marked as second in these 'Speculations on Morals' is remarkable for its subtlety and truth. I found it on a single leaf, disjoined from any other subject,—it gives the true key to the history of man; and above all, to those rules of conduct whence mutual happiness has its source and security.".

labourer arises at a certain hour, and applies himself to the task enjoined him. The functionaries of government and law are regularly employed in their offices and courts. The trader holds a train of conduct from which he never deviates. The ministers of religion employ an accustomed language, and maintain a decent and equable regard. The army is drawn forth, the motions of every soldier are such as they were expected to be ; the general commands, and his words are echoed from troop to troop. The domestic actions of men are, for the most part, undistinguishable one from the other, at a superficial glance. The actions which are classed under the general appellation of marriage, education, friendship, &c., are perpetually going on, and to a superficial glance, are similar one to the other.

But, if we would see the truth of things, they must be stripped of this fallacious appearance of uniformity. In truth, no one action has, when considered in its whole extent, any essential resemblance with any other. Each individual, who composes the vast multitude which we have been contemplating, has a peculiar frame of mind, which, whilst the features of the great mass of his actions remain uniform, impresses the minuter lineaments with its peculiar hues. Thus, whilst his life, as a whole, is like the lives of other men, in detail it is most unlike ; and the more subdivided the actions become, that is, the more they enter into that class which have a vital influence on the happiness of others and his own, so much the more are they distinct from those of other men.

> "Those little, nameless, unremembered acts
> Of kindness and of love,"

as well as those deadly outrages which are inflicted by a

look, a word—or less—the very refraining from some
faint and most evanescent expression of countenance ;
these flow from a profounder source than the series of our
habitual conduct, which, it has been already said, derives
its origin from without.   These are the actions, and such
as these, which make human life what it is, and are the
fountains of all the good and evil with which its entire
surface is so widely and impartially overspread; and though
they are called minute, they are called so in compliance
with the blindness of those who cannot estimate their
importance.   It is in the due appreciating the general
effects of their peculiarities, and in cultivating the habit
of acquiring decisive knowledge respecting the tendencies
arising out of them in particular cases, that the most
important part of moral science consists.   The deepest
abyss of these vast and multitudinous caverns, it is
necessary that we should visit.

This is the difference between social and individual
man.   Not that this distinction is to be considered
definite, or characteristic of one human being as compared
with another; it denotes rather two classes of agency,
common in a degree to every human being.   None is
exempt, indeed, from that species of influence which
affects, as it were, the surface of his being, and gives the
specific outline to his conduct.   Almost all that is
ostensible submits to that legislature created by the
general representation of the past feelings of mankind—
imperfect as it is from a variety of causes, as it exists in
the government, the religion, and domestic habits.   Those
who do not nominally, yet actually, submit to the same
power.   The external features of their conduct, indeed,
can no more escape it, than the clouds can escape from

the stream of the wind; and his opinion, which he often hopes he has dispassionately secured from all contagion of prejudice and vulgarity, would be found, on examination, to be the inevitable excrescence of the very usages from which he vehemently dissents. Internally all is conducted otherwise; the efficiency, the essence, the vitality of actions, derives its colour from what is no ways contributed to from any external source. Like the plant, which while it derives the accident of its size and shape from the soil in which it springs, and is cankered, or distorted, or inflated, yet retains those qualities which essentially divide it from all others; so that hemlock continues to be poison, and the violet does not cease to emit its odour in whatever soil it may grow.

We consider our own nature too superficially. We look on all that in ourselves with which we can discover a resemblance in others; and consider those resemblances as the materials of moral knowledge. It is in the differences that it actually consists.

A SYSTEM OF GOVERNMENT BY JURIES.

[This remarkable fragment was published by Medwin in *The Shelley Papers*, having previously appeared in *The Athenæum* for the 20th of April, 1833, with the remark, " We have considered it best to print this fragment as left by the poet, and to leave it to the reader's imagination to supply its imperfections." Like some others of *The Shelley Papers*, it was silently abandoned by Mrs. Shelley. We may perhaps infer, without any great stretch of imagination, that it is a portion of the substantive Treatise on Political Reform mentioned in the Preface to the *Essays* &c. (1840), page xviii, as "to be published when his works assume a complete shape."—H. B. F.]

A SYSTEM OF GOVERNMENT BY JURIES.

A FRAGMENT.

GOVERNMENT, as it now subsists, is perhaps an engine at once the most expensive and inartificial that could have been devised as a remedy for the imperfections of society. Immense masses of the product of labour are committed to the discretion of certain individuals for the purpose of executing its intentions, or interpreting its meaning. These have not been consumed, but wasted, in the principal part of the past history of political society.

Government may be distributed into two parts :— First, the fundamental—that is, the permanent forms, which regulate the deliberation or the action of the whole ; from which it results that a state is democratical, or aristocratical, or despotic, or a combination of all these principles.

And Secondly—the necessary or accidental—that is, those that determine, *not* the forms according to which the deliberation or the action of the mass of the community is to be regulated, but the opinions or moral

Y 2

principles which are to govern the particular instances
of such action or deliberation.   These may be called,
with little violence to the popular acceptation of those
terms, Constitution, and Law : understanding by the
former, the collection of those written institutions or
traditions which determine the individuals who are to
exercise, in a nation, the discretionary right of peace and
war, of death or imprisonment, fines and penalties, and
the imposition and collection of taxes, and their application, thus vested in a king, or an hereditary senate, or in
a representative assembly, or in a combination of all ; and
by the latter, the mode of determining those opinions,
according to which the constituted authorities are to
decide on any action ; for law is either a collection of
opinions expressed by individuals without constitutional
authority, or the decision of a constitutional body of men,
the opinion of some or all of whom it expresses—and no
more.

To the former, or constitutional topics, this treatise
has no direct reference.   Law may be considered, simply
—an opinion regulating political power.   It may be
divided into two parts—General Law, or that which
relates to the external and integral concerns of a nation,
and decides on the competency of a particular person or
collection of persons to discretion in matters of war and
peace—the assembling of the representative body—the
time, place, manner, form, of holding judicial courts, and
other concerns enumerated before, and in reference to
which this community is considered as a whole ;—and
Particular Law, or that which decides upon contested
claims of property, which punishes or restrains violence
and fraud, which enforces compacts, and preserves to every

man that degree of liberty and security, the enjoyment of which is judged not to be inconsistent with the liberty and security of another.

To the former, or what is here called general law, this treatise has no direct reference. How far law, in its general form or constitution, as it at present exists in the greater part of the nations of Europe, may be affected by inferences from the ensuing reasonings, it is foreign to the present purpose to inquire—let us confine our attention to particular law, or law strictly so termed.

The only defensible intention of law, like that of every other human institution, is very simple and clear—the good of the whole. If law is found to accomplish this object very imperfectly, that imperfection makes no part of the design with which men submit to its institution. Any reasonings which tend to throw light on a subject hitherto so dark and intricate, cannot fail, if distinctly stated, to impress mankind very deeply, because it is a question in which the life and property and liberty and reputation of every man are vitally involved.

For the sake of intelligible method, let us assume the ordinary distinctions of law, those of civil and criminal law, and of the objects of it, private and public wrongs. The author of these pages ought not to suppress his conviction, that the principles on which punishment is usually inflicted are essentially erroneous ; and that, in general, ten times more is apportioned to the victims of law, than is demanded by the welfare of society, under the shape of reformation or example. He believes that, although universally disowned, the execrable passion of

vengeance, exasperated by fear, exists as a chief source
among the secret causes of this exercise of criminal
justice.[1]   He believes also, that in questions of property,
there is a vague but most effective favouritism in courts
of law and among lawyers, against the poor to the advantage of the rich—against the tenant in favour of the
landlord—against the creditor in favour of the debtor[2];
thus enforcing and illustrating that celebrated maxim,
against which moral science is a perpetual effort : *To
whom much is given, of him shall much be required ; and
to whom men have committed much, of him they will ask
the more.*

But the present purpose is, not the exposure of such
mistakes as actually exist in public opinion, but an
attempt to give to public opinion its legitimate dominion,
and an uniform and unimpeded influence to each particular case which is its object.

When law is once understood to be no more than the
recorded opinion of men, no more than the apprehensions
of individuals on the reasoning of a particular case, we
may expect that the sanguinary or stupid mistakes which

---

[1] Compare these remarks with those in the fragment *On the Punishment of Death*, p. 252.

[2] This is the reading of *The Athenæum* and *The Shelley Papers*. It seems to me more than probable that the words *debtor* and *creditor* should change places, and that Medwin quoted the wrong text at the close of the paragraph. The text that might reasonably be expected in this place is, *For whoso-ever hath, to him shall be given, and he shall have more abundance; but whosoever hath not, from him shall be taken away even that he hath* (Matthew, xiii, 12).   That that text connected itself in Shelley's mind with this precise line of thought is clear from a passage in the *Defence of Poetry*. (See Vol. III, p. 132.)   It would be characteristic of Medwin, copying with difficulty from Shelley's rough notes, not only to have left the text for insertion at leisure, but also to have inserted the wrong one after all.

disgrace the civil and criminal jurisprudence of civilized nations will speedily disappear. How long, under its present sanctions, do not the most exploded violations of humanity maintain their ground in courts of law, after public opinion has branded them with reprobation ; sometimes even until by constantly maintaining their post under the shelter of venerable names, they out-weary the very scorn and abhorrence of mankind, or subsist unrepealed and silent, until some check, in the progress of human improvement, awakens them, and that public opinion, from which they should have received their reversal, is infected by their influence. Public opinion would never long stagnate in error, were it not fenced about and frozen over by forms and superstitions. If men were accustomed to reason, and to hear the arguments of others, upon each particular case that concerned the life, or liberty, or property, or reputation of their peers, those mistakes, which at present render these possessions so insecure to all but those who enjoy enormous wealth, never could subsist. If the administration of law ceased to appeal from the common sense, or the enlightened minds of twelve contemporary *good and true men*, who should be the peers of the accused, or, in cases of property, of the claimant, to the obscure records of dark and barbarous epochs, or the precedents of what venal and enslaved judges might have decreed to please their tyrants, or the opinion of any man or set of men who lived when bigotry was virtue, and passive obedience that discretion which is the better part of valour,—all those mistakes now fastened in the public opinion, would be brought at each new case to the . . . .

* * * * * *

FRAGMENT ON REFORM.[1]

THAT our country is on the point of submitting to
some momentous change in its internal government, is a
fact which few who observe and compare the
of human society will dispute. The distribution of wealth,
no less than the spirit by which it is upheld and that by
which it is assailed, render the event inevitable. Call it
reform or revolution, as you will, a change must take
place; one of the consequences of which will be, the
wresting of political power from those who are at present
the depositaries of it. A strong sentiment prevails[2] in the
nation at large, that they have been guilty of enormous
malversations of their trust. It is a commonplace of
political reformers to say, that it is the measures, not the
men, they abhor; and it is a general practice, so soon as
the party shall have gained the victory, to inflict the

---

[1] This fragment is from the *Relics of Shelley*. Mr. Garnett does
not assign it to any date; but it
has always connected itself in my
mind with the foregoing fragmentary essay from *The Shelley Papers*.
There seems to be nothing incompatible either in the style or in the
subject of the two fragments; and
this is probably the best place at
which to give the smaller one.

[2] This word was inserted conjecturally by Mr. Garnett.

severest punishments upon their predecessors, and to pursue measures not less selfish and pernicious than those, a protest against which was the ladder that conducted them to power. The people sympathize with the passions of their liberators, without reflecting that these in turn may become their tyrants, and without perceiving that the same motives and excitements to act or to feel can never, except by a perverse imitation, belong to both.

ON THE REVIVAL OF LITERATURE.

[Published in *The Athenæum* for the 24th of November, 1832, this composition was afterwards included in *The Shelley Papers*. Mrs. Shelley did not include it in the *Essays, Letters* &c., or make any remark on this particular item of the papers issued by Medwin, to enable us to judge of her reasons for abandoning it. Mr. Rossetti is probably right in assigning it (Poetical Works, 1878, Vol. I, page 150) to the year 1815.—H. B. F.]

ON THE REVIVAL OF LITERATURE.

In the fifteenth century of the Christian era, a new
and extraordinary event roused Europe from her lethargic
state, and paved the way to her present greatness. The
writings of Dante in the thirteenth, and of Petrarch in
the fourteenth, were the bright luminaries which had
afforded glimmerings of literary knowledge to the almost
benighted traveller toiling up the hill of Fame. But on
the taking of Constantinople, a new and sudden light
appeared: the dark clouds of ignorance rolled into distance, and Europe was inundated by learned monks, and
still more by the quantity of learned manuscripts which
they brought with them from the scene of devastation.
The Turks settled themselves in Constantinople, where
they adopted nothing but the vicious habits of the Greeks:
they neglected even the small remains of its ancient
learning, which, filtered and degenerated as it was by the
absurd mixture of Pagan and Christian philosophy, proved,
on its retirement to Europe, the spark which spread
gradually and successfully the light of knowledge over the
world.

Italy, France, and England,—for Germany still remained many centuries less civilized than the surrounding countries,—swarmed with monks and cloisters. Superstition, of whatever kind, whether earthly or divine, has hitherto been the weight which clogged man to earth, and prevented his genius from soaring aloft amid its native skies. The enterprises, and the effects of the human mind, are something more than stupendous : the works of nature are material and tangible : we have a half insight into their kind, and in many instances we predict their effects with certainty. But mind seems to govern the world without visible or substantial means. Its birth is unknown ; its action and influence unperceived ; and its being seems eternal. To the mind both humane and philosophical, there cannot exist a greater subject of grief, than the reflection of how much superstition has retarded the progress of intellect, and consequently the happiness of man.

The monks in their cloisters were engaged in trifling and ridiculous disputes : they contented themselves with teaching the dogmas of their religion, and rushed impatiently forth to the colleges and halls, where they disputed with an acrimony and meanness little befitting the resemblance of their pretended holiness. But the situation of a monk is a situation the most unnatural that bigotry, proud in the invention of cruelty, could conceive ; and their vices may be pardoned as resulting from the wills and devices of a few proud and selfish bishops, who enslaved the world that they might live at ease.

The disputes of the schools were mostly scholastical ; it was the discussion of words, and had no relation to

morality. Morality,—the great means and end of man,
—was contained, as they affirmed, in the extent of a few
hundred pages of a certain book, which others have since
contended were but scraps of martyrs' last dying words,
collected together and imposed on the world. In the
refinements of the scholastic philosophy, the world seemed
in danger of losing the little real wisdom that still
remained as her portion; and the only valuable part of
their disputes was such as tended to develope the system
of the Peripatetic Philosophers. Plato, the wisest, the
profoundest, and Epicurus, the most humane and gentle
among the ancients, were entirely neglected by them.
Plato interfered with their peculiar mode of thinking concerning heavenly matters; and Epicurus, maintaining the
rights of man to pleasure and happiness, would have
afforded a seducing contrast to their dark and miserable
code of morals. It has been asserted, that these holy
men solaced their lighter moments in a contraband worship of Epicurus, and profaned the philosophy which maintained the rights of all by a selfish indulgence of the rights
of a few. Thus it is: the laws of nature are invariable,
and man sets them aside that he may have the pleasure
of travelling through a labyrinth in search of them again.

Pleasure, in an open and innocent garb, by some strange
process of reasoning, is called vice; yet man (so closely
is he linked to the chains of necessity—so irresistibly is
he impelled to fulfil the end of his being,) must seek her
at whatever price: he becomes a hypocrite, and braves
damnation with all its pains.

Grecian literature,—the finest the world has ever produced,—was at length restored: its form and mode we

obtained from the manuscripts which the ravages of time, of the Goths, and of the still more savage Turks, had spared. The burning of the Library at Alexandria was an evil of importance. This library is said to have contained volumes of the choicest Greek authors.

ESSAY ON CHRISTIANITY.

[The *Essay on Christianity* was first given by Lady Shelley, in the *Shelley Memorials* (1859), where it is accompanied by the following note:—"The reader will observe some unfinished sentences in the course of this Essay; but it has been thought advisable to print it exactly as it was found, with the exception of a few conjectural words inserted between brackets." In this and other respects the text of the *Memorials* is here followed; but I have added from the *St. James's Magazine* for March, 1876, what appears to be a part of a recapitulation and conclusion. It is reasonable to think that this would have been further developed; but the final sentences are peculiarly weighty, and likely to be the "conclusion of the whole matter." Mr. Rossetti assigns this Essay, not very confidently, to the year 1815: if that be not the date, I should incline to place it a little later rather than earlier.—H. B. F.]

ESSAY ON CHRISTIANITY.

THE Being who has influenced in the most memorable manner the opinions and the fortunes of the human species, is Jesus Christ. At this day, his name is connected with the devotional feelings of two hundred millions of the race of man. The institutions of the most civilized portions of the globe derive their authority from the sanction of his doctrines; he is the hero, the God, of our popular religion. His extraordinary genius, the wide and rapid effect of his unexampled doctrines, his invincible gentleness and benignity, the devoted love borne to him by his adherents, suggested a persuasion to them that he was something divine. The supernatural events which the historians of this wonderful man subsequently asserted to have been connected with every gradation of his career, established the opinion.

His death is said to have been accompanied by an accumulation of tremendous prodigies. Utter darkness fell upon the earth, blotting the noonday sun; dead bodies, arising from their graves, walked through the public streets, and an earthquake shook the astonished

city, rending the rocks of the surrounding mountains.
The philosopher may attribute the application of these
events to the death of a reformer, or the events
themselves to a visitation of that universal Pan who——

*   *   *   *   *

The thoughts which the word "God" suggests to the
human mind are susceptible of as many variations as
human minds themselves. The Stoic, the Platonist, and
the Epicurean, the Polytheist, the Dualist, and the
Trinitarian, differ infinitely in their conceptions of its
meaning. They agree only in considering it the most
awful and most venerable of names, as a common term
devised to express all of mystery, or majesty, or power,
which the invisible world contains. And not only has
every sect distinct conceptions of the application of this
name, but scarcely two individuals of the same sect, who
exercise in any degree the freedom of their judgment, or
yield themselves with any candour of feeling to the
influences of the visible world, find perfect coincidence of
opinion to exist between them. It is [interesting] to
inquire in what acceptation Jesus Christ employed this
term.

We may conceive his mind to have been predisposed
on this subject to adopt the opinions of his countrymen.
Every human being is indebted for a multitude of his
sentiments to the religion of his early years. Jesus
Christ probably [studied] the historians of his country
with the ardour of a spirit seeking after truth. They
were undoubtedly the companions of his childish years,
the food and nutriment and materials of his youthful
meditations. The Sublime dramatic poem entitled *Job*
had familiarized his imagination with the boldest imagery

afforded by the human mind and the material world. *Ecclesiastes* had diffused a seriousness and solemnity over the frame of his spirit, glowing with youthful hope, and [had] made audible to his listening heart

> " The still, sad music of humanity,
> Not harsh or grating, but of ample power
> To chasten and subdue."

He had contemplated this name as having been profanely perverted to the sanctioning of the most enormous and abominable crimes. We can distinctly trace, in the tissue of his doctrines, the persuasion that God is some universal Being, differing from man and the mind of man. According to Jesus Christ, God is neither the Jupiter, who sends rain upon the earth; nor the Venus, through whom all living things are produced; nor the Vulcan, who presides over the terrestrial element of fire; nor the Vesta, that preserves the light which is enshrined in the sun and moon and stars. He is neither the Proteus nor the Pan of the material world. But the word God, according to the acceptation of Jesus Christ, unites all the attributes which these denominations contain, and is the [interpoint] and over-ruling Spirit of all the energy and wisdom included within the circle of existing things. It is important to observe that the author of the Christian system had a conception widely differing from the gross imaginations of the vulgar relatively to the ruling Power of the universe. He everywhere represents this Power as something mysteriously and illimitably pervading the frame of things. Nor do his doctrines practically assume any proposition which they theoretically deny. They do not represent God as a limitless and inconceivable mystery;

affirming, at the same time, his existence as a Being subject to passion and capable——

*　　　　*　　　　*　　　　*　　　　*

"Blessed are the pure in heart, for they shall see God." Blessed are those who have preserved internal sanctity of soul; who are conscious of no secret deceit; who are the same in act as they are in desire; who conceal no thought, no tendencies of thought, from their own conscience; who are faithful and sincere witnesses, before the tribunal of their own judgments, of all that passes within their mind. Such as these shall see God. What! after death, shall their awakened eyes behold the King of Heaven? Shall they stand in awe before the golden throne on which he sits, and gaze upon the venerable countenance of the paternal Monarch? Is this the reward of the virtuous and the pure? These are the idle dreams of the visionary, or the pernicious representations of impostors, who have fabricated from the very materials of wisdom a cloak for their own dwarfish or imbecile conceptions.

Jesus Christ has said no more than the most excellent philosophers have felt and expressed—that virtue is its own reward. It is true that such an expression as he has used was prompted by the energy of genius, and was the overflowing enthusiasm of a poet; but it is not the less literally true [because] clearly repugnant to the mistaken conceptions of the multitude. God, it has been asserted, was contemplated by Jesus Christ as every poet and every philosopher must have contemplated that mysterious principle. He considered that venerable word to express the overruling Spirit of the collective energy of the moral and material world. He affirms, therefore, no more than that a simple, sincere mind is the indispensable requisite of true science and true happiness. He affirms that a being of pure and gentle habits will not fail, in every thought, in every object of every thought, to be aware of benignant visitings from the invisible energies by which he is surrounded.

Whosoever is free from the contamination of luxury and licence, may go forth to the fields and to the woods, inhaling joyous renovation from the breath of Spring, or catching from the odours and sounds of Autumn some diviner mood of sweetest sadness, which improves the softened heart. Whosoever is no deceiver or destroyer of his fellow men—no liar, no flatterer, no murderer— may walk among his species, deriving, from the communion with all which they contain of beautiful or of majestic, some intercourse with the Universal God. Whosoever has maintained with his own heart the strictest correspondence of confidence, who dares to examine and to estimate every imagination which suggests itself to his mind—whosoever is that which he designs to become, and only aspires to that which the divinity of his own nature shall consider and approve—he has already seen God.

We live and move and think; but we are not the creators of our own origin and existence. We are not the arbiters of every motion of our own complicated nature; we are not the masters of our own imaginations and moods of mental being. There is a Power by which we are surrounded, like the atmosphere in which some

motionless lyre is suspended, which visits with its breath
our silent chords at will.

Our most imperial and stupendous qualities—those
on which the majesty and the power of humanity is
erected—are, relatively to the inferior portion of its
mechanism, active and imperial; but they are the passive slaves of some higher and more omnipotent Power.
This Power is God; and those who have seen God have,
in the period of their purer and more perfect nature,
been harmonized by their own will to so exquisite [a]
consentaneity of power as to give forth divinest melody,
when the breath of universal being sweeps over their
frame.　That those who are pure in heart shall see God,
and that virtue is its own reward, may be considered as
equivalent assertions.　The former of these propositions
is a metaphorical repetition of the latter.　The advocates
of literal interpretation have been the most efficacious
enemies of those doctrines whose nature they profess to
venerate.　Thucydides, in particular, affords a number of
instances calculated———[1]

　　　※　　　　※　　　　※　　　　※　　　　※

[1] It seems likely that it was
a part of the scheme of this Essay
to examine and illustrate the Bea-
titudes *seriatim*. The passage now
printed as the conclusion of the
Essay occupies a page and a half
of a sheet of foolscap paper: on
the other leaf of the sheet, and not
continuously with the rest, are
written and cancelled the following
passages :—

"I, the Redeemer of mankind;
I who dare to.....

Lament no more ye meek and
gentle beings: bear on against the
oppressions of the hard and un-

feeling world—with resolute and
tranquil mind; for in the calmness
of your own spirit shall be your
reward, and the.....

Blessed are the poor in Spirit for
theirs is the Kingdom of Heaven.
—Neither.....

Know in what manner to estimate the bearing of....."

These notes are followed, in the
same page, by the beautiful fragment of a translation of Moschus's
Elegy on the Death of Bion, given
in Vol. IV, p. 235, of the Poetical
Works.

Tacitus says, that the Jews held God to be something eternal and supreme, neither subject to change nor to decay; therefore, they permit no statues in their cities or their temples. The universal Being can only be described or defined by negatives which deny his subjection to the laws of all inferior existences. Where indefiniteness ends, idolatry and anthropomorphism begin. God is, as Lucan has expressed,

> " Quodcunque vides, quodcunque moveris,
>   Et cœlum et virtus."

The doctrine of what some fanatics have termed "a peculiar Providence"—that is, of some power beyond and superior to that which ordinarily guides the operations of the Universe, interfering to punish the vicious and reward the virtuous—is explicitly denied by Jesus Christ. The absurd and execrable doctrine of vengeance, in *all its shapes,* seems to have been contemplated by this great moralist with the profoundest disapprobation; nor would he permit the most venerable of names to be perverted into a sanction for the meanest and most contemptible propensities incident to the nature of man. " Love your enemies, bless those who curse you, that ye may be the sons of your Heavenly Father, who makes the sun to shine on the good and on the evil, and the rain to fall on the just and unjust." How monstrous a calumny have not impostors dared to advance against the mild and gentle author of this just sentiment, and against the whole tenor of his doctrines and his life, overflowing with benevolence and forbearance and compassion! They have represented him asserting that the Omnipotent God —that merciful and benignant Power who scatters equally upon the beautiful earth all the elements of security and happiness—whose influences are distributed to all whose natures admit of a participation in them—who sends to the weak and vicious creatures of his will all the benefits which they are capable of sharing—that this God has devised a scheme whereby the body shall live after its apparent dissolution, and be rendered capable of indefinite torture. He is said to have compared the agonies which the vicious shall then endure to the excruciations of a living body bound among the flames, and being consumed sinew by sinew, and bone by bone.

And this is to be done, not because it is supposed (and the supposition would be sufficiently detestable) that the moral nature of the sufferer would be improved by his tortures—it is done because it *is just* to be done. My neighbour, or my servant, or my child, has done me an injury, and it is just that he should suffer an injury in return. Such is the doctrine which Jesus Christ summoned his whole resources of persuasion to oppose. " Love your enemy, bless those who curse you :" such, he says, is the practice of God, and such must ye imitate if ye would be the children of God.

Jesus Christ would hardly have cited, as an example of all that is gentle and beneficent and compassionate, a Being who shall deliberately scheme to inflict on a large portion of the human race tortures indescribably intense and indefinitely protracted; who shall inflict them, too, without any mistake as to the true nature of pain—without any view to future good—merely because it is just.

This, and no other, is justice :—to consider, under all

the circumstances and consequences of a particular case, how the greatest quantity and purest quality of happiness will ensue from any action ; [this] is to be just, and there is no other justice. The distinction between justice and mercy was first imagined in the courts of tyrants. Mankind receive every relaxation of their tyranny as a circumstance of grace or favour.

Such was the clemency of Julius Cæsar, who, having achieved by a series of treachery and bloodshed the ruin of the liberties of his country, receives the fame of mercy because, possessing the power to slay the noblest men of Rome, he restrained his sanguinary soul, arrogating to himself as a merit an abstinence from actions which if he had committed, he would only have added one other atrocity to his deeds. His assassins understood justice better. They saw the most virtuous and civilized community of mankind under the insolent dominion of one wicked man ; and they murdered him. They destroyed the usurper of the liberties of their countrymen, not because they hated him, not because they would revenge the wrongs which they had sustained (Brutus, it is said, was his most familiar friend ; most of the conspirators were habituated to domestic intercourse with the man whom they destroyed) : it was in affection, inextinguishable love for all that is venerable and dear to the human heart, in the names of Country, Liberty, and Virtue ; it was in a serious and solemn and reluctant mood, that these holy patriots murdered their father and their friend. They would have spared his violent death, if he could have deposited the rights which he had assumed. His own selfish and narrow nature necessitated the sacrifices they made. They required that he should change all those habits which debauchery and bloodshed had twined around the fibres of his inmost frame of thought; that he should participate with them and with his country those privileges which, having corrupted by assuming to himself, he would no longer value. They would have sacrificed their lives if they could have made him worthy of the sacrifice. Such are the feelings which Jesus Christ asserts to belong to the ruling Power of the world. He desireth not the death of a sinner; he makes the sun to shine upon the just and unjust.

The nature of a narrow and malevolent spirit is so essentially incompatible with happiness as to render it inaccessible to the influences of the benignant God. All that his own perverse propensities will permit him to receive, that God abundantly pours forth upon him. If there is the slightest overbalance of happiness, which can be allotted to the most atrocious offender, consistently with the nature of things, that is rigidly made his portion by the ever-watchful Power of God. In every case, the human mind enjoys the utmost pleasure which it is capable of enjoying. God is represented by Jesus Christ as the Power from which, and through which, the streams of all that is excellent and delightful flow; the Power which models, as they pass, all the elements of this mixed universe to the purest and most perfect shape which it belongs to their nature to assume. Jesus Christ attributes to this Power the faculty of Will. How far such a doctrine, in its ordinary sense, may be philosophically true, or how far Jesus Christ intentionally availed himself of a metaphor easily understood, is foreign to the subject to consider. This much is certain,

that Jesus Christ represents God as the fountain of all
goodness, the eternal enemy of pain and evil, the uniform and unchanging motive of the salutary operations
of the material world. The supposition that this cause
is excited to action by some principle analogous to the
human will, adds weight to the persuasion that it is
foreign to its beneficent nature to inflict the slightest
pain. According to Jesus Christ, and according to the
indisputable facts of the case, some evil spirit has dominion in this imperfect world. But there will come a
time when the human mind shall be visited exclusively
by the influences of the benignant Power. Men shall
die, and their bodies shall rot under the ground; all the
organs through which their knowledge and their feelings
have flowed, or in which they have originated, shall
assume other forms, and become ministrant to purposes
the most foreign from their former tendencies. There
is a time when we shall neither be heard or be seen by
the multitude of beings like ourselves by whom we have
been so long surrounded. They shall go to graves;
where then?

It appears that we moulder to a heap of senseless
dust; to a few worms, that arise and perish, like ourselves. Jesus Christ asserts that these appearances are
fallacious, and that a gloomy and cold imagination alone
suggests the conception that thought can cease to be.
Another and a more extensive state of being, rather than
the complete extinction of being, will follow from that
mysterious change which we call Death. There shall
be no misery, no pain, no fear. The empire of evil
spirits extends not beyond the boundaries of the grave.
The unobscured irradiations from the fountain-fire of all

goodness shall reveal all that is mysterious and unintelligible, until the mutual communications of knowledge and of happiness throughout all thinking natures, constitute a harmony of good that ever varies and never ends.

This is Heaven, when pain and evil cease, and when the Benignant Principle, untrammelled and uncontrolled, visits in the fulness of its power the universal frame of things. Human life, with all its unreal ills and transitory hopes, is as a dream, which departs before the dawn, leaving no trace of its evanescent hues. All that it contains of pure or of divine visits the passive mind in some serenest mood. Most holy are the feelings through which our fellow beings are rendered dear and [venerable] to the heart. The remembrance of their sweetness, and the completion of the hopes which they [excite], constitute, when we awaken from the sleep of life, the fulfilment of the prophecies of its most majestic and beautiful visions.

We die, says Jesus Christ; and, when we awaken from the languor of disease, the glories and the happiness of Paradise are around us. All evil and pain have ceased for ever. Our happiness also corresponds with, and is adapted to, the nature of what is most excellent in our being. We see God, and we see that he is good. How delightful a picture, even if it be not true! How magnificent is the conception which this bold theory suggests to the contemplation, even if it be no more than the imagination of some sublimest and most holy poet, who, impressed with the loveliness and majesty of his own nature, is impatient and discontented with the narrow limits which this imperfect life and the dark grave have assigned for ever as his melancholy portion. It is not to be believed that Hell, or punishment, was the conception of this daring mind. It is not to be believed that the most prominent group of this picture, which is framed so heart-moving and lovely—the accomplishment of all human hope, the extinction of all morbid fear and anguish—would consist of millions of sensitive beings enduring, in every variety of torture which Omniscient vengeance could invent, immortal agony.

Jesus Christ opposed with earnest eloquence the panic fears and hateful superstitions which have enslaved mankind for ages. Nations had risen against nations, employing the subtlest devices of mechanism and mind to waste, and excruciate, and overthrow. The great community of mankind had been subdivided into ten thousand communities, each organized for the ruin of the other. Wheel within wheel, the vast machine was instinct with the restless spirit of desolation. Pain had been inflicted; therefore, pain should be inflicted in return. Retaliation of injuries is the only remedy which can be applied to violence, because it teaches the injurer the true nature of his own conduct, and operates as a warning against its repetition. Nor must the same measure of calamity be returned as was received. If a man borrows a certain sum from me, he is bound to repay that sum. Shall no more be required of the enemy who destroys my reputation, or ravages my fields? It is just that he should suffer ten times the loss which he has inflicted, that the legitimate consequences of his deed may never be obliterated from his remembrance, and that others may clearly discern and feel the danger of invading the peace of human society. Such reasonings,

and the impetuous feelings arising from them, have armed
nation against nation, family against family, man against
man.

An Athenian soldier, in the Ionian army which had
assembled for the purpose of vindicating the liberty
of the Asiatic Greeks, accidentally set fire to Sardis.
The city, being composed of combustible materials, was
burned to the ground.   The Persians believed that this
circumstance of aggression made it their duty to retaliate
on Athens.   They assembled successive expeditions on
the most extensive scale.   Every nation of the East
was united to ruin the Grecian States.   Athens was
burned to the ground, the whole territory laid waste,
and every living thing which it contained [destroyed].
After suffering and inflicting incalculable mischiefs, they
desisted from their purpose only when they became
impotent to effect it.   The desire of revenge for the
aggression of Persia outlived, among the Greeks, that
love of liberty which had been their most glorious distinction among the nations of mankind; and Alexander
became the instrument of its completion.   The mischiefs
attendant on this consummation of fruitless ruin are
too manifold and too tremendous to be related.   If all
the thought which had been expended on the construction of engines of agony and death—the modes of
aggression and defence, the raising of armies, and the
acquirement of those arts of tyranny and falsehood
without which mixed multitudes could neither be led
nor governed—had been employed to promote the true
welfare and extend the real empire of man, how different
would have been the present situation of human society!
how different the state of knowledge in physical and

moral science, upon which the power and happiness of mankind essentially depend! What nation has the example of the desolation of Attica by Mardonius and Xerxes, or the extinction of the Persian empire by Alexander of Macedon, restrained from outrage? Was not the pretext of this latter system of spoliation derived immediately from the former? Had revenge in this instance any other effect than to increase, instead of diminishing, the mass of malice and evil already existing in the world?

The emptiness and folly of retaliation are apparent from every example which can be brought forward. Not only Jesus Christ, but the most eminent professors of every sect of philosophy, have reasoned against this futile superstition. Legislation is, in one point of view, to be considered as an attempt to provide against the excesses of this deplorable mistake. It professes to assign the penalty of all private injuries, and denies to individuals the right of vindicating their proper cause. This end is certainly not attained without some accommodation to the propensities which it desires to destroy. Still, it recognizes no principle but the production of the greatest eventual good with the least immediate injury; and regards the torture, or the death, of any human being as unjust, of whatever mischief he may have been the author, so that the result shall not more than compensate for the immediate pain.

Mankind, transmitting from generation to generation the legacy of accumulated vengeances, and pursuing with the feelings of duty the misery of their fellow-beings, have not failed to attribute to the Universal

Cause a character analogous with their own. The image of this invisible, mysterious Being is more or less excellent and perfect—resembles more or less its original—in proportion to the perfection of the mind on which it is impressed. Thus, that nation which has arrived at the highest step in the scale of moral progression will believe most purely in that God, the knowledge of whose real attributes is considered as the firmest basis of the true religion. The reason of the belief of each individual, also, will be so far regulated by his conceptions of what is good. Thus, the conceptions which any nation or individual entertains of the God of its popular worship may be inferred from their own actions and opinions, which are the subjects of their approbation among their fellow-men. Jesus Christ instructed his disciples to be perfect, as their Father in Heaven is perfect, declaring at the same time his belief that human perfection requires the refraining from revenge and retribution in any of its various shapes.

The perfection of the human and the divine character is thus asserted to be the same. Man, by resembling God, fulfils most accurately the tendencies of his nature; and God comprehends within himself all that constitutes human perfection. Thus, God is a model through which the excellence of man is to be estimated, whilst the *abstract* perfection of the human character is the type of the *actual* perfection of the divine. It is not to be believed that a person of such comprehensive views as Jesus Christ could have fallen into so manifest a contradiction as to assert that men would be tortured after death by that Being whose character is held up as a model to human kind, because he is incapable of malevolence and revenge. All the arguments which have been brought forward to justify retribution fail, when retribution is destined neither to operate as an example to other agents, nor to the offender himself. How feeble such reasoning is to be considered, has been already shewn; but it is the character of an evil Dæmon to consign the beings whom he has endowed with sensation to unprofitable anguish. The peculiar circumstances attendant on the conception of God casting sinners to burn in Hell for ever, combine to render that conception the most perfect specimen of the greatest imaginable crime. Jesus Christ represented God as the principle of all good, the source of all happiness, the wise and benevolent Creator and Preserver of all living things. But the interpreters of his doctrines have confounded the good and the evil principle. They observed the emanations of their universal natures to be inextricably entangled in the world, and, trembling before the power of the cause of all things, addressed to it such flattery as is acceptable to the ministers of human tyranny, attributing love and wisdom to those energies which they felt to be exerted indifferently for the purposes of benefit and calamity.

Jesus Christ expressly asserts that distinction between the good and evil principle which it has been the practice of all theologians to confound. How far his doctrines, or their interpretation, may be true, it would scarcely have been worth while to inquire, if the one did not afford an example and an incentive to the attainment of true virtue, whilst the other holds out a sanction and apology for every species of mean and cruel vice.

It cannot be precisely ascertained in what degree
Jesus Christ accommodated his doctrines to the opinions
of his auditors ; or in what degree he really said all
that he is related to have said. He has left no written
record of himself, and we are compelled to judge from
the imperfect and obscure information which his biographers (persons certainly of very undisciplined and
undiscriminating minds) have transmitted to posterity.
These writers (our only guides) impute sentiments to
Jesus Christ which flatly contradict each other. They
represent him as narrow, superstitious, and exquisitely
vindictive and malicious. They insert, in the midst
of a strain of impassioned eloquence or sagest exhort-
ation, a sentiment only remarkable for its naked and
drivelling folly. But it is not difficult to distinguish
the inventions by which these historians have filled up
the interstices of tradition, or corrupted the simplicity
of truth, from the real character of their rude amaze-
ment. They have left sufficiently clear indications of
the genuine character of Jesus Christ to rescue it for
ever from the imputations cast upon it by their ignorance
and fanaticism. We discover that he is the enemy of
oppression and of falsehood ; that he is the advocate
of equal justice ; that he is neither disposed to sanction
bloodshed nor deceit, under whatsoever pretences their
practice may be vindicated. We discover that he was
a man of meek and majestic demeanour, calm in danger;
of natural and simple thought and habits ; beloved to
adoration by his adherents ; unmoved, solemn, and
severe.

It is utterly incredible that this man said, that if you
hate your enemy you would find it to your account to

return him good for evil, since, by such a temporary
oblivion of vengeance, you would heap coals of fire on
his head. Where such contradictions occur, a favourable construction is warranted by the general innocence
of manners and comprehensiveness of views which he is
represented to possess. The rule of criticism to be
adopted in judging of the life, actions, and words of a
man who has acted any conspicuous part in the revolutions of the world, should not be narrow. We ought to
form a general image of his character and of his doctrines, and refer to this whole the distinct portions of
action and speech by which they are diversified. It is
not here asserted that no contradictions are to be admitted to have taken place in the system of Jesus Christ,
between doctrines promulgated in different states of
feeling or information, or even such as are implied in the
enunciation of a scheme of thought, various and obscure
through its immensity and depth. It is not asserted
that no degree of human indignation ever hurried him
beyond the limits which his calmer mood had placed to
disapprobation against vice and folly. Those deviations
from the history of his life are alone to be vindicated
which represent his own essential character in contradiction with itself.

Every human mind has what Bacon calls its " *idola
specûs* "—peculiar images which reside in the inner cave
of thought. These constitute the essential and distinctive
character of every human being; to which every action
and every word have intimate relation ; and by which,
in depicting a character, the genuineness and meaning of
these words and actions are to be determined. Every
fanatic or enemy of virtue is not at liberty to misrepre-

sent the greatest geniuses and most heroic defenders of all that is valuable in this mortal world. History, to gain any credit, must contain some truth, and that truth shall thus be made a sufficient indication of prejudice and deceit.

With respect to the miracles which these biographers have related, I have already declined to enter into any discussion on their nature or their existence. The supposition of their falsehood or their truth would modify in no degree the hues of the picture which is attempted to be delineated. To judge truly of the moral and philosophical character of Socrates, it is not necessary to determine the question of the familiar Spirit which [it] is supposed that he believed to attend on him.[1] The power of the human mind, relatively to intercourse with or dominion over the invisible world, is doubtless an interesting theme of discussion; but the connexion of the instance of Jesus Christ with the established religion of the country in which I write, renders it dangerous to subject oneself to the imputation of introducing new Gods or abolishing old ones ; nor is the duty of mutual forbearance sufficiently understood to render it certain that the metaphysician and the moralist, even though he carefully sacrifice a cock to Æsculapius, may not receive something analogous to the bowl of hemlock for the reward of his labours. Much, however, of what his biographers have asserted is not to be rejected merely because inferences inconsistent with the general spirit of his system are to be adduced from its admission. Jesus Christ did what every other reformer who has produced any considerable effect upon the world has done. He accommodated his doctrines to the preposses-

[1] See Note on this subject, Vol. III, p. 312.

sions of those whom he addressed. He used a language
for this view sufficiently familiar to our comprehensions.
He said,—However new or strange my doctrines may
appear to you, they are in fact only the restoration and
re-establishment of those original institutions and ancient
customs of your own law and religion. The constitu-
tions of your faith and policy, although perfect in their
origin, have become corrupt and altered, and have fallen
into decay. I profess to restore them to their pristine
authority and splendour. "Think not that I am come
to destroy the Law and the Prophets. I am come not to
destroy, but to fulfil. Till heaven and earth pass away,
one jot or one tittle shall in nowise pass away from the
Law, till all be fulfilled." Thus, like a skilful orator
(see Cicero, *De Oratore*), he secures the prejudices of
his auditors, and induces them, by his professions of
sympathy with their feelings, to enter with a willing
mind into the exposition of his own. The art of persuasion differs from that of reasoning; and it is of no
small moment, to the success even of a true cause, that
the judges who are to determine on its merits should be
free from those national and religious predilections which
render the multitude both deaf and blind.

Let not this practice be considered as an unworthy
artifice. It were best for the cause of reason that mankind should acknowledge no authority but its own; but
it is useful, to a certain extent, that they should not consider those institutions which they have been habituated
to reverence as opposing an obstacle to its admission.
All reformers have been compelled to practise this mis-
representation of their own true feelings and opinions.
It is deeply to be lamented that a word should ever issue

from human lips which contains the minutest alloy of
dissimulation, or simulation, or hypocrisy, or exaggeration, or anything but the precise and rigid image which
is present to the mind, and which ought to dictate the
expression. But the practice of utter sincerity towards
other men would avail to no good end, if they were incapable of practising it towards their own minds. In
fact, truth cannot be communicated until it is perceived.
The interests, therefore, of truth require that an orator
should, as far as possible, produce in his hearers that
state of mind on which alone his exhortations could
fairly be contemplated and examined.

Having produced this favourable disposition of mind,
Jesus Christ proceeds to qualify, and finally to abrogate,
the system of the Jewish law. He descants upon its
insufficiency as a code of moral conduct, which it professed to be, and absolutely selects the law of retaliation
as an instance of the absurdity and immorality of its
institutions. The conclusion of the speech is in a strain
of the most daring and most impassioned speculation.
He seems emboldened by the success of his exculpation
to the multitude, to declare in public the utmost singularity of his faith. He tramples upon all received
opinions, on all the cherished luxuries and superstitions
of mankind. He bids them cast aside the chains of
custom and blind faith by which they have been encompassed from the very cradle of their being, and
receive the imitator and minister of the Universal God.

EQUALITY OF MANKIND.

"The spirit of the Lord is upon me, because he hath
chosen me to preach the gospel to the poor: he hath

sent me to heal the broken-hearted, to preach deliverance
to the captives and recovering of sight to the blind, and
to set at liberty them that are bruised." (Luke, Ch. IV.
v. 18.) This is an enunciation of all that Plato and
Diogenes have speculated upon the equality of mankind.
They saw that the great majority of the human species
were reduced to the situation of squalid ignorance and
moral imbecility, for the purpose of purveying for the
luxury of a few, and contributing to the satisfaction of
their thirst for power. Too mean-spirited and too feeble
in resolve to attempt the conquest of their own evil
passions, and of the difficulties of the material world,
men sought dominion over their fellow-men, as an easy
method to gain that apparent majesty and power which
the instinct of their nature requires. Plato wrote the
scheme of a republic, in which law should watch over
the equal distribution of the external instruments of
unequal power—honours, property, &c. Diogenes devised a nobler and a more worthy system of opposition
to the system of the slave and tyrant. He said: " It
is in the power of each individual to level the inequality
which is the topic of the complaint of mankind. Let
him be aware of his own worth, and the station which
he occupies in the scale of moral beings. Diamonds
and gold, palaces and sceptres, derive their value from
the opinion of mankind. The only sumptuary law
which can be imposed on the use and fabrication of
these instruments of mischief and deceit, these symbols
of successful injustice, is the law of opinion. Every
man possesses the power, in this respect, to legislate for
himself. Let him be well aware of his own worth and
moral dignity. Let him yield in meek reverence to any
wiser or worthier than he, so long as he accords no venera-

tion to the splendour of his apparel, the luxury of his
food, the multitude of his flatterers and slaves.   It is
because, mankind, ye value and seek the empty pageantry
of wealth and social power, that ye are enslaved to its
possessions.   Decrease your physical wants ; learn to live,
so far as nourishment and shelter are concerned, like the
beast of the forest and the birds of the air ; ye will need
not to complain, that other individuals of your species
are surrounded by the diseases of luxury and the vices of
subserviency and oppression."   With all those who are
truly wise, there will be an entire community, not only
of thoughts and feelings, but also of external possessions.
Insomuch, therefore, as ye live [wisely], ye may enjoy the
community of whatsoever benefits arise from the inventions of civilized life.—They are of value only for
purposes of mental power ; they are of value only as
they are capable of being shared and applied to the
common advantage of philosophy ; and, if there be no
love among men, whatever institutions they may frame
must be subservient to the same purpose—to the continuance of inequality.   If there be no love among men,
it is best that he who sees through the hollowness of
their professions should fly from their society, and suffice
to his own soul.   In wisdom, he will thus lose nothing ;
in power, he will gain everything.   In proportion to the
love existing among men, so will be the community of
property and power.   Among true and real friends, all is
common ; and, were ignorance and envy and superstition
banished from the world, all mankind would be friends.
The only perfect and genuine republic is that which comprehends every living being.   Those distinctions which
have been artificially set up, of nations, societies, families,
and religions, are only general names, expressing the ab-

horrence and contempt with which men blindly consider
their fellowmen. I love my country; I love the city in
which I was born, my parents, my wife, and the children
of my care; and to this city, this woman, and this
nation, it is incumbent on me to do all the benefit in my
power. To what do these distinctions point, but to an
evident denial of the duty which humanity imposes on
you, of doing every possible good to every individual, under
whatever denomination he may be comprehended, to whom
you have the power of doing it? You ought to love all
mankind; nay, every individual of mankind. You ought
not to love the individuals of your domestic circles less,
but to love those who exist beyond it more. Once make
the feelings of confidence and of affection universal, and
the distinctions of property and power will vanish; nor
are they to be abolished without substituting something
equivalent in mischief to them, until all mankind shall
acknowledge an entire community of rights.

But, as the shades of night are dispelled by the
faintest glimmerings of dawn, so shall the minutest progress of the benevolent feelings disperse, in some degree,
the gloom of tyranny, and [curb the] ministers of mutual
suspicion and abhorrence. Your physical wants are few,
whilst those of your mind and heart cannot be numbered
or described, from their multitude and complication. To
secure the gratification of the former, you have made
yourselves the bond-slaves of each other.

They have cultivated these meaner wants to so great
an excess as to judge nothing so valuable or desirable
[as] what relates to their gratification. Hence has arisen
a system of passions which loses sight of the end they

were originally awakened to attain. Fame, power, and gold, are loved for their own sakes—are worshipped with a blind, habitual idolatry. The pageantry of empire, and the fame of irresistible might, are contemplated by the possessor with unmeaning complacency, without a retrospect to the properties which first made him consider them of value. It is from the cultivation of the most contemptible properties of human nature that discord and torpor and indifference, by which the moral universe is disordered, essentially depend. So long as these are the ties by which human society is connected, let it not be admitted that they are fragile.

Before man can be free, and equal, and truly wise, he must cast aside the chains of habit and superstition; he must strip sensuality of its pomp, and selfishness of its excuses, and contemplate actions and objects as they really are. He will discover the wisdom of universal love; he will feel the meanness and the injustice of sacrificing the reason and the liberty of his fellow-men to the indulgence of his physical appetites, and becoming a party to their degradation by the consummation of his own.

Such, with those differences only incidental to the age and state of society in which they were promulgated, appear to have been the doctrines of Jesus Christ. It is not too much to assert that they have been the doctrines of every just and compassionate mind that ever speculated on the social nature of man. The dogma of the equality of mankind has been advocated, with various success, in different ages of the world. It was imperfectly understood, but a kind of instinct in its favour

influenced considerably the practice of ancient Greece
and Rome. Attempts to establish usages founded on
this dogma have been made in modern Europe, in several
instances, since the revival of literature and the arts.
Rousseau has vindicated this opinion with all the eloquence of sincere and earnest faith; and is, perhaps, the
philosopher among the moderns who, in the structure of
his feelings and understanding, resembles most nearly
the mysterious sage of Judea. It is impossible to read
those passionate words in which Jesus Christ upbraids
the pusillanimity and sensuality of mankind, without
being strongly reminded of the more connected and
systematic enthusiasm of Rousseau. "No man," says
Jesus Christ, "can serve two masters. Take, therefore,
no thought for to-morrow, for the morrow shall take
thought for the things of itself. Sufficient unto the day
is the evil thereof." If we would profit by the wisdom
of a sublime and poetical mind, we must beware of the
vulgar error of interpreting literally every expression it
employs. Nothing can well be more remote from truth
than the literal and strict construction of such expressions as Jesus Christ delivers, or than [to imagine that]
it were best for man that he should abandon all his
acquirements in physical and intellectual science, and
depend on the spontaneous productions of nature for
his subsistence. Nothing is more obviously false than
that the remedy for the inequality among men consists
in their return to the condition of savages and beasts.
Philosophy will never be understood if we approach the
study of its mysteries with so narrow and illiberal conceptions of its universality. Rousseau certainly did not
mean to persuade the immense population of his country
to abandon all the arts of life, destroy their habitations

and their temples, and become the inhabitants of the
woods. He addressed the most enlightened of his com-
patriots, and endeavoured to persuade them to set the
example of a pure and simple life, by placing in the
strongest point of view his conceptions of the calamitous
and diseased aspect which, overgrown as it is with the
vices of sensuality and selfishness, is exhibited by civilized society. Nor can it be believed that Jesus Christ
endeavoured to prevail on the inhabitants of Jerusalem
neither to till their fields, nor to frame a shelter against
the sky, nor to provide food for the morrow. He simply
exposes, with the passionate rhetoric of enthusiastic love
towards all human beings, the miseries and mischiefs of
that system which makes all things subservient to the
subsistence of the material frame of man. He warns
them that no man can serve two masters—God and
Mammon; that it is impossible at once to be high-
minded and just and wise, and to comply with the
accustomed forms of human society, seek power, wealth,
or empire, either from the idolatry of habit, or as the
direct instruments of sensual gratification. He instructs
them that clothing and food and shelter are not, as they
suppose, the true end of human life, but only certain
means, to be valued in proportion to their subserviency
to that end. These means it is the right of every human
being to possess, and that in the same degree. In this
respect, the fowls of the air and the lilies of the field are
examples for the imitation of mankind. They are
clothed and fed by the Universal God. Permit, therefore, the Spirit of this benignant Principle to visit your
intellectual frame, or, in other words, become just and
pure. When you understand the degree of attention
which the requisitions of your physical nature demand,

you will perceive how little labour suffices for their satisfaction. Your Heavenly Father knoweth you have need
of these things. The universal Harmony, or Reason,
which makes your passive frame of thought its dwelling,
in proportion to the purity and majesty of its nature will
instruct you, if ye are willing to attain that exalted condition, in what manner to possess all the objects necessary for your material subsistence. All men are [im-
pelled] to become thus pure and happy. All men are
called to participate in the community of Nature's gifts.
The man who has fewest bodily wants approaches nearest
to the Divine Nature. Satisfy these wants at the cheapest
rate, and expend the remaining energies of your nature
in the attainment of virtue and knowledge. The mighty
frame of the wonderful and lovely world is the food of
your contemplation, and living beings who resemble
your own nature, and are bound to you by similarity of
sensations, are destined to be the nutriment of your
affection; united, they are the consummation of the
widest hopes your mind can contain. Ye can expend
thus no labour on mechanism consecrated to luxury and
pride. How abundant will not be your progress in all
that truly ennobles and extends human nature! By rendering yourselves thus worthy, ye will be as free in your
imaginations as the swift and many-coloured fowls of the
air, and as beautiful in pure simplicity as the lilies of the
field. In proportion as mankind becomes wise—yes, in
exact proportion to that wisdom—should be the extinction
of the unequal system under which they now subsist.
Government is, in fact, the mere badge of their depravity. They are so little aware of the inestimable benefits
of mutual love as to indulge, without thought, and
almost without motive, in the worst excesses of selfish-

ness and malice. Hence, without graduating human
society into a scale of empire and subjection, its very
existence has become impossible. It is necessary that
universal benevolence should supersede the regulations
of precedent and prescription, before these regulations
can safely be abolished. Meanwhile, their very subsistence depends on the system of injustice and violence
which they have been devised to palliate. They suppose
men endowed with the power of deliberating and determining for their equals; whilst these men, as frail and as
ignorant as the multitude whom they rule, possess, as a
practical consequence of this power, the right which they
of necessity exercise to prevent (together with their own)
the physical and moral and intellectual nature of all
mankind.

It is the object of wisdom to equalize the distinctions
on which this power depends, by exhibiting in their
proper worthlessness the objects, a contention concerning
which renders its existence a necessary evil. The evil,
in fact, is virtually abolished wherever *justice* is practised;
and it is abolished in precise proportion to the prevalence
of true virtue.

The whole frame of human things is infected by an
insidious poison. Hence it is that man is blind in his
understanding, corrupt in his moral sense, and diseased
in his physical functions. The wisest and most sublime
of the ancient poets saw this truth, and embodied their
conception of its value in retrospect to the earliest ages
of mankind. They represented equality as the reign
of Saturn, and taught that mankind had gradually
degenerated from the virtue which enabled them to

enjoy or maintain this happy state. Their doctrine
was philosophically false. Later and more correct
observations have instructed us that uncivilized man is
the most pernicious and miserable of beings, and that
the violence and injustice, which are the genuine indications of real inequality, obtain in the society of these
beings without palliation. Their imaginations of a
happier state of human society were referred, in truth,
to the Saturnian period; they ministered, indeed, to
thoughts of despondency and sorrow. But they were
the children of airy hope—the prophets and parents of
man's futurity. Man was once as a wild beast; he has
become a moralist, a metaphysician, a poet, and an
astronomer. Lucretius or Virgil might have referred
the comparison to themselves; and, as a proof of the
progress of the nature of man, challenged a comparison
with the cannibals of Scythia.[1] The experience of the
ages which have intervened between the present period
and that in which Jesus Christ taught, tends to prove
his doctrine, and to illustrate theirs. There is more
equality because there is more justice, and there is
more justice because there is more universal knowledge.

To the accomplishment of such mighty hopes were
the views of Jesus Christ extended ; such did he believe
to be the tendency of his doctrines—the abolition of
artificial distinctions among mankind, so far as the love
which it becomes all human beings to bear towards each
other, and the knowledge of truth from which that love
will never fail to be produced, avail to their destruc-

[1] Jesus Christ foresaw what the poets retrospectively imagined.
[SHELLEY'S NOTE.]

tion. A young man came to Jesus Christ, struck by the miraculous dignity and simplicity of his character, and attracted by the words of power which he uttered. He demanded to be considered as one of the followers of his creed. " Sell all that thou hast," replied the philosopher ; " give it to the poor, and follow me." But the young man had large possessions, and he went away sorrowing.

The system of equality was attempted, after Jesus Christ's death, to be carried into effect by his followers. " They that believed had all things in common ; they sold their possessions and goods, and parted them to all men, as every man had need ; and they, continuing daily with one accord in the temple, and breaking bread from house to house, did eat their meat with gladness and singleness of heart." (*Acts*, Ch. II.)

The practical application of the doctrines of strict justice to a state of society established in its contempt, was such as might have been expected. After the transitory glow of enthusiasm had faded from the minds of men, precedent and habit resumed their empire ; they broke like an universal deluge on one shrinking and solitary island. Men to whom birth had allotted ample possession looked with complacency on sumptuous apartments and luxurious food, and those ceremonials of delusive majesty which surround the throne of power and the court of wealth. Men, from whom these things were withheld by their condition, began again to gaze with stupid envy on pernicious splendour ; and, by desiring the false greatness of another's state, to sacrifice the intrinsic dignity of their own. The demagogues of the infant republic of the Christian sect, attaining, through eloquence or artifice, to influence amongst its members, first violated (under the pretence of watching over their integrity) the institutions established for the common and equal benefit of all. These demagogues artfully silenced the voice of the moral sense among them by engaging them to attend, not so much to the cultivation of a virtuous and happy life in this mortal scene, as to the attainment of a fortunate condition after death ; not so much to the consideration of those means by which the state of man is adorned and improved, as an inquiry into the secrets of the connexion between God and the world—things which, they well knew, were not to be explained, or even to be conceived. The system of equality which they established necessarily fell to the ground, because it is a system that must result from, rather than precede, the moral improvement of human kind. It was a circumstance of no moment that the first adherents of the system of Jesus Christ cast their property into a common stock. The same degree of real community of property could have subsisted without this formality, which served only to extend a temptation of dishonesty to the treasurers of so considerable a patrimony. Every man, in proportion to his virtue, considers himself, with respect to the great community of mankind, as the steward and guardian of their interests in the property which he chances to possess. Every man, in proportion to his wisdom, sees the manner in which it is his duty to employ the resources which the consent of mankind has intrusted to his discretion. Such is the [annihilation] of the unjust inequality of powers and conditions existing in the world ; and so gradually and inevitably is the

progress of equality accommodated to the progress of
wisdom and of virtue among mankind.

Meanwhile, some benefit has not failed to flow from
the imperfect attempts which have been made to erect
a system of equal rights to property and power upon
the basis of arbitrary institutions. They have undoubtedly, in every case, from the instability of their foundation, failed. Still, they constitute a record of those
epochs at which a true sense of justice suggested itself
to the understandings of men, so that they consented to
forego all the cherished delights of luxury, all the
habitual gratifications arising out of the possession or
the expectation of power, all the superstitions with
which the accumulated authority of ages had made
them dear and venerable. They are so many trophies
erected in the enemy's land, to mark the limits of the
victorious progress of truth and justice.

Jesus Christ did not fail to advert to the ——[1]

*　　　*　　　*　　　*　　　*

No mistake is more to be deplored than the conception that a system of morals and religion should derive
any portion of its authority either from the circumstance
of its novelty or its antiquity, that it should be judged
excellent, not because it is reasonable or true, but because
no person has ever thought of it before, or because it has
been thought of from the beginning of time. The vulgar
mind delights to [abstract ?] from the most useful maxims
or institutions the true reasons of their preferableness,
and to accommodate to the loose inductions of their own

---

[1] It is at this point that the Essay ends in the *Shelley Memorials.* The rest is from the *St. James's Magazine.*

indisciplinable minds. . . . . Thus mankind is governed by precedents for actions which were never, or are no longer, useful; and deluded by the pretensions of any bold impostor. . . . . Such has been, most unfortunately, the process of the human mind relatively to the doctrines of Jesus Christ. Their original promulgation was authorized by an appeal to the antiquity of the institutions of Judæa; and in vindication of superstitions professing to be founded on them,[1] it is asserted that nothing analogous to their tenor was ever before produced.[2] The doctrines of Jesus Christ have scarcely the smallest resemblance to the Jewish law;[3] nor have wisdom and benevolence and pity failed in whatsoever age of the world to generate such persuasions as those which are the basis of the moral system he announced. The[4] most eminent philosophers of Greece had long been familiarized to the boldest and most sublime speculations on God, on the visible world, and on the moral and intellectual Nature of Man. The universality and unity of God, the omnipotence of the mind of man, the equality of human beings and the duty of internal purity, is either asserted by Pythagoras, Plato,[5] Diogenes, Zeno, and their followers, or may be directly inferred from their assertions. Nothing would be gained by the establishment of the originality of Jesus Christ's doctrines but the casting a suspicion upon its practicability.[6] Let us beware therefore what we admit lest, as

[1] Cancelled reading, *a system professing to be founded on these doctrines.*

[2] Cancelled reading, *Let us proceed to vindicate.*

[3] There is another erasure here, *The Philosophers of Greece, and their imitators, the Romans, bear...*

[4] Cancelled reading, *The doctrines were speculations of the most eminent,* &c.

[5] In the MS., *The Platonists and Stoics* is here struck out.

[6] Cancelled passage, *It promises,* and again, *would persuade man not to be tyrant of man.*

some have made a trade of its imagined mysteries, we lose
the inestimable advantages of its simplicity. Let us
beware, if we love liberty and truth,[1] if we loathe tyranny
and imposture, if, imperfect ourselves, we still aspire to
the freedom of internal purity, and cherish the elevated
hope that mankind may not be everlastingly condemned
to the bondage of their own passions and the passions
of their fellow beings,[2] let us beware. An established
religion turns to deathlike apathy the sublimest ebulli-
tions of most exalted genius, and the spirit-stirring truths
of a mind inflamed with the desire of benefiting mankind.
It is the characteristic of a cold and tame spirit[3] to
imagine that such doctrines as Jesus Christ promulgated
are destined to follow the fortunes[4] and share the extinction of a popular religion.

[1] In the MS., *our fellow men* is here struck out in favour of *liberty and truth*.

[2] Cancelled reading, *men*.

[3] Cancelled reading, *It is a cold and palsying tame thought*.

[4] In the MS. the words *share the fate* originally stood here.

THE ELYSIAN FIELDS,

A LUCIANIC FRAGMENT.

[*The Elysian Fields* is printed from a MS. in Shelley's writing, so headed, in my possession : I presume it belongs to about the same period as the Marlow Pamphlets. In a letter dated the 20th of January, 1821 (*Shelley Memorials*, page 136), Shelley thus refers to a paper by Archdeacon Hare in *Ollier's Literary Miscellany :* "I was immeasurably amused by the quotation from Schlegel, about the way in which the popular faith is destroyed—first the Devil, then the Holy Ghost, then God the Father. I had written a Lucianic essay to prove the same thing." Mr. Rossetti (Poetical Works, 1878, Vol. I, page 150) thinks the reference is to the *Essay on Devils*, withdrawn after being prepared for publication with the *Essays, Letters* &c. (1840), and never yet published. It does not seem to me certain that Shelley alludes to that essay ; but I feel pretty confident that *The Elysian Fields* is a portion of a Lucianic epistle from some Englishman of political eminence, dead before 1820, to, perhaps, the Princess Charlotte. The exposition foreshadowed in the final paragraph might well have included a view of the decay of popular belief. Those who are intimately familiar with the political history and literature of England will probably be able to identify the person represented. It is not unlikely to be Charles Fox, judging from the juxtaposition of his name, in the *Address to the Irish People*, with sentiments much the same as those set forth in the third paragraph of *The Elysian Fields.* Compare that paragraph with the relative passage in the *Address*, Vol. I, page 332.—H. B. F.]

THE ELYSIAN FIELDS.

I AM not forgetful in this dreary scene of the country which whilst I lived in the upper air, it was my whole aim to illustrate and render happy. Indeed, although immortal, we are not exempted from the enjoyments and the sufferings of mortality. We sympathize in all the proceedings of mankind, and we experience joy or grief in all intelligence from them, according to our various opinions and views. Nor do we resign those opinions, even those which the grave[1] has utterly refuted. Frederic of Prussia has lately arrived amongst us, and persists in maintaining that "death is an eternal sleep," to the great discomfiture of Philip the Second of Spain ; who on the furies refusing to apply the torture, expects the roof of Tartarus to fall upon his head, and laments that at least in his particular instance the doctrine should be false.——Religion is more frequently the subject of discussion among the departed dead, than any other topic, for we know as little which mode of faith is true as you do. Every one maintains the doctrine he maintained on

[1] Cancelled reading, *even when the grave.*

Earth, and accommodates the appearances which surround
us to his peculiar tenets.—

I am one of those who esteeming political science
capable of certain conclusions, have ever preferred it to
these airy speculations, which when they assume an
empire over the passions of mankind render them so mis-
chievous and unextinguishable, that they subsist even
among the dead. The art of employing the power entrusted to you for the benefit of those who entrust it, is
something more definite, and subject as all its details
must ever be to innumerable limitations and exceptions
arising out of the change in the habits, opinions of
mankind, is the noblest, and the greatest, and the most
universal of all. It is not as a queen, but as a human
being that this science must be learned; the same discipline which contributes to domestic happiness and individual distinction secures true welfare and genuine glory
to a nation.—

You will start, I do not doubt, to hear the language of
philosophy. You will have been informed that those
who approach sovereigns with warnings that they have
duties to perform, that they are elevated above the rest
of mankind simply to prevent their tearing one another to
pieces, and for the purpose of putting into effect all
practical equality and justice, are insidious traitors who
devise their ruin. But if the character which I bore on
earth should not reassure you,[1] it would be well to
recollect the circumstances under which you will ascend
the throne of England, and what is the spirit of the times.

---

[1] After *reassure you* there is a
cancelled reading in the MS.—*you
recollect yourself, & if the preju-* *dices of the age have not deprived you
of all that learning...*

There are better examples to emulate than those who have only refrained from depraving or tyrannizing over their subjects, because they remembered the fates of Pisistratus[1] and Tarquin. If[2] generosity and virtue should have dominion over your actions, my lessons can hardly be needed; but if the discipline[3] of a narrow education may have extinguished all thirst of genuine excellence, all desire of becoming illustrious for the sake of the illustriousness of the actions which I would incite you to perform. Should you be thus—and no pains have been spared to make you so—make your account with holding your crown on this condition: of deserving it alone. And that this may be evident[4] I will expose to you the state in which the nation will be found at your accession, for the very dead know more than the counsellors by whom you will be surrounded.

The English nation does not, as has been imagined, inherit freedom from its ancestors. Public opinion rather than positive institution maintains it[5] in whatever portion it may now possess, which is[6] in truth the acquirement of their own incessant struggles. As yet the gradations by which this freedom has advanced have been contested step by step.

---

[1] *Pisistratus* is probably a slip for the *sons of Pisistratus.*

[2] Cancelled reading, *But if these motives.*

[3] Cancelled readings, *lessons* for *discipline;* and *is to prevent* for *may have extinguished* in the next line.

[4] Cancelled reading, *evident to you.*

[5] In the MS. *them* is struck out in favour of *it.*

[6] Cancelled readings, *and this has been,* and in the same line *conquest* for *acquirement.*

ON THE DEVIL, AND DEVILS.

[In the *Relics of Shelley* Mr. Garnett published a letter from Mrs. Shelley to Mrs. Leigh Hunt, wherein mention is made of Shelley's "Essay on Devils." Mr. Garnett said in a note (page 131), "This amusing fragment was prepared for publication in 1839, with the rest of Shelley's prose works, but withdrawn, for reasons which seven other essayists have since conspired to deprive of much of their weight." The preparations went so far as setting up in type, with such omissions as pre-*Essays-and-Reviews* expediency seemed to demand. In a proof, however, which was preserved, Mrs. Shelley reinserted the omitted passages : this proof is in the possession of Sir Percy and Lady Shelley, who have kindly allowed me the privilege of first giving to the world this remarkable example of Shelley's lighter mood. The essay is given from the interpolated proof, the MS. not being at hand. Adverting to the remarks quoted at page 376 of this volume, on the subject of a "Lucianic essay," it is to be observed that, in the essay on the Devil and Devils, as preserved, there is no explicit setting-forth of the thesis that the Holy Ghost and then God the Father follow the Devil in departing from the popular belief. It is true that the Devil is described as the weak point, outwork, and so on, of the Christian faith ; and had the essay been finished the line indicated might probably have been followed. It seems possible that the preceding fragment, *The Elysian Fields*, may be a portion of an essay dealing with these matters independently in another method, or that Shelley began to approach this subject in the form of a Lucianic epistle, and then rejected that form in favour of the present.—H. B. F.]

ON THE DEVIL, AND DEVILS.

To determine the nature and functions of the Devil, is no contemptible province of the European Mythology. Who, or what he is, his origin, his habitation, his destiny, and his power, are subjects which puzzle the most acute theologians, and on which no orthodox person can be induced to give a decisive opinion. He is the weak place of the popular religion—the vulnerable belly of the crocodile.

The Manichæan philosophy respecting the origin and government of the world, if not true, is at least an hypothesis conformable to the experience of actual facts. To suppose that the world was created and is now superintended by two spirits of a balanced power and opposite dispositions, is simply a personification of the struggle which we experience within ourselves, and which we perceive in the operations of external things as they affect us, between good and evil. The supposition that a good spirit is, or hereafter will be, superior, is a personification of the principle of hope, and that thirst for improvement without which present evil would be intolerable. The vulgar are all Manichæans—all that remains of the popular superstition is mere Machinery and accompaniment. To abstract in contemplation, from our sensations of pleasure and pain, all circumstance and limit; to add those active powers, of whose existence we are conscious within ourselves; to give to that which is most pleasing to us, a perpetual or an ultimate superiority, with all epithets of honourable addition; and to brand that which is displeasing with epithets ludicrous or horrible, predicting its ultimate defeat, is to pursue the process by which the vulgar arrive at the familiar notions of God and the Devil.

The Devil was clearly a Chaldæan invention, for we first hear of him after the return of the Jews from their second Assyrian captivity. He is, indeed, mentioned in the Book of Job; but, so far from that circumstance affording any proof that that Book was written at a very early period, it tends rather to shew that it was the production of a later age. The magnificence and purity, indeed, of the poetry, and the irresistible grandeur of its plan, suggest the idea that it was a birth of the vigorous infancy of some community of men. Assuredly it was not written by a Jew before the period of the second captivity,—because it speaks of the Devil, and there is no other mention of this personage in the voluminous literature of that epoch. And that it was not written by a Jew at all may be presumed, from a perpetual employment, and that with the most consummate beauty, of imagery belonging to a severer climate than Palestine.

But to return to the Devil.—Those among the Greek

Philosophers, whose poetical imagination suggested a personification of the Cause of the Universe, seem, nevertheless, to have dispensed with the agency of the Devil. Democritus, Epicurus, Theodorus, and perhaps even Aristotle, indeed abstained from introducing a living and thinking Agent, analogous to the human mind, as the author or superintendent of the world. Plato, following his master, Socrates, who had been struck with the beauty and novelty of the theistical hypothesis, as first delivered by the tutor of Pericles, supposed the existence of a God, and accommodated a moral system of the most universal character, including the past, the present, and the future condition of man, to the popular supposition of the moral superintendence of this one intellectual cause. It is needless to pursue the modifications of this doctrine as it extended among the succeeding sects. This hypothesis, though rude enough, is in no respect very absurd and contradictory. The refined speculations concerning the existence of external objects, by which the idea of matter is suggested, to which Plato has the merit of having first directed the attention of the thinking part of mankind. . . . . A partial interpretation of it has gradually afforded the least unrefined portion of our popular religion.

But the Greek Philosophers abstained from introducing the Devil. They accounted for evil by supposing that what is called matter is eternal, and that God, in making the world, made not the best that he, or even inferior intelligence could conceive ; but that he moulded the reluctant and stubborn materials ready to his hand, into the nearest arrangement possible to the perfect archetype existing in his contemplation :—in the

same manner as a skilful watchmaker, who, if he has
diamonds, and steel, and brass, and gold, can compose
a time-piece of the most accurate workmanship, could
produce nothing beyond a coarse and imperfect clock, if
he were restricted to wood, as his material. The
Christian theologians have invariably rejected this hypothesis, on the ground that the eternity of matter is incompatible with the omnipotence of God. Like panic-
stricken slaves in the presence of a jealous and suspi-
cious despot, they have tortured themselves to devise
some flattering sophism, by which they might appease
him by the most contradictory praises—endeavouring to
reconcile omnipotence, and benevolence, and equity, in
the author of an universe, where evil and good are inextricably entangled, and where the most admirable
tendencies to happiness and preservation are for ever
baffled by misery and decay. The Christians, therefore,
invented or adopted the Devil to extricate them from
this difficulty.

The account they give us of the origin of the Devil is
curious:—Heaven, according to the popular creed, is a
certain airy region inhabited by the Supreme Being, and
a multitude of inferior Spirits. With respect to the
situation of it theologians are not agreed, but it is generally supposed to be placed beyond the remotest constel-
lation of the visible stars. These spirits are supposed,
like those which reside in the bodies of animals and
men, to have been created by God, with foresight of the
consequences which would result from the mechanism of
their nature. He made them as good as possible, but
the nature of the substance out of which they were
formed, or the unconquerable laws according to which

that substance, when created, was necessarily modified, prevented them from being so perfect as he could wish. Some say that he gave them free-will; that is, that he made them, without any very distinct apprehension of the results of his workmanship; leaving them an active power which might determine them to this or that action, independently of the motives afforded by the regular operation of those impressions which were produced by the general agencies of the rest of his creation. This he is supposed to have done, that he might excuse himself to his own conscience for tormenting and annoying these unfortunate spirits, when they provoked him by turning out worse than he expected. This account of the origin of evil, to make the best of it, does not seem more complimentary to the Supreme Being, or less derogatory to his omnipotence and goodness, than the Platonic scheme.

They then proceed to relate, gravely, that one fine morning, a chief of these spirits took it into his head to rebel against God, having gained over to his cause a third part of the eternal angels, who attended upon the Creator and Preserver of Heaven and Earth. After a series of desperate conflicts between those who remained faithful to the ancient dynasty and the insurgents, the latter were beaten, and driven into a place called Hell, which was rather their empire than their prison, and where God reserved them, first to be the tempters, and then the jailors and tormentors of a new race of beings, whom he created under the same conditions of imperfection, and with the same foresight of an unfortunate result. The motive of this insurrection is not assigned by any of the early mythological writers. Milton supposes that, on a particular day, God chose to adopt as his Son and *heir*,

(the reversion of an estate with an immortal incumbent,
would be worth little) a being unlike the other Spirits, who
seems to have been supposed to be a detached portion of
himself, and afterwards figured upon the earth in the well-
known character of Jesus Christ. The Devil is represented
as conceiving high indignation at this preference, and as
disputing the affair with arms. I cannot discover Milton's
authority for this circumstance;[1] but all agree in the fact
of the insurrection, and the defeat, and the casting out
into Hell. Nothing can exceed the grandeur and the
energy of the character of the Devil, as expressed in
Paradise Lost. He is a Devil, very different from the
popular personification of evil, and it is a mistake to
suppose that he was intended for an idealism of Evil.
Malignity, implacable hate, cunning, and refinement of
device to inflict the utmost anguish on an enemy, these,
which are venial in a slave, are not to be forgiven in a
tyrant; these, which are redeemed by much that ennobles
in one subdued, are marked by all that dishonours his
conquest in the victor. Milton's Devil, as a moral being, is
as far superior to his God, as one who perseveres in a
purpose which he has conceived to be excellent, in spite
of adversity and torture, is to one who in the cold
security of undoubted triumph inflicts the most horrible
revenge upon his enemy—not from any mistaken notion
of bringing him to repent of a perseverance in enmity,
but with the open and alleged design of exasperating him
to deserve new torments.

Milton so far violated all that part of the popular

---

[1] For Milton's purpose there is quite sufficient authority in the second Psalm and the twelfth chapter of the Revelation. The Revelation, though purporting to relate to the future, of course draws upon tradition and antecedent literature for its imagery.

creed which is susceptible of being preached and defended
in argument, as to allege no superiority in moral virtue to
his God over his Devil. He mingled as it were the elements of human nature as colours upon a single pallet,
and arranged them into the composition of his great
picture, according to the laws of epic truth ; that is, according to the laws of that principle by which a series of
actions of intelligent and ethical beings, developed in a
rythmical tale, are calculated to excite the sympathy
and antipathy of succeeding generations of mankind. The
writer who would have attributed majesty and beauty to
the character of victorious and vindictive omnipotence,
must have been contented with the character of a good
Christian ; he never could have been a great epic poet.
It is difficult to determine, in a country where the most
enormous sanctions of opinion and law are attached to a
direct avowal of certain speculative notions, whether
Milton was a Christian or not, at the period of the composition of Paradise Lost. Is it possible that Socrates
seriously believed that Æsculapius would be propitiated
by the offering of a cock ? Thus much is certain, that
Milton gives the Devil all imaginable advantage ; and the
arguments with which he exposes the injustice and impotent weakness of his adversary, are such as, had they
been printed, distinct from the shelter of any dramatic
order, would have been answered by the most conclusive
of syllogisms—persecution. As it is, Paradise Lost
has conferred on the modern mythology a systematic
form ; and when the immeasurable and unceasing
mutability of time shall have added one more superstition to those which have already arisen and decayed
upon the earth, commentators and critics will be learnedly
employed in elucidating the religion of ancestral Europe,

only not utterly forgotten because it will have partici-
pated in the eternity of genius.[1]   The Devil owes
everything to Milton.   Dante and Tasso present us with
a very gross idea of him.   Milton divested him of a sting,
hoof, and horns, and clothed him with the sublime
grandeur of a graceful but tremendous spirit.

I am afraid there is much laxity among the orthodox
of the present day, respecting a belief in the Devil.   I
recommend to the Bishops to make a serious charge to
their diocesans on this dangerous latitude.   The Devil
is the outwork of the Christian faith; he is the weakest
point.   You may observe that infidels, in their novitiate,
always begin by tremulously doubting the existence of
the Devil.   Depend upon it, that when a person once
begins to think that perhaps there is no Devil, he is in a
dangerous way.   There may be observed, in polite society,
a great deal of coquetting about the Devil, especially
among divines, which is singularly ominous.   They
qualify him as the evil spirit; they consider him as
synonymous with the flesh.   They seem to wish to
divest him of all personality; to reduce him from his
abstract to his concrete; to reverse the process by which
he was created in the mind, which they will by no
means bear with respect to God.   It is popular, and
well looked upon, if you deny the Devil "a local habitation and a name."   Even the vulgar begin to scout
him.   Hell is popularly considered as metaphorical of
the torments of an evil conscience, and by no means

---

[1] Compare this and the preceding paragraph with that passage in
The Defence of Poetry which begins with the words *The poetry of
Dante* (Vol. III. p. 126); and note
how admirably Shelley was able
to adapt his profound criticism
alike to the purposes of satire and
those of a higher strain.

capable of being topographically ascertained.[1] No one likes to mention the torments of everlasting fire and the poisonous gnawing of the worm that liveth for ever and ever. It is all explained away into the regrets and the reproaches of an evil conscience, and, in this respect, I think that the most presumptuous among us may safely say—

"One touch of nature makes the whole world kin."

On the other hand, Heaven is supposed to have some settled locality, and the joys of the elect are to be something very positive. This way of talking about a personage whose office in the mythological scheme is so important, must lead to disbelief. It is, in fact, a proof of approaching extinction in any religion, when its teachers and its adherents, instead of proudly and dogmatically insisting upon the most knotty or unintelligible articles of their creed, begin to palliate and explain away the doctrines in which their more believing ancestors had shewn a reverential acquiescence, and an audacious exultation of confidence. It is less the opinion of the person himself than that of those by whom he is surrounded, which gives that air of confidence by which the most absurd tenets have been transmitted from generation to generation. A man may, in truth, never have considered whether there is or is not a Devil ; he may be totally indifferent to the question ; yet it may occur to him to state his positive opinion on one side or the other. The air of confidence with which he does this, is manifestly determined by the disposition with which he

---

[1] *Cf.* Marlowe's *Faustus*, Act II, Sc. 1 :

Hell hath no limits, nor is circumscribed
In one self place ; but where we are is Hell,
And where Hell is, there must we ever be :

And to be short, when all the world dissolves,
And every creature shall be purified,
All places shall be Hell that are not Heaven.

expects his opinion to be received. One illustration of this view of the subject is afforded by a circumstance in the life of Dr. Johnson, the last man of considerable talents who shewed any serious attachment to the ancient faith, and whose life and death, as compared with that of his contemporary, Hume, affords a just standard of the consolations of the Christian or the Infidel systems. A gentleman inquired of Johnson what he meant by *being damned*? "Sent to Hell and punished everlastingly," he replied.

The Devil is Διάβολος, the Accuser. In this character he presented himself among the other Sons of God before his Father's throne, to request to be allowed to tempt Job by tormenting him. God, it seems, had some special reason for patronizing Job, and one does not well see why he spared him at last. The expostulations of Job with God are of the most daring character; it is certain he would not bear them from a Christian. If God were a refined critic, which from his inspiration of Ezechiel would never have been suspected, one might imagine that the profuse and sublime strain of poetry not to be surpassed by anything ancient, much less modern, had found favour with him. But to return to the Devil, the Accuser. In this view he is at once the Informer, the Attorney General, and the jailor of the Celestial tribunal. It is not good policy, or, at least, cannot be considered as constitutional practice, to unite these characters. The Devil must have a great interest to exert himself to procure a sentence of guilty from the judge; for I suppose there will be no jury at the resurrection—at least if there is, it will be so overawed by the bench, and the counsel *for the crown*, as to ensure whatever verdict the court shall please to recommend. No doubt that, as an incentive to his exertions, half goes to the informer. (What an army of spies and delators all Hell must afford, under the direction of that active magistrate, the Devil!) If the Devil takes but half the pleasure in tormenting a sinner which God does, who took the trouble to create him, and then to invent a system of casuistry by which he might excuse himself for devoting him to eternal torment, this reward must be considerable. Conceive how the enjoyment of one half of the advantages to be derived from their ruin, whether in person or property, must irritate the activity of a delator. Tiberius, or Bonaparte, or Lord Castlereagh, never affixed any reward to the disclosure or the creation of conspiracies, equal to that which God's Government has attached to the exertions of the Devil, to tempt, betray, and accuse unfortunate man. These two considerable personages are supposed to have entered into a kind of partnership, in which the weaker has consented to bear all the odium of their common actions, and to allow the stronger to talk of himself as a very honourable person, on condition of having participation in what is the especial delight of both of them, burning men to all eternity. The dirty work is done by the Devil, in the same manner as some starving wretch will hire himself out to a king or minister, with a stipulation that he shall have some portion of the public spoil, as an instrument to betray a certain number of other starving wretches into circumstances of capital punishment, when they may think it convenient to edify the rest, by hanging up a few of those whose murmurs are too loud.[1]

---

[1] *Cf.* Paragraph IX of the *Address to the People on the Death of the Princess Charlotte* (Vol. II, pp. 110 and 111), in which Shelley puts this point with desperate earnestness.

It is far from inexplicable that earthly tyrants should employ these kind of agents, or that God should have done so with regard to the Devil and his Angels ; or that any depositary of power should take these measures, with respect to those, by whom he fears lest that power should be wrested from him.   But to tempt mankind to incur everlasting damnation, must, on the part of God, and even on the part of the Devil, arise from that disinterested love of tormenting and annoying, which is seldom observed on earth.   The thing that comes nearest to it is a troop of idle dirty boys baiting a cat ; cooks skinning eels, and boiling lobsters alive, and bleeding calves, and whipping pigs to death ; naturalists anatomizing dogs alive, (a dog has as good a right and a better excuse for anatomizing a naturalist,) are nothing compared to God and the Devil judging, damning, and then tormenting the soul of a miserable sinner.   It is pretended that God dislikes it, but this is mere shame-facedness and coquetting, for he has everything his own way and he need not damn unless he likes.   The Devil has a better excuse, for, as he was entirely made by God, he can have no tendency or disposition, the seeds of which were not originally planted by his Creator ; and as everything else was made by God, those seeds can have only developed themselves in the precise degree and manner determined by the impulses arising from the agency of the rest of his creation.   It would be as unfair to complain of the Devil for acting ill, as of a watch for going badly ; the defects are to be imputed as much to God in the former case, as to the watchmaker in the latter.   There is also another view of the subject, suggested by mythological writers, which strongly re-

commends the Devil to our sympathy and compassion,
though it is less consistent with the theory of God's
omnipotence than that already stated. The Devil, it is
stated, before his fall, was an Angel of the highest rank
and the most splendid accomplishments, who placed his
peculiar delight in doing good. But the inflexible
grandeur of his spirit, mailed and nourished by the
consciousness the purest and loftiest designs, was so
secure from the assault of any gross or common torments,
that God was considerably puzzled to invent what
he considered an adequate punishment for his rebellion ;
he exhausted all the variety of smothering and burning
and freezing and cruelly-lacerating his external frame,
and the Devil laughed at the impotent revenge of his
conqueror. At last the benevolent and amiable disposition which distinguished his adversary, furnished God with
the true method of executing an enduring and terrible
vengeance. He turned his good into evil, and, by virtue
of his omnipotence, inspired him with such an impulse,
as, in spite of his better nature, irresistibly determined
him to act what he most abhorred, and to be a minister of
those designs and schemes of which he was the chief and
the original victim. He is for ever tortured with compassion and affection for those whom he betrays and
ruins ; he is racked by a vain abhorrence for the desolation of which he is the instrument ; he is like a man
compelled by a tyrant to set fire to his own possessions,
and to appear as the witness against, and the accuser of
his dearest friends and most intimate connexions ; and
then to be the executioner, and to inflict protracted torments upon them. As a man, were he deprived of all
other refuge, he might hold his breath and die—but God

is represented as omnipotent and the Devil as eternal. Milton has expressed this view of the subject with the sublimest pathos.

It is commonly said that the Devil has only precisely so much power as is allowed him by God's providence. Christians exhort each other to despise his attacks, and to trust in God. If this trust has ever been deceived, they seem in a poor way, especially when it is considered that God has arranged it so that the Devil should have no inconsiderable portion of the souls of men. A pious friend of mine tells me that she thinks that about nineteen in twenty will be damned. Formerly it was supposed that all those who were not Christians, and even all those who were not of a particular sect of Christians, would be damned. At present this doctrine seems abandoned or confined to a few. One does not well see who is to be damned, and who not according to the fashionable creed.

The sphere of the operations of the Devil is difficult to determine. The late inventions and improvements in telescopes have considerably enlarged the notions of men respecting the bounds of the universe. It is discovered that the Earth is comparatively a small globe, in a system consisting of a multitude of others, which roll round the sun ; and there is no reason to suppose but that all these are inhabited by organized and intelligent beings. The fixed stars are supposed to be suns, each of them the centre of a system like ours. Those little whitish specks of light that are seen in a clear night, are discovered to consist of a prodigious multitude of suns, each probably the centre of a system of planets. The system of which our earth is a planet has been discovered to belong to one of those larger systems of suns, which, when seen at a distance, look like a whitish speck of light; and that lustrous streak called the milky way is found to be one of the extremities of the immense group of suns in which our system is placed. The heaven is covered with an incalculable number of these white specks, and the better the telescopes the more are discovered, and the more distinctly the confusion of white light is resolved into stars. All this was not known during the gradual invention of the Christian mythology, and was never even suspected by those barbarians, in the obscure extremities of the Roman Empire, by whom it was first adopted. If these incalculable millions of suns, planets, satellites, and comets are inhabited, is it to be supposed that God formed their inhabitants better, or less liable to offend him than those primordial spirits, those angels near his throne, those first and most admirable of his creatures, who rebelled and were damned? Or has he improved like a proficient in statuary or painting, proceeding from rude outlines and imperfect forms, to more perfect idealisms or imitations, so that his latter works are better than his first? Or has some fortunate chance, like that which, when the painter despaired of being able to depict the foam of a horse, directed the spunge so as to represent it accurately, interfered to confer stability and exactness upon one, or how many, among the numerous systems of animated nature? There is little reason to suppose that any considerable multitude of the planets were tenanted by beings better capable of resisting the temptations of the Devil than ours. But is the Devil, like God, omnipresent? If so he interpenetrates God, and they both exist co-essentially; as metaphysicians have compared the omnipresence of God, pervading the infinity of space

and being, to salt mixed with water. If not he must
send some inferior Angels, either to this or some other
planet, first to tempt the Inhabitants to disobey God, and
secondly to induce them to reject all terms of salvation;
for which latter purpose, it seems equally requisite that
he should take up his residence on the spot; nor do I
see, how he or God, by whose providence he is permitted,
that is to say, compelled to act, could commit a business
of such high moment to an inferior Angel. It seems
very questionable whether the Devil himself, or only some
inferior Devil, tempted and betrayed the people of the
Earth; or whether Jupiter, a planet capable of containing a hundred times more inhabitants than the earth,—to
mention only the planets of our own system,—or the Sun,
which would contain a million times more, were not
entitled to the preference.

Any objection that might arise from the multitude of
Devils, I think futile. You may suppose a million times
as many devils as there are stars. In fact you may
suppose anything you like on such a subject. That there
are a great number of Devils, and that they go about in
legions of six or seven, or more at a time, all mythologists
are agreed. Christians, indeed, will not admit the actual
substance and presence of the Devils upon Earth in
modern times. Or, in proportion as any histories of them
approach to the present epoch, or indeed any epoch in
which there has been a considerable progress in historical
criticism or natural science, they suppose their agency to
be obscure and superstitious. There were a number of
Devils in Judea in the time of Jesus Christ, and a great
reputation was gained both by him and others, by what
was called casting them out. A droll story is told us

among others of Jesus Christ having driven a legion of
Devils into a herd of pigs, who were so discomfited with
these new invaders that they all threw themselves over a
precipice into the lake, and were drowned. These were
a set of hypochondriacal and high-minded swine, very
unlike any others of which we have authentic record ; they
disdained to live, if they must live in so intimate a society
with Devils, as that which was imposed on them, and
the pig-drivers were no doubt confounded by so heroical
a resolution. What became of the Devils after the death
of the pigs, whether they passed into the fish, and thence
by digestion, through the stomach, into the brain of the
Gadarene Icthyophagists ; whether they returned to Hell,
or remained on the Earth, the historian has left as subject for everlasting conjecture. I should be curious to
know whether any half starved Jew picked up these
pigs, and sold them at the market of Gadara, and what
effect the bacon of a demoniac pig, who had killed himself, produced upon the consumers. The Devils requested Jesus Christ to send them into the pigs, and the
Son of God shewed himself more inclined to do what was
agreeable to the Devils than what was profitable to
the owners of the pigs. He had, no doubt, say the
Christians, some good reasons. Poor fellows ! They
were probably ruined by this operation. The Gadarenes
evidently disapproved of this method of casting out
Devils—they thought probably that Jesus shewed an unjust preference to these disagreeable beings ; and they
sent a deputation to request him to depart out of their
country. I doubt whether the yeomen of the present
day would have treated him with so much lenity.

Among the numerous theories concerning the condition

of Devils, some have resorted to the Pythagorean hypo-thesis, but in such a manner as to pervert that hypothesis, from motives of humanity, into an example for cruel tyranny. They suppose that the bodies of animals, and especially domestic animals, are animated by Devils, and that the tyranny exercised over these unfortunate beings by man is an unconscious piece of retaliation over the beings who betrayed them into a state of reprobation. On this theory Lord Erskine's Act[1] might have been entitled "An Act for the better protection of Devils." How devils inhabit the bodies of men is not explained. It cannot be that they animate them like what is called the soul or vital principle because that is supposed to be already preoccupied. Some have supposed that they exist in the human body in the shape of teniæ and hydatids, but I know not whether those persons subject to vermicular and animalcular diseases, are the most likely to be subject to the incursions of Devils from any reason *a priori*, although they may safely be said to be tormented of Devils. The pedicular diseases on this view of the subject may be the result of diabolical influence, the sensorium of every separate louse being the habitation of a distinct imp. Some have supposed that the Devils live in the Sun, and that that glorious

[1] More strictly speaking Lord Erskine's Bill ; for Shelley did not live to see an Act passed on this subject. Lord Campbell tells us in his Lives of the Lord Chancel-lors that Erskine "almost entirely confined himself for some years to a subject which he made peculiarly his own, and with which his name will ever continue to be associated." On the 15th of May 1809, he made a memorable speech, in moving the second reading of his Bill "For the Prevention of Cruelty to Animals," which, however, was thrown out by the Commons after passing the Lords. Erskine re-introduced it with amendments in 1810, but withdrew it after it had passed the Committee of the Com-mons. It was not until the 22nd of July 1822, a fortnight after Shelley's death, but while Erskine was still alive, that the measure, having been brought forward by Mr. Martin, M.P. for Galway, became law, and set the example which has since been so largely followed by legislators throughout the civilized world.

luminary is the actual Hell; perhaps that every fixed star is a distinct Hell appropriated to the use of its several systems of planets, so great a proportion of the inhabitants of which are probably devoted to everlasting damnation, if the belief of one particular creed is essential to their escape, and the testimony of its truth so very far remote and obscure as in the planet which we inhabit. I do not envy the theologians, who first invented this theory. The Magian worship of the Sun as the creator and Preserver of the world, is considerably more to the credit of the inventors. It is in fact a poetical exposition of the matter of fact, before modern science had so greatly enlarged the boundaries of the sensible world, and was, next to pure deism or a personification of all the powers whose agency we know or can conjecture, the religion attended by the fewest evil consequences.

If the sun is Hell, the Devil has a magnificent abode, being elevated as it were on the imperial throne of the visible world. If we assign to the Devil the greatest and most glorious habitation within the scope of our senses, where shall we conceive his mightier adversary to reside? Shall we suppose that the Devil occupies the centre and God the circumference of existence, and that one urges inwards with the centripetal, whilst the other is perpetually struggling outwards from the narrow focus with the centrifugal force, and that from their perpetual conflict results the mixture of good and evil, harmony and discord, beauty and deformity, production and decay, which are the general laws of the moral and material world? Alas! the poor theologian never troubled his fancy with nonsense of so philosophical a form. He

contented himself with supposing that God was some-
where or other; that the Devil and all his angels
together with the perpetually increasing multitude of the
damned were burning above to all eternity in that prodigious orb of elemental light, which sustains and animates that multitude of inhabited globes, in whose company this earth revolves. Others have supposed Hell
to be distributed among the comets, which constitute,
according to this scheme, a number of floating prisons
of intense and inextinguishable fire; a great modern poet
has adopted this idea when he calls a comet

"A wandering hell in the eternal space."[1]

Misery and injustice contrive to produce very poetical
effects, because the excellence of poetry consists in its
awakening the sympathy of men, which, among persons
influenced by an abject and gloomy superstition, is much
more easily done by images of horror than of beauty. It
often requires a higher degree of skill in a poet to make
beauty, virtue, and harmony poetical, that is, to give them
an idealized and rhythmical analogy with the predomi-
nating emotions of his readers,—than to make injustice,
deformity and discord poetical. There are fewer Raphaels
than Michael Angelos; better verses have been written on
Hell than Paradise. How few read the Purgatorio or
the Paradiso of Dante, in the comparison of those who
know the Inferno well. And yet the Purgatorio, with
the exception of two famous passages, is a finer poem than
the Inferno. No poet can develope the same power in
that part of his composition where he feels himself insecure of the emotions of his readers, as in those where
he knows that he can command their sympathy.

1. Byron's Manfred, Act I, Sc. 1.

As to the Devil, and the imps, and the damned living in the Sun, why there is no great probability of it. The Comets are better fitted for this; except that some astronomer has suggested the possibility of their orbits gradually becoming ecliptical, until at last they might arrange themselves in orbits concentric with the planets, lose their heat and their substance, become subject to the same laws of animal and vegetable life as those according to which the substance of the surface of the others is arranged. The Devils and the damned, without some miraculous interposition would then be the inhabitants of a very agreeable world; and as they probably would have become very good friends from a community of misfortune and the experience which time gives those who live long enough of the folly of quarrelling—would probably administer the affairs of their Colony with great harmony and success. But there is an objection to this whole theory of solar and planetary Hells; which is, that there is no proof that the Sun and the Comets are themselves burning. It is the same with fire as with wit. A man may not be witty himself as Falstaff was, though like him he may be the cause of wit in others. So the Sun, though the cause of fire, may only develope a limited proportion of that principle on its own surface. Herschel's discoveries incline to a presumption that this is actually the case. He has discovered that the cause of light and heat is not the burning body of the Sun itself; but a shell as it were of phosphoric vapours, suspended many thousand miles in the atmosphere of that body. These vapours surround the sphere of the Sun at a distance, which has not been accurately computed, but which is assuredly very great, encircling and canopying it with a vault of aetherial splendour whose internal surface may perform the same office to the processes of vital and material action on the body of the sun, as its external one does upon those of the planets. A certain degree of plausibility is conferred on this notion by the observation that the interior surface, as far as can be collected from a view of the sides of the chasm, is of an obscurer colour than the external one: what are called spots in the sun, being no more than immense rents produced probably by streams of wind in the incumbent mass of vapours, which disclose the opaque body of the sun itself. All this diminishes the probability of the sun being a Hell, by shewing that there is no reason for supposing it considerably hotter than the planets. Not to mention that the Devils may be like the animalculæ in mutton broth, whom you may boil as much as you please, but they will always continue alive and vigorous.

The idea of the sun being Hell, is an attempt at an improvement on the old-established idea of its occupying the centre of the earth. The Devils and the damned would be exceedingly crowded in process of ages, if they were confined within so inconsiderable a sphere.

The Devil and his Angels are called the Powers of the Air, and the Devil himself Lucifer. I cannot discover why he is called Lucifer, except from a misinterpreted passage in Isaiah, where that poet exults over the fall of an Assyrian king, the oppressor of his country:—
"How art thou fallen, Lucifer, king of Morning!"—The Devil after having gradually assumed the horns, hoof, tail, and ears of the ancient Gods of the woods, lost them again, although wings had been added. It is

inexplicable why men assigned him these additions as circumstances of terror and deformity. The Sylvans and Fauns, with their leader the great Pan, were most poetical personages, and were connected in the imagination of the Pagans with all that could enliven and delight. They were supposed to be innocent beings in habits, and not greatly different from the shepherds and herdsmen of whom they were the patron saints. But the Christians contrived to turn the wrecks of the Greek mythology, as well as the little they understood of their philosophy, to purposes of deformity and falsehood. I suppose the sting with which he was armed gave him a dragon-like and viperous appearance, very formidable.

I can sufficiently understand why the author of evil should have been typified under the image of a serpent ; that animal producing merely by its sight so strong an associated recollection of the malignity of many of its species. But this was eminently a practice confined to the Jews, whose earliest mythology suggested this animal as the cause of all evil. Among the Greeks the Serpent was considered as an auspicious and favourable being. He attended on Æsculapius and Apollo. In Egypt the Serpent was an hieroglyphic of eternity. The Jewish account is, that the Serpent, that is the animal, persuaded the original pair of human beings to eat of a fruit, from which God had commanded them to abstain, and then in consequence God expelled them from the pleasant garden, where he had before permitted them to reside. God on this occasion, it is said, assigned a punishment to the Serpent, that its motion should be as it now is along the ground upon its belly. We are given to suppose, that before this misconduct it hopped along

upon its tail; a mode of progression which, if I was a
Serpent, I should think the severer punishment of the
two.[1] The Christians have turned this Serpent into
their Devil, and accommodated the whole story to their
new scheme of sin and propitiation.

[1] See note on Shelley's letter to   1821, given in Vol. IV of this
Byron of the 13th of December   edition.

FRAGMENT OF AN ESSAY
ON FRIENDSHIP.[1]

I ONCE had a friend, whom an inextricable multitude of circumstances has forced me to treat with apparent neglect. To him I dedicate this essay. If he finds my own words condemn me, will he not forgive?

The nature of love and friendship is very little understood, and the distinctions between them ill-established This latter feeling—at least, a profound and sentimental attachment to one of the same sex, often precedes the former. It is not right to say, merely, that friendship is exempt from the smallest alloy of sensuality. It rejects, with disdain, all thoughts but those of an elevated and imaginative character. I remember forming an attachment of this kind at school. I cannot recal to my memory the precise epoch at which this took place ; but I imagine it must have been at the age of eleven or twelve.

[1] Given in Hogg's *Life of Shelley*, Vol. 1, pp. 22-4, as having been "written not long before his death." Hogg takes to himself the dedication.

The object of these sentiments was a boy about my own age, of a character eminently generous, brave and gentle; and the elements of human feeling seemed to have been, from his birth, genially compounded within him. There was a delicacy and a simplicity in his manners, inexpressibly attractive. It has never been my fortune to meet with him since my schoolboy-days; but either I confound my present recollections with the delusions of past feelings, or he is now a source of honour and utility to every one around him. The tones of his voice were so soft and winning, that every word pierced into my heart; and their pathos was so deep, that in listening to him the tears have involuntarily gushed from my eyes. Such was the being for whom I first experienced the sacred sentiments of friendship. I remember in my simplicity writing to my mother a long account of his admirable qualities and my own devoted attachment. I suppose she thought me out of my wits, for she returned no answer to my letter. I remember we used to walk the whole play-hours up and down by some moss-covered palings, pouring out our hearts in youthful talk. We used to speak of the ladies with whom we were in love, and I remember that our usual practice was to confirm each other in the everlasting fidelity, in which we had bound ourselves towards them, and towards each other. I recollect thinking my friend exquisitely beautiful. Every night, when we parted to go to bed, we kissed each other like children, as we still were!